Richard Scott

D1560354

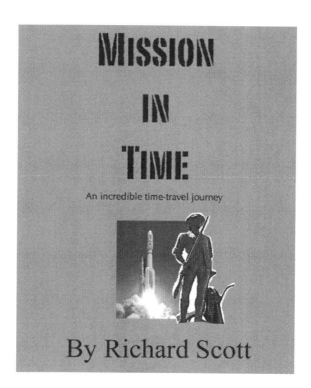

MISSION

IN

TIME

An incredible time-travel journey

By Richard Scott

Cover design: Richard Scott

Title page image: NASA

I

For Jeanne

OTHER BOOKS BY RICHARD SCOTT

Tony Dantry Thrillers
The Reluctant Assassin: Paper and ebook
The Eager Assassin: Paper and ebook
The Assassin Chip: Paper and ebook
The Assassin Series: Boxed set of three Tony Dantry thrillers: ebook

Other books by Richard Scott
Murder on Third Avenue: Murder mystery in the publishing industry: Paper and ebook
The Second Assassination: Historic mystery: Paper and ebook
Salem, the novel: Historic fiction: Paper and ebook

Major Characters

Fictional
Ames, Jimmy: Kitchen worker serving Governor Gage household
Cabot, Samuel: Trustee of the Social Library
Carver, Chris: Scientist who visited the Salem Athenæum.
Eppes, Nathaniel: Trustee of the Social Library.
Foster, Toby: *Essex Gazette* writer
Hall, Samuel (Sam): Publisher of the *Essex Gazette*.
Howard, Thomas (Tom): Space/time traveler
Inglesby, Jennie: Granddaughter of Martha and girlfriend of Thomas Howard.
Inglesby, Martha: Widow and owner of rooming house in Salem.
Kilmartin, Lawrence: Aide to Governor Gage
Lee, Gilbert (Gil): Space/time traveler
O'Connell, Trish: Library director of the Salem Athenæum in 2016.
Oliver, Captain Hugh: Representative sent by Governor Gage to threaten Sam Hall
Pratt, Oliver: A printer in Salem and a Tory
Pynchon, Thomas: Trustee of the Social Library. Created by the author
Waite, Benjamin (Ben): Owner of apothecary shop in Salem and a Tory.
Weeks, Jeremiah Librarian at Social Library in 1775.
Woodbury, Catherine: Robert's wife
Woodbury, Elbridge: Son of Henry
Woodbury, George: Son of Henry
Woodbury, Henry: Father of Josiah, George and Elbridge
Woodbury, Jane: Wife of Henry
Woodbury, Josiah: Young cattle herder and son of Henry Woodbury
Woodbury, Robert: Brother of Henry

Actual Historical Figures
Barrett, Colonel James: 1710-1779. Commander of militia in Concord
Buttrick, Major John: 1731-1791. Militia leader who led the attack at old North Bridge
Dawes, William: Shoemaker and fellow rider with Paul Revere
Derby, Richard: 1712-1783. A sea captain and shipping merchant, Derby was active in the defense preparations leading up to the American Revolution. Father of John Derby
Derby, John: 1741-1812. Son of Richard Derby and captain of the ship *Quero* that brought news of the battles of Lexington and Concord to England.
Felt, Captain Jonathan: 1723-1785. A shipmaster. Faced up to the British at the Leslie's Retreat standoff.
Gage, Governor Thomas: 1719-1787. General in the British Army and Governor of the Massachusetts Bay Colony
Lee, Arthur: 1740-1792. American agent in London leading up to the

American Revolution
Leslie, Lieutenant Colonel Alexander: 1731-1794. British commander of force that retreated at North Bridge in Salem. Later became General in British army.
Mason, Colonel David: 1726-1794. Head of Salem Committee of Safety. Served in French and Indian War
North, Lord: 1732-1792. Prime Minister of Great Britain from 1770 to 1782
Parker, Captain John: 1729-1775. In charge of Lexington militia
Pickering, Timothy: 1745-1829. A leader of Salem militia troops at Leslie's Retreat. He later became Postmaster General in George Washington's new government. Subsequent to that he became Secretary of War and eventually Secretary of State.
Thomas, Isaiah: 1749-1831. Publisher of the *Massachusetts Spy* in Boston and later Worcester
Warren, Dr. Joseph: 1741-1775. Leader in Patriot cause in Boston and the one who orchestrated
the Revere/Dawes ride.
Whicher, Joseph: Foreman in Sprague's Distillery and only person injured during the Leslie's Retreat event **Revere, Paul:** Famous for his midnight ride to Lexington and Concord

MISSION IN TIME

Prologue: Retrieving the Package

October 2015

My name is Chris Carver. I work at a remote Nellis Air Force Base test facility located in Nevada. The popular name for this test site is Area 51, but people who work here refer to it as Groom Lake. It's become famous over the years as a testing facility for secret weapons and secret aircraft. At least that's what people suspect. Much of that is true, of course, and I'm not at liberty to reveal more than that. Frankly, I know very little about many of the other projects at Groom Lake. Each project is deliberately kept isolated from neighboring projects. The project I'm working on is super secret, and I can only disclose the truth about that project if it proves to be successful. Hopefully, I *will* be able to talk about it soon.

On this particular October day I was flying coach on Southwest Airlines from Las Vegas to Boston. I always enjoy going to Boston because I'm from Boston and still have family and friends in the area. Usually I can sleep on a flight, but not on this one. As I looked at the screen with our flight path on the back of the seat in front of me, I could see that we'd be arriving in Boston in about 30 minutes. For the entire flight from Las Vegas I'd been antsier than I ever remember being—and with good reason. If things worked out the way my colleagues and I hoped they would, I would be the first to know with certainty that Einstein had been wrong. Most people don't really understand what Einstein said. They just know he was smart and that he was respected by the best scientists in the world. I won't bore you by trying to explain his theory of relativity or the conclusions he drew from that theory. Suffice it to say that if my scientist colleagues were right, before the week was over the world would never be the same.

When I arrived at Logan Airport I immediately took a cab north to Salem. From Logan it was about a half hour. First thing I did was check into the Hawthorne Hotel, an old established and very comfortable place to stay. I suppose I should explain why someone from an Air Force testing facility in Nevada would need to go to Salem, Massachusetts, a town known for its Witch Trials in the past and tourism in the present. The reason is this: The Salem Athenæum. The Salem Athenæum is an old and very well respected membership library dating back to 1760. In the 18th and 19th centuries there were many such membership or subscription libraries in America. Now there are only 16 or 17. All this is very interesting, but why should someone from a scientific test facility come all the way to Salem to visit its Athenæum?

Here's where it gets a lot more interesting. The Salem Athenæum possesses, or more properly I should say, holds, a package addressed to me and two of my colleagues. Again the reader may think, interesting, but only mildly so. Why would a scientist fly from Nevada to Massachusetts to see this package since the Athenæum could very easily send it on to Nevada?

If there wasn't a very good reason I wouldn't be writing this. I came to Salem because the Athenæum wouldn't let us have the package because it appears to be some sort of time capsule and the folks at the library want to be present when it's opened. I'm sure this is beginning to sound bizarre. That's because it is *extremely* bizarre. That, dear reader, is what makes it so important.

After checking into the hotel, I went to the Athenæum. It was late afternoon, and I wasn't sure I'd be able to see the capsule then, but I needed to get the lay of the land and introduce myself so that I could get my hands on the package as soon as possible. Believe me, there was a lot about this that was far from certain.

Bottom line: If the package *was* there, Einstein was wrong, and we were right.

Creating the Package

I wrote this journal with the hope that my mission partner, Thomas Howard, and I could somehow get it to people in charge of this historic project. I am hopeful, but not at all certain that it will ever be read. — Gilbert Lee

Chapter 1

2015

We left Earth in September of 2015. The instrument panel told us we were now nearly one-half a light year from Earth. A light year is the distance light travels in one year, which is just under six trillion miles. In other words, we'd traveled almost three trillion miles so far. Part of my assignment on this mission was to write a record or journal of everything from liftoff to landing.

The spacecraft or time-craft, if you prefer, was traveling almost as fast as light. The scientists back on Earth had assured me before we lifted off that as we approached the speed of light we would age more slowly, and we would begin to go forward in time. The plan was to reach approximately 90 percent of the speed of light traveling out from Earth for four Earth months. We would then turn around head back toward Earth reaching 90 percent of the speed of light on this four-month return trip. By doing so we would find ourselves back on Earth approximately two years into the future. In other words we'd travel for eight months, but when we got back to Earth it would be September 2017. As we approached 100 percent of the speed of light we would go farther and farther into the future. If we exceeded the speed of light we would start going back in time. At least most scientists believed that. Everyone working on the project agreed that exceeding the speed of light was pretty much out of the question. To do so would be to defy the known laws of physics. Actually they weren't laws, but accepted theories.

Yes, the best scientists in the world believed that as you approached the speed of light you would move forward in time, but if you continued to accelerate and started to exceed the speed of light you'd go backward. Thinking back to when we were still preparing for this mission I recalled that the prevailing thinking was that any error in our ETA would be in how far into the future we would find ourselves because travel faster than the speed of light was thought to be impossible. Nobody seriously even considered that we might find ourselves going back in time.

But back to my story. By my calculations we'd now been in space for nearly the four months we'd planned for our trip out from Earth. Four months of Earth time, that is, even though we were roughly half a light year away from our home planet. Four months is a long time to be away, believe me. Especially when you only see one other human being for the entire time. And this is just for the outward trip.

I'd just awakened from a state of hibernation. In order to keep our sanity we alternately put ourselves into hibernation so that, in our minds at least, the time would seem to pass a lot faster. Hibernation slows down your body metabolism, and that includes the aging process. At least that's what our fellow scientists had told us would happen. Only time would tell. No pun intended. Despite the hibernation, it still meant that there were vast periods when time seemed to stand still. When you're in outer space, nothing much changes for thousands or even millions of miles. You look out the portholes and you see space, which essentially is nothing. Off in the distance you see millions of stars, galaxies and nebulae, but they always seem to be as far away as they appeared when you were back on Earth. Once in a while you see space debris, which is a little scary, because if you collide with some of that stuff it could be fatal.

I looked over at Thomas Howard, my fellow time traveler or chrononaut. Chrononaut is a term that I think was first used as the name of a board game in the year 2000, but it's a term which is fairly accurate in describing our roles.

Thomas was 27 when we left Earth. I was 26. Oh, I'm Gilbert Lee. We'd both been selected because we were young and extremely fit. Another reason was that we both had a good education in science and math. In my case they liked the fact that I was a writer, too. They needed someone to record what happened on this trip and at the destination, which we hoped would be the year 2017. The scientists were confident in their science, but they were not that confident about pinning down a specific date.

I'm a bit of an anomaly, I suppose, because I'm good at math and science, but I also like the printed word. I happen to be a voracious reader. Always have been. When I was accepted into the time travel project I read everything I could about time travel. I started with *The Time Machine* by H. G. Wells and then found Jack Finney's *Time and Again*. I even read *A Wrinkle in Time* by Madeleine L'Engle and Twain's *A Connecticut Yankee in King Arthur's Court*. Loved every one of them. Guess I'm a born time traveler. Even though I thoroughly enjoyed those books, it was easy to see that the science behind them was flawed or completely lacking. These writers were good enough to make the stories entertaining, but they were not convincing scientifically. Of course, I read nonfiction material about time travel, too. Some of it was written to prove that time travel could never happen. Others admitted to the theoretical possibility, but feared that we on Earth would never be able to make it happen. I think these were the books that inspired our Nevada scientists. They made a believer out of me, and I'm now living proof that going forward in time may be possible. Dear God, I hope so, since Thomas and I are in it up to our necks.

We also had to be loners or at least people who could live on their own devices for extended periods of time. I guess our psychological profile fit. We had to meet certain other criteria, too. We had to be single and presently unattached. We had to have no close living family members or at least no family members we cared about. In my case I was an only child and my parents had been killed in a plane crash. I'd been raised by foster parents on Boston's North Shore. In Tom's case, his mother and sister had been killed in a car crash, but his father was alive. Tom had no problem never seeing his father again because the man had left his mother with two young kids years ago and had never even made an effort to see them. Obviously, we had to be risk takers. Some would say a little nutty. And finally, because it would not be possible to return to our present life, we had to be willing to go forward in time and carve out a new life. We could resume science careers because two years into the future we'd only be two years older and we'd still know most if not all of our former contacts. Actually we'd be a few months younger because of the effect of traveling at such a high speed.

It would only be two years, but we would have been out of touch for those two years, so we'd be behind the learning curve. On the other hand we'd be well ahead of the learning curve in the sense that we'd be celebrities. Sort of like Neil Armstrong after returning from the Moon. Tom and I weren't really worried about our future, but we did figure there'd be some tough adjustments. Planning for those adjustments was part of our psychological training for the mission. This planning was necessary because the scientists hadn't figured out how to bring us back to the present yet. Hell, they weren't even sure this trip to the future would work.

When we volunteered the scientists looked at us with a mixture of awe and disbelief. Not many healthy young men would be willing to leave Earth as they knew it, knowing they would never be able to return to their present lives. At least not to lives as they'd known them.

We were human guinea pigs. Our scientists back in Nevada wouldn't know if the project was successful until two years from now. We had a simple plan for letting them know we had made it into the future. If we were close enough to the Nevada lab, we'd simply present ourselves. If we were farther away as we expected to be, we'd simply call them and let them know. The Nevada scientists will have waited two years to hear from us, while we'd only have to wait eight months.

The project lab is called the Center for Advanced Exploration. We just call it CAE or simply Nevada. This project all started decades ago in Area 51 in New Mexico and Nevada. Area 51 is a remote part of Nellis Air Force Base, which straddles both Nevada and New Mexico.

It's known for testing advanced aircraft and weapons systems. It's also know for alleged UFO sightings. It has always been a highly secret facility. What no one knew and no one even suspected was that for decades a team in the Area 51 facility has been working on developing a time-travel technology so that man could literally go into the future or back to another period in history. Hopefully Thomas and I will be living proof that they succeeded.

As I said, I had just awakened from my hibernation. The scientists had developed a means of putting oneself into a state of hibernation similar to what bears do to get through long winters. It's partly achieved by lowering body temperature, partly by mastering mind control techniques and partly by consuming a tablet. We were able to stay in hibernation for as long as two months at a time, but Thomas and I had decided through trial and error to do it in one or two-week chunks because one of us had to stay awake. More accurately, one of us had to maintain something approximating a normal circadian rhythm of wakefulness alternating with sleep. The awake one started to get bored fairly quickly despite the movies, games and ebooks we'd brought along with us. One or two weeks was bad enough, but a couple of months would be intolerable. When we were awake we slept in normal cycles, but that is not the same as hibernation. Waking up from hibernation is a slow process. It's not something for someone who needs to be alert at a moment's notice.

Anyway, I was now fully awake, and soon Tom would put himself into hibernation. But not for a day or two, so we could both have human company, for a while, at least.

The first and only voice I heard was from Tom.

"You don't look any worse for wear. Feel okay?"

"Little stiff, but otherwise okay. Starving, though."

Tom grinned, "I can offer you a filet mignon or lobster. The chef recommends the steak."

"I'll settle for another B ration." We had an assortment of eight different rations, each prepared for their nutritional content first, flavor second and appearance third. They did resemble food on Earth in flavor, but definitely not in texture or appearance. Still, if you've been hibernating for two weeks you'd be surprised at what tastes good. After wolfing down a few bites, I said, "Seen anything interesting?"

I was already full. You don't need much nourishment in hibernation, and when you come out of it, it doesn't take much to satisfy you. Actually, you need exercise more than you need nourishment, for there's a tendency for the muscles to atrophy in hibernation. Fortunately, our cabin was large enough to permit various exercises. The risk of atrophy is another good reason to limit hibernation to weeks; not months.

"Bunch of spiral nebulae and a few fairly close stars," said Thomas. "Don't know their names. Nothing as dramatic as when we went by Sirius." Thomas had been awake for Sirius and had shot some photos of it for me. It was 8.6 light years from Earth, but from our position in space a half light year from Earth it appeared a lot closer than that. It looked like the moon did from Earth only a thousand times as bright, and we could feel its heat. Or at least I thought we could. Your mind plays tricks on you in space.

Right now as I looked out my porthole all I could see were a million pinpoints of light. Occasionally the view was occluded somewhat by interstellar dust, but other than that the view rarely changed. I turned to Thomas and said, "We must be close to our *terminus ad quem*." That was the point at which we were supposed to stop, turn around and head back toward Earth, but not the Earth we'd left. It would be Earth two years into the future. "What does the panel say?"

"Wow, you wake up sharp. Yeah, we're closing in on the *terminus*. We should start to slow down automatically in about an hour. If we don't, I'll be a little nervous."

"We can always go manual."

"Yes, but if the auto-programming is not working, you have to wonder what else might not work."

I understood how Thomas felt. Our lives were in the balance. If our systems stopped working we couldn't very well call 911. "I hear ya," I said, "But we can only do what we're trained to do. If the auto-programming fails to work it's important that we go manual within 15 minutes or we could continue to accelerate. The closer we get to 100 percent of the speed of light, the further into the future we'll end up. We could end up a hundred years into the future." Exceeding the speed of light never crossed our minds. We were convinced that it was impossible.

The way this was supposed to work was simple. Simple in concept, but the science behind it was unbelievably complex. Our people back in Nevada had calculated that if we traveled close to one-half a light year out from Earth we would go forward in time approximately one year. As we approached our *terminus ad quem*, or furthermost point out in space of our trip, we would gradually slow our spaceship to a complete stop. Then, on the return trip to Earth we would go forward in time an additional year. Don't ask me how they figured all this, but Thomas and I were convinced that they knew what they were doing. I know, I know. Easy for them to say. If things don't go well, they're embarrassed, but they're still alive.

Thomas forced a smile, "I didn't sign on for 2050."

We traded wisecracks and mindless banter for the next hour, trying to pass the time while at the same time fearing what could happen if the lab guys back in Nevada were wrong. The worst thing that could happen would be that nothing happened.

Chapter 2

As our digital clock dial ticked off the final seconds, I prayed to God that our team back in Nevada knew what they were talking about. It all came down to these next few seconds. I counted them off to myself as the numbers ticked off on the digital dial. Twenty-nine, 28, 27... This seemed like an hour; not seconds. Time really did slow down in space. Sixteen, 15, 14, 13, 12, 11... I looked over at Thomas. His eyes were closed and he seemed deep in thought. I verbalized the last few seconds. "Six, five, four, three, two, one.... " Thomas's eyes were open now and he seemed paralyzed as I tolled those final seconds.

The digital read-out showed that the neutrino emissions continued to accelerate. We were going faster than ever; not slowing down. I heard Thomas draw in a lungful of air and hold it. I felt myself on the verge of hysteria.

The neutrino accelerator continued to function. Something was wrong. Our speed indicator showed that we were now traveling at 91 percent of the speed of light and still accelerating.

Tom finally expelled the breath he'd been holding and yelled, "What the hell! It was supposed to shut down." I saw fear in his eyes.

I tried to stay calm, though I was feeling the same thing that Tom felt. "Okay," I said with false optimism. "It's a glitch. Hopefully only a small one."

"Nothing's small when you're traveling almost the speed of light. We just traveled another million miles while we were talking about it. We've gotta go manual."

"Let's give it a few minutes. Worst thing can happen is we go farther into the future than the lab planned on."

I could see Tom struggling to control himself. "Hell no. The worst thing that could happen is we go on like this forever. This is not what I had planned for the rest of my life."

"I hear ya. I hear ya. Okay, let's try manual mode and slow this baby down."

To go into manual mode required a two-step process designed to prevent hasty or impulsive decisions. Overriding the computer was not recommended unless it was done as a last resort. We exchanged looks and finally I said, "She's not stopping. Not even slowing down. I don't think we have any alternative. Shall we?"

"Yes! Let's do it," he said.

We pressed the two buttons in proper sequence to put the ship into manual mode and said a little silent prayer.

We both held our breath. I stared at the digital clock that measures Earth time. It approached 30 seconds since we'd pressed the two buttons. Nothing was happening. On the 30 the female computer voice said with absolutely no emotion, *"It is not advisable to go into manual mode at this time. The neutrino accelerator will continue functioning for 61 more days. De-acceleration will commence on day 61. At that time side thrusters will be activated so that the ship can begin its return trip to Earth."*

"Holy shit!" I said. "She's superseding our instructions. Where did this come from?"

"It's like Hal in that old movie."

"If this were a movie, I'd laugh." I pressed the two buttons again. Nothing. "Hey this is not good. Why would the computer do this?"

"Maybe it's not the computer," said Tom, "Maybe it's the software. Wouldn't be the first time someone screwed up a software program.

"Yeah, but this was tested a million times."

"That's what we were told. I'm sure it was. Still, you can't test for everything."

I said, "We have a back-up computer. I'm gonna switch over to that. Agreed?"

"Do it."

"That's a risk in itself," I pointed out. The very thought of switching over carried possibilities of some kind of a foul up.

"I know, but what we have now is not so great, either."

"Yeah, but at least we'll get home eventually. It'll take longer, but it looks as if we'll at least get there."

Tom nodded disconsolately. "I agree, but I'm willing to give the second computer a try if you are."

Again I found myself holding my breath. If this didn't work, we were out of options. It took a little over two minutes to switch over to the back-up computer. For a moment our dials went blank. That alone was enough to give you a heart attack. The two minutes seemed like an hour. Then our screen displays started coming alive, one screen at a time. Finally our instrument panel looked normal. Okay, one hurdle overcome. I then attempted to enter manual mode. Silence for a few seconds.

Then she spoke: *"It is not advisable to go into manual mode at this time. The neutrino accelerator will continue functioning for 61 more days. De-acceleration will commence on day 61. At that time side thrusters will be activated so that the ship can begin its return trip to Earth."*

"That's it, my friend," I said. "Settle in for a longer trip."

"Do we have enough food now?"

"Good question. We should. I know they stowed a lot more than I thought we'd need, though I doubt if they figured on an extra four months. This could get interesting." I left a pregnant pause before adding, "Worse than running out of food could be seeing your ugly face for an extra four months."

"Nice. Yeah, this togetherness could get a little much. Seriously, though, let's think about the implications of going another two months away from Earth. What could that do to our ETA?"

"I'm already thinking about it. We're already past 91 percent of the speed of light. The folks at CAE figured we'd end up approximately two years into the future after traveling only eight months in Earth time. If you go faster than 90 percent, you go ahead farther. Who the hell knows how far? Maybe another year. Maybe five. Maybe ten. Face it, bro, this is virgin territory. Who the hell really knows?"

"That's what I'm thinkin'. If we end up say ten years in the future, how do we explain that to the people we know?"

"Listen," I said, "That's the least of our problems. Think of how far behind we'll be on what's happened in our absence. We figured that after two years we'd have a lot of catching up to do. Imagine after ten years."

"Yeah. It'll be as if we lost ten years of our lives."

"In one sense, yes, but on the other hand, we'll be years younger than we would have been if we'd lived those ten years on Earth, so barring unforeseen calamities, we should live longer than we would have."

"Good thing we don't have somebody waiting for us."

"Yeah," I said. "They'd've given up a long time ago if the wait was ten years." Then something hit me. "If you extrapolate from how fast we go after four months, wouldn't you exceed the speed of light after another two months?"

"Jesus, Gil, you're scaring the hell out of me. Unlikely, though, since most scientists believe it gets harder and harder to increase your speed once you reach 90 percent. Sort of like a marathon. The first 20 or so miles are not too bad, but the last six knock a lot of runners out of the race."

"I like that analogy, except that it's not perfect."

"How so?" asked Tom.

"In a marathon, some runners do complete the 26 miles."

Suddenly something came to mind that I'd completely forgotten. "Hey, that contact we missed back on day six is beginning to take on a new significance." I was referring to a garbled contact we'd heard from mission control six days into our trip. At that point in our trip we'd left Earth orbit and were under neutrino power. I don't know if it was the distance from Earth or sunspots or what, but we couldn't make out the words in the garble message. There was emotion in the voice, but we couldn't tell if it was enthusiasm for the mission or an indication of a problem. We could only understand about every fifth word. Then nothing. We'd speculated at the time about what the message was about, but gradually become caught up in the day-to-day necessities of the trip itself. Things were going so well we just assumed the message had been a farewell good luck from the team back on Earth.

Tom and I agreed now that there was nothing we could do about the message. Very likely it had been an attempt to tell us that the computer programming had a glitch and that we should abort while we still could abort or just adapt to the changed itinerary. Either way, it was way too late to worry about now.

The worst thing about this delay was that we really had no idea how far into the future we were going to end up. When we thought we'd be coming back to Earth two years into the future, it was easy to get into a mindset that we could handle. Two years presented some hurdles, but it was kind of exciting. Now the prospect of landing many years into the future, or God forbid, the past, was kind of scary.

We knocked this around for God knows how long. Probably a good eight or ten hours. Our emotions ran the gamut from near despair to a relatively positive view of the situation. Face it, we were risk takers or we'd never have come on this mission in the first place. This was a setback, but we knew there'd be some glitches. No one had ever done this before, so we didn't expect it to go perfectly. We finally agreed that we'd have to settle down for the additional months. Staying agitated would accomplish nothing other than possible ulcers. We might as well enjoy the ride.

Of course it would mean more hibernation for each of us, and that would help the time pass a little faster. One plus was that while we were traveling we were getting fantastic shots with our onboard cameras. These are shots of the cosmos that earthbound stargazers would never get. Eventually we'd be able to share this treasure trove of astronomical data with folks back on Earth. So if we didn't run out of food and if the computer stuck to its new plan, we were probably okay. We'd be farther into the future, but eventually we'd be safe on Earth.

◆ ◆ ◆

The next two months went by ever so slowly, but they did go by. However, as the days became weeks, we noticed that we continued to accelerate. The dial crept up to 92; then 93, 94, 95, 96 percent of the speed of light. We were rapidly approaching a speed no one believed achievable. Nobody back at the CAE in Nevada had anticipated anything like this. Or if they did, they hadn't shared it with us. The implications of what was happening were enormous. With every advance of the dial I could see us eventually landing on Earth farther into the future. We were now into the 49th day since our computer had shocked us with its new schedule. If the ship continued to accelerate, we would equal the speed of light.

◆ ◆ ◆

It was day 53 and we were at 99.7 percent of the speed of light, with no indication that the acceleration was slowing down. If I were the kind of person who chewed his fingernails, they'd'␣ve all been bitten down to the quick by now. The last few days had been stressful in the exremis. I noticed that Tom, who was openly agnostic, had taken to saying a few prayers. I confess that I said a few myself. It's one thing to be willing to take risks when you believe in the science behind the mission, but it's much, much harder to accept these risks when you see the very science you believe in not holding up. Add to that, it's even more stressful when you discover you have an onboard computer that seems to have a mind of its own.

As the ship hurtled further out into the universe, Tom's eyes and mine were glued to the neutrino accelerator dial, which was now at 99.9 percent and inching forward. Tom turned to me and said, "I feel kind of funny. Weird."

"Yeah," I said. "Me too." Then the dial registered 100 percent. We were traveling at the speed of light. The odd feeling became more intense. It wasn't exactly painful, but it was strange and extremely unpleasant. "You still feel it?" I asked.

"Yeah. More. Not a great feeling."

Then it happened. The dial said 101. We were exceeding the speed of light. "You think this thing is working right?" I asked.

"I don't know. No reason to believe it isn't."

"Except for a lot of science that says it couldn't happen. Either we're going faster than light or this thing is malfunctioning. Christ! Now it's saying 102.4. The funny physical feeling had passed, but as we continued to accelerate, it became harder and harder to accept what was happening."

"I think, my friend," said Tom somberly, "that we should take it at face value. If we're wrong, the error's in our favor. If not, we'd better prepare ourselves for the worst."

The amazing thing was that neither of us knew what that worst meant. We had an idea, of course, but there's no way we could know precisely what might be in store for us. I'm not saying that two intelligent, well-trained scientists would risk a journey such as this and not consider the possibility of overshooting or undershooting the estimated year of our arrival, but the truth of the matter was that we had not considered this much of a variance from the original plan.

As intelligent scientists, we knew what our predecessors had believed would happen if you could exceed the speed of light. Most of them believed it was impossible, but they theorized that *if it could be done* you would begin to go back in time.

"Holy crap," yelled Tom. "I'm not dressed for this."

I forced a weak smile. "Glad you still have a sense of humor. Right now I'm not thinking this is so funny. I'm not at all sure I'm ready to spend my life in the past."

We had brought normal clothing from 2015, figuring it would be fine only two years later. What we hadn't bargained for was the possibility of living in the past. Now that we were faced with that very real possibility, we had no idea how far into the past it would be.

Would it be last year or a hundred years ago? Or would we find ourselves living in ancient Rome, or worse yet, some cave looking out at roaming dinosaurs? Clothing was the least of our problems.

Chapter 3

We were now at the beginning of day 61 of the extension of our original trip outward from Earth. This was the day we were supposed to reach our new *terminus ad quem*—if we could trust our computer. I say new *terminus ad quem* because for some reason the onboard computer had recalculated our journey and sent us further out into the cosmos. If the ship didn't turn around within the next few hours, 14 to be exact, we would then have a legitimate reason to panic. So far, since the adjustment just under 61 days ago, the computer had operated smoothly. However, the computer had given no indication that we were approaching our new *terminus ad quem*. Usually, when something significant was supposed to happen, the computer would alert us a day or two in advance. Since that hadn't happened in advance of the *terminus ad quem* , it reignited our suspicions that the computer had taken on a personality of its own. It wasn't totally out of the question, as we both knew that the computer was by far the smartest, most advanced electronic brain ever to go into space. The folks back at the CAE constantly bragged about how intelligent it was and jokingly said that we really weren't needed on the mission.

The hours clicked by, seemingly at a faster pace than they had in the first few months of our trip. No doubt, this perceived rapidity of the passing of time was caused by the fact that we still had heard nothing from the computer. There was no sign of slowing down, and we both knew that we had to decelerate soon or things would look extremely bleak.

◆ ◆ ◆

Now we were down to the final six hours of the 61st day. If we didn't begin to slow down in the next two or three hours, we had little faith that we'd ever turn around and head back to Earth.

Four hours remained on the 61st day, and the ship continued to accelerate. We were now at 112 percent of the speed of light, and Tom and I were gut-wrenchingly taut with fear of the great unknown. I hadn't eaten in hours and had zero appetite for food or drink. Now we were down to three hours. Now two. I was torn between screaming and rolling up into a ball. You don't know how you deal with something like this till you're faced with it.

Then we heard it, the robotic female voice of our system computer. "The neutrino accelerator is shutting down. Side thrusters will initiate in exactly 74 minutes."

The blood came back into our faces as we high-fived each other. I felt like I'd just finished a marathon.

Tom beamed at me, the color back in his face as he said, "Looking good. Had me worried there for a minute."

"A minute. You haven't breathed in six hours. Okay, now we wait a little more than an hour for the side thrusters. Keep your fingers crossed."

A little background on the neutrino accelerator might be instructive. Back in the twentieth century scientists discovered subatomic particles they called neutrinos. Neutrinos have virtually no mass and can travel through two feet of lead with no trouble. Scientists believed that neutrinos could travel almost as fast as light. At one point scientists at CERN discovered that neutrinos had weird properties. This led them to believe that under certain circumstances neutrinos could travel even faster than light. CERN, by the way, is a French acronym for Conseil Europeen pour la Recherche Nucleaire. It's located just outside of Geneva. It's where the World Wide Web was born and is most noted for its particle accelerators.

In these CERN accelerators they discovered what neutrinos could do. Our scientists in Nevada later learned how to use neutrino acceleration as a means of propelling a space vehicle. I suppose in our case space vehicle should more accurately be called time ship. The thrust from neutrino emissions is not powerful, so we had to lift off using conventional liquid hydrogen and liquid oxygen oxidizer thrusters. We needed that initial burst of power to overcome Earth's gravity and get us through its gaseous atmosphere.

Once free of gravity and the atmosphere, the neutrino accelerator took over. At first the weak propulsion of the neutrinos was negligible, but in outer space there is no atmosphere, which means no resistance. As the neutrino emissions continued, the ship gradually increased speed. Each second it was going faster than the previous second. After awhile we were really moving. When we'd been in space for about four months (Earth time) we were moving at 90 percent of the speed of light. As I've already explained, that was supposed to take us approximately two years into the future by the time we had returned to Earth.

However, things didn't quite work out the way the project team planned. We continued to accelerate, eventually reaching the speed of light. From that point on we figured that we must be going backward in time. Faster and faster back in time. When I first entered the project and heard about traveling almost as fast as light, I wondered how that could be possible, and even if it were, how would I feel going that fast? The science team explained that our Milky Way galaxy travels 2.7 million miles an hour through the Universe; yet we aren't aware of it. Thomas and I were assured that since our acceleration would be steady, but gradual, we wouldn't sense that we were traveling nearly as fast as light. We would, however feel the thrust of the conventional liftoff from Earth, but after that, when we were in outer space, there would be very little feeling that we were moving at all. Well, as it turned out, when we did hit the speed of light, both Tom and I felt very strange. Like no feeling either of us had ever experienced. Fortunately that feeling passed and we now felt fine. Physically anyway. We were still scared shitless about what we would find when we finally came back to Earth.

We were nearing the *terminus ad quem* and waiting for the side thrusters to go into action. We needed to come to almost a complete stop before the side thrusters were activated. Here's what blew my mind as we neared that stopping point. At that spot in space we were approximately 1.4 light years from Earth. That's 8.4 trillion miles. The human mind can't deal with distances like that. We couldn't see our Sun from where we were. Not with the naked eye anyway. To put things in perspective, after traveling 1.4 light years from home, we were still in our own galaxy, the Milky Way. I remember reading in *Scientific American* that the Milky Way alone had about 4.5 billion Earth-like planets. Scientists have estimated that there are somewhere between 100 to 200 billion galaxies in the Universe, each with billions of stars. So, on the one hand, Thomas and I have traveled farther than any human in the history of Earth, but that enormous distance is a drop in the bucket when you understand the enormity of the Universe. I get dizzy just thinking about it.

The clock tells us the side thrusters should begin to operate in 30 seconds. Thomas looked at me and nodded knowingly. We both knew that this was another momentous moment.

"Here we go again," he said. There wasn't much else to say until the half minute elapsed.

Again our time-ship computer system came through with flying colors. As the countdown reached zero the computer voice announced, "Side thrusters activating." We needed these side thrusters to function because they were the thrusters that would turn us around 180 degrees so that we could begin the trip back to Earth, but not the Earth that we'd left six months ago. No, because we'd exceeded the speed of light, we'd be going back to the Earth as it was sometime in the past. At least that's what some of our fellow scientists thought would happen. The scary part was we had no idea how far back we'd be going if we did go back. I felt the effect of the thrusters, probably the first sense of movement for our ship since we'd blasted off from the Nevada desert six months ago. That feeling of movement was one of life's small pleasures. At least it was for us. Aside from the initial lift off, our environment had changed very little in those six months. Just that sense of movement from turning around was something different.

In another six months we'd be back on Earth, the Earth we'd read about in our history books. But which history books?

Naturally I couldn't avoid worrying about the accuracy of the turnaround. We needed to be headed exactly in the right direction or we could miss Earth by thousands of miles. There would be course corrections along the way, of course, but with each correction we were told we would pay a price in time. Two many corrections would adversely affect our arrival time. Since we had no idea what that would be, we didn't worry about it too much. Still, we figured that if we had a lot of course corrections it would take us longer in Earth time to get back, which would mean that by accelerating longer as we exceeded the speed of light, we'd land farther back in history.

Chapter 4

Return trip to Earth

The return trip went as well as could have been hoped for. By that I
mean, from an engineering and technical standpoint, it went flawlessly.
Nevertheless, despite all the measures we took to reduce the tedium of
traveling in the narrow confines of a spacecraft for a total of 12
months, it was still boring, boring, boring. Sure, as I mentioned earlier,
we had on-board entertainment, and of course, we took advantage of
hibernation to minimize the tedium, but after a few weeks in space it
was still boring. Thomas and I got along fine in the beginning, but
familiarity does build a degree of contempt. Fortunately we were both
aware of this danger and worked hard not to let it lead to something
disastrous. Despite our efforts, though, there were times when we got
awfully tired of seeing each other. Our cabin was about seven feet
across and 12 feet from front to back. We could leave our seats, but
because we were in space we couldn't even walk in those 12 feet inside
the cabin. We could float and pull ourselves about, which we did a lot,
but that relatively confining cabin often felt more like a prison cell than
the inside of a vehicle that was taking us somewhere to an unknown
destination.

As we neared the final third of our trip back to Earth of an earlier
time, we came closer than humans have ever come to many of the stars
that I had seen through telescopes when I was younger. Off in the
distance we saw an amazingly bright 61 Cygni, which is 11 light years
from Earth, but appeared huge to us from our position in space. Again
we saw a huge-looking Sirius, the brightest star in the sky when you're
looking at it from Earth. Then we saw Alpha Centauri, the closest star
to Earth. To us, it was the biggest of them all.

I mentioned before that our scientists on Earth thought they would
know in just two years if we succeeded in going into the future. Now
that we thought we were going backward in time we would have to

find another way of letting them know where and when we ended up. Since it would take 12 Earth months for our round trip, one would think that the scientists at CAE would have to wait at least that long before they'd know what happened to us. But if you think about it, maybe they wouldn't have to wait that long.

Since we'd be sending them a message from the past, we should be able to make contact sooner than that. Hell, we should be able to contact them before our space craft even left the Nevada desert, which would mean that we could tell them to abort the trip. The more I thought about this the more it boggled my mind. Would it be possible after we arrived in the past to send a message that would prevent us from ever landing in the past? It was a logical paradox that was enough to blow your mind.

Of course all this depended on how far back in the past we landed. If we landed in the time of the dinosaurs, there was no chance in hell we'd ever get a message to CAE. If we landed in, say 1960, it might be possible, but it wouldn't be simple even then. How do you send a message to someone in the future if that future is years ahead? Sure, we communicate with the future all the time when we send snail mail or even email, but 60 or 70 years into the future is not that easy. Tom and I wrestled with all of this on our return trip.

One thing we did agree on was that we had to write some kind of journal or accounting of our trip and our destination and then, somehow, get that journal to Nevada. Obviously if we went very far back in time we couldn't use the post office or Fed Ex or email. If we went only one or two years back in time, I suppose we could simply walk into the CAE lab in Nevada and present ourselves. Tom and I thought about this scenario for quite awhile, since it would mean that we'd be presenting ourselves to the folks at the CAE before we had even lifted off in our space vehicle. How this would work out was a total mystery.

The more likely scenario, though, was that we'd go back in time a lot further, which could be a lot more interesting, but clearly a much bigger adjustment and present much bigger problems. Anyway, if that's what happened, and it seemed likely it would, we'd need to write our journal and then deposit it with some organization that we knew would still be in existence in 2015. Whew! We couldn't even begin to identify such an organization until we knew where and when we were going to land. If it was the time of the cave man, then there would be no such organization. I know it's confusing. It's confusing to us.

Our reverse thrusters would be starting up soon. We were approaching the time when we'd be making some final course corrections prior to the activation of those reverse thrusters. The project managers had consulted with Tom and myself and agreed that they would try to land us just off the coast of New England. Hopefully near the coast of Massachusetts, because both of us came from the Bay State and would at least have some familiarity with the geography. If we landed in 2017, adjustment would be a piece of cake. That was the plan, but obviously the plan had gone seriously awry. We both hoped and prayed that we'd still land near Massachusetts. It would be a different time, but at least we'd have familiarity with the terrain in our favor. Wasn't much, but it was something.

The reader can imagine the feelings I had knowing that we would be back on Earth within 72 hours. My nerves crackled with an edginess I'd never experienced before. On the one hand, I found myself trembling with fear of the unknown. On the other hand, I'd never been this excited. We were going to be back on Earth. Not the old familiar Earth, but Earth nevertheless. And almost certainly an Earth filled with challenges we'd never anticipated back in Nevada.

Thomas and I both tried to sleep. Conventional sleep, that is; not hibernation. He slept like a baby, but I slept fitfully. Nevertheless the time passed, and now we were only about two hours from landing.

We could see Earth now. At first just a speck. Then a pale blue dime in the distance. Gradually the dime became a nickel; then a quarter and gradually it grew to be as big as the Moon appears from Earth.

The blue orb of Earth looked huge now. We could make out the shapes of North and South America. There's no feeling like the feeling of actually being in space looking at your home planet. If nothing else went right on this trip, this alone would make everything worth while.

The reverse thrusters continued to slow us down. We had to reduce speed dramatically in order to enter an orbital flight path around Earth.

I won't go into details, but soon we were in orbit. The computer system told us that the reverse thrusters would slow our forward speed even more so that we could gradually fall out of orbit and reenter the Earth's atmosphere. The computer and various cameras and sensors calculated our landing speed and synchronized it with the geographical position we wanted to land on Earth. We had the ability to use GPS to help position us, but I knew that, if we were very far back in time there were no man-made satellites to link up with. The scientists back at CAE had ingeniously found other ways to make the positional calculations with or without satellites, though, since they knew that if our ship approached Earth at certain angles or at certain locations, they couldn't depend on satellites.

Tom looked a me and smiled. "This was supposed to be the time when we changed into fresh clothes for when we greeted the folks of the future. I'm pretty sure our wardrobe is not going to be suitable for where we're going."

"We have no idea where we're going," I said grinning weakly. "Though it's a good bet we don't have the right clothes."

"Okay, but looks like we have no choice. Our new friends are going have a lot of yucks at our expense."

"At least a lot of questions," I pointed out. "We should probably come up with some kind of reason why we dress this way. You know, this is the way they dress where we come from. Somethin' like that."

"You think it's important to explain how we dress?"

"Yes, I do. Face it, if we end up in a totally different era, we need to be accepted. We can't be seen as aliens from another planet or whatever. Who the hell knows how they treat strangers?"

Tom nodded his understanding. "See your point. Okay, once we find out where we've landed we tell them we're from someplace at least 500 to a 1,000 miles away. Chances are, if it's far back in time, the folks we meet have never been that far away so what we tell 'em won't be challenged."

"Have you considered that we may still be going forward in time? Face it, the computer screwed up big by adding four months to our trip.

Maybe this effing speed gauge has been off and we never did exceed the speed of light. Maybe what we're wearing will be the latest 'in' thing?" I thought for a few seconds as I digested the distinct possibility that we might actually not have been going *back* in time."

"Yeah, that thought has occurred to me. We have no idea where or when we're ending up. It's not as though what we're doing happens all the time."

"Look at the bright side."

"There's a bright side?" I asked.

"If we do land in the future, we'll be able to see another Patriots game."

"That would be nice, but don't count on it."

Chapter 5

The Earth loomed larger and larger now. It filled most of our forward view. Then the computer spoke again. "Landing site has been determined. Vehicle will set down in the Atlantic Ocean near the coast of Massachusetts." Then it went silent.

Thomas said, "That's pinning it down. The coast of Massachusetts is a lot of water."

"Isn't that what we were shooting for? The Massachusetts coast and in the water so we can dispose of the ship."

"Yeah, but I thought they were going to be able to narrow it down a little more."

Then the robotic voice resumed: "Vehicle will set down off Great Misery Island near Salem, Massachusetts. Vehicle will touch water in 17 minutes."

I punched Thomas on the shoulder. "Is that close enough for you?"

He smiled. "That'll do. Jeez, I can't believe it's finally happening. God, I hope the name of that island isn't as ominous as it sounds."

Unlike the old Space Shuttle landings, which were similar to the way airplanes landed, we were heading straight down into the ocean. The reverse thrusters in the nose of our vehicle had slowed us down from faster than the speed of light out in space to 30 miles per hour according to our instruments. Now it was 26, now 22. This whole trip was amazing, but this landing itself was enough to blow your mind.

Then the cloud of uncertainty as to how far back in time we would find ourselves was lifted. Tom grabbed my shoulder and pointed toward what looked like Boston, about 15 miles to the south. But it was not the Boston we both remembered. This Boston was not much more than a large village. Well maybe a bit more. Maybe a small town. We immediately noted that the Shawmut Peninsula, which is the piece of land on which Boston is situated, was a lot skinnier than the modern peninsula. It looked a lot like maps I'd seen of Boston in the eighteenth century. Over the years between the founding of Boston and twenty-first century Boston, the section called the Back Bay had been filled in. As we looked down at the peninsula now, the town of Boston was at the end of the peninsula. The part of the peninsula leading to the populated end was a narrow strip of land. My heart dropped as the meaning of this hit me full force. It seemed to me that we were looking at Boston as it was hundreds of years ago! Salem just below us looked to be almost as big as Boston. Clearly this was not the twenty-first century. We had no idea exactly what year it was, but the terrain below definitely looked like eighteenth century Massachusetts. I swallowed hard as the import of this hit me.

"Jesus!" I blurted out. "Get ready for a major adjustment in lifestyle, my friend."

Tom's expression was unlike anything I'd ever seen before. Finally he said, "I always loved this period in history. Now we get to live it. I suppose the shock will hit us soon, but right now I can't wait. Say good-by to your iPhone, Gil."

I shook my head, but said nothing. We were never going to live in the twenty-first century again. We were about to leave our lives as we'd known them, and he was excited about it; not despondent. Space travel does strange things to you

We were about 300 feet above the surface now. Off to our left I could see a few cattle grazing on Great Misery Island. It was nighttime, but there was a full moon, which made it fairly easy to make out objects below. I knew from visiting the North Shore of Boston when I was younger that there was also a Little Misery Island not far away. Our speed was now down to 12 mph. Landing in darkness had been part of the plan from the very beginning because the Nevada brainiacs didn't want our vehicle to be noticed as it settled into the ocean. Certainly the fewer people who saw us land the better. Our landing was supposed to be on the far side of the island—the side facing open sea, so that would minimize even further the likelihood of our being seen. The scientists and leaders of the project figured in their infinite wisdom that it would be better all around if people on the ground didn't see our space vehicle.

The ocean seemed calm. Getting to shore was going to be hard enough without contending with a rough sea. Actually, if we wanted to, we could get to shore easily, as the brain trust back in Nevada had designed our spacecraft so that part of it could be converted to a boat-like craft. All we had to do was press a button and the boat-like portion of the spacecraft would break away from the rest of the space vehicle. We could then ride into Great Misery Island in style. However, since Great Misery Island was only about a half mile from the mainland, getting in to the mainland probably wouldn't be too difficult. Tom and I had decided on the way down that we'd only use the boat if we landed well out to sea. In such an event we'd be stranded if we didn't use it. If we were fairly close to shore, though, we felt it wiser to make it to land on our own. If we used the boat we'd have a major problem disposing of it so that we wouldn't have to explain it to the locals. That wouldn't be easy. Wouldn't be worth the temporary convenience. If we were miles out to sea, of course, our priorities would be different. Under those circumstances it would be better to live and face the problem of explaining it. Right now it looked like we'd land fairly close to the island.

Our reverse thrusters had us down to 5 mph now. We would touch down in seconds. I took a deep breath and held on for dear life. When we hit the surface of the water it was a little like doing a cannonball into a swimming pool. No great shock, but you knew you'd hit something. As we hit there was this big hiss and a huge cloud of steam surrounded us. The nose of our vehicle had heated up tremendously on reentry, hence the steam. The steam dissipated in a few seconds and we knew we'd made it. We weren't sinking. The ship was water tight and would only sink when we opened two valves that would let water in. We weren't quite ready to do that, though. We needed to take one last look around to be sure we had everything we wanted to take with us.

I knew I would miss the computer games, access to our recorded movies and TV shows, and of course, the computer itself. We would never see anything like these things again in our lives. Well, we'd been willing to make sacrifices when we signed up so we weren't going to waste time lamenting their loss now. We had to get out of the vehicle and make our way to land as quickly as possible. Actually there wasn't much we could take with us—none of the high-tech stuff that would be so cool if you showed it to the eighteenth century folk we would soon meet.

The only things we took with us were the clothes on our backs. I realized that we *should* be wearing breeches, rough linen shirts and hand-cobbled shoes, so as soon as we met our first local we were going to stand out as different.

We had a few thousand dollars in U.S. paper money, but that wasn't going to help us at all, as the United States didn't exist until the end of the eighteenth century. We also had with us a few one-ounce bars of gold. Several such bars were sewn into the lining of our clothing. In total we each had 15 ounces of gold on our person. The folks at CAE had figured the gold would allow us to make small purchases if we landed in a remote part of the world. We could convert the bars into the local currency. My guess was that the gold we had with us would be roughly the equivalent of the annual salary of a small-town craftsman or schoolteacher in the eighteenth century. It would probably be enough for us to get by until we could begin to earn a living. We wouldn't have to beg when we met people. We could immediately be accepted. That was the hope anyway.

We took inflatable life preservers with us to be on the safe side, though we really didn't need them. We figured it wouldn't be too hard to bury two preservers after we'd deflated them on land. Certainly it would be a lot easier than disposing of the boat.

As Tom and I exchanged prolonged looks of understanding, I said in a tone that for me was atypically solemn, "Say goodbye to the twenty-first century."

"Man, I can't believe this is happening."

I forced a very weak smile, "Talk about a big decision. Well, *in for a penny, in for a pound* was never more appropriate than it is now." At this moment the import of what was happening had me on the edge of panic, but I couldn't afford to give in to it. For better or for worse, we had to be strong now. I wasn't going to collapse in front of Tom. Right now we needed each other so I said, "Let's get on with it. Let's open the hatch and get some fresh eighteenth-century air." With that I pressed a button as Thomas pressed another one. The simultaneous procedure was designed to prevent accidental opening of the hatch in outer space. The hatch door was above us, all part of the engineering design so it wouldn't open in the water. There was a cracking sound as the seal was broken. Slowly the hatch opened. As it did I felt a rush of cool air welcoming us to the past.

Chapter 6

I can't tell you what a rush of thoughts I experienced as I poked my head out into the eighteenth-century night. The sky was clear. A full moon was visible, and the cool air was a delight. Great Misery Island looked to be close, probably less than the length of a football field away. I wondered if they played football here? Of course I knew the answer. Strange how your mind works. I did wonder if they played any games. Especially any team sports. I'd soon find out, wouldn't I?

Right then I wished we'd packed an inflatable raft to get us to the island. We hadn't because it was deemed unnecessary by the project team. Waste of space and unnecessary weight in the ship. I suppose they were right. Besides, a little contact with ocean water was going to be welcome after being confined to our time-craft for 12 months.

"Ready?" I asked.

"Ready. I'll open the petcocks and say goodbye to this baby."

We climbed out of the ship and lowered ourselves into the water. We were both good swimmers so we were confident we'd have no trouble making it to the island. We'd both speculated on the way down from Earth orbit as to whether our muscles might have atrophied so much that it would make swimming difficult and tiring. Fortunately we had our life preservers to rely on if we got tired.

"Damn, that water feels good. Cold, but good," I said as we took our first few strokes toward the island. "How's it with you?"

"Great. Swimming's like riding a bike. Even with wobbly legs."

"They feel wobbly?"

"Not really. At least not in the water. Tell you more when we get on the island and try to walk."

After a few minutes I looked back and saw that the vehicle we'd spent a year of our lives in was almost submerged. We were now about halfway to the island. There were no lights—at least none that we could see. Looking off toward the mainland, which was maybe a third of a mile away, I *could* see dim lights. Not many, but some. There were people not far away.

The shoreline of the island was rocky, so we had to watch our footing as we waded in. We kept our inflatable preservers with us until we knew how we were going to make it to the mainland. We shook ourselves off and slowly climbed the small incline up to what had appeared to be a pasture. As we got acclimated to the moonlight we made out cows sleeping on the grass. There seemed to be no humans in the immediate area.

Thomas asked, "What time do you suppose it is here?"

"My guess would be about midnight."

"And what do you base that on?"

I grinned. "I glanced at our Earth clock just before we splashed down. It said 11:30."

"So we can assume that things'll be pretty quiet around here until morning. Maybe we should try to get some shuteye before we set off for the mainland. It's cool, but not that cool. We won't freeze. Maybe our clothes will dry out so we don't look like drowned rats when we meet our first person."

"Good idea. Here or down on that little beach we came in on?"

Thomas had obviously thought it out. "Up here. The beach is pretty rocky and we don't know if it's low or high tide. If it's low now, we'd get pretty wet by morning."

I couldn't sleep because I wasn't exactly comfortable in my wet clothes. I dearly missed a dry shirt and jacket. The lack of physical comfort combined with my active mind made for a long night.

It suddenly hit me that when we'd embarked on our journey I was 26 years old. Now, according my calculations, I'd be older. Probably somewhere between 28 and 30. Thomas would be somewhere between 29 and 31. My calculations were based on scientific theory that said if you were able to go back in time, you would age somewhat. The scientific community didn't agree on how much, but they all agreed it would be enough to be noticeable.

The only humans we'd seen in 12 months were each other. As I looked at Tom, I think he did look a bit older, but it's hard to be sure because, except for hibernation, we'd seen each other every day of those 12 months, so any changes would have been gradual. Then I realized something else: I was not just eager to see someone else, I was excited about it. At the same time, I was more than a little frightened. How would we be received in this new century? I was like a kid on Christmas Eve, excited, but extremely nervous. Knowing that the people we would meet would be from the eighteenth century was itself enough to make you nervous. I wondered what year this was. I was pretty sure it was in the eighteenth century, but that was a huge span. It could very well have been late seventeenth century. I based my guess that it was eighteenth century because of the moonlit view of Boston from the air and comparing that view with my memory of having seen antique maps of the period.

Was it before the Revolution or during? In my wakeful periods on the lonely island I was struck by how quiet everything was. No planes, no highway noise, no sirens, no accelerating cars. The only thing I heard was the steady sound of the surf against the rocky beach below.

Finally the first few hints of sunlight appeared off to the east. As I looked about I realized that I was shivering. I had no idea what the temperature was, but I guessed it to be around 50 degrees Fahrenheit, and I was shirtless. I'd taken it off because when wet it was colder than going without it. I quickly donned my shirt. It was damp, but better than nothing. Thomas was still asleep. I gave him a gentle poke on the shoulder and he awoke. "I'll have the eggs Benedict, please," he said. I was glad he still had his sense of humor. We were going to need it.

I looked out over the ocean and said, "I'm afraid we'll have to wait for awhile before we have our breakfast. I doubt if we'll get anything here on the island." The eastern horizon gradually turned a soft orange pink as the familiar orb slowly made its presence known. A new awakening for the coast of Massachusetts and a new awakening for Tom and myself. Surprisingly, despite my lack of sleep and the early morning chill, I felt refreshed and ready to meet colonials.

Chapter 7

We brushed ourselves off and set off to see what was on the island. Hopefully we'd meet someone who could take us to the mainland. As we made our way leisurely across the grass we saw that it was a good-sized island. My guess was somewhere between 50 and a 100 acres. Off in the distance we could see a small house. If it had ever been painted, it was a long time ago, as the boards were gray from years of weathering. We couldn't tell from where we stood if anyone lived or occupied the little building. It became quickly apparent that much of the island was devoted to cattle. Most of the cows we'd seen lying down on the grass were now up or in the process of getting up. We now saw that there were a lot of cows in the pasture so Thomas and I concluded that there must be someone on the island tending to them. We were both city boys, so we had no clue how one tended to cows, but we supposed that would be something we'd be learning in the days to come.

Great Misery Island was proving to be one of the quieter spots on Earth. Cows are not noisy anyway, and there didn't seem to be any people around. Ever-practical Tom said, "Who takes care of these cows? Who milks them? What good are they if you don't milk them?"

"Excellent questions my good man. Excellent questions. Let's check out the old house. Maybe we'll get some answers."

Tom said, "Maybe we'll find some food. I'm starving."

"Didn't you take a couple rations with you when you left the ship?"

"I did, but I'm starving for real food."

"Yeah. I know what you mean." As we neared the house, I said, "Looks like our first human sitting on the steps. Let's go make contact."

"We stick to our fur trader story, right?"

"It's as good as any. Let's go. This should be interesting."

When we were about a 100 feet away we saw that our first human was a teenage boy, probably not more than 15 or 16. He was sitting on the rickety steps of the house, which now appeared to be not much more than a shack. "Looks like he's having his breakfast," said Tom.

The boy looked up as we approached. I guessed that he was about my height, which is 5'11". He was slim, but not really skinny. Just lean and sort of wholesome looking. He seemed startled by our presence. He stared at us as if we were the strangest beings he'd ever seen.

"You surprised me. Do you have business with me, sirs?"

I said, "No. we need a way to get to Salem. We were hoping you could help us. Is there someone on the island who can take us in?"

"I'm the only one on the island till later this day. You puzzle me. Why are you on the island?"

"I'm Gilbert and this is Thomas." We'd decided while still in flight that we would not use our nicknames in eighteenth century New England. "We purchased passage from Halifax to New York with fur traders in their ketch. The boat was heavily laden with furs. After we'd been at sea for a few hours it came out that they were not legitimate traders, but thieves. Thomas and I had to make up our mind quickly about staying in the boat with those two. We decided we wanted to get off. This brought out the temper of the thieves, and we said just take us to the nearest land and give us back our money. They brought us in close to this island and rowed us to shore, but they kept the money. Thomas and I were glad to be free of them even if they have our money. They were headed for trouble we wanted no part of."

As I spoke whatever concerns the boy was feeling seemed to recede. "My name is Josiah," he said. "I think you were wise to leave that ketch. They say there's much fur stealing up the coast. I'll help get you to shore, but I'm alone here till after midday, when my father or one of my brothers comes out from Beverly Farms to relieve me."

Thomas couldn't resist asking, "That would be great. Say, mind if I ask you a question?"

"No. What is your question?"

"These cows seem to take care of themselves. What do you do out here on the island?"

Josiah had never been asked such a question, and he was surprised to hear it. "I keep an eye out for sick cows. I watch for cows that are calving. I take care of the pasture, fill in holes so the cows don't twist their legs. Most of the time, though, I fish, think a lot or, if I can lay my hands on one, I read a book." Josiah thought for a moment; then said, "You gentlemen have never lived on a farm, have you?"

I laughed. "No, we're both town boys. Both grew up in Portland. About ten years ago we went up to Halifax looking for work. We've been up there most of the time since."

I couldn't help but notice that Josiah was still staring at us. Finally he said, "You dress yourselves quite differently up there, don't you?"

I looked at Tom and then at myself and realized how strange our twenty-first century clothes must seem to this young man. Khakis and golf shirts were everyday wear for us, but far different from what our new friend was wearing.

I said, "Yes, I suppose we do." Josiah seemed to be warming up to us so I had to ask, "Don't suppose you'd know where we could get a bite to eat. Haven't eaten since yesterday afternoon."

"I don't have much with me, but you're welcome to what I have. There's a bit of bread, cheese and six or seven apples in the house. Oh, and there's a jug of small beer if you're thirsty. I'd appreciate it if you'd leave something, though, as my pa or my brother'll be needin' a bite sometime later, I'm sure."

It is no exaggeration when I say that that simple fare was the most delicious meal Thomas and I had eaten in our lives. The two of us ate sitting on the steps of the house as Josiah, leaning against a large rock a few feet away, studied us. We could see that he was curious. "Can't put my finger on it, but you gentlemen don't talk like anyone I know.

Never met anyone from Portland or Halifax. Do they all talk like you?"

Tom and I both laughed. Then I said with a grin, "I never gave much thought to it. Come to think of it, I thought you sounded a bit different, too. Not like us up north. I think the folks in Portland sound about the same as you. When you get up to Halifax, though, they do talk differently. I suppose after living there for ten years we must have picked up some of their speech."

Josiah asked, "What takes the two of you to New York, if you don't mind my askin'? New York's a long way from Halifax. Come to think, it's a long way from here."

"We're printers. Lost our jobs when our print shop went out of business."

"Couldn't find jobs with another print shop?" Josiah asked with apparent concern.

"Halifax is a big town, but not that big. There's only one other printer, and he didn't need us."

"Maybe you can find something in Salem or Boston. You may not need to go all the way to New York. My pa may know someone in Salem who might could help you."

Thomas said, "What if it's not your pa this afternoon, but one of your brothers? Will they know about any printers in Salem or Boston?"

"If it's Elbridge, he might. He's older than me. If it's George, probably not. He's a year younger than me."

"When you're not watching the herd out here on the island, what do you do," I asked. "Do you go to school?"

"I attended the parish school for three years where I learnt to read and write English and also some arithmetic. Then I moved to a Latin grammar school where I learnt Latin, read books from England and studied mathematics. I hope someday to study the law, but it's not at all certain, as Pa needs my help now with the herd."

"Doesn't your pa want you to study for the law?" asked Thomas.

"Oh yes he does. He says I should begin now, but I know he needs me. I can't leave him now."

I asked, "If you don't mind my asking, how old are you?"

"I'll be turning 16 next month. Time I should be supportin' myself."

I knew that this was a completely different period from the time in which we'd grown up, but I said, "You're still young. There's plenty of time to study law."

From his expression I knew that I had shocked him. "I can't delay my law study for many years. I should be studying law now."

"Won't you be a better lawyer if you acquire more knowledge before you go out into the world on your own? Isn't there a secondary school you could attend now, at least for a few years?"

"There's an academy in Salem, but it would cost Pa more money than he can afford. I'll continue to read everything I can until I feel that I can begin my law study."

I felt I'd pushed too far, especially since we'd just met, and clearly my perspective wasn't exactly in sync with his eighteenth century perspective. Thomas and I had a few hours to kill until someone came out to replace Josiah, so I said, "I think we'll just walk around the island for awhile. We'll let you tend to your herd."

"Tis not a bother. I'll walk with you unless you wish to be alone. I can point out some things as we go around the island." I could tell that he found us fascinating. Apparently our new perspective intrigued him.

It looked as if he was going to make a complete circuit of the island. After walking westward past a small beach we continued on till we came to a narrow peninsula. He pointed to the mainland. "That's Beverly Farms. It's the northernmost part of Beverly. To the right is Manchester. If you continue on north you come to Gloucester. To the left of Beverly Farms is Beverly. South of Beverly on the other side of the river is Salem. That's the biggest town this side of Boston. Beverly used to be part of Salem."

"How does one cross the river into Salem?" asked Thomas. "Is there a bridge?"

"No, there's a ferry. Cost you two pence." We continued south along the perimeter of the island. We'd gone about 200 feet when he stopped and pointed southward. "That's Salem Harbor. You can see the ships." I was amazed at how many ships there were. I had read years ago that in the late eighteenth century Salem was the most important port north of Boston until you reached Halifax. I could believe it because the harbor was teeming with ships and smaller boats.

Josiah then said, "Just to the left of Salem Harbor you can see Marblehead. Another seafarin' town, but not as big as Salem. Marblehead was a part of Salem, too, but broke off over a hundred years ago." When he said this I was reminded that as young as America was in the 1700s, it had already been around for over a hundred years.

Josiah did a complete circuit pointing out other nearby islands including the biggest one of all, Baker's Island. His tour took a little more than an hour, so I judged that we still had quite a bit of time till someone came out to relieve Josiah. We sat down with our host and chatted amiably for the next few hours. It was relaxing and informative, but I was restless and eager to set foot on the mainland.

We'd been chatting for some time when I asked Josiah, "Do you know what time it is?" He looked at me as if thinking that I should have as good a sense of the time as he had.

"I would judge it to be past mid-morn, but not yet midday. Would you not agree?"

"That would be my guess," said Tom. We would have to adjust to less precision in time than we were used to. Few folks in the eighteenth century had watches, so when they were away from home they had to be good at observing the position of the sun in the daytime and the moon at night.

Then Josiah said, "When we hear the church bells in Beverly Farms you'll know it's noon. Can't always hear it, but the wind is coming off shore, so we'll hear it today, I reckon."

It seemed like less than a half hour before we heard the bells. I heard one deep-throated bell, followed only a few seconds later by a higher-pitched bell that rang twelve times.

"Why the one bell followed by the twelve bells?" I asked Josiah.

"It's two churches. I think they like to sound different."

It wasn't long after that that we saw a sailboat approaching from the mainland.

"That your dad coming out?" asked Thomas.

Josiah looked puzzled. "You mean my father, if I take your meaning?"

"Yes," recovered Thomas. "I mean your father. Where I come from we sometimes say dad."

"I think I've heard the word, but tis not in common usage among the folks I know," explained our new young friend.

"The boat looks like it's a Bermuda rig," I said searching to see if they used the term in this part of the world in the eighteenth century. It was a bit larger than the ones I was familiar with, but still quite similar.

"I think it is, though I'm not certain of it. I think it may be my pa's version of a Bermuda rigged boat, but to be sure, it's close enough."

Thomas and I exchanged glances. A substitute for high-fives. At least some things haven't changed.

As the small, two-sailed boat landed near the beach I could see that it was trailing what looked like a tiny rowboat or dinghy. A man, who I guessed to be about 40, anchored the boat a few yards off shore and rowed himself into the beach. Thomas and I were standing just behind Josiah as he waved down to his father. His father waved back. As he climbed the rocky approach up to the pasture I could see that he was someone who spent much of his time outdoors. His face had a ruddy complexion and his arms were tanned and muscular. Dark, wavy hair framed a sharp, angular face.

"Name's Henry Woodbury. And who might you fellers be?" he asked as he drew close. It wasn't a challenge, but more of a show of curiosity.

Thomas and I introduced ourselves as we shook hands. A custom that hadn't changed over the years.

"They're from up north, Pa. Halifax. They're on their way to New

York looking for work as printers."

Woodbury stroked his chin pensively. He was eyeing us suspiciously. "Hmm. And why would you be in Salem if you want work in New York?"

"This is Salem?" asked Tom. "It's not part of Beverly or Beverly Farms?"

"No, all these islands belong to Salem. This one is a lot closer to Beverly Farms than Salem, but it's part of Salem." Woodbury continued to stare at us, and I realized it was probably because of the way we were dressed as much as anything.

We explained how we'd ended up on the island because we'd discovered that our fur traders were thieves. I felt bad about the lie, but it had seemed a good way to explain an otherwise unusual stopover in Salem if New York was our destination. We went over to the old house and sat as Josiah made us coffee. He said they no longer drank tea since the imposition of the Port Bill. After about half an hour, I sensed that, if Woodbury had at first harbored suspicions about our intentions or our honesty, he was now more comfortable with us. He seemed to have taken a liking to us.

As we'd gotten to know each other somewhat, he was apparently comfortable enough to ask, "Is there something about New York that attracts you? Would not Boston do just as well? Or even Salem?"

"We've never been to New York," I said. "Hear it's growing fast. Plenty of jobs."

"Boston's growing, too. So's Salem. No need to go as far as New York. I know a printer in Salem. You can tell him I sent you. And the *Essex Gazette is* in Salem, too. They might need printers. Is it possible you fellas would be interested, or have you set your hearts on New York?"

Except for one small detail, this was about as ideal a beginning as we could have hoped for, so I exchanged a quick look with Tom and said, "No, we'd be interested in looking for a job in Salem." The small detail, of course, was that neither of us had worked for any length of time with an eighteenth century printing press. The only printing we'd done was with laser and inkjet printers. Fortunately, as part of my history major, I'd had the opportunity to become familiar with a working English press we had at the college. It was used in the art studies program and was shared by the history department. I'm mechanically minded and found that I was quite good with the press and with setting type. I'd even printed up a simulated page from a period newspaper, so I felt that, if we found jobs I could get up to speed fairly quickly. Unfortunately, the first day on the job I'd probably look like a klutz. Tom would no doubt take longer than me to get up to speed. But we weren't in the time travel program because we were dullards. Both of us scored near the top in nearly every aptitude test we took, so I was confident that we could pull it off.

"Good, I'm going into Salem on the morrow for supplies. You can ride with me in the wagon if you like. We can put you up at the house until you see how you do in Salem or Boston."

Tom and I exchanged looks again. He said, "We should probably stay at an inn or rooming house, but that's very generous of you, Henry."

"Nay, I won't have it. Save yourselves the money till you have yourselves a job."

"We'll compromise with you, Henry," I said. "We'll accept your hospitality for a night or two and find ourselves a rooming house or inn when we're familiar with the town."

Woodbury continued to protest, but finally relented and we reached an agreement based on my suggestion. Henry then addressed his son. "Josiah, why don't you take the boat in to the Farms and show our new friends around our little town. Ask your Ma to fix them up some dinner and I'll join everyone later for supper. I'll take the dory in. No need to come out for me."

Dinner, I later learned was the noon meal and usually larger than supper, the evening meal.

Chapter 8

At first, Jane Woodbury didn't seem as enthusiastic about having unfamiliar guests in her house as her husband was, but she gradually rallied and made us feel welcome. We learned that we weren't the first guests her husband had invited without discussing it with her. She didn't seem to resent it though. As our conversation progressed it came back to me that I'd read that people in the eighteenth century were used to having travelers as guests. It was common to stay with friends when traveling. If you couldn't stay with friends you stayed at an inn or a guesthouse. Sometimes you might be lucky to find a tavern that had a couple of rooms upstairs. Mrs. Woodbury told us that in Beverly and Salem it was not unusual for travelers to share a room with a perfect stranger if the inn was crowded or if the traveler wanted to share the expense. I remembered from my history readings that that was generally the case throughout the colonies.

I think Mrs. Woodbury liked having two young men in her home. We were a decade or so younger than her husband, but not that young in relation to her. I imagine she was about six or seven years younger than Henry. I'm not suggesting that she was in the least bit improper in the way she carried herself, but Thomas and I have been around long enough to know when a woman finds a man interesting.

She'd effortlessly gone about the process of giving us lunch, or dinner as she called it. We'd protested and said just a bit of bread and meat or cheese would be fine, but she gave us that and more at the plank table in a room that served as a kitchen and dining room combined. It was a modest dwelling, but far from Spartan and better than some we passed on our way there. It was only Jane Woodbury, her son Josiah, Tom and myself at the table. The conversation was lively and pleasant as we all got to know each other. Jane was full of questions.

"So you are both from Halifax. I've never been to Halifax. Is it big?"

"Fairly big," I said. "Halifax's much bigger than Beverly Farms. It's the largest town on the Atlantic north of Salem, I believe." said Thomas. "Both of us were born and brought up in Portland. We only went up to Halifax to find work. We wanted to come back to the American colonies, though. If you spend too much time up in British Canada, you could forget where your roots are."

"I not only have never been to Halifax or Portland," said Jane, "I've never been anywhere but here and Salem. Oh, once I was in Boston. It's difficult to travel, and it cost a great deal of money unless you have someone to stay with. Not that we want for money, mind you. Henry does right well in his work. He works too much, though."

"He makes his living with the cows?" asked Thomas.

"He makes something from that, but mostly he's a housewright. Right now he's free, but he expects to start on a new house next week. Elbridge, our oldest is out in the sound fishing right now. You'll meet him tonight. And George is with Mrs. Pinckney. She runs a small art school. He's only there two days a week. The remainder of the week he helps Henry with his building work. George has big ideas for how he'll help his father in the design of new houses. He thinks he'll get ideas from his art lessons. He's very good at drawing, but I don't see how this will help with building houses. Oh well, I suppose we shall see."

"George is clever, Ma," said Josiah. "He's going to surprise us all someday."

Jane smiled affectionately. "Josiah has always defended his younger brother."

"That's because no one in this family thinks he'll amount to anything."

"Not true, Josiah. Your father believes enough in his drawing skills to pay for his schooling with Mrs. Pinckney. And I, too, see that he has a certain talent. I just don't see how being good at drawing pictures can help with building a house."

Josiah dipped his head in silent assent and then changed the subject. "Pa suggested that I take Gilbert and Thomas around the village so they can get familiar with the town. We might even go into Beverly if we have time." Then he turned to us and said, "We can walk, or if you'd like we have horses. We could go into Beverly if we took the horses."

Tom and I exchanged looks. Finally I said, "We don't ride much, but I suppose it would be good if we could see Beverly, too." Tom seemed to wilt. I realized that I'd given the wrong answer, but it was too late to back out now. I'd taken riding lessons once, but never stayed with it. I don't know if Tom had ever been on a horse.

I had no trouble getting up on my horse. Tom had a little trouble, but tried to make it look as if he'd just slipped.

Josiah wasn't fooled. It was obvious that he couldn't believe his eyes. Everyone he knew rode well. "How do you fellers get around up in Halifax if you don't ride?"

"Believe it or not, we lived in town up there and hardly ever traveled out of town. Most of the time if we went anywhere it was usually in someone's cart, carriage or wagon. Country folk up there ride, but a lot of us townspeople mostly walk. We ride, but not that much."

Josiah just shook his head in disbelief. "Well, I reckon we'd best not go too fast. Just follow me and we'll take it real slow, though I calculate that we could move just as fast on foot."

I winced. Thomas whispered to me. "God, I feel like such a wimp."

"Me, too," I whispered back. Then I said in a louder voice, "We'll get better at it, I reckon."

The streets in the center of the village were cobblestoned, but the peripheral streets and lanes were packed dirt. We passed a stable, a bake shop, a central open-air market, which reminded me of our twenty-first century farmers' markets. We clip-clopped past a freestanding butcher shop with carcasses hanging in front of the store.

After about 20 minutes my back was killing me. I was coming down when the horse was going up. Gotta learn to synchronize.

"Josiah, I'm curious. You seem to have plenty of food and other merchandise right here in Beverly Farms. Why does your father go all the way into Salem for supplies?" It was none of my business, but I was curious.

"He needs to see Colonel Mason in Salem. We can get a lot of supplies right here in Beverly Farms or Beverly proper, but Salem's a bigger town. Sometimes it's the only place you can get certain things. I think Salem's over 5,000 now. Almost as big as Boston. And growing every day. But you're right. If he didn't have to see Colonel Mason, he wouldn't need to go into Salem tomorrow. I usually go into Salem with him, but not when he sees the Colonel. I keep hoping that someday soon he'll take me with him."

"What's so special about Colonel Mason?" probed Tom.

"I probably shouldn't tell you, but you'll find out soon enough anyway. The colonel is helping Massachusetts so it can defend itself. He's been commissioned by the Massachusetts Committee of Safety to build up stores for our protection."

"Defend itself from whom?" I asked, already knowing the answer.

"The regulars."

"The redcoats?"

"Yes, the redcoats. Surely feelings must be the same up in Halifax?"

"Of course," said Tom. "I don't think the feelings are so strong up there, though. The English Canadians are in a difficult spot. They resent the unreasonable taxation from England, but they hate the French even more. Because of that they seem to be more accepting of the English rule than we are here in New England. Frankly, that's one of the reasons we left Halifax and headed for New York. We feel a lot more strongly about defending the colonies against the abuses coming out of England. We wanted to be down here where we could do our part for the colonies."

I hoped that Tom sounded properly grounded in the politics of the time. We had read about this period in school, but, frankly, it was all rather abstract and didn't mean much to me then. I assume that was true of Tom, too. Suddenly it all meant much, much more. For example, my readings about the Stamp Act of 1765, which at the time had made me yawn, made a lot of sense now. Through this act the British Parliament demanded that many printed materials in the colonies had to be made on stamped paper produced in England and had to carry an embossed revenue stamp. Revenue from this tax had to be paid in British currency; not Colonial money. I'd memorized all this back in school and done reasonably well, but quite frankly, it hadn't gotten my juices flowing. Now, all of a sudden, Tom and I were thrust right square in the middle of the dull stuff I'd read about in school. Only now it wasn't so dull.

Suddenly I remembered that, to add insult to injury, the proceeds of these taxes were used to pay for British troops stationed in America. These troops were in America in the wake of the French and Indian War, which was called the Seven Years War in Europe. London felt that the Americans were the main beneficiaries of the troops on American soil, so they should help pay for them. The American colonies resisted vigorously, since they sent no representatives to Parliament in London and had no influence over their own taxes. Eventually, after numerous protests including the destruction of Lieutenant Governor Hutchinson's house, Parliament repealed the Stamp Act.

Less than a year later, though, London imposed something called the Revenue Act, which placed heavy taxes on glass, paper, paint and tea. The colonies quickly reacted by abstaining from using all foreign commodities in so much as it was possible. Imports from Great Britain were reduced by 75 percent. The king demanded through the governor of the colony that the policy of abstention be rescinded. The Massachusetts House voted 92 to 17 to refuse to obey the governor. Salem was indignant that her two representatives voted with the minority and called a town meeting in which they voted to thank the majority. The next year the town replaced the two representatives with Richard Derby and John Pickering.

"I think you did not hear me, Gilbert," said Josiah, waking me from my thoughts.

"Sorry, my mind wandered. I was thinking of how different things are back home. What did you say?"

"I was saying that we accept English rule. He's our king, too, and we're proud of it. What we don't accept is when Parliament imposes taxes on us when we have no one in Parliament to speak on our behalf."

"You seem to know a great deal about such affairs for such a young man," said Thomas.

"Most of my mates think the same as I. I am not so young, either. Most men my age are working or apprenticed to some tradesman. Is it not so in Halifax or Portland?"

"If they're not studying for the law," I said with a twinkle in my eye.

Josiah didn't catch the twinkle. "Very few people around here study for the law," he said seriously. "Even fewer study medicine. Most young people work at trades. Most men in this part of the world begin working when they are 13 or 14, usually as apprentices. It's important to learn a trade alongside an experienced tradesman. Of course, all of us, boys and girls, have our chores long before that."

"It's the same in Halifax and Portland," I assured our young friend.

"I would think that would be so. I have heard that people are resisting the heavy hand of Parliament up and down the coast as far to the south as Carolina."

"Yes, I think that's true. You said that, while the people in this area have resisted the taxes from Great Britain, they still remain loyal to the king. If that be true, then why is this Colonel Mason, with the Authority of the Committee of Safety, helping the colony defend itself? The redcoats aren't going to attack Massachusetts over a tax disagreement."

Josiah seemed to struggle with this. "I think I may have already said too much. May be that Pa will want to tell you more, but I think it's not my place to say more. Per chance I have said too much already. Do you mind if I ask about something else?"

I smiled. "Not at all. What's on your mind?" At that moment, a two-wheeled carriage passed us at a furious pace. It was obvious that the horse was out of control. The driver yelled and people in the narrow street jumped aside. The commotion startled my horse and I had to hold on for dear life.

Josiah grinned at my nervousness. "Very good, Gilbert. You held on. Your horse is getting to know you and remained under your control. That bodes well for your riding future."

"He was under control?" Didn't seem so to me, but what do I know. I couldn't let on how scared shitless I was. "Well, Josiah, what's on your mind?"

"It's the way you and Thomas talk. I've met folks from up north: Andover, Newburyport, Portsmouth, and they talk more like us here in Beverly. It's not important, I suppose, but it's just that I find it strange."

"You've not met someone from Halifax, though?" I said.

"No, that's true, but I cannot believe they talk so different from us."

"What is it about our talk that you find so strange?" asked Tom.

"I cannot say, I suppose. Just different. Tis not important. Here, we're at the town market. Let's tie up and you can look around."

In many ways the outdoor market was much like our farmers' markets, but there were some clear-cut differences. Merchants yelled at shoppers, either trying to get their attention or telling them to take their hands off the merchandise. Never have I seen the carcasses of a pig, sheep or deer hanging out in the open at a farmers' market. The flies around the meat seemed to bother no one but Tom and myself. Live chickens and geese and free-running pigs added to the lively tumult. In all, it was a lot more fun than a twenty-first century farmers' market, but not nearly as sanitary.

Sanitation was not at the top of the list of priorities in the eighteenth century. The marketplace made this point loud and clear, but it was brought home even more later when were back at the Woodbury's house.

Chapter 9

About a half hour before we sat down to supper, Jane Woodbury said something that forced us to come face to face with the reality of our trip back in time.

"If you need to use the privy, it's out back just to the left of the pathway. Or maybe you'd rather use a pot. She pointed to a chamber pot on the floor in the corner of the room. You can take it upstairs to your room if that suits you."

Tom looked at me and said with a grin, "Why don't you go first."

I said, "I'll use the privy."

"There's a pile of leaves and a few corncobs there. Suit yourself."

There you have it. It was about a hundred years too early for toilet paper. This could be a hell of a career opportunity for me in my new century. I'd have to think about this.

The privy was a gray wood plank building about the size of a phone booth. Now there's an interesting phenomenon. The phone was also about a hundred years in the future and the phone booth even later than that, though at the time Tom and I left Nevada there were hardly any phone booths left. A new creation come and gone.

It was a two-seater privy. Two ten-inch holes cut through wood boards. Splinters and all. I tried to imagine two people sitting side by side doing their business in this cramped space at the same time. I'd have to ask about that. But who would I ask, and would I want to? There were no dry leaves or corncobs in the privy, so I backed out and saw that they were right there next to the structure in a little pile. Hmmm..... more primitive than camping out in our own century. I realized right then and there that it was going to be like this for the rest of my life. Might as well get used to it.

When I went back into the house my first inclination was to go to the sink and wash my hands. But, of course, there was no sink and, of course, no running water. Just another tangible reminder that what you learn from books remains fairly abstract until you actually experience it. Now I was experiencing it, and it was a whole lot more real, believe me. Jane pointed toward a murky bowl of water, which I could use to dip my fingers in if they were dirty. I followed the local protocol, wondering as I did so if I wasn't making my hands dirtier. She did have a towel in the kitchen, which I used to dry my hands. It was going to take awhile to get used to eighteenth-century hygiene.

Jane had given us a bedroom to share. It wasn't that much different from a twenty-first-century bedroom. Bed, bureau and window. I was used to reading my Kindle Fire in bed, so I hadn't needed a light. Now the only light available was a candle. I'd have to learn to read from printed books by candlelight, or wait for daylight. I could see, too, that I was going to get used to reading the classics. No John Grisham, Dorothy Sayers, Patricia Cornwell, Nelson DeMille, Vince Flynn, P. D. James, Dan Brown or Michael Connelly.

Henry Woodbury came through the door just as Jane was putting dishes on the table.

"Did Josiah show you about our little town, gentlemen?" he asked heartily.

"We had a good tour. Josiah's very knowledgable about this area." I said. "Seems like a fine community."

Josiah spoke up. "We took the horses so we could see a bit of Beverly, too."

"We're not very good horsemen, and Josiah showed us a few things to make us more comfortable in the saddle," said Tom.

Henry looked surprised. "I'd have taken two healthy fellows like you to be excellent horsemen."

"I'm afraid we spent too much time in town up in Halifax and even when growing up in Portland. Not much occasion to ride. We rode a little, but not much. After today's experience, though, I think we'll want to ride a lot more."

I could tell that Henry didn't quite believe such a lame reason for healthy men not riding, but he was too much of a gentleman to question us further. I caught him shaking his head slowly from side to side in silent disbelief, but he said no more on the subject.

"What have you in mind for the morrow? Still wish to ride into Salem with me?"

"Yes, definitely yes," I said, hoping that we'd meet this Colonel Mason, a man I vaguely remember reading about in some book about this period in history.

At the supper table in addition to Mr. and Mrs. Woodbury we were joined by Josiah and his brother George.

"You know Josiah. And you just met George, here. I hope you will meet my older boy, Elbridge soon. If his boat is in, he'll be having supper with his young wife Rebecca. They live not far from here. Mayhap on Sunday you'll meet them. George here studies drawing at Mrs. Pinckney's school when he's not helping with the herd or at my building sites. All three of the boys have spirit. All of them have ambition." He proudly extended an arm in the direction of Josiah and George.

Jane served up a leg of roast mutton, with potatoes and hard cider. I'd never had mutton. What I'd heard was that it was tough, but this was not at all tough.

"Mrs. Woodbury, this is delicious. You're a fine cook."

She beamed, and Thomas chimed in with another compliment. "This is fantastic. Outstanding!"

She seemed slightly off balance and not with the compliments themselves, but the way they'd been expressed—especially by the way Tom had praised her food. I don't think such terms as fantastic and outstanding were used much in the eighteenth century. "I have never had anyone say such things before. Thank you, gentlemen."

Henry then said, "I hope you fellers don't take me wrong when I say this, but you do have a strange way of speaking. Not what we're used to around here. I suppose we'll get used to it, though." He paused as if deciding how blunt he should be. Finally he said, "We should probably stop by a shop and get you some new clothes. Hope you don't mind my sayin' it, but you'll be accepted a lot quicker if you dress like we do around here."

George, who'd spoken very little until now, proved to be quite outspoken when he did speak. "Pa, you said what I was thinkin'." He looked at Tom and myself and forced a nervous smile. "Hope you don't mind my saying that, but we're not used to sech clothing. Jest look a bit strange to me."

I couldn't help but laugh. If they only knew the whole truth about us, they'd know what strange was.

Jane looked embarrassed. "Please forgive us, gentlemen. We haven't traveled much and are unfamiliar with the ways of other parts of the world."

"No need to apologize," I said. "Things here are just as different for us, but despite our differences, we're all Americans." As soon as I said that I realized that it might sound a bit strange to our hosts.

A broad smile crossed the rugged features of Henry Woodbury. "I'm mighty glad to hear you say that, Gilbert. Mighty glad. After we finish here, why don't the three of us take a little walk. I've got something I'd like to discuss with you."

Chapter 10

After a scrumptious dessert of baked apple with brown sugar and fresh cream from Woodbury's herd on Great Misery Island, we three men adjourned for a walk. Before we left the house, Henry pushed tobacco into a briar pipe with his thumb and lit it from the embers of the fire in the kitchen fireplace where Jane had done all of her cooking. He generously offered Tom and me puffs, which we refused politely. I restrained myself from addressing the hazards of smoking. No doubt my advice would be received no better by Woodbury than it would be by a confirmed smoker in the twenty-first century.

Darkness was beginning to descend upon Beverly Farms. It was a peaceful time of day. I immediately noted that there were no streetlights in the village. Or at least not in this part of the town. I decided to ask our host about this. "Henry, do you have street lighting in the center of the village?"

"Aye, but just on Hale Street for a short distance. Keeps a man busy lighting those candles and trimming them. Village can't afford to light more of the town."

I was tempted to tell him that gas lighting would be invented before the end of the century, but decided I'd either spook him or he'd think I was daft. I needed Henry as a friend, and for that to happen, he had to see me as fairly normal—by his standards; not mine.

Henry turned serious now. "You said at supper that we're all Americans. Do you mean that?"

I thought for a minute before responding. What was he looking for? I guessed that he was hoping that Tom and I were fed up with the way Parliament in London had been treating the colonies, so I said, "I hope I don't offend you, but Thomas and I have lost patience with John Bull. For the last ten years or more we've both felt that London takes us colonials for granted. They forget that we're British citizens, too. I think it was the Tea Party in Boston that finally decided for me that I wanted to do more than complain. That's one of the reasons we left Halifax. Most folks up there have a lot more patience with the king and parliament than Thomas and I have."

Henry smiled. "You'll remember, then, that after the Tea Party, Parliament passed the Boston Port Bill that would move the Boston Custom House to Salem. It meant that all the shipping revenue would then come through Salem. The bill, as I'm sure you know, made for bitterness in Boston and resentment of Salem. But Salem possessed too much magnanimity to let herself benefit at the expense of Boston. At a town meeting they voted in favor of the colonies stopping all importing and exporting from Great Britain until the Boston Port Bill was repealed.

"London refuses to treat us like British citizens. Most people I know don't see things getting any better, either. What I'm saying to you both is you've landed yourself in the right place if you want to fight on behalf of the colonies." He studied our faces, trying to read our minds, no doubt.

This was getting a bit uncomfortable. Not the politics of the issue, for I was fairly certain we were all on the same page, but I was unsure of the timing of our conversation. Tom and I still didn't know what year it was. We learned something when my comment about the Tea Party went unchallenged. So we knew that today was later than December 16, 1773—probably months or even a year or two later, for Woodbury had reacted as if the Tea Party were sometime in the past. What we didn't know was what other important events had happened since the Tea Party. His comment about fighting on behalf of the colonies was a bit cryptic. Did he mean fighting against taxation without representation or did he mean fighting in the Revolution? Could the war already be underway? Based on what Henry had been saying, it probably had not yet begun. I was hoping we'd come across a newspaper soon so we'd know the date. We couldn't just ask Henry. I was sure he already considered us strange. I didn't want him to think us stupid as well. After a rather extended pregnant pause, I said, "Once we settle ourselves into positions with a printer and find ourselves some rooms, I think we'd both like to do our part. What kind of fight are you talking about?"

"We're hopin' things don't come to actual fighting with weapons, though we fear, unfortunately, that it may come to that. That's why the Committee of Safety is preparin' for the worst, while hopin' for the best."

"I sense that you believe war can't be avoided?" said Tom.

"You read me clearly, Thomas. "I think the last straw was when Parliament passed the Act for Better Regulating of the Government of the Province of Massachusetts. It rescinded the colony's charter and gave the governor supreme power. He now appoints and remove judges. He appoints all other officers of power. How can you expect proper decisions of these officials and judges when they serve at the pleasure of the governor? The act even prohibits town meetings from being held without first gaining written permission from Governor Gage or his lieutenant governor."

So now we knew that the war had not yet started. I estimated that at that very moment we were somewhere between early 1774 and the spring of 1775. It appeared that we'd not only gone back in time, but gone back over 240 years. Going back in time had not been our goal. We'd gone the wrong way and then some. Still, on the bright side, we'd proven that you could travel in time. On the dark side, though, I was not sure going back this far was going to end happily for any of us. As I considered this I was reminded of the garbled message we'd received in the space vehicle six days into our trip. Could it have been a warning that something was wrong and that we should have aborted the trip? We'd never know now.

I slowed to a stop and faced our host. "So, Henry, if you and your friends think war is a real possibility, I assume you're preparing for it so that you won't be at too much of a disadvantage when it happens?"

"We are, but I'm afraid I can't tell you much more about it, Gilbert. I know so little about you and Thomas. We can't afford to be too open about all this. I'm sure you understand."

"I do understand, Henry, but tell us what we must do to earn your trust." As I was saying this I thanked God that I'd been a history major in college. I had an idea and thought there was no better time than this to give it a try. "Henry, when I was barely 15 years of age I tried to sign up with our local militia up in Portland. The commander of the militia turned me away. Said I should wait till I was 16 and then he'd welcome me with open arms. I told him I wanted to do my part in the war. Wanted to fight the French and the Indians. At the time the French were laying siege to Quebec. The commander told me that the Portland militia wasn't going to be involved in Quebec because the British army under General Wolfe had enough troops. I told my father that if the Portland militia wouldn't have me I wanted to go to Quebec and join the regulars under Wolfe. My father just laughed."

"I can understand why he did," said Henry with a kindly smile.

"I know. I was young and reckless. I only tell you this because I think it might show you that even at an early age I was willing and eager to fight for a just cause."

"I'm not sure how just that cause was, Gilbert, but I do take your point. Certainly it was a patriotic cause. Do you still feel the same fervor for the British cause?"

I winced. Hoist by my own petard. "No, no. Certainly not. I only tell you this because I want you to know that I'm willing to fight for a cause If I believe in it. I was just a boy at the time. I don't know if we were right in fighting for French territory then. I know we were right when the French encroached on our territory. I know we were right when we defended ourselves at Fort William Henry. But no, I don't know if we had a right to take Quebec. And certainly I cannot defend Parliament and British regulars who rule this colony by military force. This is not what our ancestors came here for. Britain's policy toward us has changed for the worse. I will fight against those abuses with every fiber of my body. I can tell you right now that Thomas and I intend to join the Salem militia soon. We want to do our part."

"I like the sound of what you say, Gilbert."

"Believe me, Henry, Thomas and I have strong feelings about the Patriot cause and want to do whatever we can to support it. I know that you've only known us for less than a day, but I'm sure you've had to trust all of your friends who declare their willingness to fight for the Patriot cause. The only true test is to see how people behave. Let us help and you'll see that you can trust us. I'm willing to trust you and what you're trying to do." I hesitated a minute before saying, "The only thing I'd like to know is will you and your friends be the ones to start a war if it comes to that?"

"My friends and I would never initiate a war against our own king, but we would defend ourselves if he started such a war. All right, if you really want to help defend the colonies, I'd like you to meet our local leader. Tomorrow, when I ride into Salem, I'll be meeting David Mason. Mason's a colonel in the Massachusetts Committee of Safety. David has been authorized to collect military stores in preparation for the possibility of a future conflict. These are secret preparations, and I must extract from you your promise not to disclose any of this unless it be to someone you know to be working for the committee."

"How would we know that?"

"If you have any doubt, speak to me first. In time you'll know who these people are. You'll meet Colonel Mason tomorrow. He'll be a might cautious about trusting you. I'm puttin' my reputation on the line, so I expect that you'll need to convince him of your desire to help the cause. Don't be put off if he asks you to wait in another room during our meeting. He's extremely cautious about who he lets into these sessions. Needs to assure himself about who he can trust. So if he excuses you from the meeting, don't take offense. With time I'm sure you'll prove yourselves."

♦ ♦ ♦

Thomas and I shared a room that night. We slept in a rustic bunk bed—he on top and myself on the bottom. Our mattresses were made of straw. They were not as uncomfortable as I feared when I first saw what I was in store for. I usually read for a few minutes when I go to bed, but that was not in the cards that first night. For one thing there were no lights and for another, there were no books. I later learned that the Woodbury house did possess one book: The King James edition of the *Bible.*

I also learned the next day that they had recent copies of the *Essex Gazette* neatly piled in one corner of the kitchen. In the morning, at breakfast, I asked Jane Woodbury if I could look at the latest edition of the paper. Aha! Finally! The masthead said it was for September 19 to September 26, 1774—a weekly.

Jane said it was yesterday's paper. She apologized for not having that morning's paper, but said it would be delivered later in the morning. As I scanned the front page I saw that Governor Gage had adjourned the Provincial Assembly, which was now meeting in Salem. According to the account, Gage feared that the legislature, which was made up of representatives from the various communities, would vote to resist the latest aggressive acts of Parliament. The legislature did convene anyway, but neither the governor, nor his representatives showed up to administer the usual oaths that would qualify the legislators to convene. The legislators waited another day, but Gage still did not show up, so the assembled legislators chose John Hancock chairman and passed resolutions that declared that the governor, by adjourning the House before it had even met, had violated the terms of the *Massachusetts Bay Charter*. The *Gazette* article went on to say that the charter was essentially the constitution of the colony, so the governor had acted unconstitutionally. Before the legislature closed its proceedings, they resolved themselves into a congress and agreed to meet later in the month in Concord.

I was fairly familiar with all of this, because of my history major and because I was still somewhat of a history buff. What happened in the Salem legislature and the Congress in Concord only a few days later was in essence a preparation for conflict with Great Britain. Delegates from most of the colonies met soon after in Philadelphia to discuss their grievances with Parliament. In Massachusetts, the Committee of Safety was considered by many to be the executive authority of the colony. They dedicated themselves to collecting munitions and weapons for the protection of the colony in the event that war should break out.

I had just finished the article when Henry entered the kitchen.

"Mornin' gents," he said heartily. Henry seemed like a morning person. "Sorry to interrupt your reading. Anything interesting?"

"I just read about how Gage tried to shut down the latest meeting of the legislature. And when it did convene, he didn't show up to administer the oaths. Things don't seem to be getting any better, do they?"

"You speak the truth, Gilbert. Gage will never take the side of the Americans. What is sad, they tell me, is that he likes Americans. He likes being here, too. Hell, he married an American girl. He's been in America since '55 when he fought the French. Led a regiment at Ticonderoga. Later became military governor of Montreal. When the war ended he became commander-in-chief of British forces for all of America. So he's been here for 20 years and has many friends here. But he will not act in defiance of the king. He's a good soldier to the core. As much as he supposedly likes us, he apparently feels it's his duty to keep us in line."

I said, "Up in Halifax many people are siding with the king. Not everyone, but I'd guess that more than half of the folks up there are loyalists. What's the thinking down here?"

"I don't like the term loyalists. Prefer Tory. Most of us here are loyal to our king, even when he turns on us and treats us like non-citizens. We're proud to be British, even though many of us have never set foot in England. Massachusetts, after all, is just another province of the mother country. At least that's the way my friends and I see it. But to answer your question, Gilbert, I'd say that maybe a third would side with the king regardless of the abuses of Parliament. They think the term loyalist belongs to them alone. My own brother's in that group. Another third, myself included, have had enough and feel something has to be done to put an end to these abuses. The other third will probably wait and see which way the wind is blowing."

"So you and your brother don't agree on politics.

He laughed nervously, "That would be an understatement. Somehow, though, we've managed to stay close. Until recently we've tried to avoid politics as much as possible. Lately, though, it's been harder to steer clear of the subject because it's on everyone's mind now. Hopefully he and his wife'll be joining us for supper tonight so you'll see for yourselves. I'd best go over there after my coffee this morning and let them know they're invited. They just live a few houses from here."

"I look forward to meeting him. So you drink coffee and not tea?"

"Won't drink tea till the Port Bill is rescinded," said Woodbury with finality.

Chapter 11

The trip across the river into Salem was interesting. The ferry was a flat-bottomed barge. We rode our horses onto the barge and then dismounted for the short trip across to Salem. The entire process took less than 20 minutes. Tom and I were still getting used to horses, so the unsteady gait of our horses as they got onto the barge made for more than a little bit of instability. Getting off the barge on the other side was even more precarious. I couldn't help noticing Henry Woodbury as he took it all in. I think he was still astounded that two otherwise robust men couldn't ride worth a damn.

Salem was obviously the metropolis of this part of Massachusetts. Well, not exactly a metropolis, but certainly a hell of a lot more imposing than Beverly or tiny Beverly Farms. Salem had originally encompassed most of the towns of the North Shore. Beverly, Marblehead, Swampscott, Danvers, Peabody were all part of Salem in the early part of the seventeenth century. Then they gradually broke off for various reasons. I had to be careful now not to mention Peabody because that wouldn't become a separate entity until 1855.

The harbor was teeming with vessels of every size and configuration: sloops, schooners, barks, yawls. I knew from my reading that in the 1700s Salem competed with Boston for the shipping trade of New England. It was a growing bustling town compared to sleepy Beverly and Beverly Farms. Woodbury took us down busy Front Street where merchants of every type hawked their wares. Then he led us ten or twelve blocks to a quieter more residential neighborhood.

"Colonel Mason lives here," said Woodbury pointing to a stately house that marked the owner as a man of substance. The houses in this area were clearly several notches above the ones I'd seen in other neighborhoods as we rode through Salem.

"A very nice house," said Tom.

"It's a fine home. The Mason's have roots here." We tied up our mounts at street-side hitching posts and proceeded toward the house. Woodbury rapped twice with the brass door knocker. Within moments we heard someone approach from the inside. The massive door swung open, and we were greeted by an imposing man of above average height. I guessed he was eight or ten years older than Henry. He was clearly a man of military bearing who was used to be being in charge. Yet despite this self-assured manner, I immediately felt comfortable in his presence. He smiled and addressed Woodbury.

"Henry, I see you've brought friends with you. Come in, come in." The interior of the house was more impressive than the exterior. Woodbury's house was comfortable, but it was easy to see that the Mason family was very well off. I wondered where their wealth came from. Mason was an officer in the Committee of Safety, but I was fairly sure that he didn't get rich in that role. Usually, military officers in this century became officers because they already had money.

After brief introductions, Mason invited us to sit down in his library. What a treasure that was. Far more than the one holy book in the Woodbury household.

"Would you like some tea?" asked our host. Before any of us could answer, he said, "Almost forgot, Henry, that you're off tea for the present. You still adhering to that vow?"

"Yes, but you go ahead. I don't know what Gilbert and Thomas drink."

Coffee was fine with Tom and myself. We'd become addicted to it a long time ago so it was no sacrifice to accept it now.

"I think I'll have coffee," I said. "The least I can do is support my new friend."

"Coffee sounds good for me, too," said Tom.

"I trust you have business to discuss with me, Henry. Should you and I excuse ourselves for a moment or two? I'm sure your friends wouldn't mind perusing my library." He smiled proudly. "I've devoted my adult life to collecting books. It's been a slow process, but I wager I have one of the finest collections this side of Boston—other than the Social Library, of course." He was referring to a small subscription library that opened in a brick schoolhouse in Salem in 1761. A Boston minister had been hired to purchase books in London and stock the little proprietary library, the first library of any kind in Salem. The collection consisted of the books bought by the minister, plus books donated by library members.

"Please, excuse yourselves," I said. "Thomas and I can occupy ourselves with the library. Haven't seen this many books in one place in my life." I could see that Mason was pleased that we appreciated his collection. He started to leave the room and then stopped. It was obvious he wanted to make a point.

"Henry and I go way back," he said. "We both fought in '57 at Fort William Henry against the French and those red savages. Nearly lost our lives in the massacre. Montcalm granted us generous surrender terms, but we had to lay down our arms and march away peaceably. As we left the fort the Indians descended upon us and slaughtered hundreds of unarmed men, women and children. It was the most horrible experience of my life. The French didn't pay the Indians the way they paid French soldiers or Canadian militiamen. They bought them with a simple promise: When the fighting is done, take whatever booty you can find for yourselves. On this occasion, though, the redskins went crazy scalping, beating, ripping children from the bosoms of their mothers. One Indian was seen running with a human head in his hands, blood dripping from the thing. Believe, me when I say 'twas a terrible thing."

"Some of us managed to make our way to Fort Gilbert in Western Massachusetts, with the help of a French escort, but we left behind so many friends and fellow comrades in arms, that....never mind. When you've gone through something like that you can see why I trust Henry's judgement."

Woodbury said, "David commanded an artillery company at Fort William Henry—a battery of brass cannon. Fired the last ball before the fort fell. He then led a group of us including troops and some women and children to safety at the height of the massacre and then on to Fort Gilbert. Normally we would've fought the devils, but we were defenseless because we'd already laid down our weapons. David saved fifteen of us so you can see why I trust him."

"We trust each other implicitly," intoned Mason soberly. "I hope you understand my caution when meeting new folks. Until I get to know them or know enough about them, I can't afford to share certain information. Not when lives depend on it. So if you'll excuse us for a minute or two, Henry and I will retire to another room."

◆ ◆ ◆

In the kitchen Mason addressed Woodbury.

"Fine looking men, Henry. I assume they wish to join us.?"

"Aye. Wanted you to meet them. I'll be keepin' an eye on them. I think they'll be good, but admittedly I just met them. They're definitely interested."

"Good. Keep me apprised. We can use as many good men as we can get. You have something else, I suspect?" he said knowingly.

"I've found at least two more cannon at Fort William. We can add them to your stores at Foster's workshop on the North River. Not much compared to what you got from Derby, but every cannon helps." He was referring to Richard Derby, who'd made his money from the shipping trade. Derby's ships had mounted cannon to defend against privateers during the French War. His contributions to Mason's cache of cannon were from both his own ships and privateers his ships had outgunned.

"Aye, every cannon helps. That's good, Henry. Good. What else have you got for me?"

"Six more muskets and a quantity of balls."

"Good, good. It all adds up. It's slow going, because we don't want to alert the wrong people. Far too many people think we're alarmists and disloyal to the king when we make these preparations. Already Gage has people combing the countryside for weapons that have been set aside for the worst. They know they can't confiscate every weapon, but when there's a large cache of them, they go after 'em. That's why I'm being cautious with your two new friends. No more cautious, I might add, than I would be with any new people.

"I know, I know. But I wanted you to meet them. Hopefully I'll know more about them soon. I'd like for them to work out. They don't know anybody here, which in a way is a good sign."

"It could be. Then again, it could be because they've been planted here. Keep an eye on them and we'll see how it goes." Then Mason softened his tone a bit. "My greatest fear is that one of our own will somehow inadvertently or even intentionally reveal the locations of where we store our ordnance and ammunition. We've all worked hard to put these defense supplies away in the event we might need them. Careless talk could set us back months. It could also mean that some of us would end up behind bars or worse. The very reason we're doing all this is because the sad truth is that our king and his Parliament are not nearly as benevolent as we once naively believed them to be. If I'm worried about those among us, you can understand why I must be doubly cautious about newcomers."

"Yes, of course." Woodbury then changed the subject. "Have we any new men in the last week, David?"

"Aye. We've got two from up in Andover, three from Danvers, one from Beverly and two, maybe three more from Salem. We could get more if we weren't so careful." Then he added, "And it looks like we may eventually have two more here from....I don't think you've told me where they're from?"

"Halifax. Originally from Portland. Moved to Halifax after the war. Looking for work in the printing trade. They're here because they lost their jobs in Halifax and took passage on a commercial boat bound for New York. That boat turned out to be in the hands of fur thieves. Gilbert and Thomas wanted out and they set them ashore on Great Misery Island. So they know no one here in Salem."

"That's quite the story. I repeat, keep an eye on these fellows. They seem good, but you admit we know nothing about them. If you want to help them, though, I know Sam Hall, the publisher of the *Essex Gazette*. Good man who supports our cause. He might have something. There are at least two printing houses here in Salem, too."

"Yes," said Woodbury, "I plan to take them around to the *Gazette* to meet Sam after we leave here. If need be, we'll visit the two printers, too."

"Good, good. Now I think we should go back into the library."

♦ ♦ ♦

As they reentered the book-laden room, Mason said, "I hope you gentlemen haven't become bored in our absence."

Tom said, "I could never become bored with this collection. I'm in awe of your library, Colonel."

Mason beamed. "It's good of you to say that. I appreciate it. You don't find many book lovers in this part of the world." Then he cleared his throat and said, "Before you take your leave, gentlemen, I want to impress upon you if your desire is to join our ranks at some point you will become part of something much bigger than our organization here in Massachusetts. As I'm sure you know, our Committee of Safety is part of the Sons of Liberty movement that functions in virtually every colony in America. John Hancock of Boston is our leader in Massachusetts, and he is looked upon by Sons of Liberty members in colonies up and down the coast as the titular leader of this great American movement. One way or another, we will put an end to Parliament's tyranny."

Tom and I left Mason's house fully aware of how the under-manned colonists were eventually able to overcome British power. There was a dedication here in the colonies that I was sure the Brits across the pond couldn't imagine. Surprisingly, the movement was fueled by all walks of life. From the tradesmen to the fishermen to the shipping magnates and scholars, people seemed to be willing to risk their treasure and even their lives to halt what they considered major abuses by their fellow Englishmen from across the sea.

As we rode away Tom raised the question that was on both our minds. "Henry, I take it Colonel Mason wants to wait before he accepts us as members of the Committee of Safety?"

"I'm sure you can understand why. He doesn't know you, and we can't afford mistakes. He was properly impressed by both of you, and I think he's hoping he'll feel comfortable with your joining soon. After all, you're new in town and we know nothing about you. If you're still interested, I'll bring your name up again."

We both understood. I changed the subject.

I raised an issue that I assumed was on the minds of many colonists, no matter which way they leaned.

"London thinks we owe them for the French war, don't they?"

"Both the king and Parliament maintain that we colonists were the primary beneficiaries of Britain's victory over the French back in '63. They believe that because we benefited, we should be expected to pay at least part of the cost of that victory and also of maintaining 10,000 regulars here on American soil after the war. Obviously, we don't agree. Certainly we should pay our fair share of the cost of victory, but we've already done that with the lives of our young men. What we object most to is the presence of those 10,000 regulars here long after the war was over. We don't need 'em and we don't want 'em. We definitely don't want to be taxed for anything if we don't have the right to send delegates to Parliament, which as I'm sure you know, we don't. We should at least have the right to have a say in what levies are imposed on ourselves. We might not always agree, but at least we should have our say."

Our next stop in Salem was at the office of the *Essex Gazette*. Henry knew Samuel Hall, the publisher and introduced us to him. Hall was a short stocky man with a big round head that matched his body. He was bald with a ring of hair around his head that hung well over his ears. He was perhaps 20 years older than us, but moved with a surprising quickness and ease in view of his size and shape. He smiled warmly as he asked Henry, "Who are your new friends? Never seen these gents around Salem, and I think I know nearly everyone in town."

"Gilbert and Thomas have just moved here from Halifax. They're printers and looking for work. I thought you might have something for them."

"Tell me a bit about yourselves, lads. I do need one man. We'll be moving the paper to Cambridge soon, and I think we'll need a second man when we do. What have you done up in Halifax?"

"Usual typesetting, of course," I said as casually as I could. "We've both worked with wood and metal type. I've even done wood-letter collages. All of our presses came over from London, of course, so we're more familiar with that kind of press, but we could learn to work with any press. Oh, and toward the end they let me write a few short political essays." As I said this I noticed that Hall frowned ever so slightly, but made no comment, but to say,

"Our presses are from England, too, so that won't be a problem."

"I've designed printing blocks and etchings for illustration purposes. We're fast workers, and I think you'll find us reliable."

A pensive look had transformed Hall's face. "You said a moment ago that you've done some political writing up there. As I understand it most of the folks up that way think the king and Parliament are their friends. Is that what you lads think?"

Uh oh. Had to head this off fast. "Not at all, sir," I said. "Thomas and I were fortunate to be working for one of the few men in Halifax who disagreed with how London has been handling the colonies. He encouraged me to write some opinion pieces that were rather critical of the king and Parliament."

"Sounds good to me. By the by, who'd you work for up in Halifax?"

"For a short while," I said, "we set type at the *Nova Scotia Chronicle*, but they failed after we'd been with them only a few months, so we worked at a private printing house. I don't know of any newspaper up there right now. Halifax is not as big as Salem, from what I can tell by looking around here." I amazed myself with this one. Somehow I'd remembered reading about the *Nova Scotia Chronicle* and it stayed with me. Being a history buff paid off.

"I'll give you both jobs now if you're willing to work on a probationary basis. If I like your work, you can stay on. If I don't think you can do the work, then I'll have to let you go. As I said, I don't need both of you right now, but since we plan to move down to Cambridge at some point, it would be good to have an extra hand. Assuming you'd both be willing to move to Cambridge."

We agreed to terms. It was more pounds than either Tom or I had ever earned, since we'd worked for dollars all our young lives. In eighteenth century terms, I estimated it was fair, but far from lavish. Moving to Cambridge would be no inconvenience, since we weren't settled in Beverly or Salem. We chatted for a half hour or so before Henry said, "We've taken too much of your time, Sam. I thank you for taking a chance on my new friends."

The jovial Hall smiled. "Don't usually take on new help so fast. I would normally give a little consideration to the matter before I bring someone on, but I trust your judgment, Henry, and frankly, there's something about these two friends of yours that intrigues me. Maybe it's the way they speak. It's a vocabulary or a way of speaking that you don't hear around here. Can't put my finger on it, but you fellas have my attention. I'll expect you both here next Monday at eight o'clock."

Chapter 12

Dinner that night at the Woodbury house was not dull. It started off pleasantly enough as you might expect at such a meal. Jane Woodbury had gone to considerable trouble to put a bountiful meal of leg of lamb, potatoes, squash and corn on the table. She and Catherine Woodbury, their sister-in-law, chatted animatedly, frequently pausing to ask Tom and me how we liked our visit to Salem and how we liked Beverly Farms.

Henry's brother, Robert was not as big a man as Henry, but looked to be four or five years older. We knew he was older because Henry had introduced him as his big brother. The meal proceeded in lively fashion for 20 or 30 minutes until Robert set his mug of ale down on the table, leaned back in his chair and changed the mood in the room dramatically.

"So, Henry, I assume you're recruiting these two gentlemen to your rabble-rousing cause?"

The room fell silent. It was obvious that everyone there—everyone that is, but Tom and myself—was familiar with the topic just raised by Robert. A look of dread transformed the comely face of Jane Woodbury. Catherine Woodbury, whose face was less classically beautiful than Jane's, but still warm and pleasant, also bore a worried look. Henry seemed to be counting to ten, if they did that in the eighteenth century. Finally, he expelled a long breath and spoke. He looked at Tom and me when he spoke.

"If you haven't already deduced it, I think you can see that Robert and I don't agree on how we in the colonies should feel about King George. Robert thinks the king can do no wrong. I, on the other hand, thinks that lately he has done no right."

Robert turned grim. "You and your hot-headed ingrate friends always view matters of state simplistically. It's not as simple as you would have it, Henry."

Jane cleared her throat and said, "Do you think it will rain tomorrow, Henry? I was hoping to ..."

"Not now, Jane. Not now. Can't you see that my brother is up to his old tricks?"

"Gentlemen," said Robert, addressing us now, "I hope you will not be taken in by my otherwise well-meaning brother. He's a good man, but he's allowed himself to be deluded by these Sons of Liberty rabble rousers who would undermine our king and take us to war with our own fellow citizens."

Catherine Woodbury made a weak effort to defuse the conversation. "Robert, this is no time for such discussions. We're guests in Henry and Jane's home, and we're in the presence of their new friends. Leave your politics for the tavern."

"I'm sorry, Catherine," said Robert, "but avoiding these issues just encourages this kind of disloyalty to the king. The more we bring it out in the open, the less their arguments have a chance to survive." He paused for a moment; then said, "Though, I suppose we're beyond talk now. They tell me that Henry's friends up and down the coast have been gatherin' muskets and even cannon for the war they want to fight. What kind of British citizens start war with their own country? Traitors, that's what kind!"

"That's enough, Robert!" roared Henry as he rose from his seat in a fury. His face was red and the veins in his neck were bulging. "You call your own brother a traitor. I fought for my country against the French, and you know it. The Sons of Liberty and the Committee of Safety are made up of some of the finest men in America. All men leaders of their communities and loyal to the crown. I don't know one of them that wants to start a war against the regulars, but that doesn't mean we shouldn't prepare for the worst. You seem to have conveniently forgotten the Quartering Acts that allowed the king's soldiers to occupy our inns, public houses, barns and other private property. Then, to add insult to injury, we had to pay for the regulars' food and other costs. The king has treated us shabbily and you know it, Robert. The very presence of the king's troops on these shores in time of peace suggests that Parliament is thinking war. If Parliament feels the only way it can impose its will on us is by force, we aim to be prepared. If that's disloyalty, I plead guilty. Frankly, though, I see the very need for these preparations as an indication that the king and Parliament have shown no loyalty to us, loyal British citizens, who just happen to live here and not in England."

"Sooner or later one of your so-called Sons of Liberty will talk too much about where you've been storing these munitions, and when he does, those of us loyal to the crown will get that information to Gates. That'll put an end to all this talk of civil war. There can't be a war without weapons."

"Who's talkin' about civil war?" fumed Henry. "Far as I can tell it's you lickspittle Tories who cow-tow to arrogant British authorities that care nothing for you and your fellow colonists. You're the ones talking civil war. Since you're my own brother I hope and pray that you are not the one to betray your own kind to Gates or any of his hand-picked officials. I'm sure you haven't forgotten what they did to Governor Hutchinson's mansion after the Stamp Act."

"Damn right I remember. The rabble you're so proud of ransacked the place and left it in a nearly worthless state. This is the way you and your friends deal with people who see things differently."

Henry looked like he was about to explode. "The way Hutchinson saw things was that it was impossible for residents of New England to have the full rights of those who lived in the home country. Is that not outrageous!"

"I'm sure there are good reasons for that. Generally speaking, the crown has not done badly by us. Maybe a few miscalculations, but it's not easy to rule when you're 3,000 miles away."

"If they're unwilling to give us the same rights as those in England, then maybe they shouldn't be ruling."

Robert smirked as he said, "If that doesn't sound like talk of civil war or revolution, I don't know what does."

Henry fought to control himself for a moment before saying,

"Seriously, my brother, if you talk like this around town, I fear for you. Don't forget that fellow they tarred and feathered in Salem a few years ago because he informed on a merchant who smuggled a cargo of molasses to avoid the outrageous duties imposed by Parliament. Tempers are heating up in the colony and who knows how people will react if they think you're defending the king and his Parliament. I think you're wrong, Robert, but you're still my brother. Don't bring down the wrath of the good people of this town on you and your family."

It went on like this for about fifteen more minutes. Suddenly Catherine Woodbury rose from her chair and said, "I'm awfully tired of this fighting between you two brothers. You're both good men, but when you act like this I'm ashamed. Gilbert and Thomas, I apologize for my husband's behavior."

The awkwardness had come to a head, and I groped in my mind for the right thing to say.

"Mrs. Woodbury, there is no need to apologize. These are important issues being discussed. I'm sure both Robert and Henry mean well. They just see things differently. We men sometimes get carried away with our emotions." Both women stared at me as if I were from another planet. Little did they know how close they were to the truth.

Both men glared at me. They'd never experienced twenty-first-century diplomacy. Still, they both metaphorically put down their swords and made an effort to get through the rest of the meal as graciously as possible. An undercurrent of anger and resentment still lingered, but the evening was at least tolerable.

The next morning Tom and I were greeted cheerfully by Jane and Josiah. Josiah had spent the supper part of last night's evening with Martin Woodbury, his 19-year-old cousin, while Martin's parents were at Josiah's house.

Josiah grinned playfully at the morning breakfast table. "I understand you calmed the troubled waters here last night. Maybe in time you'll bring father and Uncle Robert to the same side of these political issues."

Thomas smiled back. "Oh I doubt that. They seem far apart when it comes to politics."

"I'm afraid you're right, Thomas. They've disagreed on this as long as I can remember. If we get them off this subject they get along fine, but lately it's been harder and harder to get them off the subject. From what I can tell, the entire town is divided. It's not good for anybody as far as I'm concerned."

"Sometimes I think Josiah has more sense than his father," said Jane. "Best you don't tell him I said so, though."

"It won't leave this room," I said.

"Is it this bad up in Halifax?" she asked.

"No, it's not. Most people up there view the king and Parliament more kindly, but that's because they fear the French more. Up there, the French threat is always in the back of their minds, so they feel more secure with the king on their side. Better the king and Parliament, than the French." I said this, not knowing for sure if it was true or not, though I seemed to recall from my history readings that that's the way things were in Canada at the time.

It was Saturday. Tom and I asked Henry if we could take a couple of horses into Salem to get familiar with the town. While there we would look for a place to stay. We didn't want to take advantage of Henry and Jane's hospitality for much longer. We also wanted to stop in at the *Gazette* and take a closer look at the presses and type cases. Maybe even get a little practice in. We were both a little nervous about working with an old press and setting type. Samuel Hall had told us that the press we'd be working with was an English common press. The type we'd be setting was Caslon. I'd been given printing lessons in college and eventually was able to set type and print broadsheets similar to those used in early American newspapers. I actually got pretty good at it by the end of the three weeks. So I felt I'd be able to cope when we reported to work on Monday. Still, I wanted to hit the presses running, and I hoped by this visit to be able to point some things out to Tom so he wouldn't start work with absolutely no clue.

We'd sold ourselves to Hall as experienced printers. We couldn't go in and look like beginners or we'd be out on the street with no hope of work. At least no work as good as printing. A good printer could progress in many directions.

Henry had been very accommodating in entrusting two of his horses to us, as he knew we were neophytes when it came to riding. Somehow we'd snowed him into thinking we were dependable.

Before we left the house he had to say, "Last night, when you intervened between Robert and me, I got the impression you saw his side of things as much as you did mine. Have I made a mistake in introducing you to Colonel Mason?"

I said, "Do you mean can you trust us?"

"Yes, I suppose that's what I do mean."

I nodded my head up and down and said, "Yes, Henry. You definitely can trust both of us. We can see how your brother and other loyalists can think the way they do, but that doesn't mean we agree with them. They think it disgraceful to turn on their king. But Thomas and I are of a mind on this. While we would prefer not to challenge the king and Parliament, we feel that they have forced our hand and that if they go much further we will have no alternative but to defend ourselves. I spoke the way I did last night because I hate to see two brothers so far apart. You are both good men."

Henry smiled cautiously. "Good God, Gilbert you keep surprising me with your good sense. Thank you for explaining your words. I appreciate it. You know, Robert and I were not always in such disagreement. Until a few years ago we agreed on most things. It's only recently that we've grown apart. Unfortunately, I don't know what can be done to change that. I think back to when I was a boy. He was my big brother, and he came to my defense on many occasions. I looked up to him. Now, as you can see, we are worlds apart on how we view Parliament and the king." He sighed and said, "Enough of that. Have a good trip into Salem."

♦ ♦ ♦

As Tom and I rode through Beverly Farms and then Beverly toward the river crossing to Salem, I reflected on how Tom and I had become residents of 1774 Massachusetts. The Time Travel Project's recruitment of volunteers to make a trip in time had not been easy. Even considering the fact that the intent had been to go into the future a mere two years. The project leaders did not want to place ads in the papers or on the Internet, as it was important that the project remain secret until they knew whether the attempt was successful or not. Either way they eventually intended to announce that they'd made the attempt. It's just that they knew that if they announced it in advance, they would spend years fending off arguments against it. It was going to be hard enough sending people forward in time without diverting all their energy and resources to defending the project.

What they did was make contact with people who fit certain criteria. I think I've already said that candidates had to be single, unattached, and without close family ties. They also had to be fairly well educated and obviously, people who liked to take risks. They had to be venturesome without being loony. This narrowed down the pool of contenders quite a bit. Nice to know they didn't think I was a nutcase.

Not surprisingly, they went to the military, because right from the outset they knew they were dealing with a subset of the population with proven training and skills. Both Tom and I were in the service when we were contacted. I was in the navy and Tom was a marine.

Okay, that explains how the project found us. But why did we agree? Let's see if I can make it sound somewhat reasonable. By going forward in time just two years we would ultimately be reunited with the few people we knew and cared about—mostly our colleagues on the project and a few friends we'd made in college and in the military. The two-year separation would be comparable to when someone moves away for a couple of years and then comes back. Nothing traumatic. Not that big a sacrifice really. No big deal. No big deal, that is, if it's only two years into the future. Of course everything changes when you find yourself 240 years in the past with almost no likelihood of ever getting back to where you started from. Then it is a big deal. I'm not at all sure either of us would have volunteered for this scenario.

What truly amazed both Tom and myself now that we were in the eighteenth century was that we didn't find it more traumatic. Don't get me wrong. At first the shock of it all was devastating, but gradually, as inconvenient and sometimes uncomfortable eighteenth-century life was, we knew that our ancestors had endured it and that they probably were just as happy then as twenty-first century Americans are in their century. Happiness didn't seem to have much relation to technology. The difference for us was that we knew what we were missing. Still, it was already fascinating to see how the folks in the eighteenth century coped. The fact of the matter was, we were seeing our own ancestors in everyday conditions. We both felt that it was going to be fun knowing that we knew more about the future than they did. Our biggest problem would be not sharing what we knew about the future. The urge to share would be great, but if we indulged that urge, the colonists would soon consider us crazy as loons.

Obviously, the hardest part of adapting was knowing you'd never, ever be going back to the twenty-first century.

I remember reading that an organization called Mars One was considering sending people to colonize the planet Mars. The trip would be one way, since there would be no way to bring them back. The idea was that the Mars settlers would multiply and eventually, when technology figured out how to get them back, they or their descendants would have the option to return to Earth. Amazingly I had read that they got over 200,000 men and women volunteers. I think the first manned Mars trip was planned for around 2024.

I wondered more than once whether the Mars mission was riskier than what Tom and I were now undergoing. At least we were on Earth —an Earth that even in the eighteenth century was a lot less primitive than Mars in the twenty-first century. As I recalled, Mars temperatures dipped to more than 200 degrees Fahrenheit below zero at the poles. Worse than that, you couldn't breathe the atmosphere that surrounded Mars.

We were approaching the landing for the ferry now. I had to come back to the present and concentrate on getting my horse on the ferry without falling into the river. Tom smiled and said,

"Where've you been? You've been in another world for the last ten minutes."

"Just thinking about how we got here. Still can't quite believe it, can you?"

"Not really. But these horses seem real and so does this ferry. I know it wasn't here when I was a kid living in Beverly. The bridge was a lot easier." He grinned and added, "And there were a lot more cars."

"Not so loud. How would you explain that?"

Chapter 13

The premises of the *Essex Gazette* were centrally located,
appropriately enough on Essex Street in Salem. Tom and I tied up our
horses in front of the building. We were quickly getting more
comfortable on horseback. I casually surveyed the street. It was busy
with two-and-four-wheeled carriages and wagons. A few pedestrians
were on the street, too.

As we entered the premises, we observed Hall and a thin, gaunt
man with wild long wisps of pewter-colored hair in heated discussion
at the rear of the room. Hall heard the bell as we opened the front door
and looked to see who it was. His face lit up for a moment as he
recognized us, and he said, "Be with you in just a moment lads." Then
he turned back to his gaunt visitor. The visitor picked up where he'd
apparently left off. He was speaking so loudly that we could easily hear
what he said.

"You will not be getting' my business if you keep this up, Sam.
We've known each other for a long time, and I thought the world of
you until recently. But I'll not be spending my money in yer rag if you
persist in writin' such inflammatory stuff."

"If that's the way you view a man who stands up for his fellow New
Englanders, then I don't want your business. If I were you, though, I'd
think it through. I'm the only paper in town, so I don't know where
you'll do your advertising in the future."

"You'd like that, wouldn't you, Samuel?"

"I'm not the one who threatened to take his business elsewhere."

"My God, man, can't you see how your writing is fanning the
flames of the hotheads in our midst?"

"I know a good number of these hotheads as you call them, and I'll vouchsafe their good sense in the face of a heartless Parliament. True, a few of them might be eager for a fight, but most just want to protect themselves and their families against the encroaching exploitation of what's become an insensitive Parliament. Not to mention a king who sees us as little more than a source of revenue for the home country." Hall paused a moment as he apparently considered just how far he wanted to let the argument with his visitor go before reigning it in. "Listen, Ben, we're never going to agree on this. I'm sorry to see it go this way, but I must do what I believe in. If you still want to advertise in the *Gazette*, I'll accept your business. I don't have to agree with everyone I do business with. If you've read the paper, you know that we're open to a free exchange of opinions. I've published letters from folks like yourself who don't agree with our views on things. What I won't do is give up my right to express my opinion in my own paper."

"I'm sorry, too, Sam. I miss our old friendship, but I'll not be supporting the radical ideas you so eagerly print in the *Gazette*. Guess I'll just have to find another way to tell folks about the good remedies we have in the apothecary. What's more, if I could, I'd find a way to shut down this travesty of newspaper. You may not have heard the last of me yet, Sam. G'bye, Sam." With that the spindly grim-faced fellow stormed out of the building, passing Tom and myself without even a nod.

As we walked back to where Hall was standing somewhat disconsolately, he forced a smile and said, "Sorry you had to hear that. We have a lot of disagreement in this community lately. Salem is more divided than I can remember. Sad. Well, it's nothing for you to worry about. I didn't expect you until Monday. What can I do for you today?"

"We just wanted to take a closer look at the presses and the type cases so we'll be better prepared for work on Monday. Is it inconvenient now?"

"No, no. It's a fine idea. Here, let me show you. I'll answer any questions you have."

"By the way, Mr. Hall," I said, "no need to apologize for what just happened. From what I can tell, it's happening everywhere. I *am* surprised that when we met the other day you didn't ask us what our views were about Parliament and the king. As it happens, I think we're on the same page as you, but if we weren't, would you still want us working for you?"

"Same page, huh? Must be some sort of expression you people use up in Canada. I think I take its meaning. I should, shouldn't I, being in this business, but I have never heard nor read it before." He smiled. "As a man of the printed word I'm pretty much up on the latest locutions."

Oops! *Same page* definitely was an import from a different century, but I couldn't say so. I knew right then that I was going to like this man. As committed as he was to his views on the rights of colonists, he still cared enough about the language that he had to comment about that first. I tried to be disarming in my response.

"Yes, I suppose we do use it up in Halifax. Never gave much thought to it, but interesting that you took note of it."

He nodded his acknowledgement and said, "As for your political thinking, I don't care so long as you do your job and don't undermine what I say or what I print in the Gazette. Oh, I suppose if you were a Tory zealot, I'd soon find out and push you out the door. But if we don't always agree, that's healthy. I'll just expect you to recognize that I'll have the final say on what goes in the paper."

"I doubt if we'll disagree on the important things," I said.

Hall scratched his head contemplatively. "That fellow I had the row with, old Ben Waite—he's a good man. Runs a fine apothecary shop. Troubles me no end that he feels the way he does. I'm not sayin' that because I'll lose his business. I'm more concerned that I'll lose his friendship—if I haven't already. Here at the *Gazette* we see too much of this: Friends turning on friends. Family turning on family. All because bloody Parliament treats us not much better than hired help." He smiled sheepishly. "Egad! Come Monday, you'll be hired help won't you, but I warrant that I'll be treatin' you better than Parliament treats us. Parliament has driven a wedge into New England. Actually, all of the colonies up and down the coast. They've forced people to take sides—folks who once considered themselves good British citizens." He paused for a few seconds; then changed the subject. "But back to Ben. He's been shooting his mouth off so much lately that I fear for him and his family."

Tom had a puzzled look on his face. "I'm not sure I understand, Mr. Hall. Just what is it that you fear could happen to him or his family?"

"I don't know what it's like up in Halifax, but here in Salem, Beverly and Marblehead, and down in Boston, Tories who shoot their mouths off often incur the wrath of the mob. I'm sorry to say it, but among the many good Patriots here in New England, we have a few firebrands who sometimes go overboard. They throw water, eggs, and other things at Tories and their family members. Tarred and feather an unfortunate soul here in Salem a few years ago. Don't know if you heard about it. Down in Boston they tarred and feathered a customs man. There's been property destroyed, too. Stores have been ransacked and looted. Things have gotten ugly of late. Men like Ben Waite are good men, but their loyalty to the king and Parliament in the face of a mountain of evidence that Parliament and the king no longer deserve that loyalty could get him into trouble. I'd hate to see that happen. He's misguided in my opinion, but he's still a good man. See, that's the problem, isn't it? We all consider ourselves good British citizens, but not for the same reasons. *They* say the king can do no wrong. *We* say he can and does a great deal of wrong. We say the king is not treating us as the good citizens we think we are." He stopped to draw a breath and then said, "All right, my friends, enough of that. Let's take a look at these two presses."

I had to marvel at Hall and the way he took such a thing in stride. If I were Sam Hall I'd be concerned about Waite's threat to find a way to close down the paper.

Chapter 14

We'd been working for Samuel Hall about three months. Each day had gotten better as we grew comfortable in our jobs and saw that Hall was extremely satisfied with our work. Much of the routine was similar enough to what I'd done with the old press in college to make it easy for me to get up to speed fairly quickly. I guided Tom, who is a quick study anyway, and soon he was a whiz at typesetting and using the presses.

When it came to the news we seemed to always be one or more steps ahead of his other workers. It wasn't really fair, of course, because we knew things that they couldn't possibly have known. When major historic events occurred we would suggest that Hall or his two reporters cover angles that we knew would develop as the event unfolded. At first he would balk, but after seeing on several occasions that we'd had the "foresight" to accurately predict events, he would follow our advice. It made the *Gazette* the most accurate and incisive paper north of Boston. I called his employees reporters, but it didn't take long to discover that the word "reporter" hadn't yet been invented. Hall sometimes called his reporters gazetteers, but usually used the term writers, so we did, too.

One thing Tom and I didn't know, though we probably should have, was that Christmas in 1774 New England was a far different thing from Christmas in the twenty-first century. As December 25th neared, both of us were disappointed to discover that most families in New England either didn't celebrate Christmas at all or did so in a very low-key way.

Tom had lived in foster homes most of his young life, and my parents died in an auto accident when I was 19. Despite such beginnings we both had fond memories of festive Christmas celebrations. It's not that either of us came from overly religious backgrounds, but most of Tom's foster families had made an effort to make the holiday festive. My parents, too, had done that. Sure, it often veered away from its religious *raison d'etre*, but it left me with warm and fuzzy feelings about Christmas and the holiday season. I was disappointed to find that the Puritan influence in Massachusetts in 1774 was still a lot stronger than I would have guessed. Cotton Mather, the seventeenth century Puritan clergyman, had protested violently against celebrating Christ's birth on December 25. The Puritans no longer ran the colony, but it turns out that many clergymen of the time still believed that December 25th was a pagan holiday co-opted by some Christians who wanted to celebrate it as Christ's birthday. Pagan Romans originated what they called Saturnalia, which was a period of virtual lawlessness celebrated from December 17th to the 25th in the Julian calendar.

When Tom and I asked Hall about the lack of celebration at Christmastime, he said he'd heard that it was a lot more festive down in Virginia, where the Puritan influence had never been as great, but here in New England things generally went on as usual on December 25th. That was true, too. Tom and I were both shocked when we found that young George Woodbury would be going to Mrs. Pinckney's art school on the 25th. Hall said that as far as he knew all the schools in the area would be open that day.

It turns out that New Year's Day was far more of a celebration in New England than Christmas. People would visit friends and relatives and enjoy food, drink and conversation. It was also the time when people with debts would settle up with their creditors—if they could— so that they could start the new year free of debt.

We were invited to the Woodbury house on New Year's day. They had a few friends and relatives over, and, unlike December 25th, it was very festive. To some degree it reminded me of the holiday seasons I'd enjoyed before my parents passed away. The entire day wasn't festive, though. Henry's brother Robert and his family were there, and before the day was over Robert and Henry couldn't avoid a heated discussion of the brewing political situation. Governor Gage had sent troops to a number of locations in recent months to take possession of weapons the patriots had stashed away. Fortunately, they were mostly insignificant stores of guns and munitions, but just the act of troops storming into the private property of civilians continued to raise tempers and inflame attitudes toward Gage, Parliament and the king. Things were not getting better. They were getting worse. Much worse.

As Henry Woodbury raised his glass in a toast to the New Year, I thought we were going to get through the holiday meal without friction between the two brothers. Unfortunately, it wasn't meant to be. As we set our glasses down, warm with a spirit of conviviality and the flush of alcohol, Robert rose and said, "I'd like to drink another toast." Henry and the wives present appeared somewhat startled, as apparently this wasn't done. At least not on this occasion. Robert continued, "I'd like to drink to His Majesty's health."

Henry was appalled. "I'll not have a toast to His Majesty in this house," he roared. "Not in this house."

"Are you not loyal to your own king?" taunted his brother.

"I have never been disloyal, and you damned well know it, Robert Woodbury. But I'll not drink to his health till he shows by his actions that he cares about *my* health."

Robert surveyed the table and said, "Anyone care to join me?"

His wife, Catherine, blanched and said, "Robert, you're in Henry's house. You're deliberately being provocative. That is not the spirit of the new year." Then she looked at Henry and Jane and added, "I apologize for Robert's bad manners. I think we should go."

It had been a pleasant day until then. Robert and Henry did not make up. As far as I know, they didn't see each other for weeks after that unfortunate incident. In retrospect I look back at New Year's Day 1775 as a microcosm of the New England community at the time.

Chapter 15

As we moved inexorably into the year 1775, relations between Whigs (or Patriots as they called themselves) and Tories, (or Loyalists as they called themselves), continued to deteriorate. Patriot extremists broke windows in the homes of Loyalists. Patriots stole livestock and destroyed property. I sided with the Patriot cause, but have to admit that the Loyalists were better behaved for the most part.

When Tom and I arrived at work one morning in early February, Hall greeted us with a wrinkled brow and sad countenance.

"Good Lord, men, have you heard the news?"

"What is it, Sam? What's happened?" I asked. I could see he was in an unusual state of distress. Sam Hall rarely let his emotions take control, but today he was close to losing it.

"They destroyed the presses at Oliver Pratt's print shop. I've known Oliver for nigh onto 20 years. 'Tis a sad day when this sort of thing happens."

"If I'm not mistaken," said Tom, isn't he a Loyalist?"

"Aye, he is, but he's not one to tell the world about it. He's not nearly as vocal as Ben Waite. Good God, gentlemen, what is becoming of us?"

"He does, however, print those Tory pamphlets," I pointed out somewhat hesitantly, not wanting to further agitate our friend and employer. "Patriots find them more than a little offensive. The printed word can often generate more intense emotions than an occasional one-on-one outburst like those of your friend Ben Waite. In his own way, by issuing these inflammatory pamphlets, he is telling the world about his Loyalist views."

Hall shook his head in incredulity at his own naiveté. "Yes, of course you're right. I know him so well that all I see is his personal reserve and reticence. Of course his written words do speak to a much larger audience." Suddenly he relaxed and smiled. "You've done it again, Gilbert."

I wasn't sure what he was talking about. "I have. What have I done again?"

"It's not important. Just another of your Halifax locutions."

Still not sure what he was getting at I asked, "which locution was that?"

"You said 'one-on-one'. I have never heard that spoken before today. Actually I like it. I like it a lot. It captures your meaning with concise precision. Excellent term."

"Glad you like it." Funny how you take things for granted I reflected inwardly. Obviously the English language had evolved in 240 years. After thinking about this a few seconds I forced myself to focus on the issue at hand. "I assume we'll cover this attack on Pratt's shop in our next edition?"

"Very definitely. We'll have to be careful, though. I don't want the same thing happening to us."

"By careful, do you mean avoid condemning the attack and just describe it briefly on a page somewhere inside the paper?"

"Dear God, no, Gilbert. We shall describe it and condemn it on the front page. I don't agree with the Tories, but I don't condone physically attacking them. They have a right to live among us as long as they don't interfere with our right to protest against Parliament. Would I prefer that they help us? Yes, yes, of course I would, but I understand their point-of-view even if I don't agree with it. If we allow only one point-of-view, then we are just like the government we protest against." He paused to see how we reacted to his words. Then his eyes lit up, and he went ahead. "How would you two mates like to cover this story?"

We were pleasantly surprised by his offer. Tom said, "Speaking for myself, sir, I would be delighted. But don't you want Richard or Simon to cover it? They do most of your news stories."

"They have their hands full already. We have more news this week than we can handle. Besides, I know already that you can write, for I've seen what you do on rewrites and on the little things I've asked you to do."

I was pleased, of course, but knew it wouldn't be as easy as Sam made it out to be. Both Tom and I were still struggling with the erratic spelling and the cultural idiosyncrasies of the eighteenth century. We could easily screw up this story.

"We'll do our very best not to disappoint you, Sam," I said, meaning every word.

"Quite candidly, you fellows bring a new way of looking at things that I believe is important for a story like this."

I grinned. "And we're not friendly with any of the principals in this story, so no one can accuse the *Gazette* of playing favorites."

"Yes, there's that, too," he said with a twinkle.

◆ ◆ ◆

Oliver Pratt was an older and larger version of Sam Hall. Stocky, though not really fat, he was perhaps three or four inches taller than Hall. His bald head was a bit larger than Hall's, too. When we entered he was in the midst of sweeping with a ragged straw broom. He looked up and said, "Sorry, but we won't be open for business for a few days."

I said, "I understand. I know that you've suffered some damage to your presses. I'm Gilbert Lee and this is Thomas Howard. We're from the *Gazette*. I wonder if we could speak with you for a few minutes?"

"I'm afraid not. Isn't it enough for Sam Hall to know that I'm out of business without him wantin' to make money out of it? He won't have me writin' the truth about his so-call Patriots now. You'd think he'd be happy with that."

"He's not at all happy with that," said Thomas. "He doesn't agree with some of what you say, but he believes you have the right to say it. And he doesn't approve what just happened to your presses. Surely you know that's not Mr. Hall's way."

"Yes, I suppose you're right. I've never known Sam Hall to do a bad thing in his life. You'll have to excuse me, gentlemen. I'm feeling bitter. What just happened here is a mite discouraging. Bad enough that half my friends hate me because I remain loyal to George III. Now some of those friends who hate me apparently hate me enough to damage my presses and put me out of business. A man loyal to his king doesn't have the right to support himself and his family anymore. Good God, man, what has become of these colonies? This wouldn't happen back in the home country."

"Do you mind if I use some of your ink so I can write down what you say?" I asked Pratt. "I have my own paper."

"Yes, I suppose so. Help yourselves."

"Could we see what was done to your presses?" I continued.

"Over here. Two English Common Presses. I think they're much like what Sam uses at the *Gazette*."

"Yes, they appear to be quite similar," said Tom.

"You can see," said Pratt, "that they overturned my type cases. The type is all over the floor. 'Twill take me forever to sort it all out and put it back in the proper spots in the two cases. In truth, this is the worst of the damage. They didn't or I suppose I should say, couldn't, damage the platens or the spindles. 'Twould take a lot to ruin them. Thank God." He was right, of course, as the platens and spindles were quite solid and sturdy. So was the devil's tail. The devil's tail was the lever used to lower the platen onto the type. It would indeed take a lot to damage them. Sam Hall's information had not been entirely correct. The presses had not been damaged, but the overturned type cases were bad enough.

"Did they damage anything else?" queried Tom. "Anything else around the shop?"

"Not that I've come across. No, most of the damage is in overturning the type cases. That'll set me back a day or two I'm afraid. Oh, they did break the lock on my door. That'll take some fixin', too."

"Were you here when these people came into the shop and did

this?" I asked.

"No, I was home in bed with my wife. Minding my own business. Whoever did this broke in in the middle of the night so I wouldn't see 'em. Cowardly bastards they were. Didn't have the gumption to face me."

"Who do you think did this?"

"Some goddamned Patriots, that's who."

"You might be right, but can you be sure that's who it was?"

"Aye, I'm sure. They bragged about it. Look over here on the wall." He pointed to a line scrawled in lamp black on the wall not far from the empty type cases: **Keep yer pamphlets to yerſelf, Tory.** It was signed, **—Patriots for the cause.** I noted that the spelling was far from perfect, but I wasn't shocked by that because I'd observed over the past few months that people generally spelled things the way they sounded to them. Sometimes they spelled the same word differently in the same document. Nobody seemed to care or maybe not even notice. I had only come across one dictionary so far in the eighteenth century. That was Dr. Johnson's dictionary, and it made no attempt to include most of the frequently used words in English. Instead it included what were considered hard words. I think there were one or two other dictionaries in existence, but they apparently didn't compare in quality to Johnson's, and as I say, that omitted many of the words people used and spelled in everyday life. In short, there was no standardization of spelling. As long as people got the meaning of a word, they were happy.

I noticed on the scrawl on the wall that the shop invaders had used the long *s*, that closely resembled a lower-case *f*. This was common in eighteenth-century usage and I had now grown accustomed to seeing it and setting it in my type compositing duties.

I was sorry to see those roughhewn words on the wall. I believed in the Patriots cause, but I was opposed to these methods. So far, I was convinced that the vast majority of Patriots were not the sort that would resort to this kind of destructive act, but every time I came across it I cringed. I turned to Pratt and said, "I'm very sorry this happened to you, sir. Very sorry. I know Mr. Hall will be, too."

"Aye, I thank you for that. I'll get these fonts back in shape soon. What I can't rectify is my standing in the community. Half the people in Salem hate Loyalists. Half of my friends are Loyalists and agree with me, but half of them are afraid to show it. Even if I get the type back into the cases, my business'll be a fraction of what it was a few years ago. I'm seriously thinking of getting out of here and going to England. If I can't afford that, I may go up to Canada. There's no place for me here anymore. Do you hear what I'm saying, gentlemen? What I'm saying is that I'm going to have to leave the place in which I was born and raised. The place I call home. And all because some of my fellow New Englanders disagree with the crown's taxation policies. My God, have you ever known anyone to enjoy taxes?"

I didn't want to add more grief to the poor man's problems, but I couldn't let that pass.

"I don't think that's the issue here, sir. I think it's because we are not allowed anyone in Parliament to represent us; yet they feel free to tax us anyway. We're a growing colony as are most of the colonies up and down the coast, so we're a rich source of revenue for Great Britain, but despite our growing importance, we are not allowed representation. Worse, the Crown's troops are authorized to seize our property and occupy our private buildings."

Pratt then sat down hard in a nearby chair and placed his hands together in thought. After reflecting a moment he said, "I understand how you Patriots think. I suppose there is something to it, but it doesn't give you license to attack those who are willing to overlook the excesses of Parliament because allegiance to Great Britain is still to be preferred to going it alone. Good Lord, man, do you think we could have fended off the French and their Indians without the aid of the regulars?" He sighed, as if the fight had gone out of him. "Right now, though, I'm tired of arguing. I need to get my shop in order. As you can see, once I reorganize my type I'll be able to go on as if everything were normal. Only you and I know that everything isn't normal. Not anymore. Not for any of us."

Chapter 16

It was about two weeks after Tom and I had interviewed the Tory printer Oliver Pratt that Henry Woodbury entered the *Gazette* office and asked Sam Hall if he could speak to Tom and myself for just a moment.

Shortly after we'd begun working at the *Gazette*, Tom and I had taken two small rooms in a house on Essex Street owned by a widow named Martha Inglesby. For a small fee in addition to the rent she'd included a modest breakfast and supper. There were six roomers including Tom and myself at Mrs. Inglesby's place. Most of the others were pleasant enough, though we really didn't know them all that well. Mrs. Inglesby was a rather prim, but kindly sort, and we settled in fairly quickly. Once ensconced at her house we saw the Woodbury family maybe once a month. We did, however, see Henry more often than that as we attended local meetings of the Committee of Safety at Colonel Mason's house at least once a week. After we'd been in Salem a few weeks Colonel Mason had become persuaded that we were good risks and granted us membership in the Committee. Lately meetings had become even more frequent as things in the colony seemed to be heating up. We'd become close friends with Henry, and he often came to us to discuss politics. We seemed to know more about politics and events than many of his friends and fellow Sons of Liberty members. No surprise there, as much of what was discussed at our meetings had already been reported in various history books two centuries later.

Henry took us aside and spoke in a quiet voice.

"My friends, I need your advice."

"What's up, Henry? You look a wreck."

"It's Robert. He's gone off and reported our stash of cannon and other munitions to the troop commander in Boston. Gage'll know about it and almost certainly send troops to confiscate them."

"How did you learn this? I'm sure he didn't tell you."

"He was drinking at the George and Dragon tavern in Beverly with a gaggle of his mates. A friend of mine overheard him say that he and three other Tories had gotten through to the commander at the British headquarters in Boston and informed him about our stash. Said one of the Tories was an old countryman employed by Colonel Mason. My brother was proud to tell his mates that Mason didn't know about the Loyalist in his midst."

I felt for Henry. "What will you do? You have to tell the colonel, but if you do, you'll be informing on your own brother. It's a terrible problem."

"Indeed. Mason must know, though, and soon. I have to tell him about Robert. Robert has made his own bed, and he obviously feels no remorse. Nay, he seems to revel in what he's done. I also must discover how he found out about the location of our stash."

"It probably wasn't that hard to figure out. A stash of cannon can't be hidden from everyone. When the cannon were hidden in Foster's workshop, someone may have witnessed it. What will you do when you confront Robert?"

"I'll let him know that he is no longer welcome in my house and that I cannot protect him if there comes a conflict with Britain. You and I know that such a conflict is almost inevitable."

"Dear God, Henry, I'm truly sorry about all this. Nothing could be worse than brother against brother."

"My heart goes out to you, Henry" said Tom.

"I thank you, Gilbert. And you, too, Thomas. I know you both care. If this weren't bad enough, I must also alert Mason to the fact that he has a traitor in his midst—someone in his employ or maybe someone on the committee. It could have been one of the men who helped move the cannon to Foster's place." Then, realizing that he'd taken us away from our work for several minutes, he said, "I'd best let ye get back to your work. I'm glad it's been working out for you. Sam tells me he's never had such fine workers. I expect I'll see you tonight at Colonel Mason's."

Chapter 17

February 24, 1775

In Cambridge a curious Lieutenant Colonel Alexander Leslie faced an exhausted General Gage over the vast mahogany desk that was at the general's disposal as governor of the colony. Gage had been offered the use of an elegant home on Brattle Square owned by a Loyalist by the name of William Brattle.

Thomas Gage's tenure in office had been plagued by constant and increasingly frequent testing of the Crown's authority in colonial America. He was not so much physically exhausted as he was mentally tired from coping with the struggles he'd inherited from his unpopular predecessor, Thomas Hutchinson. It was not an easy assignment for anyone, but it was made all the more difficult for Gage as he sometimes considered himself as much American as he did British. After all, he'd spent the last 20 years on this side of the Atlantic. He'd even married an American woman—the feisty New Yorker, Margaret Kemble. Immediately upon his appointment to replace the hated Governor Hutchinson, Gage had become the most popular Brit in America. He'd enjoyed the popularity and celebrity of being the "good" governor. He'd held the office less than a year now, and already things had been turned upside down. The colonists had not rolled over and docilely accepted the dictates of Parliament. Far from it. They'd reacted as if they were entitled to the same treatment their fellow British citizens in England expected.

The colonists, particularly, the Patriots as they called themselves, had at first quietly challenged the unpopular taxes levied upon the colonies. When merely complaining had come to naught, they'd openly protested. This had become annoying to Governor Hutchinson and later, to Governor Gage. Protestation was followed first by rioting, then the Tea Party and in recent years the organized hiding of weapons that the Patriots claimed would be needed to defend themselves against the Crown. Gage empathized with the feelings of the colonists, but also believed that the king and Parliament were justified in imposing taxes on a somewhat ungrateful group of American colonies. After all, had not Parliament fought a costly war so that the French could no longer encroach on western territory?

Now, Gage found himself just as unpopular as his predecessor. It was not a feeling he enjoyed. Unfortunately, his unpopularity would only worsen if he did his job right. He had to quell the dissenting Patriots. He hoped, at least, that he could do it without escalating tensions. The last thing he wanted was to be the one who triggered a civil war that pitted British citizen against British citizen, but he was a soldier to the core and would do his duty no matter where it led.

Leslie remained expressionless as he waited for Gage to speak.

"Colonel Leslie, I have a little mission for you and the 64th. We have a problem up in Salem."

"Yes, governor. I assume it's about the cannon?"

Gage looked surprised. "How do you know about the cannon?"

"Rumor, sir. Nothing official."

"But who told you, Colonel?"

Leslie squirmed in his chair. "One of my men, sir. He heard it from someone in town, I believe."

Gage closed his eyes and shook his head slowly from side to side. "Then it's even more urgent if it's become common knowledge. Yes, it's true. The colonists have stashed away something between 11 and 17 cannon, plus powder and balls. Apparently they're in a blacksmith's shop up in Salem. I'll give you the exact location later. If it's become common knowledge that we know about their stash, then we have to get to that stockpile before they move it."

"Yessir. I'll put together a plan and we'll take care of it."

Gage leaned forward and placed his palms on the surface of the desk. "Colonel, I want you in Salem within two days. No later. Understood?"

"Yessir, it won't be easy, but we'll do it. I'm told the road up to Salem this time of year is rutted and sometimes covered with snow in places. If there's a thaw, it's almost impassable because of deep mud. If that weren't enough, there's a few river crossings to slow us down even more. It'll be slow going, sir."

"I don't want you going by land, Colonel. I want you to go by sea. You'll sail up to Marblehead and from there march your men over to Salem. By sea you'll gain the element of surprise. No one will know about you and the troops until the last minute. And you'll avoid the treacherous roads except for just a few miles from Marblehead. You'll use a naval transport vessel. Best you sit down with your staff and start planning."

Chapter 18

February 25, 1775

I counted ten men already assembled in Colonel Mason's parlor when Tom and I arrived. By now I knew all of them. Henry Woodbury was already there, as was Sam Hall and Joseph Whicher, the foreman of Sprague's Distillery in Salem, Jonathan Felt, a shipmaster, and Richard Derby, the man who'd provided most of the cannon now stored at Foster's workshop near the North River. Whicher was a jovial, exuberant sort who made being in his presence a joy. Derby was probably the wealthiest man north of Boston. He was more serious than Whicher, but then who wasn't. Still, he was a true gentleman and in good physical condition. Richard Derby was a truly likable sort. Nobody in the room gave the slightest indication that they resented his good fortune.

Mason, himself, seemed well enough off. I don't know where he'd made his money. He'd been in the military for a good many years. Usually British military officers had to have substantial resources because they had to purchase their commissions. Among the others present were a greengrocer, a lawyer, a banker and two shipping merchants like Derby, though neither of them came close to being as rich.

As head of the Committee of Safety north of Boston, Colonel Mason was the de facto leader of the shadow Patriot government of the region. Usually, before we began our meetings, we enjoyed a libation of some sort. Sometimes a pint of ale. Occasionally some rum or Irish whiskey. Today Mason began on a somber note and dispensed with the drinks.

"Gentlemen, I have some serious information to share with you. I learned of it not one hour ago from Henry Woodbury." He nodded in the direction of Woodbury. "Henry left work early to tell me about it so that I would have a little time to digest the implications of what he told me." By now everyone was leaning toward Mason both apprehensive and eager to know what the problem was. Mason continued, "It was not easy for Henry to tell me what he had to say. Not easy at all."

"What is it?" said Whicher excitedly.

"Yes, what is it, man?" urged Sam Hall.

Mason continued, "Apparently four Loyalists have gotten word of our cannon stash and other supplies. Worse, they discovered their location and went into Boston to notify the troop commander there. 'Tis a *fait accompli*, I'm told. As serious as this is, it's been made doubly difficult for Henry because one of the four is his own brother, Robert."

A deep murmuring rose up from the men in the room. A few pointed accusingly at Woodbury.

Henry rose to defend himself. "Friends, I assure you I did not share the existence or the whereabouts of these cannon with my brother. For that matter, I have not shared the location with anyone other than you men in this room. I knew Robert was a Tory and could do nothing about that, but I would never do anything to better his cause. I have already notified him that he is not welcome in my house, and if there should be a conflict of arms, I fear that we will be enemies. This I said to my own brother. I will not turn against this colony for any man." Henry sat down and leaned forward, placing his face in his hands. My heart went out to him.

I surveyed the room and saw that by his heartfelt words Henry had erased any doubts in the minds of the others. Rather, they clearly empathized with him. I was sure such intrafamilial conflict was now all too common in New England.

Mason rose and said, "'Tis not fair that Henry Woodbury should be tested this way, but the times we live in test us all too much, I fear. I thank God—and I thank Henry—that he saw fit to come to us. Now it is we who must face the consequences of what has been set in motion by these four Tories. Someone has revealed what we wanted kept hidden. We must discover who that is, but right now we have a more pressing problem. That more pressing problem is what will come of this disclosure? It is almost certain that Gage will send regulars to claim our cannon. We cannot let this happen, for to lose these cannon would be a double disaster. First, we would lose valuable weapons for our own defense and second, we would cede to Gage the conviction that he can deny us anything that Parliament wants to deny us. In short, we would grant them the use of martial law as a means of governing these American colonies. Our brothers and sisters in England send their own neighbors to Parliament to represent them. Our ancestors came here for the right to govern themselves in the same way; not to be dictated to with no say in the matter. We cannot allow their efforts to be in vain."

"Here! Here!" roared the committee members.

Mason raised his hand signaling his intention to continue. "I would like for us to leave this meeting with a plan of action. Do I hear any suggestions?"

Richard Derby spoke. "It's almost certain that Gage will send troops here to confiscate our cannon. They may even want to spread fear amongst us and use their muskets against us if we resist. I believe we should have an immediate call to arms of the Minutemen. We need to alert our fellow Patriots that as soon as we become aware of advancing troops they should make their way to Salem so that we can present a formidable presence in the face of these troops. We need enough men so that the redcoats and their commander will think twice about using force. When we leave here each of us should reach out to our contacts so that they in turn can reach out to theirs and so on. We have practiced this more than once. Now, we need to get serious." He looked about the room and said, "Does this make sense to the rest of you?"

The plan Derby had proposed was similar to the way a chain letter worked. Each committee member was to contact at least two known Minutemen, each of whom in turn was to contact two others and so on. All of the people in the chain had either volunteered or agreed when asked to participate. The list of volunteers was organized so that the earliest responders—the Minutemen—would be contacted first. Minutemen were a rapidly deployed force trained to respond to aggressive action against the colony. Most of the Minutemen were under 30 years of age and were the most eager to respond. The remainder of the list formed the rest of the militia and consisted of volunteers of all ages who would respond as soon as they were able. All of these Patriots had some sort of weapon they would bring with them—usually a musket.

Everyone in the room nodded or spoke their assent, so Mason took the floor again.

"All right then, we seem to be in agreement. The message we pass along is this: We believe there is a strong likelihood that Gage will send troops here within a matter of days. Their mission almost certainly will be to take possession of our cannon. We must resist any such effort. A strong Patriot presence is needed to resist these redcoats. If we can assemble enough men, I believe we can avoid bloodshed, but I'd be lying if I said bloodshed was impossible. Gage and his officers have been frustrated in recent months. The governor may believe that he needs to teach us all a lesson in order to keep us in line. Every man who answers our muster must be prepared for the worst and pray to God for the best."

"Here! Here!" roared the people in the room. Mason was about to adjourn when Jonathan Felt rose and asked a question.

"How many do you think it will take to put the fear of God into these damned redcoats?"

"I'm hoping we can bring together several hundred. A hundred present plus the knowledge that more are on the way, should deter them. We've never sent out a call from Salem before, so we shall see. We must all pray that the turnout is a good one."

Chapter 19

Meanwhile, in his workshop, blacksmith and retired Captain Robert
Foster, had nearly completed his work on the several cannon that had
been placed in his care by Colonel Mason. The cannon, most of which
came from Richard Derby, were in various states of repair. Some of
them needed to have the iron work affixed to the carriages. It was a big
job and one that kept him from most of his normal work as a
blacksmith. The cannon had ended up in Foster's blacksmith shop
because his was one of the few places big enough to store all the
weaponry and still keep it from the view of his customers, and because
he was willing to take the enormous risk of housing such weaponry.
While Foster and his employees worked on the cannon, Colonel
Mason's wife and daughters had been packing five thousand flannel
cartridges for the cannon.

   When word first reached Mason that Tories had notified Gage and
his military staff in Boston, the colonel had discussed with Foster the
possibility of moving the cannon to another location so as to evade any
troops who might try to confiscate the stash of weapons. Foster had
convinced Mason that it would be impractical to try such a move now
that the Tories were aware of the cannon. Almost certainly they'd have
lookouts watching every move and would know the whereabouts of the
cannon after any such move, so why bother. Better to defend against
any confiscation, since they'd have to do that no matter where the guns
were located. If the Patriots couldn't protect their weapons now, said
Foster, they had no hope of prevailing in the face of future British
aggression.

♦ ♦ ♦

The troops of the 64th Regiment were stationed on Castle Island in
Boston Harbor. Lieutenant Colonel Leslie busily prepared his men for
the upcoming mission. They would all be taken to Marblehead by

naval transport ships. From there they would go on land to neighboring Salem. The regiment embarked two hours after sundown on Saturday, February 25th, and were told that, while the trip could easily get them to Marblehead later that night, they would remain just off the coast until Sunday morning.

In the morning, the large vessels sailed slowly toward Marblehead Neck, the remotest part of Marblehead, so that it would be less likely the local residents would take notice of them. Until the last minute the soldiers remained below the hatches so any early risers in the town would think nothing of seeing two more ships off their shore. Marblehead was a seafaring town and ships were part of their economy.

The timing of the assault was designed to take advantage of the apparent lack of security offered the citizenry because it was Sunday. Ironically, the time chosen by Gates and Leslie flew in the face of the governor's recent pronouncements encouraging piety and virtue on the Sabbath. The ships were now anchored just off Marblehead Neck. The crews lowered dories as the hatches flew open and the troops emerged loading their muskets and affixing their bayonets. In less than an hour 300 men had been rowed to shore and were now in formation marching toward Marblehead proper.

As the troops crossed the narrow sandbar connecting the Neck to Marblehead proper in single file, they played "Yankee Doodle," openly mocking the Patriots and inflaming residents as His Majesty's soldiers passed by.

The locals dispatched several messengers to notify Mason of the advancing troops. At this point, Leslie erroneously believed he had the advantage of surprise on his side. He knew that at some point word would get to the rebels in Salem, but assumed that by the time they knew, it would be too late to do much about the presence of nearly 300 British troops. His second in command, Major Simon Blackwell, said somewhat hesitantly out of deference for his commander, "Sir, I fear that we're announcing our arrival and giving the people in Salem a chance to prepare their resistance. Perhaps we could silence the fife players."

"Good God, Blackwell. Why does it matter if they know we're coming? What can they do about it anyway?" It was a critical mistake to underestimate the intense feelings that Marbleheaders felt toward Britain's oppressive measures in recent years. There was no way they would fail to alert their friends and neighbors in nearby Salem. It would have been far wiser of Gage and Leslie to plan the troops' arrival for Salem Harbor, thereby giving the Patriots far less warning.

As Mason was preparing to leave his house for church he was startled by a loud pounding on his front door. "Who is it?" yelled his wife, Susanna, from their bedroom.

The annoying pounding was repeated, only louder it seemed to Mason.

"Just a minute, just a minute," he said as he made his way to the door.

He pulled open the heavy door, wondering who on God's earth would be calling of a Sunday morning. As he did so he was greeted by a man he'd never seen before. The man appeared to be in his early 30s and was sweating. Mason looked past the man and saw that the man's horse was tied up at the hitching post. The horse was panting and wet with sweat, too.

"Good Lord, man," said Mason. "What's so important that you surprise us like this on the Sabbath?"

"Sorry, colonel. I'm with the Marblehead militia. Come to warn you that there's a few hundred regulars on the march toward Salem."

"Come in, come in. Tell me everything you know and then the wife'll get you something to wet your thirst."

"Thank you sir. Let me catch my breath." He took a few deep breaths and then proceeded. "My guess is there's close to 300 of 'em, sir. They came by ship and anchored off Marblehead last night. First thing this morning the ships came in close to Marblehead Neck, anchored, and sent the troops to shore by longboat and dories. Leastwise, that's what I'm told. They're headin' this way right now. We tried to slow 'em down by removing some planks on a bridge, but they're comin' now."

Mason quickly explained to Susanna what was happening and asked her to give the militiaman something to drink.

"We may not make it to service this morning." I've got to rally the men right now, and I suspect we'll be occupied for some time."

"Will there be shooting?" she asked fearfully. Susanna was accustomed to her husband's involvement with the Committee of Safety and the local militia, but it had never involved actual fighting. The last time he'd been to war was over ten years ago against the French. Still, she was married to a soldier and tried to give him as much support as she could.

"I hope not, my dear. I hope not. But I don't like the smell of this. Stay in the house till I come home. You'll be safe here."

As soon as he left the house he ran to the North Church on the corner of North and Lynde Streets and announced to the congregation and minister that "the regulars are coming." Mason told those present how close the troops were and urged them to spread word to their fellow citizens. The congregation dispersed immediately and within minutes the town was abuzz with excitement. Friends told friends and soon the word reached the far reaches of Salem and even neighboring towns.

Nervous energy infected everyone. While people naturally feared the advancing redcoats, many felt that, finally, this was an opportunity for Patriots to stand up for their rights and send a message to Gage and the Crown that British citizens on this side of the Atlantic would not be pushed around. Suddenly a quiet Sunday morning had become a tense, but exciting moment in their lives.

But everyone didn't share the same feelings. Neighbor looked at neighbor, wondering where their true sentiments lay. People suspected friends and kin folk of holding views that were dangerous or stubborn or ignorant depending on their point of view. It was a moment of high excitement, charged with suspicion and considerable fear.

Once the alarm had been raised in Salem, Mason mounted his horse and rode directly to Foster's blacksmith shop to see if Foster and neighboring Patriots could move at least some of the cannon to other locations. It was a reversal of Mason's previous thinking, but the pressure of the moment reinforced by the knowledge that the advancing troops numbered in the hundreds convinced him that every effort should be made to hide the cannon in case the Patriots were unable to stop the advancing soldiers. For some reason, until this morning, Mason and his fellow Patriots had assumed that troops sent out to seize the cannon would number far fewer than the hundreds that had been reported by the messenger from Marblehead.

Local residents were seen with their teams of horses hurrying to Foster's to haul whatever they could handle. A few cannon were taken to a nearby neighborhood called Buffum's Hill. There was a dense woods there with a deep fall of dry leaves. There was no snow on the ground so the cannon were separated from their carriages and buried under a thick layer of these leaves. Other teams took cannon as far away as Danvers. There wasn't enough time to remove all of the big weapons, but at least they could do something.

Chapter 20

As the British troops approached the Forest River separating the southern entrance to Salem from Marblehead, Lieutenant Colonel Leslie saw that the plank bridge was impassable. He turned to Major Blackwell and said, "It looks like we're not going to surprise them. They work fast, I'll give them that."

Blackwell said, "Yes, they've removed just enough planks to make it impossible to get across safely. You can see that they've just recently been removed." He scanned the immediate area and said, "Over there, sir, they've piled the planks just over there."

"So they have, major, so they have. Quickly, select ten men and let's replace those planks."

Within a half hour the missing planks had been replaced. They weren't held fast with spikes, but temporary repairs would have to be adequate as long as the troops used care in crossing the span. As soon as some of the men tested the bridge, Leslie gave the order to proceed into Salem.

"We underestimated these rebels, Blackwell. Let's not do that again. They're not fools."

"No sir."

"Let me see the map again, major."

"Here, sir. We follow this road until we come to the center of the town. Then we have a few streets to negotiate in order to get to North Street, which should lead us toward the blacksmith shop of this fellow Foster."

"Another hour and a half should take us there, major. Unless we meet more obstacles like this one."

"Yessir, we can probably expect more obstructions. Frankly, sir, it seems rather silly to me. They know we'll get there eventually. Why not just capitulate and get it over?"

"You haven't been in America very long, have you, major? You don't know these people. Don't make the mistake of concluding, because they live in roughhewn conditions and their towns are unsophisticated by comparison to London, that they are simple people. They're surprisingly resourceful. Many of them are well versed in British law and classical philosophy. Don't underestimate them."

♦ ♦ ♦

Not quite two hours later an advance unit of the regiment was emerging from Lynde Street onto North Street. Leslie had decided that if the townspeople saw a smaller group of troops they would not be certain as to their real intent. This would allow the soldiers to get closer to the cache of weapons in Foster's workshop before the locals could make any attempt to further conceal the arms. Having encountered no further obstacles since the plank-less bridge, Leslie and his men were feeling confident that their mission would be accomplished with minimal effort. Expecting no resistance, they marched onto North Street with muskets loaded, bayonets fixed, colors flying and drums beating with all the arrogance of a conquering army.

Shortly after turning north onto North Street, Leslie was approached by two young Tories. One of them was a well-known Salem lawyer. Both of these men wanted to assure Leslie of their support and offered their help in any way possible.

Colonel Mason had just returned from supervising the removal of several of the cannon from Foster's shop when he saw in the distance the advancing troops. With a little more focus he noticed that the commander of the troops was conversing with the two known Tories. Mason immediately turned and went back to his position on the north side of the North Bridge.

As the advance unit resumed its march down North Street, the bridge came into view. It was a drawbridge, and as soon as the Patriots saw the troops, they raised the leaf, which fortunately for them was on their side of the river. To Leslie, it was immediately clear now that the rebels were determined to resist. Leslie brought his troops to within a few yards of the bridge before he yelled, "Halt!"

As Leslie surveyed what lay before him he saw that a large number of citizens had assembled on the north side of the bridge. Many of them carried muskets. Some held axes, shovels, hatchets and all manner of objects that could be used to defend themselves if the forces on the other side of the bridge decided to attack. On either side of the street could be seen women and children on their stoops and leaning out windows taking in what they knew could be a day that might change their lives forever.

Chapter 21

I heard the call to arms from the street. I was surprised that this should be happening on a Sunday morning. From my few months in the eighteenth century I had found that most people honored the Sabbath. Even those who were not particularly religious honored it out of respect for those who were. At the very first call Tom and I had dashed to North Street and the north side of the bridge. Sam Hall and several nearby merchants I knew were already there. Shortly after we arrived at the bridge a steady flow of recently acquired friends and acquaintances joined those of us who were already there. Men came from all directions and slowly turned our small group into a multitude. As men arrived they kept reminding us that others were coming. Off in the distance I made out the approaching figure of Henry Woodbury.

The highly respected Reverend Thomas Barnard was there with a friend of his, who told us that when Colonel Hamilton's regiment of regulars was stationed at Fort William on Winter Island last year he, Reverend Barnard, had met many of the troops. He had come today to see if he might recognize any of the men he'd met last year.

I smiled as I saw that a number of younger residents had now climbed up on the upraised bridge leaf and sat there smiling as if this were all some sort of game. I didn't know the name of the commander of the regulars, but someone said he was a lieutenant colonel. Regardless of his name or rank I could see that he was enormously frustrated and displeased by the reception he'd received from the local populace. The lieutenant colonel, who I was soon to learn was named Leslie, demanded that the leaf be lowered immediately. I could tell by the way he said this that he was used to being obeyed. When no one responded and no action was taken, I could see the frustration take over. Leslie began to stomp and swear. He again demanded that the bridge be lowered.

"I give you fair warning," roared Leslie, "I have orders to cross this bridge, and I will do so if it costs me my life and the lives of my good men." Hearing no response from the inhabitants on the other side of the river and seeing no movement of the bridge leaf, the dilemma that faced him began to sink in. To advance without the consent of the great throng across the river was impossible. Yet retreat would be humiliating, a total disgrace and clearly the end of his military career. Faced with two bad choices he conferred quietly with Major Blackwell. The two of them decided to retire to West's Wharf a short distance away on the south side of the river. Leslie and Blackwell were followed discreetly by Captain Jonathan Felt, a Salem shipmaster, who was able to catch some of what the two British officers were discussing. Felt was one of the members of the Committee of Safety that Colonel Mason had come to depend on and I had come to respect.

Still enraged, Leslie turned to Blackwell and said, "We must order the men to fire on these people. We cannot let these rebels defy His Majesty's army."

Felt had quietly moved closer to the two British officers and cried out, "Damned you if you fire! You have no right to fire. Even Gage wouldn't have given you those orders." He then pointed to the great mass of Patriots across the river and said, "If you fire, you're all dead men." Captain Felt said this loud enough so that many on the north side of the river heard him. Until now the multitude assembled across the river had had no apparent leader. Upon hearing Felt openly defy the commander of British forces, the crowd was uplifted with confidence. Felt had become the unifying force that the aroused citizenry needed. Leslie and Blackwell could sense this latent energy in the assembled Patriots and decided to think some more before acting. As they returned to their regiment, Leslie pointed to flat-bottomed gondolas tied up on the south side of the river. Fearful that Leslie might use them to transport troops across the river, Captain Felt got several men to help scuttle the gondolas with axes and other tools that some in the crowd had brought with them.

Leslie was not about to ignore this so he ordered soldiers into the gondolas to prevent the Patriots from destroying the boats. The citizens continued their efforts, ignoring the bayonets of the soldiers. A scuffle broke out with considerable pushing and shoving. Two Patriots opened their shirts and dared the soldiers to use their bayonets. One soldier poked Joseph Whicher with his bayonet, drawing a small amount of blood.

Leslie could see that the inhabitants were determined to resist at all costs. Instead of submitting, the locals had become bolder and more confident. He briefly conferred with Blackwell and one of his lieutenants. Upon emerging from this brief confab, Leslie announced boldly, "I am determined to pass over this bridge before I return to Boston. I will cross this bridge if I have to be here till autumn.

I found his stand fascinating. I'd been watching the troops standing in a rather loose formation. It was an extremely cold day and the troops had become sweaty from their march over from Marblehead. Now, as they stood more or less motionless, the sweat was obviously evaporating and intensifying the bitter cold. Many of the men were shivering. They were losing their enthusiasm for the whole enterprise.

Now Leslie was saying, "If necessary I will make barracks out of the two stores on West's Wharf."

Captain Felt, now unofficially representing the locals, said, "Nobody would care for that."

"By God, I will not be defeated," retorted Leslie, clearly annoyed by the disrespect intended by Felt.

"You must accept that you have already been defeated," said Felt defiantly.

On hearing this, I had the feeling that by taunting Leslie and his men, Felt was inviting bloodshed.

As I observed the tense verbal fencing between Leslie and Felt, my eye caught sight of Henry working his way through the mass of people toward me. We exchanged greetings and then focused our attention on Leslie on the other side of the narrow river.

For a moment no one was speaking. Then a gentle voice from the crowd addressed Leslie.

"I urge you not to fire upon these innocent people, colonel. I beg you not to use your bayonets anymore."

Hearing this, Leslie inquired, "Who are you, sir?"

"I am Thomas Barnard, a minister of the gospel, and my mission is peace." I had heard good things about Barnard, but had never met him. I was surprised at how young he was.

Seemingly respectful of Barnard's ministerial position, Leslie said, "My soldiers and I are greatly insulted by our reception here in Salem. We are determined to cross this bridge, sir. We are on the king's highway and should not be kept from passing freely on it."

A man in the crowd yelled, "It is not the king's highway. It is a road built by the owners on both sides of it and no king, country or town has any control over it."

"That may be the way you view it, sir," said Leslie, "but that is not the way I see it."

The man then said, "I think 'twould be best and safest for you to conclude that the king has nothing to do with it."

More than an hour and a half had transpired since the initial demand made by Colonel Leslie. It appeared to me as I watched events unfold, that Leslie was at a complete loss as to what he should do next. He now conferred again in a huddle with Major Blackwell and his lieutenant. Apparently they concluded that it would be wisest to attempt some sort of compromise via diplomacy, since it was clear that force was not going to be viable. Not if he wanted to leave Salem with his regiment intact. Having come to this conclusion he spoke openly with Captain Felt, asking if he had the authority to demand that the leaf be lowered.

"I have no such authority," said Felt, "but I might have some influence."

Sensing an opportunity to resolve a bad situation without bloodshed and still preserving a modicum of his dignity, Leslie spoke with Felt and a few other leaders of the opposition. Among them were Colonel Mason, the Reverend Barnard and a prominent Salem resident, Timothy Pickering. I would have thought that Mason would take charge, but he seemed to have deferred to Felt. The conference was conducted openly, and all present were able to hear what transpired. Mason had climbed a ladder and now sat atop of the raised bridge leaf facing Leslie across the river. Leslie and Mason knew each other, and both found it difficult being in the situation they now found themselves.

I couldn't hear everything, but I did hear a brief exchange between Felt and Leslie.

"'Tis a good arrangement, sir," said Felt. "We allow your troops to cross over and continue on for 50 rods, but no more. At that point you can honestly report that you persuaded the difficult colonials to let you pass. We gave in to your demands. You retain your honor, and we retain our dignity."

"And your cannon," said Leslie bitterly.

"And our cannon. But only for defensive purposes. They will not be used unless we need them to defend ourselves. So, Colonel Leslie, I think we have a bargain we can both live with. Yes, the more I think about it, the more I think that we all come out ahead because nobody gets hurt."

"You're a smooth talker Mr. Felt. A sly one and a smooth talker. We'll agree to these terms, but I advise you and Colonel Mason, too, that if there's a next time, you colonials may not fare as well."

I couldn't hear it because of the chatter from both sides of the road, but I later learned that Leslie had given his word of honor that if the citizens on the opposite side of the bridge would lower the leaf and allow him and his men to pass, they would march peacefully not more than 50 rods beyond the bridge and then return. They would not injure person or property, he promised. Upon return to the south side of the river they would proceed on to their transport ships in Marblehead harbor and then return to Boston.

Mason assured the vast crowd that the word of Colonel Leslie was unimpeachable. Felt, however, was less certain of Leslie's honor and hesitated to give his okay until Mason assured him that most of the cannon were now secured in places the troops would never find. Finally Felt assented and the leaf was lowered to catcalls and murmurings from the now enormous crowd of Patriots. Leslie and his troops marched across the bridge and continued up the narrow road less than 300 yards whereupon they turned around and marched back across the bridge, all the while submitting to the taunting of men, women and children on both sides of the road. As the troops marched away in disgrace, a woman by the name of Sarah Tarrant leaned out of a window and taunted the soldiers as they passed by.

"Go home and tell your master he has sent you on a fool's errand and has broken the peace on the Sabbath. Do you think we were born in the woods to be frightened by owls?"

A soldier pointed his musket at her, and Tarrant yelled, "Fire if you have the courage, but I doubt it."

As Leslie and his troops marched into the distance down North Street, Henry Woodbury said, "Good Lord, Gilbert, that was a close one. This will happen again somewhere, and it may not end so well."

"It's a good thing it did end well," bellowed a large man standing next to Henry. "No thanks to your traitorous brother."

"I don't know you," responded Henry. It was an inappropriate response, but I could see that Henry was taken by surprise.

"No, you don't, but I know who you are, Henry Woodbury, and I know who your brother is. A Tory traitor, that's who. It was him and some of his Tory friends that brought these redcoats to our town. You can tell that brother of yours that if he knows what's good for him, he'll get the hell out of Beverly Farms and go back to England where he belongs."

"He's not from England," said Henry, still somewhat inappropriately, as he was clearly quite shaken by the attack from a complete stranger. "I don't agree with him, but he has a wife, who was also born here."

"Well, they've made their bed, so they need to lie in it. If they don't want England, then they'd best go to Canada, for there's no place for 'em here in America."

"Ay," said a second man nearby. "We know where Robert Woodbury lives, so tell him he better get out fast if he knows what's good for 'im."

Henry's neck was now as red as a beet. "I'll not defend what my brother did, but he is my brother, and I'll not listen to threats against him, either."

"Sorry, Woodbury, but you've already heard 'em," said the large man. "It's not just us he has to fear. There's a lot who would tar and feather your Tory brother. Get the word to him first, or someone'll get to him. We don't want no more of 'im around here."

I could see that Henry was torn as to what he should do. Lashing out at fellow Patriots whose sentiments closely approximated his own would only make matters worse. Besides, there were too many to lash out at. He would lose and gain nothing. He turned away from his antagonists, trying to ignore them. They in turn found other interests and moved away to brag to friends about their small verbal victory.

It took a while for the crowd to disperse. There was a heady feeling of jubilation running through the surging body of patriots, and people lingered to share the experience. It was the first time in their lives that they'd seen anyone go head to head with the king's forces, and it was energizing. They all knew of the Tea Party in Boston in '73, and they'd heard of a confrontation in Cambridge just last September similar to this one in Salem, but this was the first time they'd actually witnessed such a thing, and it was the most exhilarating thing many of them had ever experienced. The Cambridge clash had ended differently, though. The king's troops had actually taken control of a stash of cannon and powder there. Today Salem had shown firsthand that the crown's power had its limits. It could be thwarted by a determined Patriot citizenry.

Chapter 22

As the crowd thinned, Mason approached Henry, Tom and me to let us know that he was calling an immediate meeting of the Committee of Safety at his house. He and Felt were convening the meeting in half an hour even though he wasn't sure how many he could round up on such short notice. Then he excused himself saying he had to reach as many as possible and urged us to notify as many as we could, too.

Not surprisingly, we had a good turnout at the meeting. Mason and Felt, who in recent weeks had played increasingly important roles in the committee, announced that they wanted to move the cannon and other armaments to Concord, where the recently formed Provincial Congress was amassing a large store of weapons in preparation for the growing likelihood of battle with the king's forces. That possibility seemed even more likely after today's events. Mason also made it clear that we should all be on the alert for that unidentified someone who had leaked information to Robert Woodbury and his fellow Tories.

The Provincial Congress had been formed just last October when Governor Gage dissolved the Provincial Assembly in Salem under the terms of the new Government Act. One of the most onerous parts of the Government Act was the dramatic revision of the colonial charter. Under the colonial charter Massachusetts was an independent colony allowed to govern itself for all intents and purposes.

The dramatically altered charter treated Massachusetts as a province of Great Britain. Its provincial status meant that Massachusetts was now part of the British imperial structure. The governor's powers were greatly expanded. The governor, who was appointed by the king, could now veto acts of the General Court. The governor became commander-in-chief of the militia. Up till now the governor had formed a Governor's Council consisting of 28 men he'd selected from the House of Representatives. The Government Act said that members of the Governor's Council would no longer be elected representatives, but henceforth would be appointed by the king and remain in office at his pleasure. These new powers of the governor inflamed the colonists.

A few days after the dissolution of the Provincial Assembly by Gage, the members of the Assembly had met anyway and adjourned to Concord where they formed the Provincial Congress.

As far as Governor Gage and Parliament were concerned the Provincial Congress was illegal. Nevertheless it controlled nearly all of Massachusetts except Boston. More than half of the colony's citizens recognized it as their government and rejected more and more of what emanated from Gage's British-controlled Boston.

Chapter 23

Henry invited Tom and me back to his house in Beverly Farms. He called it a celebration because Leslie had been forced to retreat with his tail between his legs. He said everyone was celebrating and he'd like to do it with us. Henry hadn't seen much of us lately and he was sure Jane and the boys would love to see us, too. He said if the night drew on too late, we could stay over so no need to trouble ourselves because of the hour. If we left a little over an hour early in the morning we could be at the *Gazette* in time for work, and Sam Hall would not be put out. Little did we know at the time that Henry had a second motive for asking us to his house.

Tom looked forward to the celebration, and I did, too, so we retrieved our horses and rode through Salem and then took the ferry into Beverly. It had been a cold day, but because of the tense events I had not noticed the cold that much until now. As night approached it grew much colder out, so I was glad to finally settle myself in front of the inviting fire in the cozy Woodbury cottage.

Jane brought Tom and me mugs of ale that were pleasantly cool because the keg was stored in the cellar. As we relaxed while Jane prepared something for supper, Henry opened up to us.

"You witnessed my encounter with those two men today, so you can imagine what I'm feeling."

"Yes, Henry, I think I can," I said, trying to show as much concern as I could. "I know you didn't want to create more of a stir there, but I can imagine what it's doing to you."

"They were right, you know."

"About your brother?"

"Yes. Because of him we came within a hairsbreadth of open battle with the regulars. Fortunately, thanks to Jonathan Felt and David Mason, it didn't happen."

"And Colonel Leslie, too," I suggested.

"Yes, clearly Leslie didn't want bloodshed either. But another time and another place, and it will happen. You know it, and I know it."

Tom nodded his agreement, saying, Yes, Henry, it was a close one."

I said, "I know you blame your brother for what happened today, but I know it's not that easy for you to condemn him. As much as he's angered you, I sense that you don't want to see anything happen to him, either?"

"He deserves something for his treachery, but he is my brother. No, dear God, I don't want harm to come to him. I have to warn him. Probably should tonight. I have no doubt that some of these hotheads will do something, and soon."

"What can Robert do, Henry? Short of leaving Massachusetts."

"I fear that that is exactly what he and Catherine must do, at least until things blow over. There'll be no peace for him here. Not now anyway. Do you see any other way, Gilbert?"

"I wish I did. No, he probably should leave the colonies entirely— or at least Massachusetts."

"Tis a terrible problem, and it can't be avoided, I fear. Would you two mind terribly going over to his house with me tonight? There is so much between the two of us, he might listen to you more. I don't think we'll be there long."

"Right now? Before Jane puts supper on?"

"She knows I have to do this, and she'll wait supper, but I'd appreciate it if the two of you would accompany me. I know it's not a pleasant thing I ask of ye, but you've become good friends, and I think I'll need your help."

Roberts house was not ten minutes away by foot. When Robert came to the door, he stared at Henry, clearly at a loss as to what to say or do next.

After an awkward pause, Henry said, "Would you kindly let me and my friends in for a minute, Robert. It's cold out here."

"I can imagine what you have to say to me," said Robert. "Oh well, come in, it is cold out."

An anguished Catherine Woodbury tried to make us feel welcome, though I knew she feared something bad was going to happen.

We tried to appear relaxed as we sat in front of the fireplace in their small sitting room. Catherine offered tea or cider, but we deferred, knowing this was no social call. Finally, a grim-faced Robert said, "Well, you didn't come here to enjoy our hospitality I reckon. What is it, Henry? What brings you and your friends here on a cold Sunday night?"

"'Tis not a pleasant task, I assure you, brother. The three of us were at the North Bridge today when the king's regulars led by a Lieutenant Colonel Leslie attempted to cross the river and confiscate weapons that the Committee of Safety had collected to protect the colony from the oppressive...."

"You mean collected so you and your fellow rebels could stage a rebellion against the lawful authority in these British colonies."

"No, I mean so that the good citizens of this colony can defend themselves against the kind of oppressive government the king and his parliament have become in the last few years. Somehow, our king and

Parliament now view us as lesser beings and not as British citizens with equal rights. You should be ashamed of yourself, Robert. You are part of an American civilization that we and our ancestors have built here; yet you think the Crown has the right to dictate to us as if we were menial servants. I can't believe you think so little of what we have built here."

Things were getting out of hand quickly, and I feared that we'd be sent back to Henry's place before we accomplished our mission. Tempers were going to make a bad situation even worse.

"Henry, Robert," I said firmly, "I know you both and I respect you both. You are not going to agree on this matter. At least not tonight. It is not an easy matter to resolve." I then directed my next words to Henry. "Thomas and I urge you to remember why we came here tonight."

Henry was furious. I'm sure it was at the very thought that his brother would attempt to justify supporting the king and Parliament after all the injustices they had perpetrated. Worse than that, I suspected, he was livid because Robert had turned on his fellow citizens putting them at risk of being fired upon by redcoats.

"I'm sorry, Gilbert, I know your intentions are good, but I'm not sure Robert deserves our good intentions. He says that we would rebel against the lawful authority of the Crown. The Crown has annulled our charter. The Crown denies us the right to elect our legislators, the Crown denies us the right to vote on our levies. Is this the legal authority we should obey? Does the Crown deserve our loyalty?"

"Without the support of the Crown," roared Robert, "we would all be speaking French, if we were not scalped first. You and your so-called Patriots, Henry, are a bunch of ingrates."

"I think we'd best leave, my friends, before one of us does something he regrets."

"No, Henry," I said, "I'll not let you leave before you deliver your message. If you leave first you will regret it the rest of your life." I briefly took my eyes off the two brothers and saw that Catherine was bent over in fear. As if what she was hearing wasn't bad enough, I sensed that worse was coming. And I was right.

"What the hell is it you came to say?" blurted Robert. "As if what you've already said wasn't enough for one night."

Henry closed his eyes a moment, and through sheer force of will, overcame his anger enough to say, "We came to warn you, my brother, that there were threats made today by Patriots. Threats against you."

"What kind of threats?"

"That if you didn't go back to England or up to Canada, you and your family would suffer."

"I never lived in England. You know that. What do they mean, go back? What do they mean by suffer? And why take it out on Catherine?"

"Good God, Robert, I know you were born here, as was I. They weren't specific about what they'd do, but Gilbert, Thomas and I believe they were serious. God knows, we haven't gotten along lately, but I don't want anything bad to happen to you or Catherine or the boy. They said they know where you live, Robert. I think you should take this seriously. I think you should move out of here until things settle down at least."

"Where would we go?" shrieked Catherine from the other side of the room. "We can't just leave everything we have here."

"We'll not run from these people, Catherine. I'll not let them scare me out of my own home."

"What about Martin and me, Robert? What about us?"

Robert turned back to us. "You said leave until things settle down. You and I know that things are going to get a lot worse around here before they settle down."

"I know that. I know that. But if you and Catherine stay, there's no telling what could happen to you. Do you want to risk that?"

"See what kind of people you associate with, Henry. These people say they would defend their independence, but think nothing about terrorizing fellow British citizens. What kind of rabble are they?"

"Only a small minority of the Patriots would do this, but whether you like it or not, Robert, you inflamed them and their more moderate fellow citizens, too, when you revealed their secrets to Gage. By doing so you set British troops against the good people of Salem and their neighbors. Thanks be to God and a few level heads, too, that we didn't have a bloody massacre today." Henry took a deep breath and then said, "Listen, Robert, I'm not here to debate which side is right. I'm here to warn you to do something for your own safety."

"If we leave, what's to prevent them from burning our house down?"

"What's to stop them from burning it down with you in it?"

Robert thrust his head into his open hands and moaned. After a moment he looked up and said, "I need time to think. Where would we go? Do we have enough money? This is the only place we know. Damn these ungrateful rebels! Damn them all!"

Chapter 24

We left Robert and his wife agonizing over what they would do next. Catherine had reminded him that they had an uncle in Nova Scotia who might help them resettle up there.

During our delayed supper Henry told us that he knew that Robert's funds were limited.

"He has a few bills of credit issued by the Crown. Has some Spanish dollars and other coins. Most of what he has, though, is in that house, and they can't take that with them. They don't have a lot, but maybe enough to get him through till he finds work in Canada. I'm sure there's just as great a need for cod fishermen up there as there is here. With the Canadians being a lot happier with the king than we are down here, he should fit in up there."

Jane Woodbury spoke up. She didn't often intrude in conversations between men, but she did now. "We could put them up here for a few days until they get things straightened away. We have the room. Oh, Henry, I feel so bad for them. Especially Catherine. I happen to know she doesn't share Robert's views on political things. She doesn't speak up, though, because he doesn't like it when she does. I feel for both of them, but Catherine in particular. She's an innocent victim in all this. She and young Martin." She smiled at Henry and added, "I know you're going to say that it would be dangerous for us if we had them here. Maybe it wouldn't, though, if people didn't know."

Henry smiled lovingly back at his wife. "They would know, Jane. They would know. I'm almost certain that they have Robert's house under close scrutiny. If he leaves soon, they will probably let him and Catherine go. If he lingers too long, who knows what will happen. The Patriot community has little patience right now. If they ignore what Robert did, they would be encouraging the very sort of treachery that brought the troops to Salem today. No, if he doesn't leave, they will want to punish him. I fear what that punishment might be. If we bring Robert and Catherine here, it will bring God knows what manner of misery upon you and the boys. No, he's my brother, but you are my dear family. Robert brought this on himself. I've alerted him to the danger. Now it's up to him. When I think about it I wonder why he didn't anticipate this himself. The man doesn't live in a cave, for God's sake."

"Surely these friends of yours would not do something tonight?" asked Jane.

"They are not my friends. We are all Patriots, but my friends would not attack my brother."

"You hope."

He looked at the floor before saying, "Yes, I hope. In any event, no one would blaspheme the Sabbath by doing something today."

"No one," I interjected, "but the redcoats."

"Aye, you see why we hate the bloody Crown so much these days."

♦ ♦ ♦

Tom and I had been at work at the *Gazette* for a couple of hours when Henry entered and asked Sam if he could have a minute with us. Hall called us from the back to join him and Henry.

Our boss, who'd known Henry for years and liked him, saw the frantic look in Woodbury's eyes and said, "What in God's name is wrong, Henry? You look a fright."

"I don't know why I'm here really. I had to tell someone, but these days one can never be sure it's safe to talk too openly. I trust the three of you." Henry was trembling now. Clearly not himself. "I shouldn't have come. You all have your own troubles. You don't need mine. Sorry to interrupt your work." With that, he started to leave through the door.

"Wait a minute, my friend," said Hall firmly. "Don't leave in that state of mind. Sit down and I'll bring you some coffee. I prefer tea myself, but I'll drink coffee before I'll spend two pence for tea from a British merchant. Wait, if you must have tea I have some that was smuggled in from the Netherlands."

"No, Sam, thank you, but I'm in no condition to enjoy coffee or tea right now. I should go."

"You'll not go until you tell us what's troubling you. Sit over here and tell us what's got you so lathered up."

"Just for a few minutes, then." He dropped into a rough wooden chair, drew in a deep breath and then unloaded. "You know that my brother was one of the Tories who went to Gage and informed about the cannon." We all nodded. "And you know that some of the folks over on North Street near the bridge yesterday made threats against him?" We nodded again.

Sam said, "I heard about it. Yes."

"Well, he's not come to bodily harm, but when he went down to Beverly Harbor to his boat this morn to ask the owner, who's also the captain, if he would take him and his wife to Halifax or even to Portland, he got a flat no for an answer. Mind you, he's worked on that boat for over six years now. Said he was even willing to pay his passage, but figured it wouldn't cost the owner much since he goes up there to fish for weeks at a time."

"I take it the owner's a Patriot," said Hall.

"Aye, they used to argue a bit on the boat, but as long as Robert did his job that was it. They talked and debated. Usually it was friendly verbal fencing. At least that's what Robert told me. Once in a while it got a bit testy, and they'd change the subject. They could always work together, though. But when the crew got wind of how Robert and those other fellows went down to Boston to see the commandant, they weren't so tolerant. Owner said Robert would never set foot on the boat again. Even if he and Catherine stay, which I think would be foolish, he'll never get work here. Now he has to go, and he has to find a Tory boat to go on."

"Damn shame," said Hall sincerely. "I don't know your brother much, but I met him once or twice. Seemed like a decent chap. Sorry about all this, Henry."

"He is a decent man. Just muleheaded. Loves his king. King can do no wrong."

"Well, I suppose in his own way he thinks he's the patriot staying loyal to his king."

"So were we all until recent years," said Henry. "So were we all."

"Wish I could help you, Henry, but I don't see what I could do, and quite honestly, I don't think I'd be inclined to help your brother. Not after what he did."

"I know, Sam. I know. I didn't come here askin' for help. Just needed someone to talk to. Needed to get this off my chest."

"Well, there's probably a few silent Tories with boats down at the harbor. He should probably look for one of them, if he wants to get out of here fast. Otherwise I think he'll have to get himself to Boston to find a boat."

"I told him that this morning. I expect that's what he'll do." Henry stared out the heavily mullioned window for a moment and then said, "It's hard to believe now that Robert and I were so close once. As boys we played together and learned to fish together. Shared secrets. We did everything together. Now we're worlds apart. Frankly, I don't see how it'll ever get better. Worse, if he and Catherine go to Canada, we'll probably never see each other again."

"Yes, 'tis a terrible thing what these times are doing to all of us," said Hall. "Many are suffering now. But when it's your own family, it brings the suffering much too close. Here at the paper we see family against family, friend against friend all too often. Henry, I can't wish your brother good fortune, because I don't believe he deserves it, but if he and his wife leave Massachusetts safely then I'm happy for you. To be honest, I'll be happy he's gone, too."

Chapter 25

American history means a lot more to you when you actually experience it. Sadly, I remember 9/11. I also remember when we got Osama bin Laden. These events were a lot more real to me than reading about Pearl Harbor and World War II, neither of which I experienced.

I read American history in school. It never really came alive till now. Tom and I are actually experiencing the history that we've read about.

We both read about the events that led up to the American Revolution. We read about how the colonies were almost 100 percent pro British at the end of the French and Indian War. British troops with the help of colonial militiamen defeated the French, took control of much of North America and tamed the Indians, all in one ten-year period. Prosperity followed in the wake of the war, and our relationship with Great Britain was close. American colonists all felt British and all felt loyalty toward their king.

But the war had drained British coffers, and Parliament looked for ways to help pay for those expensive ten years of conflict on the North American continent. They needed to rebuild the British economy. Britain had been fighting the Seven Years War in Europe at the same time, so they really did need money. They looked across the sea to the American colonies and began imposing all manner of new taxes. It started with the Sugar Act in 1764. Then came the Stamp Act in 1765 followed by the Townshend Revenue Act in '67 and the Tea Act in '73. Those are just a few of the oppressive acts imposed against the colonists so it's not hard to see why things reached a breaking point in 1775.

One day I told David Mason that I understood why so many

colonists were fed up with the way Britain governed the American colonies, but that many people around the world would probably think being a colonist under British control was not too bad.

Mason was taken aback by my query. "I thought you felt the same way we do, Gilbert. Are you becoming a Tory?"

"No, no. Of course I feel the same as you do. It's just that I sometimes wonder how our fellow British citizens in the mother country feel about our complaints. Do they think we are unappreciative ingrates or do they agree with us?"

"I've spoken with many from the home country. Some agree with us, and some simply don't understand why we complain. When I tell them we send no delegates to Parliament, they tell me that some in England cannot vote for delegates, either, but that Parliament says that all Englishmen enjoy *virtual representation*. I rebut this explanation by telling them that maybe British subjects in England 'enjoy' virtual representation, but we British on this side of the ocean get no satisfaction from it. How could we if it means we have no say in our own governance? I tell these people that what they don't seem to understand is that we've been voting for our leaders here in the colonies for over 100 years. Virtual representation is a major step backward for us.

"They counter that with a question of their own. The ask me to tell them if we can honestly say that we suffer because of British laws imposed on us? Do we not have a viable economy? Can we not do as we please?"

I smiled at Mason and interjected my own answer. "And I imagine you say that, yes we have a viable economy that has been greatly curtailed by taxation without representation. Probably the first examples were the Sugar Act and Stamp Act ten years ago when Britain imposed taxes on legal documents, newspapers—even playing cards. Then came the Townshend Act, which put levies on paper, paint, and all manner of things. Things got much worse when British troops landed in Boston to enforce these levies. Bostonians resented the very presence of these troops. Now we have real martial law and virtual representation. To make matters worse, because these troops were so poorly paid, many of them took work in Boston. In so doing, they took jobs that Bostonians should have gotten." As I paused for a moment I studied Mason's expression. I think he found my little speech interesting. I don't think he could quite figure me out. He thought he knew me, but now he was finding me a bit more complex.

"Then, just last year," I continued, "came the latest indignity. Parliament passed the Intolerable Acts, which closed the Port of Boston and allowed troops to be quartered in private property such as taverns and vacant buildings. Some say even private homes. Worse yet, we, the colonists are expected to pay to provision these troops." I took a breath and smiled at my friend. "Still worse, of course, is the fact that Parliament has by these laws turned Gage into a dictator. "So no, David, I'm not becoming a Tory. I was just taking a minute to try to view the situation as others might see it. You see, if we understand their point of view, maybe it will help us better explain our views to them."

"You are a strange man, Gilbert. I like you, but you have strange ideas."

Chapter 26

Tuesday morning when Tom and I arrived at the *Gazette*, Toby Foster, one of Sam's two writers, came up to us and said, "Did you hear what happened to your friend's brother?"

Toby saw the puzzled look on my face and explained.

"Robert Woodbury, up in Beverly Farms. He was tarred and feathered yesterday."

"Dear God, no! Where?"

"In Beverly, down at the harbor. Here, I've already written the story. You'll be setting the type, so you might as well have it now." He handed me a sheet of foolscap on which he'd scrawled a brief article. I held it up so that Tom could read it along with me.

Beverly—Several fishermen reported witnessing the tarring and feathering of one Robert Woodbury of Beverly Farms at Beverly Harbor Monday. These witnesses told the *Gazette* that Woodbury was attempting to hire passage to Halifax for himself and his wife when several of their fellow fishermen left their boats and seized the man, tying him to a dock post on Bailey's Wharf. Whilst Woodbury was tied up the men fetched a barrel of pitch from the stores available on the wharf and a quantity of dry waste material, there being no feathers available at that moment. The barrel of pitch was heated to near boiling and then poured over the bare upper body of Woodbury, who was then rolled in dry waste that had been collected.

The witnesses, who refused to give their names, said that the tarring and feathering was retaliation for Woodbury's disclosure

of the location of cannon secured in Salem by the local
Committee of Safety. It was because of Woodbury's action, said
one witness, that nearly 300 British troops descended upon Salem
Sunday. Only through the diplomacy of Captain Jonathan Felt,
Colonel David Mason, Timothy Pickering and Rev. Thomas
Barnard was the commander of the British regiment persuaded to
return to Boston empty handed, thus averting what might have
been a bloody disaster. Such a disaster would have been
rightfully attributed to the treachery of Robert Woodbury.

I set the type, not entirely comfortable with my efforts. It was
clearly yellow journalism, but since the term had not even been
invented yet, I felt I had best avoid that fight right now. I liked Toby,
but he had obviously inserted his and probably Sam's opinions into the
article, which a good journalist shouldn't do. Well, that was a battle I'd
lose because virtually every journalist did that in the eighteenth
century. It was expected of them.

As soon as Tom and I finished work we rode down to the river, took
the ferry across and rode as quickly as we could to Henry's place. Tom
and I had become rather good with a horse and actually enjoyed riding
now.

When Jane opened the door she just pointed to the kitchen where
we found Henry pacing back and forth. Upon seeing us, he said,
"Gilbert, Thomas. You heard?"

"Yes, yes, we heard," I said. "How is he?"

"Catherine went for Doc Orme, who said she should just scrape off
the tar and expect him to be in pain for a long time."

"He didn't go to Robert and give him something for the pain?"

Henry seemed puzzled by this. "What could he give him? Besides,
Catherine said he didn't seem too eager to help. She begged him, and
finally he just said scrape off the tar and try not to take too much skin
when you do it. He said no need for him to go and see Robert."

"No sympathy there, I see."

"None at all. I don't suppose Robert should expect much, but I always thought physicians lived by a certain oath."

"Yes, but it sounds as if this doctor feels your brother doesn't deserve his best efforts, regardless of the oath."

"I suppose I understand, but Good Lord, I can't bear to see my brother go through this no matter what he's done. I've been over there a couple of times. She's gotten much of the tar off, but Robert is in terrible pain. She couldn't avoid scraping skin off so he has bloody raw patches all over his body. The melted tar left terrible burns on most of the skin that remains. The man's in agony. Can scarcely move because of the pain." Henry peered out the window at the graying sky. Finally, he turned back and said, "I expect it will heal after some time. A great deal of time I'm afraid."

"Do you think his tormenters will still want him to leave town," asked Tom.

"Do you mean will they be satisfied now or will they want him to suffer more? I imagine they'll be less inclined to force him out of town now. Doesn't matter, though. He and Catherine have already decided that they'll leave this area. How could they ever have a normal life here?"

"Where will they go?" I asked.

"He told me just an hour ago that as soon as he's able to get about without too much pain they'll head for Boston. There's a bigger Loyalist population down there. If they think they can survive down there, they may settle there. If it looks as unwelcoming as it is here, they'll book passage on a ship headed to Halifax."

Chapter 27

In the middle of April Sam Hall asked me to go to Boston for him and speak with Isaiah Thomas. Thomas was the publisher of the *Massachusetts Spy*, the most influential newspaper in the 13 colonies at the time. Hall had told me that Thomas started out as a nonpartisan paper open to all views, but beholden to none. It had proven to be impossible to maintain that neutrality for the same reason Sam Hall was unable to be nonpartisan. People who bought subscriptions to the paper and advertisers demanded that he stand for what they believed in. Faced with needing to openly defend a position, Sam had favored the Whig or Patriot views in his paper. Thomas felt the same way and had made the same decision. Apparently it had not been at all easy for Thomas as he was a very young man to be publishing a paper. He'd started the paper back in '71 when he was only 21.

Sam wanted to know how young Thomas was handling the increasing pressure Whig newspapers were getting from the Royal authorities in Boston. Sam was getting that pressure, too, though so far it was not nearly as bad as what Thomas suffered in Boston. Clashes were more common now as the friction and tension between the Patriots and the Loyalists intensified. Sam figured things would get worse and wanted to get another view on how to deal with these worsening conditions. That's what I admired about Sam. He was smart and successful, but he didn't rest on his laurels. He was always thinking ahead.

Thomas looked like he was still 21. Sandy haired, he stood just under six feet tall and combined an outward animal energy with an easy manner that made him immediately likable. He offered me some cider. Most Patriots avoided tea on general principal now. It was not easy to make coffee in a place of business, so cider was often the beverage of choice in such situations.

I smiled inwardly as I realized that the practice of drinking water virtually everywhere you went had not caught on yet in colonial New England. Maybe it was the lack of plastic bottles and the lack of running water.

"Glad to meet you, Mr. Lee," said Thomas. "I take it Sam could't make the trip himself."

"He sends his greetings and apologies for not being able to come here himself. Has some personal problems he needs to attend to, and he wants me to get to know some of our fellow journalists anyway. He thought it would be a good chance for me to meet you and see how you run a newspaper in Boston. He admires your work. Says you put together the best paper in all of New England."

"Old Sam Hall. Ever the charmer. You know, Sam and I collaborated back in February of '73 and published a joint edition under both names. Nice idea, but we discontinued it as it proved to be a bit impractical. Still, I'm glad we did it. So far as I know, no other papers have ever done it before or since." He paused, savoring the memory, before saying, "Well, I am glad to meet you, Gilbert. What can I help you with?"

"We've heard that Gage and his officials have been harassing you here at the paper, making it difficult to publish. Can you tell me what sort of thing they're doing and how you cope with it? We figure it's only a matter of time before we'll be facing the same interference. Actually, we've already lost subscribers and some advertisers. Fortunately, though, we've gained almost as many as we've lost."

"I know Sam, and I think pretty much the same way he does, so I expect what you're experiencing with your advertisers and subscribers will continue in about the same way. You'll lose some who don't agree with you and gain some from folks who want to support a voice for liberty. What I fear far more is interference from Gage and his people. We get under their skin, and they look for ways to interfere with our business.

"What Gage and the Crown authorities back in England seem to mind the most is our practice of printing essays by anonymous commentators."

"Yes, I know," I said. "They go by such names as Centinel, Leonidas and Mucius Scaevola. They sometimes recommend open rebellion. I can see why Gage and the officials back in London don't like to read such things. Still, you break no laws."

"Exactly. It's the Crown that violates our laws. Turned Gage into a virtual dictator. Abrogated our charter. Took away our assembly—our right to vote for our representatives. They're making it harder on newspapers such as ours. I'm pleased to say that the paper's commentators are read everywhere in the 13 colonies now, since other papers have asked for the right to reprint them."

I'd become a fan of the *Spy* myself. It was more outspoken than the *Gazette* and because of that fanned the flames of patriotism in a disgruntled populace. Or I should say, in a large part of the populace. "Mr. Thomas, —"

"Isaiah is fine."

"Isaiah, you said you feared the actions of Gage and his people more than loss of advertisers or subscribers. What kind of actions are these?"

"I've had several visits by one or more of his officials telling me to be less 'strident' as they put it. Said that open statements against the Crown were disloyal and seditious. Possibly even treasonous."

"How can it be treasonous to merely disagree with government pronouncements?" As soon as I said it I realized that I was influenced by 250 years of struggles for the right to freedom of speech and freedom of the press. Obviously King George and Isaiah Thomas did not have the benefit of those 250 years. Thomas looked at me as if I were the naivest person he'd ever met.

"Come, Mr. Lee, surely you can understand why they'd say that. Almost certainly what we print is seditious. I'll argue against it being treasonous, but in fairness, you must see that they would think so."

"Please call me Gilbert. I suppose I can, though I don't like such a label in this case because I believe in your cause."

"I assumed you did or old Sam Hall wouldn't have sent you as his emissary."

"Have you been harassed in any other way recently?" I asked.

"We've had delays in delivery of paper and other supplies. My vendors tell me they've been pressured by Gage's authorities to delay deliveries to me or they might find themselves subjected to investigation into their loyalty to the Crown. They have been threatened with increased levies on their supplies. They've been told they might have to close while undergoing scrutiny of various sorts. Of course I've already been subjected to that kind of scrutiny. I had two of Gage's officials in here for three days looking into my bookkeeping, my records, subjecting my employees to endless interrogation. It was three days when we might just as well have been closed because we got no business done. The next issue of the paper was barely a paper. If it continues, I may have to close down the *Spy*." He stopped talking for a few seconds; then became even more serious. "What I tell you next must be between us only. Of course, you may tell Sam. I assume I can trust you?"

"I assure you, you can."

"I take great pride and considerable pleasure in being a voice for the cause of freedom in these 13 colonies. I am so proud of our ancestors who came here for the freedom they lacked back in England." He forced a smile before continuing. "At least that's what the people coming to New England did. I'm not so sure about our more materialistic brethren down in Virginia, but that's another story, I suppose. But here in New England we came for freedom. King Charles gave us a charter that granted us the freedoms that our ancestors were entitled to in England, but did not always receive. When our ancestors came here they lived by that charter, created their own legislature and governed themselves the way they wanted to be governed. For many years the Crown left us alone and our relationship with England was mutually beneficial. But in the last ten years we have seen a rapid erosion of the freedoms our ancestors fought for and we've tried to defend. In the past decade Parliament has tried to fill its coffers through the sweat and toil of colonists and has punished us for objecting."

"Everything you say makes sense, Mr. Thom— er Isaiah, but that isn't what you want kept quiet. You've been saying that in the *Spy* for years."

"You're right, of course. I sometimes get carried away. What I want kept quiet must remain between us and Sam Hall. Sometime soon I'm going to move the paper inland to a safer, more receptive community. Mind you now, only you and Sam Hall know this."

"You have my word. You would do this rather than just close down?"

"Yes, I can't give up."

"Have you decided where you would take it?"

"Probably Springfield or Worcester. They're both Whig towns. If I become convinced that I can't continue here, rather than close down I'll take everything west. If Gage knew that, he'd confiscate my presses or put me in a cell."

"If he were going to shut you down, don't you think he'd already have done it?"

"Here in Boston his minions visit me all too often just to put the fear of God into me. Up till now Gage believed that if I was close at hand, he could shut me down at a moment's notice. If I move the paper, though, it won't be so easy for him. The governor is losing patience, and it's only a matter of days or weeks at most before he shuts me down. Wouldn't be surprised if he put me in a cell, to make his point to other Patriot publishers. No, I must make my move soon.

Chapter 28

The next day, as I was reporting to Sam Hall on what I'd learned in Boston, the bell rang, and I turned to see three men entering the premises. One of them was in the uniform of a British army captain. The second man, a stranger to me, was in civilian garb, and the third, also a civilian, was Benjamin Waite. I had only seen Waite once before, and that was when he and Sam had argued over Waite's advertising and their differences of opinion on political issues. At that time just a few months ago, he and Sam had parted on bad terms. From the looks of things, their relationship wasn't going to improve any today.

Sam approached the three newcomers and said, "May I help you gentlemen?" Then condescendingly he added, "Oh, hello, Ben."

The captain took a step forward. "Mr. Hall, I'm Captain Hugh Oliver. This is Lawrence Kilmartin, a civilian aide to Governor Gage. You obviously know Mr. Waite."

Captain Oliver took a step forward to shake Hall's hand. Sam stood his ground, not accepting the proffered hand. Looking grimmer than I'd ever seen him, Sam demanded, "What do you people want? I have a newspaper to get out."

Kilmartin took a half step forward and said, "Mr. Hall, we're here as representatives of the Crown. We've had a number of complaints about your newspaper and are here to advise you that we believe it would be in your best interest if you refrained from criticizing His Royal Majesty, Parliament and Governor Gage in your newspaper. As one of the governor's legal advisors I am obligated to tell you that we, as representatives of the Crown believe, that your paper has been guilty of libel, sedition and possibly even treason. In short, sir, you are treading on very dangerous territory. Should you persist, it is highly probable that your newspaper will be shut down and that you, yourself, will be put on trial for these and possibly other offenses."

Sam Hall glared at Ben Waite. "So, Ben, I see you found a way to make good on your threat. I'm disappointed in you. Thought our friendship, despite our differences, meant more to you than that." He then turned to Kilmartin and said, "Then liberty of the press accepted in England does not extend to these shores. That appears to be what you're saying."

Looking superior, Kilmartin said, "Liberty of the press in Great Britain does not grant the press the right to libel the king or his representatives; nor does it grant the press the right to print ideas promoting the overthrow of His Majesty's government. As I said, sir, you are on shaky ground. Captain Oliver is here to make it clear that we are serious. If you do not change your practices in this newspaper immediately, Captain Oliver has orders to shut down this establishment and to arrest you for defying the Governor's orders." Then Kilmartin drew himself up haughtily, as if he were speaking to a common street urchin. "I hope I have made myself clear."

When the three men left, Tom and I tried to offer Hall our support, as minimal as it was. "Listen, Sam," I said soberly. "Gage is cracking down hard on—" Before I could continue, I saw the blank look on Sam's face and realized that I'd used an expression completely unknown in the eighteenth century. I awkwardly tried to get out of it by saying, "Cracking down is an expression we used up north. Means a decision to enforce the laws—or something to that effect. Anyway, after what Isaiah Thomas told me yesterday, it's quite clear that Gage is putting pressure on newspapers that don't agree with him." I was referring to Thomas's telling me that almost the same thing had already happened to him—that he'd been harassed by government officials and that he was seriously thinking of moving the *Spy* to Springfield or Worcester."

Sam was shaking now. "Oh for the love of God, things keep getting worse for all of us. I may have to move the *Gazette*, too. As you know, I'd been thinking of Cambridge, but that's out of the question now. Too close to Boston. Now I may have to consider someplace in the western part of the colony. I may have to do what Isaiah is doing. Not yet, though. Not yet." He paced back and forth a few steps; then added, "By the way, dear boy, I understood what you were saying. The expression is new to me, but it pretty well speaks for itself."

I smiled, but felt it best not to say more on the subject, since apparently I'd already insulted one of the most verbally proficient men I'd ever met. Seeing that I had nothing to add, Sam said, "I think we can all agree that Gage is getting worried. Obviously Isaiah Thomas and I are getting under his skin. That's good, but it may also mean that he and his officials are becoming so desperate that they will act recklessly. We have to stay on the alert." I could see that Sam had recovered his composure now. In a businesslike voice he said, "Let's put that aside for now. Yesterday I received a message that Colonel Mason is calling a special meeting of the Committee of Safety tonight at his house in North Salem. It's an early meeting. Six o'clock. I hope the two of you can be there."

"Did the message say what the meeting was about?" asked Tom.

"No, only that it was important that all members of the committee council be there."

♦ ♦ ♦

As Tom and I left work and headed toward Colonel Mason's place, Tom said, "This meeting is not good timing for me."

"Why is that?" I asked.

"Believe it or not I have a date."

"You sneaky devil. I see you at the paper all day. When did you find the time to meet a girl? And where?"

"It's Mrs. Inglesby's granddaughter, Jennie."

Jennie was an extremely attractive young woman who lived at the rooming house with her grandmother. We'd learned that her mother had died during Jennie's birth. Her father had died in 1760 in the French War at the Battle of Sainte-Foy, or Battle of Quebec as some called it.

Jennie lived with her grandmother and sometimes joined us at breakfast or supper, or occasionally both. Tom and I had judged that she was in her early twenties and very marriageable, as she radiated a warm beauty that one seldom sees.

She was teaching in a small grammar school for children of the more affluent residents of Salem. I say she looked marriageable, but that was more from a twenty-first century perspective, I suppose, than from an eighteenth century perspective. As attractive and pleasant as she was, she had very little to bring to the table (a twenty-first century expression if there ever was one) in 1775 Salem, where families expected to gain more than just a daughter-in-law when their son got hitched. In eighteenth-century New England both families expected something more from a prospective daughter-in-law or son-in-law than a pleasant mien or good looks. In the America Tom and I had left, most people got married because of love, or at the very least, lust. It was not unusual for a twenty-first-century man or a woman to overlook factors such as modest income or low social standing if the two people were truly in love.

I'd learned in the few months since arriving in the eighteenth century that families played a much bigger role in the decision to marry. Families expected the other family to either complement, equal or exceed their own family's wealth and social standing. Love was considered a shallow and trivial reason for marriage. If a couple was of good will they might eventually grow to love each other. If things did not develop into love, it was hoped that they would learn to be compatible.

"Awesome! That's great. Where does one go on a date in this century?"

"I'm still learning. Tonight, since it's not too cold, we're going for a walk around town. Jennie said, when we got back we could sit in the parlor and have tea or beer if I preferred." He grinned nervously. "As I said, I'm still learning. I'll take it slowly and see where it takes me. Hope the meeting doesn't last too long, or I'll be getting off to a bad start."

As we walked toward Colonel Mason's place (we walked most

places in Salem and only took our horses from the stable when we were going more than a couple of miles), I reflected on my own views of dating in the eighteenth century. Since arriving in this century I'd met or seen a number of women I would have liked to have known better, but something had kept me from taking the first step. It wasn't shyness, either. I'd seldom hesitated back in the twenty-first century if I wanted to ask a woman out.

Here in 1775, though, it was kind of weird. For awhile I couldn't get past the idea that I might become intimate with a woman who would be almost 250 years my senior. I know, in one sense she'd be younger than me, but I had had a hard time getting the image of a 250-year-old woman out of my head. In my 26 years on earth before coming to the this century, I'd met some elderly people. Some I liked; some I didn't. But of the old women I'd met, there was not one I would have been attracted to physically. I know that sounds shallow, but I don't think I'm unique in my thinking on this. Now that I was living in 1775, for the longest time I couldn't help imagining what a 250-year-old woman would look like. I know, any woman I'd be attracted to would appear to be my age or younger and would not look like she was 250, but in one sense, she'd be more than two centuries older than I was. I shook my head. The whole temporal contradiction was crazy, and I knew I had to get it out of my head and put myself mentally as well as physically 100 percent into the eighteenth century if I wanted to be happy here. Certainly if I wanted to maintain my sanity. I think I was now past this, but it took me some time to make the mental adjustment. After all, I'd already accustomed myself to being somewhat comfortable in 1775. I never thought it would happen this fast. It's amazing how adaptable we humans are.

"Helloooo.... Earth to Gil." It was Tom noticing that I was in another world.

"Sorry, just thinking."

"About me and Jennie?"

"Yeah. I think it's great. I was also wondering what Mason has that's so important."

"We'll know in a few minutes."

Chapter 29

"Gentlemen, I'm glad so many of you could make it on such short notice." Mason paced the room as he spoke. He was clearly agitated. "I have just heard from one of our people in Boston that Gage was infuriated by the way Colonel Leslie and his men were treated here in Salem. He was also at his wit's end to learn that Leslie had proven to be so ineffectual here when he and his troops encountered our opposition. Make no mistake, I'm proud of all of you and many others who helped defend against the reach of the regulars on that remarkable Sunday, but I fear that Gage will feel the need to prove the efficacy of British forces. If we Patriots can turn them back at every turn, they lose their ability to govern.

"They have already shown that they will not allow us to govern ourselves by charter law. Rather, they have taken it upon themselves to resort to military force to govern here in the colonies—whether we like it or not. *And we do not like it!* We must therefore expect greater and less humane use of force in the near future. Of that I am certain.

"I am therefore issuing a call for renewed efforts to train able-bodied men to take up the cause of defense, should a future conflict arise. Such future conflict, I think we all agree, is more likely than ever now. I urge each of you to look for recruits to serve in our standby militia. Training should continue as in the past with renewed emphasis on defensive tactics that we believe can be effective against British-style military action. In view of Gage's new state of mind, I also urge each of you to quicken your efforts to find recruits for Minuteman status. Keep in mind that our Minutemen must be of sound physical and mental condition because these are the men who are likely to be called to action first in the event of British provocation. They must possess their own weapons and be able to move swiftly at the first call to arms. These are the men who will be in the vanguard of any actions taken by our on-call militia. Our largest force, our Salem militia, will be led by Colonel Pickering. He has not been able to attend all of our meetings, but I believe many of you know him. Are there any questions?"

A heavyset, middle aged man asked, "Are these calls for more recruits just local here in the Salem area or are they doing this in Boston and other parts of the colony, too?"

"I met with Hancock, Revere and Dr. Warren in Boston yesterday to insure that all members of the committee are aware of each other's efforts and will be ready to come to the aid of any member, should the need arise." Dr. Warren had been chairman of the Committee of Safety for all of Massachusetts until recently when John Hancock succeeded him. "It was up to Hancock to make the final decision on our future policy, and as I expected, we're in full agreement on what I've just told you. Mr. Hancock has dispatched a messenger to Rhode Island, Connecticut and New York informing their committees of the measures we're taking up here in Massachusetts. He's also sent a courier with the same message north to Maine territory and another to New Hampshire. Now do we have any questions?" He paused briefly and getting no questions continued.

"Before we end our meeting I'm requesting volunteers to move our cannon, powder and other provisions to Concord, where Mr. Hancock and his fellow committee members in Boston think they will be more secure from Gage's intrusions. In the event of a conflict, our brethren will be able to rally there for necessary large weapons. As for small arms—muskets and the like—I expect each and every Patriot to keep at least one at the ready. If you know of anyone in need of a musket, we're expecting a shipment to arrive on Misery Island next week. Henry Woodbury will help us there, as he has cows on the island and knows the best way to approach it. Gilbert Lee and Thomas Howard have offered to assist Henry." He nodded in our directions as he said this; then continued. "As you know, we can't bring a shipment into Boston Harbor, Salem Harbor or any other port because of the import ban on firearms and gunpowder." A number of hands went up to volunteer and Mason took down their names. He then said, "Now then, have I forgotten anything? Are there any questions?"

I figured I'd better speak up. "Sam Hall is sorry he couldn't be here, but he's asked me to speak for him. When I've finished, you'll understand why Mr. Hall had to remain at his office. Colonel, your sense of urgency was brought home to Thomas and myself earlier today at the *Gazette*. Sam Hall had three surprise visitors from Boston." I went on to relate the threats made by Gage's messengers and how these threats were almost identical to those made recently to Isaiah Thomas at the *Massachusetts Spy*." I concluded by saying, "So I think all of us here in this room should expect Gage and his troops to intensify their intrusions and attacks almost immediately. What Colonel Mason just told us can't be stressed too much. Sam Hall, as you might imagine, is working feverishly to be prepared for whatever Gage and his people might attempt."

Mason seemed to appreciate this reinforcement of his message. "Thank you, Gilbert, for that report. You see, gentlemen, as Gilbert has just pointed out, we have ruffled the governor's feathers."

Chapter 30

It was the middle of April and the sun would be setting in less than half an hour. It was not too cold for this time of the year, but Mrs. Inglesby reminded Jennie to wear her winter coat anyway. "You never know if it will turn chilly at a moment's notice," she'd said. Then she'd added, "And I'll expect you back here within an hour. You shouldn't be out there without me or someone from family. I'm only making this exception because I know Thomas." Then she winked at him, "Don't you disappoint me young man."

Tom Howard and Jennie were about to leave the house for what Tom considered their first date. He'd called it a date after she'd agreed to go for a walk with him, and she'd looked confused at the time, saying, "Sometimes you use the most uncommon expressions, Thomas. Why do you refer to tomorrow when we'll be seeing each other as if the date on the calendar were *our date*, a date that only we possess? Certainly it is a date on the calendar, but it is not *our* date. Not that I mind your making it so. I suppose it's actually rather romantic." She grinned mischievously, "Though it would appear to some as being a bit premature. We haven't known each other very long now, have we?"

As they walked around Salem they came to the common where they saw cows grazing peacefully. Some were lying down in the tall grass; most were standing.

Jennie said, "Now that it's spring they'll sleep here at night. In the colder weather most of them are brought back to their barns at night." Tom, who'd been to Salem in the twenty-first century, couldn't resist saying, "Someday there will be no cows on the common. Someday there will be paved pathways for strolling and comfortable benches to sit on. The grass will be cut short and even. I know it's hard to believe, but that's what I predict."

She looked up at him, smiling. "You are the strangest man, Thomas. Where do get such ideas?"

"I just know how things evolve. As time goes by towns and cities improve, slowly, but surely. The changes in the common will not be the only changes, either. Believe me. I know it sounds strange to you but I can predict any number of changes that someday people will consider normal."

She couldn't resist grinning. "My Lord, Thomas, you do have quite an imagination. And you use so many words I have never heard before. What is this evolve?"

"Gradual change for the better. Development, improvement."

"People must be awfully smart up in Halifax if you're an example. Now you've made me curious. What sort of changes do you predict?"

"Believe me, people are no smarter in Halifax than they are here in Salem." He went silent for a minute resting his chin between his thumb and forefinger. "All right, I'll give you a couple predictions. "Someday horse-drawn carriages and carts will be replaced by carriages or vehicles that are propelled or powered by machines or engines. They will go much faster than today's carriages and carts."

"You are something, Thomas Howard. You're pulling my leg with such fantastical ideas."

Tom was dying to tell her the truth—that he had experienced everything he was telling her about in the century in which he'd spent most of his life. He admitted to himself that he wanted to impress her, wanted to take her breath away with his firsthand knowledge of what he was telling her, but another part of his consciousness warned him that instead of being awed, there was a very real chance that she'd think he was crazy and tell others that he was crazy.

"Of course I can't prove that these vehicles will exist someday, but I honestly believe that they will."

She grinned. She was enjoying his little game. Most of the people she knew could never have imagined such things. "I'm listening. Tell me about another one of your predictions."

"I predict that someday people will fly through the air in vehicles the way birds fly. The vehicles will be big enough to carry hundreds of people, and they'll go faster than birds."

Jennie burst out laughing. "Now that's a good one. That's even better than the first one. Where do you get such ideas?"

He pointed to his head. "Up here. I told you I have a vivid imagination. Imagination is what makes things better in this world. You can't invent something new if you don't first have the idea in your head. Someone had to imagine the wheel before the first wheel could be made. Take my trade: printing. Gutenberg invented moveable type, which made modern printing as we know it possible. Before he invented it, though, he had to imagine it. It was an idea before it became a reality."

She stood back a few feet and stared at him. "You are truly a remarkable man, Thomas Howard. Truly remarkable."

He beamed. "I don't know about that, but I'm hoping it means that you will be willing to go for another walk with me soon."

"Of course I will."

"Is there anything else we might do sometime?" he asked hopefully, knowing things were dramatically different in 1775 from the way things were in 2015.

"Now what in the world do you mean by that?" she said with a smirk.

He decided he'd better play it straight and asked, "I was wondering if sometime we might go to a local tavern for lunch or even for supper?"

"Good Lord, Thomas. You know women don't go to taverns. Certainly not unmarried women. We might be able to sup at the Salem Inn, but we'd need to bring grandmother with us."

He feigned a frown. "I was justing hoping." Then he announced, "I have another prediction. Someday unmarried women will be able to go to a tavern or a dining room in an inn."

"By themselves?" she said incredulously.

"Usually they will go with another woman or a man."

"And just what in the world makes you think such craziness will happen?"

He couldn't help himself now. He was drunk with infatuation. He felt something for this woman, and he wanted to confide in her—no doubt partially because it would be fun to share such an amazing secret with someone, and partially because it would make it a lot easier for her to understand him in the future.

Sure, there was risk in revealing his secret, but he couldn't spend the rest of his life not trusting anyone. Who better to trust than Jennie Inglesby, whom, for more than half a year now, he'd come to appreciate mightily. No, it was more than appreciate, he admitted to himself. Much more than mere appreciation. He'd grown fond of her through the mostly superficial interactions they'd had in her grandmother's rooming house. Jennie had a certain sparkle in her eye when she talked to him that was awesomely seductive. She was attractive, charming, intelligent and had a great sense of humor, although sometimes he didn't always get some of her attempts at humor. She didn't always get his either. He understood why, of course. It was more than just a generational gap. It was a gap of more than two centuries. He'd amazed her many times, but she amazed him at how quickly she picked things up. He knew he was hooked on Jennie and rationalized that he could share a secret with her that he and Gil Lee had agreed they must keep to themselves.

"Because I've seen it happen," he said.

She stopped walking and asked, "And just where have you seen such things, Thomas?"

Okay, there was no going back now. "In Boston in the twenty-first century. Also in California and Nevada."

"Thomas, it's all right to joke with me like this, but promise me that you won't say such things in front of my grandmother or at the supper table with the other tenants. And where are these imaginary places: California and Nevada? Do you make up everything you tell me?"

This was going to be interesting, he thought.

"I know you will think me insane, Jennie, but I am telling you the truth. I know it's hard to believe."

"Hard to believe. You don't really want me to believe what you just told me. I find it entertaining and humorous, as I do so much of what you say, but certainly you can't expect me to believe you are serious this time?"

This was not going to be easy.

"Suppose I could prove what I've said. Would you believe me then?"

"If you could prove it, I suppose I would have to believe you, but I don't think you can prove it. Thomas, how do you get off on these flights of fancy?"

"The scientists in the twenty-first century discovered a way to travel back in time. People in the twenty-first century don't believe in time travel any more than you do, but a small group of scientists working for the government believed that they had found a way. Gilbert and I were the guinea pigs when they tested their theory. Gilbert and I are living proof that these scientists were right."

"You're making me dizzy with such crazy talk. You continue to use words that are unfamiliar to me. Or if not unfamiliar, the way you use them is unfamiliar. You say that you and Gilbert were guinea pigs. I have a very difficult time imagining that. And scientists? What on earth are they?"

"Scientists are men and women of science. They do not accept things on faith alone, they..."

"Then our minister would not think very highly of them. We have been taught from childhood that faith in God is essential for the good Christian life."

"Many scientists in the twenty-first century believe in God, but they believe there are some things that we must be able to prove or demonstrate. Their job is to investigate ways to improve the way we do things. Many of them do research..."

"My head is spinning. I think I have heard this word research, but perhaps not."

"It's another way of saying they investigate, look into the facts about a thing."

"You can tell me about research later." She smiled. "What I really cannot wait to hear is how you and Gilbert were once guinea pigs. This imagination of yours is too much, Thomas."

"Some scientists use guinea pigs in their laboratories when they do research." She rolled her eyes at this. As Tom said this he realized more and more how much of a time gulf he and Jennie had to overcome. "Many scientists work in laboratories. When I said that Gilbert and I were guinea pigs, it was just an expression comparing us to the real guinea pigs."

She nodded, trying to be patient with him. "I think I see what you are trying to say, but you said that you could prove to me that you and Gilbert were from another century. You haven't done that yet."

He grimaced, realizing that he was at a crucial moment in their relationship. He needed to convince her that he was not some entertaining, but crazy lunatic.

"If I could predict something that came to pass, would you believe me?"

"I would believe you were a seer. That would be fascinating in itself, but I'm not sure that it would prove you came from the future. Besides, you've already predicted that women would go to taverns, that people will fly through the air in flying machines and that people will ride in carriages pulled by machines. None of these things have happened, Thomas," she taunted playfully.

"None of those things will happen for decades. The flying machines and horseless carriages will not happen for centuries. Supposing, though, that I could predict what will happen this month or this year? Would that convince you?"

She was enjoying this game. She hoped it was just a game. Either way, Thomas was the most interesting man she'd ever met. She wasn't sure, though, if he was playing a game or really was a little bit crazy. That he was from the future was not a real possibility. If he was crazy, though, it seemed a harmless sort of lunacy, though she would not want others to suspect that of him. People did not treat lunatics kindly.

"I suppose it would. Can you predict something that will happen this month? I'd really like to be convinced sooner rather than later?"

"Anything I tell you remains a secret between us, right?"

"You don't really believe I'd want anyone else to know what a crazy man you are, do you?" she said impishly.

"No, I suppose not." God how he liked this woman. "All right, then, I predict that there will be bloody battles in Lexington and Concord later this month. They will be battles between the Minutemen and the British regulars."

"My goodness, Thomas, why would you say such a thing?"

"I'm not saying I want them to happen. What I'm saying is that I know they will happen because I learned about them in my history class at school."

"I sincerely hope you're wrong about this, but what little I do know about such public affairs tells me that many in the colony expect a conflict sometime this year. But you, Thomas, are saying it will be in April. We are already halfway through April, so it will have to happen soon if you are to prove your point."

"Believe me, Jennie, I know that. I can tell by what you've said that even if it does happen you will just think I made a good guess based on what everybody knows is likely to happen. If I told you the exact date would you be more inclined to believe me?"

"Of course, but now I think you are likely to fail. The more precise your prediction, the less likely you are to be right. However, I said I wanted to hear your prediction so tell me the exact day these conflicts will take place?"

"They will happen on the 19th of the month—just four days from now. Sam Adams and John Hancock are hiding out in Lexington even now. Gage will send troops to Lexington to arrest Adams and Hancock for treason. Gage feels he must arrest them because they've criticized the British rule here in the colony. Hancock gave a speech condemning the Crown and the regulars for the massacre that occurred in Boston four years ago, and Adams was personally active in the Boston Tea Party incident. While in Lexington, the troops will look for weapons and other supplies the Patriots have stashed away in preparation for just this sort of conflict. What the Redcoats won't know is that the Minuteman militia will resist. Shots will be fired and men on both sides will die."

She couldn't help but be fascinated by all this, as frightening it might be. "Thomas, I must ask you this now. If you are so certain about this, shouldn't you report it to someone so that the bloodshed you predict might be avoided?"

"It's a good question. Unfortunately I can't. First of all, who would I tell? If I told Colonel Mason he'd want to know how I knew all this. You know how hard it is for you to believe me. Here's your chance to use your own imagination. Imagine if I told Mason or even Hancock. They would laugh me out of the room. Worse than that, they would wonder how I got the information and think that I was working for Gage. I can't even tell Sam Hall, for the same reason. Even if I could convince them, which I'm sure I couldn't, it wouldn't help. What I'm predicting actually happened. What's actually happened can't be undone."

"Now I do think you're crazy," she said, clearly wondering what she'd gotten herself into. "How could something that's going to happen in four days have already happened. Where's the sense in that?"

He nodded his agreement. "You're right, of course. It makes no sense. Any sane person would say that. Yet I know that when I was looking back to 1775 from the twenty-first century the battles of Lexington and Concord were history. There were documents recording these events, old newspapers describing it, monuments in Lexington and Concord commemorating the battles. It was as real to me in 2015 as it will be to you four days from now." Her look of disbelief forced Tom to pause before he continued. He totally understood how she felt, but he pressed on. He wanted her to believe him.

"I know you still think I'm making this up. I'm either a lunatic or playing some elaborate game. I can see that I need to tell you more details so you'll know that no one could be that good a guesser. Before the battles begin, Dr. Warren, the leader of the Committee of Safety in Boston, will send Paul Revere and William Dawes, a local shoemaker, to Lexington to warn Hancock and Adams that the regulars are coming to arrest them. Their orders will also be to alert the Patriots in Lexington and Concord that the troops are coming to seize the store of weapons in the towns. Revere and Dawes will travel by different routes to alert more folks along the way and to improve the chances of at least one of them making it all the way to Concord." He stopped and looked into her eyes trying to be as serious as possible. "I think that's enough detail for you. If all this happens, I hope you'll believe me."

"If all this takes place, what choice do I have. You're either a time traveller or a man possessed by special powers. Hopefully good; not evil powers."

It occurred to Tom that he and Jennie were having their conversation only 83 years after the famous Salem Witch Trials. It was not too farfetched to believe that many people still believed in the power of demonic possession and other mystic arts. Jennie could easily be inclined to believe he was a seer rather than a time traveller.

Chapter 31

Governor Gage leaned back in his chair behind his polished mahogany desk as he listened to what Lawrence Kilmartin was telling him. He was infuriated by what he was hearing.

"You're telling me, Kilmartin, that this seditious journalist, Isaiah Thomas, and his rag the *Spy,* stole off in the middle of the night with his presses, type cases and everything else?"

"Yes, sir. We don't know for sure where he's gone, but we think it's probably Worcester. That's a hotbed of Whig fervor. Captain Oliver tells me it will be extremely difficult to shut him down there."

"We could do it, I assure you," said Gage confidently, "but he's right. It would take a lot of men, and we're already stretched thin. With all the local people so interested in defending their rights, it could get rather bloody. Would only agitate the colonials for miles around. Probably not worth it. We don't need a little war to contend with. We have enough to contend with trying to contain these radicals without stirring up a hornet's nest in Worcester."

"I'm afraid I have more bad news, sir."

Gage raised his eyebrows and clenched his jaw. "Go ahead. Out with it."

"That other paper that's been giving us such a headache—the *Essex Gazette* up in Salem."

"Yes, what about it?"

"We think they're about to move to a new location, too."

Gage pursed his lips, trying to contain himself. Finally he spoke. "What makes you think that?"

"When we were there recently we threatened to close them down if they didn't modify their criticism of you, the King and Parliament. One of our Loyalists up in Salem says there's evidence of packing and other preparations that one would expect if they were getting ready to move."

"You'd best get up there quickly with Captain Oliver and close the place down before they take everything and start printing their rubbish elsewhere. Thomas and his tripe in Worcester is more than enough." He paused a moment to consider what was happening in the colonies he'd come to love. "Good Lord, Kilmartin, what has become of this place? I like these people, but enough is enough. They must respect their king."

"On what pretext do we close it, Governor? We should have some legal reason for our actions. Shall it be sedition and libel?"

Gage gave Kilmartin a withering look and said impatiently, "Yes, yes. Of course. You've been ordered by the military governor of the Massachusetts Bay Colony to close the place down while an investigation is underway into the illegal operations of a seditious and possibly treasonous publication."

"Yessir." Kilmartin looked at his feet for a moment before saying, "Sir, there's just one small problem here."

Gage was losing patience. "What's that, Kilmartin. Haven't you brought me enough problems already?"

"Captain Oliver came down with the fever and is confined to his bed. Can we wait a few days, sir?"

The governor rolled his eyes upward. Since being appointed military governor of the colony things had gone from bad to worse. Being named military governor should have been a proud achievement. Unhappily, it had become an enormous problem that kept getting worse. "From what you tell me we may not have but a few days. By the time you and Captain Oliver get to Salem, this man and his paper could be gone."

"I may have a solution, sir."

"Pray to God you do. All right, let me hear it."

"That Salem Loyalist—Benjamin Waite—understands the importance of shutting them down quickly and said that he has an idea that may help until we're able to get up there and lock the door on the place. He says he would be willing to visit Mr. Hall, the publisher, and tell him that the Crown has dropped all charges against him so there's no need to move."

Gage smiled. "It would be a lie, but a lie in the best interests of British rule and keeping things peaceful in the colony. I don't like to operate this way, but the man gives us no choice. I was about to tell you that I could assign a different officer to this mission if Oliver doesn't recover soon, but this is better. Captain Oliver is fully briefed so hopefully in a day or so the two of you can go up there and slam the door on this inflammatory rag." Gage leaned forward, placing his chin in his hand deep in thought. "Didn't you tell me a few days ago that this fellow Waite, the Loyalist, was a friend of the publisher Hall? I'm glad for Waite's help, but it doesn't make him much of a friend to deceive Hall like that, does it?"

Kilmartin sneered. "No sir, it doesn't. Frankly, I don't like Waite, but if he's willing to help us, I can hold my nose."

"Yes, I suppose I can, too. But, say, how can he help us if he's already up in Salem."

"He hasn't left Boston. Says he feels more comfortable here lately. Says he's ready and willing to go back there if he can be of help to us."

"Sounds to me as if there's some sort of grudge there."

"That's what it smells like to me, too, sir."

Chapter 32

It was the morning after Tom's date with Jennie Inglesby. "So, how did it go?" I asked.

"I like her."

"You didn't answer my question."

"It went well, I guess. From an eighteenth-century standpoint, that is. This really is a different world when it comes to dating. They don't even call it dating. If you're serious, they call it courting. If it's the first date, you're spending time with the other person. If you date more than once or twice, you're seeing them."

"That last part is not so different from what it is in the twenty-first century."

"Yeah, that part is, but so much is different. If her grandmother didn't already know me fairly well, I'd need a chaperone to go out with Jennie. I could never take her to a tavern with or without a chaperone. If I wanted to take her to a performance like a lecture or something of that sort, I'd have to bring her grandmother or some other relative along. Even then *where* you go is really limited as I'm sure you can imagine. So dating is nothing like it is in the twenty-first century. Nothing."

"Knowing all this do you still want to see her again?"

"Yeah, I do. Things'll move along a lot slower than I'm used to, but when in Rome...."

I grinned. "It won't be that different for you anyway. You never got very far with women in the twenty-first century, so you should be pretty comfortable here with Jennie."

"Funny."

Tom dreaded telling his friend about what he'd confided in Jennie. He almost let the conversation end right there, but decided there was nothing to be gained by putting it off.

"There's something else I should tell you."

"What?"

"I told Jennie about where we came from. I know, I know. We agreed not to tell anyone."

"You what? Tell me I didn't hear that right? Tell me you didn't put us both at risk of being treated as nutcases? Or worse."

"I know, I know. You have to understand."

"I don't have to understand anything. Jesus, Tom, I can't believe it. Why?"

"Jennie and I have gotten pretty close."

"You're in love and lovers make fools of themselves."

"Well maybe a little. Look, I trust her. Besides, as you could have predicted, she thinks I'm either playing this elaborate game or I'm nuts."

"I know which one I'd pick," I said. "Jesus! This opens up a huge can of worms."

"I hope and pray not. If this ends up kicking me in the face, you're still okay. Pretend you agree that I'm nuts. I'll understand."

"It's tempting, believe me." I thought a moment and said, "She probably doesn't believe you."

"She doesn't. Maybe she will in a few days when my amazing predictions come true."

"What did you predict?" I stared at him in disbelief, and he didn't answer. Finally I said, "Not Lexington and Concord?" He nodded sheepishly. I was flabbergasted.

"Well, yeah. Maybe after the 19th she'll believe me."

"Or think you're a freakin' witch."

♦ ♦ ♦

As we were taking our coats off in the *Gazette* offices, Sam Hall approached us.

"Before you begin work I want to have a brief word with the two of you," he said. "As you know, I've been deliberating over the wisdom of moving the paper or keeping it here in Salem and taking my chances."

"I know it hasn't been easy for you, Sam," I said.

"You're right, it hasn't, but I'm not the only one affected. You and Thomas and Toby and the others will all either be out of a job or be faced with moving with me. I've finally made my decision. I feel I must move. I can't let the paper fall into the hands of the military government. I would hope that all of you would join me, but I'll understand if you don't."

"Where will you go?" asked Tom.

"I'm thinking Springfield. The *Spy* has already moved to Worcester. We don't need to compete with each other in the same town." I wasn't at all happy about this, but I understood why he was making the move. He could probably expect Gage's people to confiscate his presses and close the paper any day now.

"I've grown to like Salem," I said, "but I believe in what you're doing, Sam, so if you move, I'd like to go with you."

"I feel the same way," said Tom firmly. "We work well together and changing locations is disruptive enough without your having to find new press and type men."

Hall smiled for the first time in a long time.

As we left work later that day I asked Tom the question that loomed large in my mind and no doubt even larger in his: "If Sam moves the *Gazette* out of town and takes us with him, won't that put a serious monkey wrench in your relationship with Jennie?"

"Damn it to hell, yes. I couldn't say no to Sam, but I really like

Jennie. I know we could see each other occasionally if I moved, but if it's Springfield or some other town as far away as that, it won't be easy. Can't just hop on the Mass Pike, can I? Must be at least 100 miles. Maybe more. How long would that take me on horseback?"

"Probably six or seven hours if you include time for the horse to rest and you to take at least one break. Maybe more. These roads can be nasty, especially when it rains or snows. Someday they'll pave them, and someday people will make the trip by car in an hour and a half." I forced a lame smile, "But you can't wait for that, can you? Yeah, moving will put a crimp in your style. Not a good way to carry on a romance," I added seriously.

"I just told Sam I'd go. I may have to rethink that." Jeez, I don't want to back out on the man. He's a hell of a good boss, and I like the work."

"You should sleep on it. Give it overnight, or maybe another day, before you make your decision. Sam will understand—probably more than Jennie would."

Chapter 33

Ben Waite paused at the door to the *Essex Gazette*. He'd ridden hard from Boston and was dusty, tired and hungry. He'd come right to the Gazette because time was critical. He could clean up, eat and rest later.

This was his last chance to change his mind. Should he do this? If it weren't for his Whig leanings, Sam Hall wasn't such a bad sort. Bloody hell, way back they'd actually been friends. He couldn't let old times influence him now, though. These were serious times with serious issues to deal with. Sam and his paper were giving support to these rabid radicals, these so-called Patriots in their call to undermine the king and his government. He shouldn't be allowed to get away with it. Ben Waite was not going to let him get away with it. He knew that Hall would be planning to leave Salem for a safer haven in order to continue his radical journalistic ravings. Hall would have taken the warning he got from Kilmartin and Captain Oliver seriously. His packing of crates recently was evidence that the move was close. Sam Hall had to be stopped so that Gage's people from Boston would have time to come to Salem to confiscate his presses and close him down. He pushed the door open and heard the bell ring.

"I never thought I'd see you in here again," spat Hall as he came forward to meet his visitor. "What's on your mind, Ben?"

"I came to apologize, Sam. We've been friends too long. I'm sorry for even coming here with those two men. It's these times, I suppose. We get carried away. Anyway, if you'll just listen to me a minute I have something to tell you that I think you'll be pleased to hear. Can we go somewhere where we can talk quietly?"

"Come back here with me. Let's step into my office." After he'd closed the door, Hall said, "Why all the secrecy?"

"What I tell you is for your ears only. If you want to share it with someone else, that's up to you."

"Understood. Now what is it you have to say?" Hall had little patience with Waite, despite his apology.

"Remember that Lawrence Kilmartin fellow who accompanied Captain Oliver and me when we visited you?"

"More like threatened. Yes, I remember him."

"Well he told me not three hours ago in Boston that Gage had changed his mind about the threats to close you down. The *Massachusetts Spy* has already moved to Worcester. Gage doesn't want us colonials to think that he can't tolerate criticism. He feels it will only stir up more anti-Parliament protests. What I'm trying to tell you, Sam, is that you don't need to relocate the *Gazette*. You'll be fine right here in Salem."

"That's good news, Ben. Very good news. Hard to believe, though. I can't imagine why Governor Gage would do such a turnabout."

"He's feeling a lot of pressure lately. Doesn't need problems like this. Mind you now, he's not saying he approves of what you and the *Gazette* are saying, but I think he's saying he has bigger fish to fry."

"Indeed he does. Indeed he does. Well, Ben, I thank you for telling me this. I didn't want to move. I appreciate that you made the effort to tell me. You've restored my belief in our friendship. I value that, despite our differences." Hall reached forward and shook Waite's hand.

After Waite had gone, Hall asked his staff to come into his office.

"I have some good news. I just spoke with Ben Waite. He told me that he has it on good authority that Governor Gage has relented. He's changed his mind and will not close us down here in Salem."

I had to interrupt. "Sam, wasn't it Waite who came here recently with two of Gages officials to threaten to close you down? Why would Waite come here today with an entirely different message? Aren't you the least bit suspicious of this man that used to be your friend and turned on you like that?"

"I supposed I should be a little suspicious, but Ben told me that he got carried away and gave in to his emotions. He apologized, said our friendship was too important. I think he felt really quite bad about even being in the company of those two men when they delivered their message."

"But Sam, it's almost certain that Waite was the one who convinced Gage's people that you were a threat. That means Waite turned on you. How can you trust him now?"

"I must trust him, Gilbert. We've been friends too long. I can't reject his show of goodwill today. I'm inclined to believe him."

I had come to respect Sam Hall as much as any man I'd ever known for his integrity, intelligence, and generally kind manner, but if he had any flaw it was his tendency to be a little too trusting. He might be right about Waite's turnabout, but if he was wrong, it meant he was out of business and maybe even behind bars. Nevertheless, I could see that there was no point in pursuing this any further so I said, "Then that means we don't have to look for someplace to live in Springfield."

He beamed. "That's right. We can all stay put."

On our way back to the presses I pulled Tom aside. "Looks like you and Jennie are still an item."

"I can't tell you how great that is," he said.

"I can see it in your eyes."

Getting back to my work, I placed the last piece of cast metal type into a form, added a slug to allow for a space and tapped the face of all the type with a wooden mallet to be sure all the letters and punctuation marks would make contact with the paper when the spindle was turned to force the platen down on the paper. Before I continued, I caught Tom's eye and said, "Still can't believe that old Ben Waite made a complete 180. I didn't pursue it with Sam because it's not my place, but I hope he's right about Waite."

"Yeah, I agree. Why would a sleaze like Waite magically become such a good guy? But you're right, it's Sam's decision. Just hope it was the right one or we all lose out. Well, until I hear otherwise, I'm happy."

"I'll bet you are."

Chapter 34

April 18, 1775

Eighteen-year-old Jimmy Ames worked in the kitchen of the Murray mansion, the finely appointed and majestic Cambridge house in which Governor Gage was staying and used as his base of operations. Thomas Murray was a wealthy Loyalist friend of William Brattle, another Cambridge Loyalist who'd recently moved to Boston. Brattle had made his money in sugar plantations in Jamaica and Antigua. He often fed information to Gage when he heard of things the Patriots were planning. Without such Loyalist support, life would have been even more difficult for Governor Gage.

Before working for the Murrays, Ames had been kitchen boy for the Brattles for over three years. Jimmy started out doing the least desirable things such as cleaning up after the cook, peeling potatoes and worst of all, disposing of slop buckets and chamber pots. Gradually the cook had seen that Jimmy was a bright boy and had given him more responsibility—even let him prepare a few dishes for the family. When the Brattles moved to Boston they recommended Jimmy to the Murrays. With the help of Murray himself, Jimmy was taught how to behave in the presence of the prominent and well-placed men and women in Cambridge, Boston and Salem. The Murrays dressed him up for formal occasions and taught him how to serve at elegant functions. Murray sometimes borrowed Jimmy from the kitchen when he wanted important errands carried out. The young man had gradually become someone the Murrays could depend on.

At the recommendation of Mr. Murray himself, Gage had kept the boy on. Murray's assessment had been spot on. The boy was bright, alert and useful. What Gage and the Murrays didn't know was that Jimmy Ames was a fervent Patriot. He only stayed on when Gage asked him to because he and his fellow Patriots thought it would be extremely useful having someone on the inside. Sooner or later Jimmy might hear something or witness something that would be valuable to the Committee of Safety and its leaders. Today was just such a day.

Jimmy had just finished serving tea to the last-to-arrive member of the small assemblage gathered before the governor. Gage had called his top officers and aides before him because he had an important announcement to make. The group included Captain Hugh Oliver, Lieutenant Colonel Francis Smith, Major Gilbert Mitchell, Major John Pitcairn and civilian Lawrence Kilmartin.

"Gentlemen, as some, but not all of you know, we have been informed by certain Loyalists in outlying communities that the rebels have been storing munitions in certain villages some distance from Boston. I have also learned that that rabble rouser Sam Adams and another prominent rebel organizer, John Hancock, have stolen off from Boston and hidden themselves away in one of these villages. We think that other radical organizers are hiding out there, too." He leaned back and drew in a deep breath before saying, "In view of these events I've ordered an expedition to these villages to arrest these criminals and to confiscate the weapons and powder they have in storage up there. As some of you already know, preparations have been underway for some time now. Until today, the actual date for this expedition has deliberately been known only by Lieutenant Colonel Smith and myself. We couldn't afford to have word of this get out. I'm announcing now that the mission will embark tonight." He then gazed directly at one man sitting in the front row of chairs facing him and said, "As I'm sure most of you know I've asked Lieutenant Colonel Smith to head up the mission. Most of you are already aware of this, but I thought it important that we all be fully informed, as I expect the next two days to be critical and fraught with possible pitfalls. I don't want any misunderstandings about what we are about.

"It's critical that word of this mission not leave this room. The only people who need to know are the troops who will be part of the expedition. Even they will not know their destination until they are well underway. At the proper moment Lieutenant Colonel Smith will inform them of this destination. I'm sure that all of you can appreciate that secrecy is of the utmost importance, since we want to take these treasonous scoundrels by surprise. In doing so, it will insure that we bring them into custody, and I believe will prevent unnecessary bloodshed. If we surprise them they will not have enough time to call to arms their little Minuteman militia. I have no fear that we could dispatch them anyway, but I'd prefer we not turn this into anything but a small skirmish."

It was perhaps the arrogance of privilege or a conviction that anyone working for Governor Gage was automatically a Loyalist that enabled Jimmy Ames to circulate in the room almost as if he were invisible. For whatever reason, Jimmy was able to take in much of what was said, making his trips to the kitchen as brief as possible so that he would not miss any critical bit of information. Thirty minutes after the meeting adjourned the cook dismissed him for the rest of the day. The governor and Mrs. Gage would be dining with the Brattles at their house in Boston in just a few hours, so he wouldn't be needed to serve supper. William Brattle and his wife had recently relocated to a Loyalist neighborhood in Boston since revealing their colors as Tories. The majority of Cantabrigians had made life so unpleasant that moving to a Loyalist neighborhood in Boston had become a necessity.

Less than an hour later Jimmy knocked on the door of Dr. Joseph Warren, the head of the Boston Committee of Safety and one of the founders of the Committee of Correspondence. Jimmy related in some detail what he'd heard at the Governor's meeting.

Warren sprang into action. "Jimmy, I want you to come with me. We need to seek out Mr. Revere and Mr. Dawes for an important mission."

Warren found Revere at work in his silver shop. He sent Jimmy off to find Dawes at the tannery in which he worked. Ames was to bring Dawes back to Revere's shop so that they could coordinate a plan of action. While waiting for Ames to return with Dawes, Revere said, "I knew something was afoot earlier today. A stable boy was talking about a fight one of his stable boy mates heard about when tending to some of the officers horses this morning."

"What kind of a fight?" asked Warren.

"A fight between the regulars and the rebels as they called us. Said it was going to happen somewhere out west of here. Somewhere soon. I tried to get more out of the boy, but that's all he knew. I trust the lad. Good boy, and quick.'

"So it appears that Gage is looking for more than Adams and Hancock and our weapons. Looks like he's looking for a fight. Looks like he wants to teach us Patriots a lesson." He grew grim-faced and then added, "So, Paul, you can see how important it is that you and Billy get to Lexington and Concord before Smith does."

It was already dark out now—not ideal for travel on the rutted, hard-to-see dirt roads through the dense New England woods; yet Warren, knowing that the Crown's troops under the command of Lieutenant Colonel Smith would be setting out that very night, felt they couldn't afford to wait until morning to sound the alarm.

"All right, gentlemen, then it's agreed. Paul, you will cross over into Charlestown and ride north through Medford, sounding the alarm at every opportunity. All Minutemen and any other able-bodied militiamen who can make it must be urged to ride directly to Lexington and be prepared to go on to Concord if necessary. Once in Medford you should follow the Mystic River south to Menotomy and then ride west past Pierce's Hill and into Lexington. I know I don't need to remind you that while riding at a swift pace at night is necessary, it's also quite dangerous. You can't afford to have your horse break a leg. Choose your roadways carefully and trust your horse.

Warren turned to Dawes now and said, "Billy, you'll take a southern route. Ride out of Boston on the neck through Roxbury and Brookline. Then make your way north through the western reaches of Cambridge and find the road west past Pierce's Hill. You'll then be on the same road as Paul and the regulars. If you meet up with the Redcoats, though, keep clear and go around them. Make sure they don't see you, as it's imperative that you and Paul reach Lexington before Smith and his troops. And try to depart Boston no later than ten o'clock tonight.

"Just to be sure we get the word out, I will go to the North Church as soon as we finish here and speak with Sexton Newman about our prearranged signals." He looked at both of his riders to be sure they were with him and added, "We've discussed these signals before. In the event of just such a movement of troops as will occur tonight, Newman will hang one lantern in the steeple tower if the Redcoats are moving by land and two if they're going by sea across to Cambridge. Jimmy has just learned that the Redcoats will go by sea to Cambridge so Newman will be hanging two lanterns in the steeple tower. If the two of you make it to Lexington, this lantern signal will not matter, but I will ask Newman to hang the two lanterns just in case you meet up with trouble. Better to have two warnings than none."

Revere then said, "Understood. I'll need someone to row me across the river to Charlestown."

"I have a couple of lads that'll be glad to get you there. Just get yourself down to the waterfront at the place we've agreed on, and you'll find two young lads with a dory waiting for you. I'll have them there before ten o'clock."

"How will I recognize them?"

"Don't worry, Paul, they'll recognize you. I'll give you their names in a minute if it'll make you feel any better."

"It will. These days you have to know who you can trust."

"Indeed. When you get to the other side they'll have a good horse waiting for you."

Chapter 35

As he sat at the Brattle supper table in their elegant rented house in Boston, Governor Gage found that his attention was divided between being the charming governor he was quite capable of being and executing his role as commander in chief. His attention was constantly diverted as he needed to leave the room when an express rider interrupted or his aide, Lawrence Kilmartin, excused themselves in their urgent need to speak with the governor. Gage had only agreed to dine as a guest this evening because he knew it would be in Boston closer to the military base of operations. Besides, it was never a good idea to snub one of the colony's richest and most influential Loyalists.

Gage would normally not confide military secrets to civilians, even civilian Loyalists, but because William Brattle was so influential among the Loyalists of the colony and because the expedition to Lexington and Concord was about to be underway within the hour anyway, he felt it would do no harm to discuss the army's march toward Lexington.

"These rebels have ears everywhere. I have no doubt somehow they'll get wind of our expedition, despite our efforts to keep it quiet. I've deliberately withheld the destination from the very troops who make up the mission until they are in Cambridge. Only Lieutenant Colonel Smith knows the destination."

"I see," said Brattle seriously. "You seem to have thought of everything, governor."

"Hopefully, that's true. I see no harm in telling you, sir, and Mrs. Brattle, that Smith and his men are heading for Lexington and then on to Concord. Our intelligence tells us that that is where Mr. Adams and Mr. Hancock are staying and that it is in these two towns that they have hidden a large cache of weapons and other supplies they intend to use against us. As I'm sure you can imagine, anyone in Boston who observes the troops marching toward the waterfront and then embarking on longboats can deduce that the men will be crossing over into Cambridge. The logical conclusion will be that the troops' destination is Cambridge or somewhere west of Cambridge." Then Gage engaged in a little lie because it was easier than admitting the embarrassing truth. "I don't think they'd expect us to go north as we've already rooted out the weapons they had up in Salem. In any event I think we can expect that the rebels will send a rider out to alert their so-called Minutemen in advance of our troops' arrival."

"I suppose there is nothing you can do about this?" queried Brattle.

Gage smiled proudly. "Well, sir, I think there is. I have already sent 20 riders of my own out to Cambridge and the surrounding towns to block any such messengers sent by Dr. Warren and his fellow rebel leaders. Any rider they send out is likely to be apprehended by our men. It is unlikely that the rebels hiding out in Lexington will have any advance notice before our troops arrive. Or if they do, it will only reach their ears at the last moment. Too late for them to remove themselves to an even more remote location. Certainly too late to move the hidden weapons."

"You know, governor, I have mixed feelings about all of this. I was born here in Massachusetts. These are my people. I understand how they think, though I think they're misguided. They somehow fail to appreciate what the king and Parliament—and, you, sir— have done to protect this colony. They're unwilling to pay levies on goods. Levies that will reimburse the King and Parliament for their tremendous expenditures during the French and Indian War—a war that Britain won and, by doing so, virtually insured the safety of these thirteen colonies."

Gage had listened attentively and said, "In a way, sir, these are my people, too. I've lived here in the colonies for the better part of 20 years now. I have more American friends than British." He turned to his wife and smiled. "Mrs. Gage is American, as you know."

"Then you can understand my mixed feelings. I pray to the

Almighty that your expedition as you call it does not end in bloodshed. I would not like to see British soldiers from the mother country fighting British citizens on these shores. Nothing could be gained from such a tragic happening."

Gage said, "Let me assure you that that is not my intent; nor our goal in this venture." Then he grew stern as he said, "While it is not my intent, you must realize that as the military governor of this colony I cannot allow the rebels to openly defy the king. If the common citizenry witness open disobedience, they will lose all respect for British authority. My orders to Lieutenant Colonel Smith are to take the rebel leaders into custody, secure the weapons cache and return to Boston. However, those orders also stipulate that, should the rebels offer resistance, the troops are to respond in kind and gain the upper hand."

Chapter 36

April 18 and 19, 1775

While Governor Gage was dining at the home of wealthy businessman William Brattle, Robert Newman left his house and walked quickly to the North Church where he served as sexton. When he arrived at the church he was joined by fellow member of the Sons of Liberty, John Pulling.

Newman spoke quietly to Pulling, "It's dark enough now for the lamps to be seen in Charlestown. I'll go up to the steeple and hang them in full view for just a minute or so. "I'll wait a bit and show 'em again. Don't want to hang 'em too long or some Tory'll become suspicious and report us."

"Aye," said Pulling. "I'll stand watch here in front of the church. If I see anyone I don't know I'll start making noises like a sailor who's had too much rum."

◆ ◆ ◆

Tom and I later learned that at about the same time Newman was displaying the two lamps in the North Church steeple, Royal Navy seamen had just finished landing longboats and naval barges ashore on the western part of Boston's Back Bay just north of the neck. Their orders were to row 700 troops across the Charles to Lechmere Point in Cambridge. As the last boat to arrive was secured, the first of the troops began arriving. They marched in single file down the embankment toward shore where the boats lay empty and waiting. An officer formed the troops into a group formation and barked, "at ease." Lieutenant Colonel Smith had not yet arrived at the staging area, so things were off to a bad start. In less than an hour the entire 700 had assembled on the beach awaiting orders to file into the boats. It was a cold night for April, and the men faced a long night and the new day without sleep. They'd been told to get as much sleep as possible before reporting for duty, and to eat a good meal, too. They stashed some cheese, bread or dried meat in their haversacks and carried canteens with water or cider. They had no idea where or when they would get more food or water when these supplies ran out. After some time, Colonel Smith showed up and the boats were loaded. They were so tightly jammed with their human cargo that the men were unable to sit down during the passage across the river. Because of this crowding, the trip was extremely precarious. More than one soldier toppled into the cold river, which further delayed passage.

The last of the boats reached the Cambridge side sometime after midnight. The landing augured dismally for the troops as they disembarked in waist-deep water, meaning they would begin their march to Lexington with water in their boots and wet clingy breeches that only made the night colder as they proceeded on their march. They had no idea when they would eat or sleep again. Neither did they know that the Patriots on the Cambridge side were already aware that they were coming, thanks to the efforts of Sexton Robert Newman and his fellow Patriot, John Pulling.

♦ ♦ ♦

Revere had already crossed the Charles into Charlestown and was well on his way to Lexington. Somehow he had eluded detection by Gage's riders. En route, Revere had stopped at many houses along the way, spreading the alarm about the advancing Redcoats. In Charlestown and Cambridge, where the houses were close together, he'd stopped at every third or fourth house and asked people to alert their neighbors. Once out in the country he stopped at every house he came to. The message was, *Send every able-bodied man to Lexington to help defend against the advancing regulars because the Redcoats intend to capture Hancock and Adam and take possession of our weapons stored in Concord. Do not engage regulars en route to Lexington.* Warren did not want individual Minutemen to make stands against the troops as they passed by their houses because it was obvious that the odds would be against them if they did. There was strength in numbers, so it was imperative that they all assemble under the leadership of the militia commander in Lexington.

It was expected that several hundred Minutemen would assemble in Lexington. If the number was great enough, Warren hoped they would be able to face the Redcoats down and force a standstill, much as the Salem Patriots had done when they sent Leslie's troops in humiliating retreat back in February. If that could be accomplished now, Hancock and Adams would be safe and the weapons would be secure. However, it was more than likely that the regulars under Colonel Smith would not capitulate. In light of the ignominious Salem retreat under Colonel Leslie, British pride would almost certainly compel Smith and his men to make a bolder stand. It was unlikely that Smith would want a retreat on his military record, and even less likely that Gage would want word to get back to London that his troops had turned tail twice because of resistance from a few rag-tag colonials.

Rag tag, of course, was not at all an accurate description of the Minutemen and other colonial militiamen. Many of them had fought a decade earlier under the British flag in the French and Indian War. Before the British regulars arrived to back them up in the war against the French, the colonists had developed their own effective style of fighting. A style they'd learned from the Indians. Hiding behind trees, behind rock walls, on hills, avoiding open terrain and wearing clothes that were grays and browns enabled the colonists to win more battles than they lost against French soldiers who were trained to fight in large formations. That European style of fighting made the French excellent targets for the colonials who attacked them from the security of their hiding places.

The colonial style of fighting was a style that British regulars considered unconventional. It was not the way British gentlemen soldiers would fight French gentlemen soldiers in Europe. Soon, though, thanks to the example of the colonial soldiers, the regulars did adapt to the unconventional style of the locals—at least to some degree. They never did rid themselves of the eye-catching red uniforms, though.

Many of the colonial soldiers were as well prepared or even better prepared for battle than the regulars, who were more than a little bit out of their element. Many of the colonials used a gun on a regular basis hunting for food. All of them had been training regularly as militia units. All of them were on their home turf. The younger ones who had not fought in the French and Indian War were eager, well trained and quick. The advance militia guard or Minutemen expected to respond at a moment's notice. Many of these Minutemen were these eager younger men.

◆ ◆ ◆

Sometime after midnight a rider came through Salem spreading the alarm that Revere and Dawes had been spreading in Charlestown and Cambridge on their way to Lexington. As word got out, at least one Patriot rider rode north along the coast alerting others who also became riders. One of these men entered Salem when most of its residents were asleep.

Tom and I were awakened by the alarm rider's voice in the street. We quickly dressed and reported with muskets to the agreed-upon deployment spot on the Salem Common where we joined a growing number of militiamen, under the leadership of militia leader Colonel Timothy Pickering. Tom and I were eager to ride to Lexington and do whatever we could to defend Hancock and Adams and the stashed weapons. Pickering, however was not ready to move out yet. We were close enough to him to hear him tell one of his subordinates that he expected more men to respond to the alarm rider's calls and wanted to wait a bit longer until he had a full contingent before he and his men headed out toward Lexington.

While Tom and I had joined Colonel Mason's Committee of Safety, we had not yet officially joined Pickering's militia. After a few minutes of standing around we both began to get antsy. Finally I said, "Why don't we head out to Lexington. We're not officially leaving Pickering's unit since we never actually joined. We can meet up with them when they get to Lexington, but we both know that the colonel and his men won't arrive till after the fighting. I'd like to get to Lexington ASAP. Kinda like to see some of this history we read about in school. We grinned at each other.

The trick was to quietly leave the common without someone wondering why we weren't staying with Pickering's men. We didn't want to look like deserters. We walked our horses to the edge of the group nearest the periphery of the Common. Once there it was easier to slip away without drawing too much attention to ourselves.

After letting our mounts get some water we started to head out of town. We'd never been to Lexington, but I'd asked one of our fellow pressmen at the *Gazette* a few days earlier if he knew the best roads to take to get there. Tom and I wanted to meet Adams and Hancock and had planned to ride out to Lexington sometime in the next week or two with that in mind. We would deliver messages from Colonel Mason so it would be more than just a social call. Of course, we were very much aware of what was going to happen in Lexington and Concord later this morning.

In the twenty-first century you could make it to Lexington from Salem by car in 40 to 45 minutes. However, by horse in 1775 it was a different story. If all went well—meaning if we didn't get lost or a horse didn't pull up lame—we might make it in two to two-and-a-half hours. There were no "good" roads, but I had written down our co-worker's instructions and let him draw me a crude map, so we had at least some idea of what lay ahead of us. Still, it wasn't going to be an easy trip—especially at night in unfamiliar territory.

After stopping off at Mrs. Inglesby's rooming house where I retrieved my map and took along two canteens filled with cider, we headed off toward Lexington.

The map was of minimal value. Our colleague had admitted that he'd drawn it from memory and that he didn't remember the names of all the roads he'd drawn. Because of this, Tom and I had to stop periodically to ask directions. In the process, we actually killed two birds with one stone, as we would always tell the person we aroused from a deep sleep that the regulars were on their way to Lexington and Concord. If they were part of a militia they should get on the road right away. We were not three miles out of Salem when one homeowner said that he was ready to go and that he'd join us. This worked out well, as he knew the way to Lexington, so the remainder of our trip, while not easy, was at least in the right direction. What slowed us down as much as anything were the streams and rivers. There were rough-hewn wood bridges over creeks and streams, but most of them were so rough that you had to watch out for broken boards. Sometimes entire boards were missing, making the crossing extremely treacherous. Rivers were a different challenge entirely. These required some sort of ferry crossing. Most were fairly primitive. All of them required a toll, an early form of free enterprise. At one river there was a flat raft maybe 12 by 20 feet in dimension. The guy who ferried you over was sleeping in a small tent near the side of the river. He wasn't happy about being wakened, but when we told him why we needed to cross his attitude changed completely.

By the time we got to Lexington, it was after three in the morning. As we neared the village we'd seen more men making their way into town. Each one carried a musket. They all seemed to be heading toward the heart of the little town. In the center of the town the numbers were greater. By the time we arrived at Lexington Common we saw that there were close to a hundred militiamen assembled there, nervously milling about, awaiting direction from their commander. A nervous buzz of conversation filled the air as the men, young and old, had to be considering the likelihood of an armed confrontation within a matter of hours.

I approached two men who appeared to be in their early twenties.

"We just got here. What's happened?" I asked one of the young militiamen, a blond fellow with a ruddy complexion holding his musket by its barrel and resting its stock on the ground next to his left foot.

"Not much, so far. Revere and a fellow named Dawes rode into town just after midnight. Revere got here first and made a bloody lot of noise. Woke half the town up. Someone said that a sentry guarding the house where Hancock and Adams are staying told 'im to keep the noise down. I understand that Revere yelled back at the guard saying there'd be a helluva lot more noise soon when the regulars get here."

"But you've seen no regulars yet?" I asked.

"None yet, but a rider just rode through. He said they're about an hour away. There must be close to a thousand of 'em, he said."

"Looks like you've got close to a hundred here on the common," I said.

"More like two hundred now," he said. I thought he was exaggerating, but I didn't say so. "They're still coming in from all directions. We'll be a match for the bloody Redcoats, I'm sure. Can't wait."

"You mean you want to have a battle with the regulars? They'll outnumber us by a lot."

"It has to happen sometime. Might as well be now when we're prepared. Plenty of good men here, and more coming every minute. We'll have enough. No shortage of powder, either. The king's men could've won in Salem, but that cowardly Leslie was afraid to fight. Here, we can give a good accounting of ourselves if the regulars want a fight. Many of these Patriot fellows here on the common fought the bloody French and sent them running. The regulars when they're right off the boat fight the same way the French fought. During the war against the French the regulars gradually adopted some of our methods, but it took awhile for them to do it. These new regulars will fight like they do in Europe. We can beat them. That is, if they dare to fight."

This sort of bravado made me nervous. The soldier in me understood, but another part of me wondered why you would want to fight if you didn't have to? Oh, I understood how the Patriots felt about the abuses they'd endured from Parliament and the king. Still, if bloodshed could be avoided as it had been in Salem, maybe things could be worked out to everyone's satisfaction. I shook myself out of this kind of thinking. In this particular case such pacifist thinking was illogical, since I knew what was going to happen. The fighting was not going to be avoided.

I had to adopt a mindset that accepted the fact that the two sides were going to engage in a blood battle. I would be foolish to deny it, since I knew it was going to go down, and soon. With this pragmatic mindset I found myself wanting to be part of the upcoming fight. Now this is where it got really weird. Since I knew there was going to be a battle, It was logical to conclude that even if I fought in the battle, I would not die, since I would be alive over 200 years later in the twenty-first century. You'd think that I would face the upcoming clash without fear, knowing I would survive. *Au contraire.* I was scared shitless. As I said, I know it's weird, but the thought of being shot at or run through with a bayonet loomed larger than the abstract knowledge that I would be alive two centuries later. I couldn't wrap my mind around these time-travel inconsistencies.

I had another question for the blond soldier. "I have a message for Adams and Hancock from Colonel Mason in Salem. Do you know where they're staying?"

"I'm not from Lexington, but someone said they were at the Reverend Clarke's house not far from here, but I doubt if they're there now. Revere and Dawes supposedly warned 'em, and they left for God knows where." He grinned. "What these Redcoats don't get is that we have eyes and ears everywhere. Gage thinks he's smarter'n us, but he's not by a long shot."

"He may not be," I said, "but he has a helluva lot of well-equipped men at his disposal. It won't be easy meeting them head-to-head."

"Guess we'll see fairly soon, won't we?"

He was right about that. I later learned that Colonel Smith had sent ahead an advance guard of several elite light infantry companies under the command of Major John Pitcairn. Their job was to secure the bridges before the colonists could make them uncrossable. Pitcairn was so contemptuous of the colonists that he reportedly had written, *"I have so despicable an opinion of the people of this country that I would not hesitate to march with the men I have with me to any part...and do whatever I was inclined. I am satisfied they will never attack Regular troops."*

Tom and I continued talking with the young blond militiaman and his friends. Partly to pass the time and partly out of nervousness. Tom and I knew what was about to happen, but we sensed that the militiamen milling about and talking among themselves nervously, (but without our historical perspective), also knew they were on the verge of something big.

Tom and I were close enough to hear a rider notify the Lexington militia leader, 45-year-old Captain John Parker, that Pitcairn's advanced guard was nearing the common. I estimated that there were under two hundred militiamen now milling around on the common, with more joining them every minute. Parker was a veteran of Roger's Rangers, a provincial unit that was merged into the British army during the French and Indian War. He'd fought valiantly in that war and brought that experience with him. He wanted to present a strong force when the regulars arrived. It was important that the advancing troops be stopped here before they could go after the weapons cache in Concord. Parker already knew that Adams and Hancock had made their escape, so they were no longer at risk.

What he didn't know was that Revere had been captured by an advance detachment of Pitcairn's advancing troops somewhere between Lexington and Concord. He'd been riding with Dr. Samuel Prescott, a local physician and Patriot who'd been visiting his fiancee when he heard Revere's call to arms outside her house. While Revere and Prescott were being interrogated, Prescott made a bold dash to his horse and escaped his captors by jumping the horse over a nearby fence. He made it all the way to Concord where he alerted the locals. The bell in the townhouse was rung and word quickly got out about the advancing regulars.

Meanwhile, in Lexington, things were heating up rapidly. As the sky began to lighten, a man came riding breathlessly onto the common reporting to Captain Parker of more advancing British troops not far behind the advance detachment. These trailing troops were the main contingent of several hundred men under the command of Colonel Smith. The man then told Parker that he'd witnessed a rider from Pitcairn's advanced unit reporting to Smith to tell him that they'd learned from Paul Revere that there were 500 Minutemen awaiting them in Concord. The rider explained that Revere had been interrogated for over an hour and then released.

On the Lexington Common, Captain Parker told his men to let the regulars pass. "They outnumber us greatly. Don't molest them without they begin first."

He'd barely gotten these words out of his mouth when the lead column of British regulars under the command of Lieutenant Jesse

Adair marched briskly onto the common. At this point Adair had two choices: He could turn left toward Concord, avoiding direct confrontation, but exposing his flank to the colonial militia. Adair decided to turn right, thus bringing his men to a standstill facing the militia. The tension between the two opposing forces was palpable. Pitcairn, leading a larger unit of troops, then entered the common and lined up on one side of the militia. He immediately ordered Parker's men to leave the common. Parker, with major combat experience a decade earlier, was realistic and ordered his men to disperse. They slowly fell out and began to head in different directions away from the common.

Then I heard a shot. Then another. It's unclear where they came from. Then the regulars opened fire. Puffs of smoke obscured several of the British regulars. Tom and I were in the thick of it and saw two men fall not two yards away from us. There was thick smoke in our own midst. More shots and several more of the men around us fell. Tom grabbed me by the arm and directed my attention to one of the fallen men. It was our blond friend. I squatted down to feel for his pulse. Nothing. Our historical adventure had suddenly become a living nightmare. I stared in disbelief at the red spot on the forehead of a young man Tom and I had grown to like. We'd even spoken of getting together sometime for a pint when this was all over. We knew he had a sister he wanted us to meet.

I was shaken out of my thoughts by a tug from Tom, clearly the more pragmatic of the two of us in life-and-death situations.

"Grab your musket and shoot, for God's sake," he yelled.

I hadn't bargained for this, but obviously it was a case of them or us, so I aimed and fired into the advancing Redcoats. I'm not sure, but I think I missed. As I reloaded, a Redcoat came at me with the bayonet affixed to the end of his musket. I sidestepped and slammed the barrel of my musket down on the back of his head. He went down and stayed down. I was mad. I don't like it when someone fires a musket at me, or aims a steel bayonet at me. I was about to fire again when I heard someone in the ranks of the regulars bellow an order.

"Cease fire! Cease fire!" I think it was Pitcairn, but I couldn't be sure with the cacophony of musket shots, the frantic yelling from the soldiers and our own militiamen plus the desperate screaming from the wounded.

Then, from somewhere in the midst of the British forces I heard a drum roll. The history books will tell you that Colonel Smith was aghast at the breakdown of discipline among his troops. I guess the Brits were trained like Pavlov's dogs to stop everything when they hear drum rolls, because that's what happened. The shooting stopped on both sides. It was later pointed out to me that many of the militiamen who had fought under British command in the French and Indian War had reacted to the drum rolls for the same reason that the regulars did.

Captain Parker now ordered his troops to cease fire. His men, who'd reluctantly been leaving the common when the shooting broke out, had returned to fight with their comrades who had not yet left and were now being shot at. Parker barked his cease fire orders three times before the militiamen slowly, grudgingly stopped shooting, though they remained wary, lest the Redcoats take advantage of the cease fire.

Smith now had his men under control and ordered them to march in the direction of Concord. At this point, because many of his men suffered from exhaustion and slowing down noticeably, he sent 250 of his fittest men ahead as an advance unit, apparently figuring the remaining 250 would arrive as soon as they were able. As his cold, exhausted men proceeded, he reminded them of their mission to take possession or destroy the cache of hidden arms in that nearby village. It was not to engage in battle with the locals unless fired upon. In this brief skirmish they had discouraged Parker's outmanned forces so there was no need to continue the battle. Clearly, they had demonstrated the superiority of the king's forces.

Chapter 37

The last of the regulars were nearly out of sight now. Most of the acrid smoke had wafted off in the cool morning breeze. Now all that was left were eight bodies on the ground with forlorn fellow militiamen standing around them, not sure what to do next. A number of other men were wounded—some lying on the ground, writhing in pain. A few wandered around bleeding, not certain what to do. I looked around for a doctor or medic, but saw none. Captain Parker took charge of the dismal situation.

"All right, let's get these bodies on a wagon and take it somewhere where their families can come and fetch them." He pointed at several men and said, "You: Baker, Kelvin, Smith, Joslin and you Horton. Help us get these bodies on a wagon." Within minutes a wagon was brought over and the men began loading the eight bodies. As two men lifted the lifeless body of our young blond acquaintance I felt a sorrow that I hadn't felt since attending the funeral of my parents as a small, confused child. We hadn't known the young soldier well or long, but we'd taken a liking to him and would have liked to have gotten to know him better.

Our trip back in time had started out as a shock to both of us, but gradually we'd grown to accept it. Slowly we'd found ourselves accepting our new existence. We thought less about being trapped in the past and more about our newfound everyday life. Amazing how we humans adapt. Not so bad; that is until recently. Recently we'd found it a lot harder to deal with the ways of the past. First the tar and feathering of Robert Woodbury and now the death of a man we'd been speaking with only minutes ago—not to mention the other men being placed silently on the rough boards of the wagon. As the men finished loading the grim cargo, Parker's voice rose so that he could be heard by all.

"You men did well today. It's a sad day when you lose eight good men, men we all know, but it's a proud day, too. We were outnumbered and we gave enough of a fight to make them see the wisdom of moving on. We wounded a few of 'em and they knew it would only get worse if they continued the battle. They'll think twice about engaging colonials next time."

They were good words and said at the right time. Unfortunately, events in Concord would prove them not to be prophetic. Parker didn't know that when he spoke, though. The men needed a boost, and his words were just the right thing at that moment. I'm not sure Parker was right about why Smith and Pitcairn called off the fight. Might not have been out of fear so much as the feeling that they had already won. It was very likely that Colonel Smith thought there was no need for the regulars to beat up on the feisty, but inferior locals. They'd made their point.

Of course the regulars did outnumber the militia by about 500 to 100, so the Patriots had nothing to be ashamed of. Early estimates of as many as a thousand regulars turned out to be an exaggeration by nervous locals. Five hundred, though, were bad enough. As bad as the odds were, the colonials did not cut and run when the shooting began. They stood their ground in the face of overwhelming numbers.

The militia was now slowly dispersing and Tom said, "Wanna ride on to Concord and see what happens next?"

"Why not?" I said. " We need to feed these horses first, though." I did miss my Jeep. I'd grown happy in the eighteenth century, but every once in awhile, I missed some of the conveniences of a century I would never see again.

He grinned. "You miss your Jeep, don't you?"

"You read my mind. Yeah, I kind of like old Ben, but he is pretty high maintenance compared to the Jeep."

"Same with Chestnut. Great horse, but needs a lot more attention than a car. Speaking of feeding these nags, you and I could use a little sustenance, too."

"Yeah, but it better be quick for us and the horses. I want to get over to Concord ASAP."

Chapter 38

We arrived in Concord shortly after seven o'clock that same morning. Concord is about seven miles from Lexington. It took us a half hour on our tired horses. Up ahead, as we approached the center of the little town, we could just make out through the morning haze a mass of Redcoats near the common. One thing about those red uniforms—they're easy to spot from a distance. As we got closer we saw an even larger group of Minutemen deployed maybe three or four hundred yards away from the regulars. We headed for the Minutemen and fell in behind them. We estimated that there were three or four hundred of us and less than half that of the regulars. This time we outnumbered the bad guys.

The commander of the Concord militia was Colonel James Barrett. He looked to be much older than most of the Minutemen and other militiamen present—probably in his sixties. As Tom and I struck up conversations with our fellow militiamen, we learned that they came from Concord, Lincoln, Acton, Westford, Bedford and several other nearby towns. As commander of the Concord militia, it fell to Colonel Barrett to also command the militias from the nearby towns that had come to Concord's aid.

Barrett spoke to the assembled men.

"The regulars have destroyed some of our cannon, though they haven't been able to find most of them. They've burned a number of gun carriages and other supplies, too. I just learned that they've attempted to break into Wright's Tavern, but innkeeper, Ephraim Jones, stood his ground as long as he could. Then one of the Redcoat officers knocked Jones to the ground, and they eventually got to the three cannon he'd had hidden next door. These regulars will show no mercy, so be on your guard. There's not much more they can do here in town, so I'm surrendering the town and directing all units to the North Bridge area. Upon arrival they should cross over and assume position on Punkatasset Hill facing town so we have views of both bridge and town."

On our way over the bridge and on up the hill we engaged several of our fellow soldiers in conversation. None of the men Tom or I spoke with knew anything about what had happened in Lexington. We told the few militiamen we came in contact with that there had already been a confrontation and that, as far as we could tell, eight colonials had been killed and more wounded. We pointed out that it looked to us as if the Redcoats under Colonel Smith considered their main mission to be to taking control of the hidden munitions in Concord. I stressed that if we don't capitulate they will not hesitate to shoot.

One of the fellows, a local Minuteman from Concord, then said, "I'm not surprised that they're eager for a fight after their retreat in Salem in February. Well, if that's what they want, we're ready for 'em. Surprised, though, they didn't bring more troops. Is that the best the King's army can do?" I was about to agree with him when he said, "Hey, is that smoke coming from the middle of town? It looks like it's coming from the meetinghouse."

Barrett grew concerned lest the fire spread to other buildings in the village so he ordered us to move back down from Punkatasset Hill to a smaller hill closer to the bridge in order to be able to move into town faster if necessary. As we redeployed toward this lower hill we now numbered at least 500 men. We were at least five companies of Minutemen and five more of militiamen. At the foot of this hill, the field between our hill and the bridge was occupied by two or three British companies. We greatly outnumbered them. As we advanced toward them they marched in retreat toward the bridge.

More smoke could now be seen coming from the center of town. Barrett and his fellow officers thought that the regulars had set fire to the town. He ordered us to load our weapons and advance toward the bridge, but not to fire unless fired upon. The British companies that had set up formation near the bridge to guard it now were ordered to retreat across the span. One Redcoat officer ordered a few men to try to pull up loose planks from the bridge to hinder our advance. One of our officers, a Major Buttrick yelled out to the regulars to stop damaging the bridge. We, the Minutemen and the militia, advanced in a column toward the bridge.

Then, Captain Walter Laurie of the regulars made a tactical mistake. He'd sent for help from the remainder of the regular forces that arrived late and located themselves in the center of town. When no one came, he ordered his men to line up for "street fighting," near the bridge. Street fighting was a tactic used when fighting in a city, allowing heavy fire into a narrow street between buildings. It concentrated troops close together, making them an easy target. It was a tactic that made no sense out in the open near a bridge. The scene became chaotic as regulars scurried over the bridge to assume the street-fighting formation. As they made their way awkwardly over the bridge, bumping into each other in the process, they kept looking over their shoulders at us, wondering if we would shoot at them in their disarray.

British Lieutenant William Sutherland from a different company realized the error of the street-fighting formation and ordered his men out of that position. Only a few troops obeyed him, as most of the men did as the captain, a superior officer, had commanded. I have no idea if they realized that the street-fighting formation they were assuming was making them more vulnerable than they would have been had they obeyed the lieutenant. Confusion reigned.

Thanks to history books and the movies Tom and I knew what was going to happen next. I turned to him and said, "This is like a movie you're seeing for the second time. You know what's going to happen; yet you're still nervous."

"Nervous is putting it mildly," he replied. "I remember as a kid I'd close my eyes in the scary parts of movies. But this isn't a movie. This is real, and we both know that hundreds of people are going to die in the next few hours. We know that; yet we can't do a damn thing about it."

"What looks exciting in the movies," I said, "looks like a goddamn nightmare in the making when you're in the middle of it. History books and movies make killing a lot more palatable."

A tired looking militiaman old enough to be my father poked me on the shoulder.

"Am I hearin' you two lads right? Hundreds are dyin' today you say? What put that notion into yer heads? The regulars have no taste for a fight. We outnumber 'em two to one. They're nasty bastards, but they're not foolish. Gage just sent 'em out here to show he's in charge."

"Sorry my friend," interjected Tom, "but events will prove you wrong. It'd be nice if you were right, but I'm afraid we're in for a bloody fight."

"And where do you get this dismal insight, young feller? You young'uns are all looking for a fight. Well I fought in Quebec and at Fort William Henry, and I'll tell you killing's no fun. You young lads like to glorify war, but there's no glory in it. It's death and dirt and hunger and blood. Don't be looking for a fight."

I knew where he was coming from, and he was right. How could he possibly understand that Tom actually *KNEW* a battle was coming. It wasn't Tom's desire that was speaking, it was his knowledge. How could Tom explain to the old guy how he knew?

I don't know what got into me, but I figured what the hell. The situation was tense enough as it was. At that moment we all had time to kill—an unfortunate turn of phrase in light of what was about to take place. Anyway, in this waiting period before the fighting broke out, we might as well have a little fun. If the old guy thought we were nuts, so be it. He didn't know us, so it wouldn't hurt our reputations back in Salem. Hell, for all we knew the man could be wounded or even killed in the coming battle. A little entertainment could at least loosen things up for these last few tense, but peaceful, moments.

"My friend isn't looking for a fight with the regulars," I said, "He's not eager for battle any more than you are. The fact of the matter is, he really does know that we're all in for a fight, and soon."

The seasoned militiaman studied us quizzically for a few seconds. He was trying to figure us out. I think he thought we were up to something or had some kind of an angle, but was at a loss as to what it was.

"So you both know we're going into battle, do you? Far as I can see the only way you could know that is if you were regulars yourself spyin' on us. Come to think of it, you don't sound like you're from around here. Mebbe you are regulars."

"Yeah, well we sure as hell don't sound like Brits from the home country, either. You have to admit that."

"I spose that's true, but there's something odd about the both of you."

I said, "I won't deny that we're different, but I will deny that we're regulars or even siding with the regulars. We're on your side, believe me."

"Where'd the two of you learn to speak like you do?"

"If I tell you, you won't believe me."

"You let me decide that."

Tom now saw where I was going with this and said, "We're from the future. The twenty-first century. We know what's going to happen here because we read about it in our history books."

The old guy just stared at us for a minute; then turned around and grabbed another militiaman

who looked to be of the same vintage.

"Jesse, you have to meet my new friends here. They claim they're from the future. The twenty-first century. Say they know we're going to have a big battle here today. Lots of folks'll die, they say." He smiled as if he was either in on some sort of macabre joke or he was poking fun at two nut cases. I couldn't tell which.

Jesse, who loomed over us, was maybe six inches taller than our new acquaintance, and a lot thinner, grinned and said, "Tarnation!" He then tendered his hand for us to shake. Clearly he thought he was sharing the joke. "You don't say," he continued with a broad smile on his weathered face. "So you fellers know what's gonna happen here today? That's mighty interestin'. Mighty interestin'."

"I know it must be difficult to believe," said Tom, "but as things proceed today, maybe you will."

Jesse turned serious now. Obviously this was eating at him, and he was trying to figure out just what our game was.

"The way I see it, fellers, you're one of three things: You're makin' a joke at our expense, you're workin' for the regulars, or you're witches." He didn't smile when he said this, and I realized that he was probably born less than 20 years after the Salem Witch Trials and very likely believed in witchcraft. It was certainly easier for him to believe in witchcraft than that we had come from the future. Then again, I supposed that if you could believe in witchcraft, time travel might not be that big of a jump either.

Right now I was hoping that Jesse and his friend would settle on the joke explanation, as lame as that was. Even a bad joke at their expense would be easier to deal with than if they seriously thought we were witches or spies for the regulars. Our fellow militiamen were edgy, and it wouldn't take much to get ourselves killed. Being accused of spying or witchcraft could do it. I doubted if we'd have much of a trial out here on the battlefield.

We knew—or thought we knew—that we couldn't die because we knew we would be alive two centuries later. Our strategy now had to be to change the subject. Jesse hadn't even considered our real reason—time travel—as a serious explanation of our behavior. I saw now that that wasn't going anywhere. Best to let that one die. It was reckless to even suggest it. At the end of the battle our new friends would have a lot more to talk about than two crazies they met before the fighting started.

Suddenly a new thought hit me. All along Tom and I had been assuming we couldn't be killed in the eighteenth century because 240 years later we were alive in the twenty-first century. The logic of that had appealed to me because it was very comforting. But maybe that wasn't the case. Maybe we could die in the eighteenth century, since all our living in the twenty-first century had occurred before we entered the eighteenth century. The more I thought about it, the more this made more sense. Clearly we would die in this century if we were never going back to the twenty-first. And if this was true, it made a lot of sense to be careful from this point on. So far, we'd lucked out, but obviously it had only been luck. Right now we'd better not tempt fate.

"Look," I said, trying to seem sincere, "you're right. I suppose from your perspective you could say it was sort of a bad joke. Not even that, really. We were just thinking out loud about what could happen. We just have this awful feeling that something bad is going to happen today. We shouldn't have talked about it so loud, but when your friend—" I nodded toward the shorter of the two men— "overheard us, we decided to turn it into a kind of sick joke. We shouldn't have. We shouldn't be joking about death. The future thing was silly, too."

"Smartest thing you've said yet, lad," said the man without a name. "You shouldn't be goin' off talkin' like that—'specially out here. Could get yourselves killed. So you really do think somethin' bad is gonna spoil this beautiful day?"

"I'm afraid I do, sir. Hope I'm wrong." I said respectfully.

Chapter 39

We gradually mollified our new friends. We even grew friendly as we chatted amiably, all the while keeping one eye toward Colonel Barrett and listening for any change in status. As we chatted, we learned that the other man's name was Bevis. As Tom heard about Jesse's purchase of a new horse and how it was already so well trained, I drifted off in my own thoughts. For Jesse, getting a new horse was like my getting a new car when I lived in the twenty-first century. It made me think about how different things were now and yet how similar we were in some ways.

Usually, when I was busy, I didn't reminisce about my previous life. I'd gotten used to so many things now that most of the conveniences from the future were as abstract as space aliens used to be when I went to a sci-fi movie. I could envision them or remember them, but in my new environment, I didn't need them and certainly was able to get by without them. Sure, I missed things that made life easier: things such as flush toilets, safety razors, toilet paper, and a refrigerator. But surprisingly, while at times I also missed my car, my TV and my smart phone, I was amazed at how little I missed them. With a car you can travel a considerable distance quickly compared to travel by horse or on foot, but in my present world I had no need to go great distances very often. On occasion, TV would be nice, but I found myself reading more now and getting to know people better. I missed my cell phone less than any other technological convenience. I was never much of a phoner. I used my phone more for texting, email and searching the Web, none of which I can do now. I admit that in times like war or the onset of war a cell phone would give you an advantage over your enemy, but then again, if I had one, so would the enemy.

I did miss my Red Sox, though. Tom and I were both originally from the Beverly-Salem area in Massachusetts, so the Sox were in our blood. There were no professional sports in this century For that matter, there wasn't much in the way of any organized sport. Cricket, wicket and shinny were the only games I was even aware of. Shinny was something like field hockey, where you had this shovel-like stick you used to hit a ball over an end line. Wicket was a game similar to cricket that you played if you didn't have enough players to play cricket. The only other sport of any kind I was aware of was wrestling.

None of these sports was that common, as almost all able-bodied young men, meaning anyone from 13 on, were engaged in some kind of work—usually physical work. The days were long and tiring. Sunday was the only day off, and most people went to church and took it easy the rest of the day. The young men, meaning guys in their teens, were apprenticed to some trade, which was on-the-job training. The 40-hour work week was a thing of the distant future.

It was virtually unheard of for girls to play any sport. Bottom line: very few guys, girls or women had the time or energy for athletics.

"Isn't that true, Gil?" Tom said loudly. He'd obviously noticed that I was off in another world and was trying to drag me back into the conversation.

"Isn't what true?" I noticed that a third militiaman had joined our group. He was not as tall as Jesse, but a lot heavier and not very friendly looking.

"Isn't it true that folks up in Halifax speak like us? We can't help it if we sound strange here." Then he added with a grin, "Folks around here sound strange to us."

"Yes," I said, trying to look friendly, "you folks talk differently down here, Don't know why, but you do."

"Mebbe that's why we got the wrong idea before," said Jesse

mischievously.

The new man then furrowed his brow and looking suspicious asked, "What wrong idea was that?"

"Oh," said Jesse, "this here is Aaron."

I introduced myself and said, "We said that there's going to be fighting here today. Soon, too. We meant to say that we had a feeling that there'd be fighting, but your friends, Jesse and ....?"

"Bevis," said the first militiaman we'd met.

I continued, "Jesse and Bevis thought we were being smart-asses or we were working for the regulars."

"Or the both of you were witches," poked Jesse. "I take it the term smart-ass is one of your Halifax curses, though I think I take your meaning." He looked at Bevis and added, "I think we've settled on that one."

Aaron, who looked like he was on the far side of 300 pounds, and whose only expression so far had been a frown, said, "Is it normal up in Halifax to make jokes about death?"

"It's not," jumped in Tom, "and we both feel terrible about what we said. We weren't joking, we just expressed a feeling we had." It really was stupid of us, but we were now stuck with our explanation, since the other two reasons these guys were considering would get us into a lot more trouble than the embarrassing situation we now found ourselves in.

"Thank God there aren't many of you Halifax types here or you'd have us at war," spat out Aaron disagreeably.

"There's enough locals here looking for a fight," blurted Tom angrily. "You don't need anyone from Halifax to stir up a war."

That was not smart. He was right, but it was not smart.

I could see Aaron doing a slow burn.

Jesse tried to put a lid on the boiling kettle. "Let's calm down now, friends," he said. Then, he added diplomatically, "we're all a mite skittish today. Let's not be sayin' things we'll regret tomorrow. We're all on the same side. Let's not forget that. Let's remember who the enemy is."

"I'm beginning to wonder," said Aaron. "Maybe we're lookin' at 'em."

I was tempted to take a swing at his ample chin when a shot rang out.

Chapter 40

Unlike Lexington, where it was unclear who fired the first shot, in Concord there was no confusion. We were marching in a column two abreast toward the bridge. I was somewhere in the middle of the column, and I could clearly see the shot and puff of smoke in the midst of a cluster of confused regulars on the far side of the bridge. Very likely it was an exhausted, nervous young soldier who'd never seen battle. Maybe that wasn't the case. Maybe it was an intentional warning shot. Whatever the reason, two more regulars then fired. Both shots splashed in the river, harming no one. Within seconds a volley of shots issued from the regulars. This time at least two Minutemen fell dead and several more were wounded. And still we continued marching toward the bridge and directly into the face of the enemy fire. I looked at Tom. We were both thinking, *Why don't we stop and begin firing?*

No sooner had we thought this than Major Buttrick yelled, "Fire! For God's sake, fire!" At this moment we were in deadly close range. The colonial forces were separated from the regulars by the narrow river and perhaps only another 50 yards. Our Minutemen struggled to fire over each other's heads. This was not at all like what we'd read about the fighting style of our forces in the French and Indian War and the American Revolution. Most of us now were right out in the open. We were not hiding behind walls, trees and buildings because there was no such protection in sight. We had no choice. This was British-style fighting, and the only thing that gave us a chance was that we outnumbered them by as much as five to one. That didn't help the men at the head of our column, though, and many of them fell to enemy fire. Tom and I both managed to get off a couple of shots. Admittedly, we were slow at reloading. I honestly don't know if either one of us hit anyone. If we did, did it in any way alter the course of history?

The regulars suffered great losses in this exchange. Not knowing who's command to follow left them outmaneuvered. While the colonial forces were unable to fight in their preferred style, their superior numbers, their familiarity with the terrain and their experience in previous battles gave them a decided advantage over the youthful regulars, most of whom lacked battle seasoning. As their casualties mounted and the colonial forces moved relentlessly toward them, the regulars abandoned their wounded and fled toward the relative safety of the approaching reinforcement companies coming from the village.

Shocked by their success, some of the Colonials continued their advance toward the retreating regulars. Some, though, went home, thinking they had done their duty. Colonel Barrett slowly gained control over the remaining Minutemen and militiamen and moved the militiamen back to the original hilltop. He positioned the Minutemen near the bridge. His intention was to watch over the entire area until it was certain that the regulars had lost their desire to fight.

Colonel Smith, the commander of the British forces positioned in the center of Concord, had heard the battle from a far. He immediately led two reinforcement companies of grenadiers toward the bridge. As they neared the scene of the recent battle they encountered remnants of the fleeing companies. Seeing the Minutemen beyond the bridge, he halted his grenadiers and proceeded with a few of his officers to get a closer look.

Up on the hill Tom and I could see all this unfolding, and it was clear as could be that if the Minutemen had opened fire, they would have killed Smith and his officers with no trouble. While we militiamen were yards to the rear, I could distinctly hear Colonel Barrett order the Minutemen not to fire. The tension all the while was tighter than a bowstring. Strangely, though, even in life-and-death situations, sometime things happen that lighten up the mood of all involved. Hard as it is to believe, we saw a man wandering among the Minutemen and then among the regulars selling hard cider. At least that's what most of the men around me said he was doing. Apparently he was a local known to most of his neighbors as mentally off. Nobody harmed the man, and it looked from our vantage point that he actually made some sales.

Colonel Smith and his officers did a quick survey of the battlefield. In so doing they passed unmolested by Barrett's militia and saw numerous bodies and wounded comrades lying on the bridge. As they returned over the bridge they passed safely by Buttrick's Minutemen and made their way back into the center of Concord. While this was going on the regulars were within range of the colonial forces; yet not a shot was fired by either side. I'm sure that Smith and his regulars had had their fill of the Minutemen and the militia. It was clear that the colonial forces were not the disorganized rabble that they'd expected to encounter. The battle near the bridge was not a big one, but it served to inform the king's army that the rebels knew what they were doing and could be mustered in sufficient numbers to be a serious military threat.

I think what surprised me most was not our victory, because, after all, I knew about that before it happened. No, what surprised me most was how much restraint the colonials showed even when they possessed superior numbers.

Another thing that took me by surprise was the bizarre behavior of the Redcoats at times. I later learned that while they were burning our military supplies in town and setting the town hall on fire, they quickly joined the locals in forming a bucket brigade to save the very building they'd set afire. After Smith and his regulars returned to town they proceeded to burn more of our supplies, then eat lunch and begin their march back toward Boston.

Military behavior is not always consistent. One surprise that seriously detracted from the gentlemanly behavior of the British officers was their treatment of their wounded. Or more accurately, their lack of treatment. As far as I could tell, they left them on the battlefield to fend for themselves. Bear in mind that most of these soldiers were teenage or early twenties. They'd signed up for army service because it promised them a paycheck and service for their country. Maybe I missed it, but I didn't see any regulars going to the aid of their fallen comrades.

◆ ◆ ◆

When the last of the regulars had left Concord, Colonel Barrett and Major Buttrick excused the men and thanked them for their service.

They asked for volunteers to go back to the battlefield and help the wounded and bring in the dead. He said he also needed men to help clean up the damage left in town by Colonel Smith's regulars. I approached the weary Barrett and asked him if he knew where Adams and Hancock had gone when they left Lexington. I explained that we had a message for them from Colonel Mason. He said he did not know and chances are my message could wait considering the fighting that just took place. Adams and Hancock, he suspected, would keep a low profile until they could relocate to a safer town. I found out later that they'd gone to Woburn.

Not knowing that at the time, though, Tom and I decided to go into town for something to eat. It had been a long night and a hard morning. It would be good to sit down and enjoy a little sustenance. Maybe not sleep, but at least rest for awhile. What better place than Wright's Tavern. Ephraim Jones could probably use our business after what the Brits had done to him and his place. Meanwhile, it would give our mounts a little more time to rest before we headed out.

Before we did that, though, we decided to help out with the wounded. As far as I could see there were still no medics or nurses to be seen. There was no medical aid at all. We didn't have to look far for the wounded. They were on both sides of the bridge and a few were on the span itself. A quick assessment of the situation told us that most of the wounded Minutemen and militiamen were being tended to by their fellow soldiers. However, many of the fallen Redcoats who were still alive were ignored by the colonial forces, or at least, left for last. Tom and I went to the nearest injured regular, a fellow who couldn't have been more than 18, and carefully helped him to his feet. He was white as a sheet and seemed half out of it when we asked him his name. On closer scrutiny we could see that he'd taken a ball in his right bicep and one in the thigh. He was bleeding profusely. Probably not fatal if we could stop the flow, but clearly painful as hell. We took the shirt off one of his dead comrades and made rough tourniquets to stanch the bleeding. Then we slowly walked him into town, not knowing exactly what we'd do with him when we got there, but thinking he could at least get some attention there as opposed to out here in the open field. We realized that by helping this regular we might in some small way be changing the course of history. In sort of a perverse way, I hoped that he would have survived anyway and that our efforts were more cosmetic than lifesaving. I know one thing, though, it would have been hard to ignore him when we didn't have to go out of our way to help him.

Once in town, we were shocked by the number of bodies and wounded lying on the ground. At least one doctor was busy tending to a long line of colonial wounded. A militia officer was directing traffic, trying to bring a semblance of order to the chaos. I went over to him and asked who could attend to our wounded soldier.

Without looking he barked out, "Take 'im to the end of the line. He'll have to wait his turn. There's only one doc now. We've sent for another, but he hasn't arrived yet." So there was at least one doctor at the scene.

"He's a regular," I said, "will he get care like everybody else?"

This got his attention and he said, "Not sure we'll get to him today. Our boys get help first." Then he glanced our way and saw how young and helpless the lad was and changed his tune. "Put him in line and we'll see what we can do. As you can see, it'll be awhile before anyone sees 'im."

I thanked the officer and Tom and I started toward the end of the long line waiting to see the harried physician.

"What's your name, soldier?" I asked the pale regular.

"Simon Barker, sir?" he managed.

"You heard what the lieutenant said. We'll put you in line here and you'll have to wait till the doctor can get to you. You want some water?"

"Yessir. If you have it."

I saw that his wooden canteen had taken a ball and was splintered. It held nothing. He had no water, but the canteen may have saved his life. I gave him my canteen, which was also wooden, and he drank as if he hadn't seen water in a week. War will do that to you.

Tom and I then left him. We'd done what we could. Now we needed to take care of ourselves. It wasn't easy leaving him. He was just a kid. As we walked away he looked toward us, almost as if he saw us as his only hope. We really weren't though. We'd helped him because he was in pain, but there was a limit to what we could do now. Our first allegiance was to our own. Funny how things work out. Before fighting broke out we would have considered him one of our own. Well, that's not entirely true. Tom and I would have thought of him as a Brit who came to America to keep American colonials in line. Most of the other colonials we knew, though, would have thought of him as a fellow Brit who just happened to come from the home country.

"What do you think will happen to our friend Simon?" asked Tom.

"He'll probably be taken prisoner, once the Minutemen and militia officers take stock of things here. They'll very likely pump him for info about troop formations and what Gage is planning to do next. He probably doesn't know that much, but they'll try."

Chapter 41

Wright's Tavern was abuzz with grimy faced soldiers. Innkeeper Ephraim Jones had a black eye and looked as if his nose had been bloodied, but he was beaming as we entered the place. Clearly standing up to the British assault on his place of business made him one of the boys right now. He was too old to fight, but he'd done his part.

Word had obviously gotten around because it was clear that everyone in the place knew about his brave stand against the Redcoat intrusion earlier in the day.

When we finally got close enough to place our order Jones said, "What can I get you boys? Can't be too fancy. The bloody Redcoats took most of what I have."

"Whatever's left over," said Tom. We're hungry and thirsty."

"Still have a bit of bread and some cheese. That's about it." He paused to let us decide, then added, "Plenty of beer, though."

"Bread and cheese'll be fine," I said. "And a couple pints sounds good."

Ten minutes later he handed us our food and beer. We paid him, and I said, "So they robbed you blind of all your food?"

He smiled. "Wish I could say they did, but they didn't. Paid for every damn plate and pint. Bloody regulars are bastards, but they're gentlemen bastards."

"Well they learned a lesson today," I said. "I think they underestimated us."

"That they did. That they did. I'm proud of what you fellas did out there today. I expect the bloody regulars will learn a few more lessons on their way back to Boston, too."

"You think they'll start something on their way back?"

"Not if they learned anything today. No, I think they'll march back to Boston with their tails between their legs. They just might have to fight their way back, though. There'll be a lot more of us provincials to greet 'em with lead balls along the way. Won't be an easy trip for those fellas."

"I'm a little surprised they turned tail so fast," said Tom. "As far as I could see they didn't lose that many men."

"I wasn't out there m'boy," said Jones. "Just how many do you reckon?"

"Five or six. Certainly not more than ten," said Tom. "I know they wouldn't want to lose *any*, but considering what they were up against, that wasn't bad."

Jones furrowed his brow. "Just what do you mean *considering what they were up against*?"

"I mean they were greatly outnumbered. We could've killed a good deal many more if we'd wanted to."

"Pity we didn't," said Jones. As he spoke a tall gangling militiaman got in his face and said, "Hey, Jones, get back to business. You can't wallow in your glory all day. You got thirsty men here." He had a broad grin on his angular, pockmarked face as he said this.

"You're right, my friend. Can't keep these Patriots waiting. Not after the thrashing they gave King George's troops.

The banter and verbal jousting became more animated as the beer flowed freely and more men entered the tavern. Gradually we found ourselves in the midst of friendly conversation with men we'd never met before. The more we spoke the more we seemed to stand out—not necessarily for our eloquence, but apparently because somehow we seemed different. People couldn't put their fingers on it, but they sensed that we were not like them, so they were drawn to us. Tom and I were getting used to this, but even though we tried to adopt local terminology, old habits don't die easily.

One man, a lieutenant in the militia, came over to us. As he did so, I noticed that he was followed by a small entourage. He was obviously well respected and clearly had a certain presence. The room quieted as he stopped and was about to speak. It wasn't because of great size, for he was slightly more than average in height and neither heavy nor slight. Tom and I stopped talking with others around us and turned our attention to the lieutenant.

"Name's Henry Upton. Lieutenant in the Concord militia. I hear that you two came over from Salem. Is that right?"

"Yes, lieutenant. We're about to leave for Salem shortly. What can we do for you?"

"I know that Colonel Barrett would like to send a report of today's battle to Colonel Pickering or Colonel Mason over in Salem. We like to keep each other informed. Would you two mind staying in Concord a bit longer till Colonel Barrett can finish his report?" I looked at Tom and he nodded fine, so I said, "No problem, sir. Be glad to. When do you think it will be done?"

"I estimate an hour or two. It's important we get this off soon."

As he was about to leave I spoke up. "Pardon me, lieutenant, but why did you choose us to be your couriers?"

He smiled for the first time. "I spoke with some of the boys here and they all said you two seemed a mite better informed than most of the men in my unit. They said you seemed a mite more clever, too."

I couldn't help but take satisfaction from his assessment. After all, we were like two men coming to a new country from a foreign country and not only managing to get by, but actually gaining recognition for what we knew. It was pretty gratifying to be excelling on someone else's turf.

Someone should have reminded me of the Biblical adage: *pride goeth before a fall* because we were indeed headed for a fall. I was still riding high from the lieutenant's flattering words when he said, "Because you two are so well informed I'm afraid I'm going to have to confine you to our local jail. At first I thought I'd send my report to Salem with you fellows, but I'm not sure I can trust you." He motioned to two soldiers standing just to his rear and said, "Take these two to the jail near the courthouse. If they give you any trouble, shoot 'em."

"Why are you doing this?" I protested frantically. "We've done nothing."

"That's for us to determine. The way I see it you know far too much. Much more than a militiaman should know or be expected to know."

"You're taking us prisoner because we're well informed?" asked Tom incredulously.

"That and the fact that you were seen aiding a bloody Redcoat."

"My God," I said, "the man was bleeding out. The fighting was over, and he was no more a threat than that chair."

"You've got an insolent mouth on you, haven't you? I've got an odd feeling about you two. We'll talk when you've had a chance to think about whose side you're on. Take them away, men. I'll be over later, and we'll have ourselves a little chat."

I looked at Tom as we were prodded along out of the crowded tavern. All eyes turned our way. Suddenly the rush of satisfaction turned to embarrassment and anger at our plight.

"Jesus," I said as we hit daylight, "this wasn't in the script. Is this guy a pain in the ass or is it us?"

"Good question," said Tom. "Guess we're not reading people as well as we thought. I think we're pretty normal, but maybe there's a bigger difference between our normal and their's than we thought. Not good to get too comfortable, at least until you get to know the local culture better."

"Hell, we've been here six or seven months. We should have picked up on all that by now."

"Maybe should've, but obviously we didn't." He thought for a moment; then said, "Or maybe the lieutenant really is a pain in the ass."

One of our captors then said, "That kind of talk'll keep you locked up a long time, soldier. You're not acting too smart if you ask me. I was you, I'd keep my mouth shut."

That was probably the best advice we'd had in a long time.

Chapter 42

The Concord town jail was in the basement of a three story brick building near the village green. It was cold and damp down there. Water was leaking slowly through most of the cracks. The two soldiers pushed us both into a single narrow cell. As the shock of what we were going through started to sink in I took note of our surroundings. The cell couldn't have been more than eight by ten feet. In the corner was a ceramic chamber pot. On each side was a very narrow cot with a straw mattress, if you could call it that. That was it. No TV.

After taking in our immediate situation I saw that there were three other cells in the dank basement. The entire jail consisted of four cells. That was it. The other cells were empty at the moment, but I imagined we'd be getting company soon.

After depositing us in our cell, the militiamen left, saying nothing. As they were leaving I yelled out, "When do we get to defend ourselves?"

One of the soldiers stopped and said, "You'll get your say sometime. Right now we're rather busy." That was it. He joined his partner and left.

Tom and I were exhausted, and if the circumstances were different, we would have welcomed the chance to lie down and rest. A cold, damp jail cell wasn't exactly what we had in mind, though. We were no longer hungry, thanks to our stop at Wright's Tavern. Unfortunately, we could also thank our stop at the tavern for the situation we now found ourselves in.

We had no watches so it was hard to judge how much time had passed just waiting in that cell, but I estimated that it was at least two hours before we heard someone coming. At least I hoped they were coming. Then we heard the clop, clop of boots on the stairs leading down to our basement cell area.

There were two of them. I recognized Lieutenant Upton and Colonel Barrett, the commander of the Concord militia. They were grim-faced as they approached our cell and stood outside the bars facing us. They remained silent for a full minute, I suppose waiting to see if we might break down and confess at the very sight of them. That wasn't going to happen. Finally Colonel Barrett spoke.

"Lieutenant Upton here tells me that my men think you're spies."

I wanted to say his men were full of crap, but decided that wouldn't help our case, so I said,

"Respectfully, sir, they're mistaken. Nothing could be farther from the truth."

"I don't have much time, so you're going to have to be mighty persuasive, or I'll leave you here for a military trial at the convenience of the Concord militia."

"Might I ask, sir, why your men think we're spies?"

Barrett looked at Upton and said, "Tell 'em, Henry. Make it quick."

Upton, who was a greengrocer when not fighting in the militia, was not used to such confrontational situations. It took him a moment to collect his thoughts.

"You were seen giving aid and comfort to a regular. You were heard speaking with great knowledge of Redcoat strategy. You spoke of events as if you had advance knowledge of their occurrence. When you speak you do not sound like one of us. You sound as if you come from some distant place." Barrett gave him a questioning look at this last indictment. Then he turned to us.

"I'd be obliged if you responded to what the lieutenant said."

"We already explained to the lieutenant that the regular was lying on the ground bleeding out. All we did was stop the bleeding and bring him into town where he could get medical attention. He was no longer a threat. The fighting had ended."

Upton leaped on this. "But you helped him when you could've helped one of our own."

"He was the first fallen soldier we came to. I thought we were civilized. We don't deliberately let soldiers die when the threat is over." I stared directly into the eyes of the colonel. "Do we?"

Barrett scowled and said, "No, we don't."

Then I added, "We didn't help him escape. Once he was attended to I'm sure your men took him prisoner. In fact I'm surprised he's not in one of these cells."

Barrett turned to Upton. "Where is he?"

"He's upstairs. We've taken the most seriously wounded up there. Temporary hospital. We couldn't leave 'em out in the field, could we?"

I could only imagine what the "hospital" floor upstairs looked like. More like a charnel house than anything Tom or I knew as a hospital. Few American doctors in the eighteenth century had medical degrees. Those who did had few skills of any value to their patients.

Barrett nodded grimly and confronted me again. "Where did you get this great knowledge of Redcoat strategy?"

"What little knowledge we have we got at Colonel Mason's Committee of Safety meetings in Salem." That had to satisfy him because the honest answer would have labeled us as real "nutters." It was tempting to fess up because we did know what was going to happen next between the regulars and the colonials, at least in a general sense. However, we didn't know what was going to happen to us.

If we told them that we knew how the war was going to proceed, they wouldn't believe us and they'd treat us like we were from outer space, which, in fact, we were.

The colonel was studying me, trying to decide if he could trust me. I decided to keep speaking. "As for speaking like we were from far away, we are from far away. Both of us came to Salem from Halifax, so it shouldn't be surprising that we have a different accent."

He nodded, as if it made sense to him, but said, "You could still be Tories, couldn't you?"

Tom stepped closer to the bars now and said, "I suppose we could, but why would we fight with your militia? If we supported the regulars, why wouldn't we enlist with them? Or stay out of the fight entirely?"

Upton said, "You couldn't spy on us if you fought with them, could you?"

"That makes no sense at all!" I blurted out. "As soon as I said it, I wished I'd kept quiet. Doesn't help to imply that your captors are idiots.

"I've heard enough," said Barrett. "I need to think on it." He looked at Upton and said, "Let's go upstairs. I want to talk to the wounded. We can discuss this later."

I looked at Tom and said, "I've been thinking about how we all along have believed we couldn't die in the eighteenth century. Wanna hear my latest thinking on the subject?"

Chapter 43

My mouth and eyes were open wide as I looked at Tom with my hands outstretched, palms upward. This was a helluva situation we'd gotten ourselves into. Why had the colonel not given us a clue as to what our fate was? To make matters worse, we no longer were convinced that we couldn't die in this century. Even if we survived being incarcerated, who knew how long we'd spend in this cold, dismal lockup?

For the first time since we'd arrived in the eighteenth-century, Tom was not upbeat. Just the opposite now. He looked totally defeated and discouraged.

"This is getting to you, isn't it?" I said sympathetically.

"You bet your ass it is," he said bitterly. "Traveling two years into the future seemed pretty cool from the comfort of our labs in Nevada. Exciting and even glamorous. Maybe it would have been, but we didn't bargain for this. I think we were too young to make the decision to do this."

"Hell, man, we didn't decide on this. We were younger when we thought that two years into the future would be exciting. It probably would have been, too. But, hey, you're right. We didn't ask for this. Still, when you look at it, up until now we've adjusted fairly well. You even have a girlfriend. Look, you know that we're gonna get out of this. I have no idea how, but somehow we will. You'll be back with Jennie before you know it. C'mon, we both agree that despite the old-fashioned living conditions, this hasn't been all bad. The technology is primitive, but the people are pretty much the same."

"Pretty much the same until now."

"C'mon, you can see how we might look a little suspicious."

"I suppose, but how do we prove our innocence? If we tell the truth, they'll lock us up forever in some loony bin."

"I don't think they have insane asylums in this century," I said.

"Whatever. The truth certainly won't help us."

"If we tell most of the truth, I think it will. Assuming they believe us. We just omit the time-travel part."

"Ya think."

I didn't like the way his mind was going so I brought up something that we both knew was an extreme long shot. "I suppose you're now holding onto the hope, remote as it is, that the folks back at the CAE will come up with a way to get us back? You do know how unlikely that is."

"I won't lie. It has crossed my mind more than once lately. Yeah, I know how unlikely it is. C'mon, are you saying you're totally happy in this time warp?"

"Hey, who's totally happy?" I said, "But yes, I could stay."

"If the CAE landed a ship here in the next couple of years, you wouldn't want to return home?"

"Of course. Look, you know the technology wasn't there when we left. Maybe it was in a year or two. It's including all of the fuel and initial liftoff thrust technology to enable a trip back that's iffy. Too much weight. I wouldn't count on it happening. Besides, they'd have to land at or near the same spot or we'd never find it." I thought for a moment and then added, "Look, you're in love with Jennie. If you could go back, would you?"

He shook his head disconsolately. "I guess not."

Since we first signed up for this mission I'd always thought Tom was rock solid. Frankly, at times as we were going through training, there were moments when I thought he was tougher than I was. Now, when things weren't going well, I could see that it was getting to him. As I thought about it, and unfortunately we did have plenty of time to think, I had to admit that I could understand how he felt. We were 240 years away from the only lives we'd ever known. This wasn't what we'd signed up for.

I'd adapted to the eighteenth century better than Tom had. Did that mean that I had a screw loose, or was I just better at dealing with my new reality? I certainly couldn't blame Tom for having doubts—especially now, when we were in a cell that you'd find in horror movies in future centuries. Maybe Tom's stressing out made him more human than me. Maybe I was the strange one because it didn't bother me as much. Well, that's not exactly true. At times like this, I did miss the comforts of the twenty-first century. At times like this I felt a tug of homesickness. What surprised the hell out of me was how comfortable I'd gotten living in this century. Guess I was just an old-fashioned kind of guy. As I thought about it I realized that we'd both been flip-flopping on whether we wanted to stay or not.

"When do you think we'll get out of here?" asked Tom soberly. "You seem to think it's only a matter of time."

"I want to believe we'll be out sometime today. I'm hoping we convinced Barrett, and he needs to justify in his own mind letting us go free."

It was hard to estimate the passage of time because there was no window in the cell. The only sounds we heard were faint voices from the street. I was beginning to think we would spend at least the night in the jail. As time passed and no one came, one night seemed optimistic. Had we been forgotten? Would they even feed us? Would they just let us rot here?

I wished now that I had access to paper and quill so that I could update my trip's log. Good way to kill time. Of course, if I had a cell phone I could record my thoughts and then transcribe them later. Now I *was* dreaming. As far as the log was concerned, it's something we'd agreed we'd do as soon as we got settled in Salem. The idea was that we'd somehow figure out a way to get a written accounting to the folks back at CAE. Because I enjoyed writing, I'd volunteered to do it. It was to be an accounting of our trip including liftoff, travel through space and a year or so of our time in the eighteenth century.

Recently we'd given serious consideration to making sure that our accounting got to CAE in Nevada **BEFORE** we actually lifted off from the Nevada desert. The idea was that by doing so we could tell them about the malfunction of the onboard computer that had caused us to end up 240 years in the past instead of two years in the future as planned. We would urge them not to launch the mission in the first place. I say we had given this serious consideration because we hadn't agreed on whether we wanted to go back or not. Tom, now that he was in love with Jennie, was fairly sure he wanted to stay where he was. I, on the other hand, was leaning toward returning, though even I wasn't absolutely sure that that was the right choice.

We hadn't quite figured out how, but we hoped to plant the document in some institution that existed in the eighteenth century, but had survived into the twenty-first century. After much thinking we settled on the Salem Athenæum. There were other possibilities, but this suited our needs best since it was located in Salem. Having grown up on Boston's North Shore, I was aware of the Athenæum. My foster parents had even attended events there, so I knew it had survived into the twenty-first century. Ideally we would have placed copies of the document in several such institutions for retrieval later, but as there were no copying machines in the eighteenth century and no hi-speed printers, one place would have to do.

To be perfectly accurate, there was no Salem Athenæum in 1775, but its predecessor, the Social Library, did exist, and we knew that it had merged with the Philosophical Library in 1810 to form the Salem Athenæum. Our problem was to convince the people in charge of the Social Library to preserve the document to be retrieved by a certain person or persons on a certain date in the twenty-first century. Not a small problem. Why would the Social Library director agree to such stipulations? Our thinking was that he would, provided we called it a time capsule and provided we paid them to do it. There was no guarantee that Tom or I would have enough money to extract such a commitment so we decided that we would pay a modest amount now with the commitment that the retrievers in the twenty-first century would pay one hundred times that amount so that the library of the future would benefit greatly. We would tell them that our time capsule was to be opened on the 250th anniversary of one of our parents' death. The agreement would stipulate that inside the capsule the Athenæum folks of the future would find instructions to contact our descendants.

Actually it would be instructions to contact any of our former colleagues at the CAE in Nevada.

If the Social Library folks agreed to that, wouldn't they still want to know what was so important in the time capsule? We were sure that they would, so we agreed that we would tell them that the time capsule contained our memories of our deceased parent plus some of his important documents. We figured, though, that we'd have to explain what we meant by the term "time capsule." We were fairly certain the term wasn't in use in this century.

"Gil, did you hear that?" said Tom startling me and shaking me out of my mental wanderings. It was the sound of boots again on the stairs. It turned out to be Lieutenant Upton. He greeted us with a frown.

"You boys got lucky. The colonel thinks you're innocent. I'm not so sure."

"You going to let us out?" asked Tom hopefully.

"Yep."

"Must kill you," I said.

He gave me a look, pursing his lips sourly, but saying nothing as he turned the heavy metal key in the cell door.

As the wrought-iron door clanked shut behind us I couldn't resist asking Upton why he'd been so suspicious of us.

"I thought we were having a decent conversation back at the tavern. I didn't sense that you were suspicious at the time. What made you think we were spies?" I probed.

He stopped in his tracks and put his hand to his forehead. "I think it was just the way you seemed so well informed about everything," he said thoughtfully.

"You mean we sounded like know-it-alls?" said Tom.

"Now see, that's what I mean," said Upton.

"I don't understand," I said. "What is it that you mean?"

"Know-it-alls. I have never heard anyone say that. I suppose I can guess what you mean, but people around here don't talk like that." He grimaced as he tried to explain what he meant. "But that's only part of it. You fellers seem to have a self confidence about you that I don't see around here. You seem to know too much about too many things. Just gave me a funny feeling about you from the first. I know, I know. Ain't no crime to know a lot. Wish I did myself. But I wasn't the only one. Some of the boys back at the tavern said, they had the same feeling."

"Then you really don't like us very much, do you?" asked Tom bluntly.

"Tain't that, really. Funny thing is we did take a liking to you boys. We just thought that was somethin' you put on to cover up your spyin'."

We had a real honest exchange for another five minutes or so as we walked out of the building and across the green. By the time we were near the stable where we'd left our horses, I think Upton had actually changed his mind about us. He gave us directions to Salem and bid us good riding. As we were about to leave I remembered that Colonel Barrett had wanted us to carry a message to Colonel Pickering in Salem. I asked the lieutenant if Barrett still wanted us to be his couriers.

Upton forced a sheepish smile and said, "He sent his message with another man who was goin' to Salem."

"Guess he doesn't totally trust us yet," I said.

"He does now, but he had his doubts for awhile. He needed to send it as soon as possible. When he sent it, he hadn't made up his mind about you two. As I said, he does trust you now or you wouldn't be goin' free."

"What changed his mind?" I asked.

"Said he'd talked to a few of the militia boys, and they said they saw you right in the thick of battle doin' your part. Not what some weaselly spies would be doin.' Anyway, have a good trip back, and mind the trails just east of Lexington. Lots of ruts and you could have trouble crossin' some of the creeks. Specially at night. You probably should stay till morning. Lot easier to ride those roads and trails in daylight."

We were eager to get out of Concord, though, and willing to risk the rutted trails and precarious water crossings along the way. Besides, where would we stay? I was pretty sure the few rooms over Wright's Tavern were already taken.

Our trip back to Salem was fairly uneventful. Before we even went to Mrs. Inglesby's we passed Colonel Mason's house to see if he might still be up. We guessed it was somewhere approaching midnight when we arrived at his house. Lights were still on so we knocked on the door. We were certain he'd want our report on the events at Lexington and Concord.

Mason answered the door himself and greeted us like we were long-lost brothers.

"Glad you're here, boys. Come in, come in." He stood back a step and regarded us with arms outstretched. I looked around the room and recognized a few faces: Henry Woodbury, Jonathan Felt, Richard Derby and Sam Hall. We shook hands as Mason said, "God God, lads, you look terrible. I take it you were in Lexington?"

"Lexington and Concord both," I said. "I won't deny that we're tired, but we thought it best to tell you what we know before we got ourselves some shuteye."

Mason looked at me as if I were speaking Chinese and I quickly said, "It's a term we use up north. Means—"

"I think I take your meaning, Gil. Sit, sit. Will you have some coffee or beer?"

Tom had coffee, and I accepted a pint of beer. The provincials made a good hearty beer. Not as cold as I liked it, but still damned good. As I plopped myself down I wondered how much the group knew about what happened in Lexington and Concord.

"'We're glad you're here. We got a report a few hours ago from a man who was visiting his mother in Lexington. He told us that we lost a good many men there. So far his report is the only report we have. What can you tell us?"

"To lose any is bad," I said, "but I don't think we lost many. My estimate would be somewhere between six and ten. That's at Lexington, but I think that's because the regulars stopped shooting at that point and moved on toward Concord. In our opinion it's a good thing they stopped because we were outnumbered greatly in Lexington. I'd say four to one or more. We would have taken greater losses if Colonel Smith had continued his attack. Tom and I think he concluded that he'd taught us a lesson and had no desire to turn it into a full-fledged battle. We think his object was to get to the weapons in Concord and go back to Boston without further conflict if he could avoid it."

"He leads a regiment of regulars into a town and expects us to roll over," interjected Woodbury angrily.

"I agree it's the height of arrogance," I said. "but I believe that's what he and Gage thought. The regulars had been stymied in Salem back in February, but it appears that Gage figured if he sent enough men to Lexington and Concord, we'd be cowed by the numbers and give them what they wanted. Then, after what they no doubt considered an annoying skirmish in Lexington where they killed a few of our men, Tom and I believe Smith became even more arrogant. We think he felt that after that we'd have no fight left in us. The fact is, Captain Parker, who leads the Lexington militia, called his men off when he saw that the regulars were heading off toward Concord. Parker and his men had stood their ground in the face of overwhelming British forces, even though it was clear that we would not have prevailed if the regulars continued their assault. Parker saw that nothing would be gained by further engaging the regulars once they stopped their assault. He thereby kept his losses to a minimum while showing Smith and his men that they weren't afraid to defend themselves."

"Mmm...," said Richard Derby, "so the Redcoats deliberately engaged the militia in Lexington? Gage must really want a war. How did the fighting start?"

"We honestly can't say," chimed in Tom. "It's not clear who fired the first shot. Might have been one of our militiamen, or it might have been one of the regulars."

"It seemed to me," I interjected, "that someone got nervous and fired unintentionally. Once that shot was heard, all hell broke loose."

"It's terrible what happened to those men in Lexington," said Mason but if that's the extent of it, maybe they don't want a real war. As you said, Gil," they could have continued the fighting, but they didn't.'"

"They did nothing else in Lexington," I said, "but Smith sent some units on to Concord, where things got even bloodier." This got the attention of everyone in the room.

"Dear God, Gil, go on," said our boss, Sam Hall. "We've heard nothing about Concord. What in God's name happened there?"

Tom and I went into some detail, explaining the fighting, how it began and how the two of us ended up in the village clink for a few hours. We explained how we lost more men and how this time, the regulars lost more men than we did. As we told it, it dawned on us and the others in the room that we all had rather mixed feelings about what had happened.

On the plus side, it was good to know that we had prevailed in Concord. We'd sent the Redcoats back to Boston in total disarray. I honestly don't think most of those young regulars ever expected to be in a real battle. I think they went back toward Boston scared out of their wits.

However, every last one of us in the room realized or at least suspected that what had gone down in Lexington and Concord might just be the beginning of an actual war with our home country. Of course Tom and I knew that was exactly what was happening, but we had to act as if we merely suspected it. To be honest, it wasn't that hard to act that way because, when you're living something, you're in the moment and the feelings of others around you are pretty much your own feelings. The sense of impending war was definitely in the air in the room. Little did the other men in the room know that many more would be killed as the regulars made their way back to Boston. The vast majority of deaths would come after the Redcoats left Concord. If any of the others had any doubts that Lexington and Concord was the beginning of the war, they would be dispelled the next morning when they learned about the additional fighting between Concord and

Boston.

Richard Derby, a successful shipping merchant in Salem and father to two even more successful sons, spoke for the first time. He was probably the oldest man in the room, and clearly a presence. "I think most of us expected something like this would happen sooner or later. After Leslie's retreat here in Salem it was inevitable that Gage would feel that a show of force was necessary to preserve the Crown's dominance over these American colonies. It's critical now that we learn what happened as the regulars returned to Boston. If they marched peacefully without further provocation, these incidents in Lexington and Concord may be nothing more than unpleasant and deadly skirmishes. However, if we find that there's been further bloodshed on the march back to Boston, I'm afraid we must face the unpleasant fact that we're at war with the world's greatest military power. Not a happy undertaking."

"You may very well be right, Richard," said Mason soberly, "but I'm afraid what's happened in Lexington and Concord may already have taken us too far. Both sides have gone beyond protest and diplomacy. We may already be at war with our fellow British citizens, regardless of what took place on the regulars' march back to Boston. A sad situation. In any event, I have a suggestion. I believe it's of the utmost importance that someone representing the colonial interests report on the events at Lexington and Concord to the authorities in London before Gage sends someone there with their version. We have friends in Parliament and other important parts of the government in London. If we can get our version of events their before Gage does, who knows? King George himself may begin to understand our side of things. Maybe we can yet avoid an all-out war."

Derby leaned forward, eyes wide with excitement. "Excellent idea, David. We need to send a courier to the Provincial Congress in Watertown. If they agree to this idea, I will personally provide a fast ship and my son John as its captain." The Massachusetts Provincial Congress lately had moved from place to place in order to avoid Gage's interference. It had been in Salem, Concord and Cambridge before moving to Watertown. "Derby scanned the room to see how his fellow Patriots received his offer. Seeing nods of agreement, he added,

"Things may have progressed too far for this to help, but we should make the effort anyway if there's even a slight chance of avoiding all-out war. I believe most of us are willing, perhaps even eager to defend these colonies if it comes down to it, but we all know that our chances of prevailing are not good. If we can resolve our differences peacefully, Britain and the American colonies will be better for it."

"All right then," said Mason, "I think we should vote on this. All in favor of sending a courier to London, assuming the Provincial Congress agrees, say aye."

The vote in favor of the proposal was unanimous.

It was then left to decide who would be sent to Watertown. After a brief discussion I volunteered to go if Sam Hall could get by without me for another day. He, himself, couldn't go because he had to get out a paper bringing his readers up-to-date on the report Tom and I had brought back from Lexington and Concord. Both Felt and Woodbury had offered, but I said it made sense for me to go since I had first-hand knowledge of what went on yesterday. Derby didn't offer, but no one expected him to. He was too old for such a fast trip and, besides, his offer of a ship and his son to captain the ship was more than enough. Mason, as the leader of the Committee of Safety, and a close associate of Timothy Pickering, the head of the Salem militia, was needed in Salem. There was no need to send two people to Watertown, so I went and Tom stayed in Salem to help Hall get out the next edition of the *Gazette*.

Chapter 44

April 1775

The Provincial Congress met three days after the battles at Lexington and Concord. After much deliberation, they finally voted to send an emissary to London. The depositions took a few days to complete as the congress members strove for completeness so as not to be faulted for inaccuracy or distortion of the facts. They wanted to include the accounts of all possible eyewitnesses. As they went about collecting this supporting information, they began to worry about the time this cautious process was taking. It was imperative that Derby and crew depart as soon as possible or they would arrive too late.

As soon as I returned to Salem from Watertown I focused on helping Sam and the others prepare the next issue of the *Gazette*, which would report on what happened in Lexington and Concord, as well as the brutal fighting between Concord and Boston. The march back to Boston had been bloodier than the battles in either of the two towns.

As we worked feverishly to get out the next edition, Sam told me that Mason had dropped by to try to recruit Tom and me as crew members for the *Quero*. I was flabbergasted at this, since my experience as a sailor was limited to a few outings on a 14-foot Sunfish. Obviously I wouldn't mention that. Of course I'd claimed that we'd helped crew on the ship that brought Tom and me to Salem from Portland. Since only Tom and I knew that that ship was a figment of our imaginations, we were stuck with our seafaring reputations. The fact of the matter was, Mason wanted at least one of us on that ship, not for our sailing expertise so much as for our ability to express ourselves about Lexington and Concord when we got to London. He was certain that at least one of us would be a welcome aide to Captain Derby when he met with dignitaries in the British capital.

Hall said he thought one of us should go. He agreed with Mason that we were more knowledgable than most of the crew members he was familiar with, and we did express ourselves well. However, he urged us to decide which one would go. He couldn't afford to lose both of us for several months. After some deliberation I was chosen, which was great because I saw this as an adventure and a fantastic opportunity to see the beginning of the American Revolution from the British point-of-view.

I had only one concern. I was afraid that Derby would resent me or reject me out of hand, since it seemed that I was being foisted upon him by Mason. Sam said, *au contraire*. Mason and John Derby were close friends, and Derby respected Mason's judgement. There would be no problem—so long as I held my own as a crew member. That, of course, was the rub. I wouldn't say that I was clueless when it came to sailing, but I certainly wasn't going to look like an experienced sailor. That's where Tom came in. He suggested that I make myself useful in other ways so that Derby wouldn't look to me for sailing skills. "You could help him with navigation. Remember, you told me that you studied navigating with old sextants when you were learning to use that old printing press. Your curiosity about old stuff will pay off." He grinned. "You could volunteer to write up a log or diary or some such thing to record the trip over, when you get there and then your return trip." Suffice it to say, I became a crew member.

As it was, we were not at all certain that Derby would beat out Gage's ship, the *Sukey*. Word reached the Provincial Congress that a Lieutenant Nunn had been given the task of carrying Lieutenant Colonel Smith's report to London. The *Sukey* had already sailed on the 24th of April. Derby was still recruiting a crew for his sleek, but small 62-ton *Quero*, so we were already behind the *Sukey* before we even left Salem. Our sailors were told that the mission was one of absolute secrecy. No one but Derby and I knew the destination until the ship was out at sea. The only thing they were told was that the mission was of a patriotic nature on behalf of the Provincial Congress.

Captain Derby had the crew well in hand now, and awaited word from the Provincial Congress that he should sail. Every day the *Quero* remained in port added to the *Sukey's* head-start. The *Quero* was fast, but it couldn't perform miracles. Finally, on the 27th, the Provincial Congress directed Captain Derby to set sail for Dublin or any other port in Ireland and from there to go to Scotland or England and on to London with all due haste. This circuitous route was ordered so that Derby and his ship could avoid detection by the British Navy or any enemy officials who might try to interfere with the mission.

The Provincial Congress had finally completed its report just as some of the more frustrated members were on the point of sending anything just to get to England before Nunn.

Derby was given an address to be distributed to the people of Great Britain, which clearly set forth the grievances of the colonists, stressing that their devotion to the king was in no way diminished by the expression of these complaints. *"Nevertheless,"* it added, *"to the persecution and tyranny of his cruel ministry we will not tamely submit."*

In addition to the address to the people, Captain Derby took with him depositions setting forth the views of numerous individuals who had witnessed the battles. He also carried with him several copies of our *Essex Gazette*. Derby was also given a letter to Benjamin Franklin, the colonial agent in London for the Provincial Congress, urging him to arrange for the immediate printing and dispersal of the address and the depositions throughout every town in England. A special request was also made to communicate the address and depositions to the influential Lord Mayor of London.

On the morning of the 28[th,] the *Quero* set sail out of Salem. Once out to sea, Captain Derby resisted the temptation to reveal their destination to the crew. He didn't tell them where they were going until they were off the banks of Newfoundland. It wasn't easy maintaining the spirits of the crew, as many of them felt that they'd already lost the race, since they now knew that the *Sukey* had departed Boston four days before them. True, the *Quero* was a faster ship, but it couldn't fly.

As the days passed, the trim *Quero* benefited from a following wind much of the way across the Atlantic. Derby and the crew were fortunate, too, that we ran into very little foul weather or angry seas. Many of the crew remained skeptical, but became somewhat less pessimistic as we neared the Irish coast, since the few experienced transatlantic seamen among us said they'd never had a swifter, less eventful crossing. They were sure they'd made up some of the time lost to the *Sukey*, but it was impossible to know how much, since they had no way of knowing where the *Sukey* was. It was times like this that radios and satellite phones would have come in handy. Of course, even if we and the *Sukey* had such technological conveniences, the *Sukey* wouldn't contact us. However, we *would* be able to contact London and find out if Nunn had arrived there.

But I digress. We didn't, and they didn't, so we had to hope that somehow we still had a chance, however small, to get there first.

Of course I knew what the outcome would be, but I couldn't tell anyone. I could speculate like the rest of the crew members and the captain, himself, but that's all I could do. In the meantime, I got myself a fine tan and became a better sailor than I was when we set sail. Fortunately I didn't get seasick. I was surprised to find that some of the experienced seamen did suffer from *mal de mer*.

Captain John Derby proved to be one hell of a human being. He was in his mid-thirties when I met him and the youngest son of Captain Richard Derby. His older brother, Elias Haskett Derby was to become the first millionaire in America. While not as wealthy as Elias, John had no money worries. He was respected by the crew members because he didn't just give orders. He took his turn at winches, standing watch and all manner of activities sailors were expected to do. He handled disputes between the men with a fine blend of diplomacy and firmness. Never did I see him show favoritism. Never did he show weakness. I learned later that he took no pay for executing the voyage to London, although he did submit a statement of expenses to the Provincial Congress for reimbursement for such items as *three barrels of bread, 56 pounds of beef, candles, small beer, greens, expenses at the Isle of Wight and Southampton, post-chaise hire from London to Falmouth.* In all the expenses came to £57.

Derby took a liking to me and confided in me about many of the details of the mission. In the eighteenth century you have a lot of time to get to know someone on a transatlantic voyage. Derby said that he wanted me to accompany him when he contacted Franklin and certain other important people in London. I was flattered and delighted. This would put me right square in the middle of events of great historical significance.

After we'd been out a few days, the crew got tired of dried beef and bread and decided to catch some fish. This wasn't difficult as more than a few of our sailors had also been fishermen at one point in their lives. I was as pleased as the rest of the crew to vary my diet with cod, haddock and countless other fish.

It was on reaching the Irish coast that Derby made the first of what proved to be several wise—or lucky—decisions, depending on which you prefer to believe. His instructions were to head for the nearest port in Ireland and from there to find his way to Scotland or England and then on to London. Soon after leaving Salem, he told me confidentially, that he thought of nothing else than the implications of arriving in London too late. Now, with the benefit of the *Quero's* swift crossing, he realized that, if he gambled and ignored Ireland and headed directly for the English Channel, they might reach London first. He knew he'd made excellent time crossing the Atlantic, but he still had no way of knowing if he'd beaten the *Sukey*. He figured that he was probably behind, so he had nothing to lose by heading straight for the Channel.

On May 27 the *Quero* dropped anchor off the Isle of Wight, just 29 days since leaving Salem. Excellent time for an ocean crossing. Derby and I left the ship and proceeded to Southampton on the mainland. Before leaving the ship Captain Derby instructed his second in command to take the ship to Falmouth and to wait for us there to be ready to sail at a moment's notice.

When we got to Southampton Derby hired a post-chaise at the rate of nine pence per mile. Before we set out for London, though, he inquired if anyone had heard of the fighting at Lexington and Concord. The answer was a resounding "no." Could we have actually beaten the Sukey?

The trip to London was a long 80 miles. While the roads were at times in bad shape compared with twenty-first century roads, they were a cut or two better than the roads between Salem and Boston, which were really not much more than trails. That was because the English roads had been around for a lot longer, and with the passage of time they gradually improved them. The traffic was much heavier in England because of the greater population, so they apparently felt compelled to keep the roads in tolerable condition. Despite this favorable comparison to New England roads the trip was still bumpy, dirty and tedious.

None of this mattered to Derby or myself as all our thoughts were on what we would do when we got to London. We were both eager for our meeting with the world-famous Dr. Franklin.

When we arrived at the building that Franklin and his staff were staying in on Craven Street near Charing Cross, we were disappointed to learn that the great man had returned to America and that Arthur Lee had taken his place as London agent for the Continental Congress. Franklin had learned of the death of his wife back in February, but postponed returning home until just recently. Apparently, despite receiving numerous letters from his ailing wife urging him to come home, he'd convinced himself that she was going to be all right once she got past this bout of illness. He was known for his penchant for viewing information in the most positive of ways. Some might say that despite his brilliance he was all too prone to self-deception.

Arthur Lee was well respected in London, as he'd lived many years in England. He was born in Virginia, but spent much of his young life in England. He'd attended Eton College and the University of Edinburgh, graduating in 1765. He earned degrees in both law and medicine and practiced law in London for five years. As I said, he was well respected, which gave him access to important people. An access we desperately needed.

Derby filled Lee in as to what had happened, turning to me frequently for my on-the-scenes observations. Lee quickly grasped everything we told him and was glad for the documentation we'd brought with us. When we were finished he thanked us repeatedly for all we had done and complimented Derby for beating the *Sukey* to England. He gave us a brief written letter introducing us to Lord North, the prime minister. He said he couldn't promise that the PM would see us, but he thought it likely.

Lord North did agree to see us, and I admit that I was so nervous that I felt myself shaking. I prayed that it didn't show. The Prime Minister couldn't have been more welcoming. I got the feeling that he liked us American colonials. At least that's the impression he gave. My first impression of him was that he was a bit roly poly and soft. Hardly what one would expect of one of the most powerful men in the world. I soon learned, though, that his physical appearance belied the internal strength of personality that came through as time in his presence passed. By the time we were finished I understood completely why the king and other key people had chosen him to run the government. One minute I'm noticing this overfed, soft-looking man. The next minute I realize that Lord North, by the very force of his personality, has taken over the room.

John did a fine job of presenting our version of the events at Lexington and Concord. I think my first-hand observations added a bit of authenticity to our presentation. When we finished, the PM leaned back in his chair, thumb and forefinger on his chin, and said nothing for an uncomfortably long time. He seemed to be studying us, either forming an evaluation or seeing if we would rattle. Finally he spoke.

"You must be an excellent sailor, Captain Derby. Twenty-nine days across the Atlantic is a rare feat. It seems all you Derbys are high achievers." The PM was well informed, I'll give him that.

"That's very kind of you sir," said John. "We have a schooner designed for speed and luckily we benefited from a consistent trailing wind."

"And you, Mr. Lee, are you by any chance related to Arthur Lee?"

"No, sir, I'm not."

"Well, I think you can imagine my unhappiness with what's transpired in Massachusetts. I'm afraid that so much of what we disagree on is based on misunderstandings that we should be able to work out peacefully. Does that make sense to you?"

John and I nodded our assent and almost jointly said, "Yessir, it does."

He seemed pleased that we didn't respond in a more bellicose manner.

"Good Lord, many of you colonists were born here. We're all British, after all, so why must we fight?"

"I'm sure there are two sides to this, sir," said Derby, "but we colonists believe that London treats us as lesser citizens. We sense that we are deemed of less importance than our fellow citizens here in Britain."

I studied North as John was talking and was impressed by his willingness to listen. He didn't interrupt once. John closed by saying, "We consider some of the taxes imposed on us as punitive and unfair. We also believe that if we *are* to be taxed we should have representatives in Parliament. The events at Lexington and Concord add further insult to these grievances. Governor Gage sent armed troops into our peaceful countryside. He had to know that we would resist such a warlike intrusion. The king does not send regulars into Manchester or Brighton or Newcastle against his own citizens, but he does in America." Derby left it at that. He'd been clear and direct, but he told me later that he didn't think an overly bombastic oratory would help our case with the Prime Minister. We both doubted that many would dare lecture the PM.

"You have been most eloquent in stating your case Captain Derby. I will tell you now, but in confidence, that I do not want Britain to wage war against our American colonies. I have known too many of you Americans, and I like you all. You are bright, ambitious, educated and civilized. I suppose I will eventually hear Gage's side of these sad events." He paused, then said, "You say they departed Boston four days before you left Salem. Damnation! What kind of a scow must they be using! Anyway, once I have digested their side I will make my recommendations to Parliament and King George, and we shall see what we shall see. Hopefully things have not gone too far for both parties to draw back and take a breath. Oh, one more thing. Just a formality, but a formality that will make my job easier." Lord North then told us that he wanted us to meet with the Privy Council to fill them in on Lexington and Concord.

He paused, as if deciding whether to say something else, then said, "Good day gentlemen. Thank you for the information and for your heartfelt opinions. I bid you a safe passage back to Massachusetts."

By the afternoon following our meeting with the Prime Minister, London became aware that there had been an armed conflict between British troops and American Colonials and that a number of men on both sides had been killed. The actual numbers vary, depending on who was counting, but it's almost certain that well over 200 British regulars and more than 70 American Colonials perished that one day.

A few months later it became public knowledge that Lord North had no heart for a war against British provincials in America. Newspaper reports confirmed what he had told us in our private meeting with him in London. As he saw the inevitable conflict looming just over the horizon he tried to resign, but King George would not accept his resignation.

Derby and I dreaded facing the Privy Council. The Council was made up of former high-ranking members of Parliament, a few judges and a few key clergymen. We met with Arthur Lee later that day, and he turned somber at hearing of our upcoming Privy Council meeting. We called it a meeting; he called it an interrogation. He explained to us that Dr. Franklin had gone before the Privy Council in January 1774 to present a petition and a set of resolutions of the Massachusetts Assembly and had been humiliated by a Lord Wedderburne, who distorted facts about the American Colonies, scoffed at the resolutions, and treated Franklin as a criminal; not the well-respected messenger he was. Lee said that Wedderburne had resorted to the coarsest language and the dirtiest of attacks on the character of Franklin. At times during the proceedings, Wedderburne's fellow Council members piled on Franklin, mocking and jeering him instead of presenting a fairer and more evenhanded side to the Privy Council as one would expect from such highly regarded men.

The conclusions of the Privy Council were not always decisive, but their opinions carried considerable weight, and it appeared that the Council members would be going into our meeting with a decided bias.

Before we met with the Privy Council, Arthur Lee said to expect hard questions and little respect. He feared that the Council may have already made up their mind about the American Colonies. It occurred to me for a moment that John and I had a chance to affect history. Of course that was ridiculous, since the die was already cast. Or was it?

Chapter 45

I learned that the Privy Council consisted of four or five hundred members who remain members for life. Rarely, however, does the entire Council meet. Usually it's only somewhere between 15 and 35 members who actually meet, and even then they're not always the same people. The Prime Minister summons the councilors he wants for the upcoming meeting.

Lee saw us just before we left to meet with the Privy Council. He reminded us that the Council would consider our meeting an examination. We should try to control our tempers and make the most of the "examination," no matter how unpleasant it was. The important thing was to form an assessment of how the British authorities seemed to be leaning on the matter of Lexington and Concord and whether they considered themselves at war or were still hoping they could avoid war. Once done, our objective should be to get back to the *Quero* and to head home to inform Hancock, Adams and other key Sons of Liberty members as to how London was viewing recent events. Just as Lee was wishing us luck with the Privy Council he said something that blew me away.

"Gentlemen, I think it will interest you to know that to my knowledge, the *Sukey* has still not arrived here in Britain."

"Very interesting," said John, trying to hide a smile of satisfaction. "Very interesting."

♦ ♦ ♦

Even though the Council cast of characters had apparently changed considerably from the group that had humiliated Dr. Franklin, I noted that at least one member remained the same: Lord Wedderburne. He opened the questioning.

"Captain Derby, you are before us because Lord North believes you have information that would be of interest to us. Please consider yourselves our guests and tell us what you have to say."

I knew that Wedderburne and his Privy Council colleagues had to have some idea of what we were going to share with them; yet Wedderburne acted as if he had no idea. Was he toying with us? Was this some kind of arcane tradition? Or was he the wily, underhanded fox we'd heard about? Derby wasn't rattled as he responded—at least not outwardly.

"Lord Wedderburne, members of the Privy Council, my colleague and I thank you for the opportunity to inform you of the events at Lexington and Concord in the Massachusetts Bay Colony. I'll briefly outline the serious events that transpired—"

Wedderburne sprang to his feet and interrupted Derby. "So they've sent you two to spout more treasonous lies. First Hancock and that firebrand Sam Adams send Franklin to parrot their seditious treason. Now they send you. Is there no end to the treachery coming out of Massachusetts these days?" His eyes were bulging in their sockets as he screamed these indignities toward John and myself, clearly playing to his audience. My first impulse was to stand up myself and shout, "You pompous ass. I'll remind you in a few years how badly you misjudged Dr. Franklin, John Derby and myself. You will live to eat your words." I resisted that impulse because I was the only one in the room who knew with certainty that I was right. I would have had to spend more time explaining myself than was in the best interest of the American colonies, John Derby or myself. I wisely shut up, though it was killing me to do so.

Instead, I paid close attention to how the other Council members reacted. Not one man raised his voice in support of Wedderburne as they apparently had a year-and-a-half earlier when they humiliated Franklin. The fact of the matter was that most of them were turning their heads from side to side in shocked disapproval at the discourtesy being shown to Derby and me.

Wedderburne sputtered a few more vulgar banalities, but slowly ran out of steam as he gradually began to recognize that he had virtually no support in the room. Finally he sat down and Derby proceeded to give an excellent accounting of the events at Lexington and Concord. He admitted that his accounting was based on observations by American militiamen and Minutemen, plus citizens living close by. He assumed that when the *Sukey* arrived Lieutenant Nunn would bring new observations for their consideration. I think what he said, plus a sampling of the depositions he read and excerpts from the *Essex Gazette,* left the impression that the Colonial view of events was relatively fair-minded and objective.

I spoke very little, but did give my observations as a militiaman. They seemed to accept what I said as valid. When John Derby finished his presentation, there was no applause, but many in the Council nodded their apparent approval. Some came up to us afterward and thanked us for traveling so far to give our personal impressions and to share the Colony's accounting of what happened. Still, when all was said and done, it was hard to tell if we'd swayed a majority of the Privy Council present. I suspected that we'd convinced some that we had not provoked the fighting, but most likely not enough to change Britain's thinking. My guess was that many in the room had misread their American brothers.

British government officials had for years misjudged the situation in the American colonies, and this time was probably not going to be an exception. The most cynical of the ministers considered the American colonies insolent provincials who needed to be taught a lesson. The most sympathetic ministers hoped that the outbursts on the other side of the Atlantic were little more than the frustrations of immature colonial settlements lashing out from time to time when they didn't get their way. Maybe it was arrogance. Maybe it was the vast distance. Whatever it was, neither the cynical group nor the sympathetic group fully appreciated the significance of the conflicts at Lexington and Concord.

Chapter 46

Derby, the crew and I left Falmouth on June 1.

The *Sukey* carrying Governor Gage's dispatch finally arrived in England on June 9. Before we left London we spent some time with Arthur Lee, who found it quite remarkable that we should have accomplished our mission and set sail for America before Lieutenant Nunn and the Sukey had even made an appearance on British shores.

We wanted to believe that we'd helped the American cause with our various testimonies, but before we left London Lee brought us down to earth as gently as he could.

"We American colonists have many followers here in Britain. There are many who believe we've been mistreated by the king and Parliament. Yet if pressed, I doubt if very many of these same people would support American independence. They are, after all, British and loyal to their king. They expect nothing less from their American brothers and sisters. I suppose what I'm saying is that we should not mistake sympathy and support for more than it is. Many believe that Parliament has been harsh, nay sometimes even churlish in their handling of the American colonies. They want better for these colonies, but they expect them to remain colonies. And they certainly don't approve of open rebellion. They don't approve of armed resistance to their king."

"So you think our efforts will end in failure?" I asked, having learned to value the opinions of

our colonial agent.

"It depends on what you hope to gain from your efforts. If you want to get their attention here in London, armed resistance has already done that. I have no doubt that the colonies will get tax relief in the coming year. It's too expensive to maintain a standing army on the other side of the Atlantic. It will be cheaper to provide tax benefits."

"One of the things we've been demanding is representation in Parliament," I reminded Lee. "What is the likelihood that that will happen?"

He pursed his lips at that. "I wouldn't count on that, frankly. They still think of us as provincial settlers, not quite at parity with homegrown Brits."

Derby then reminded him of how he'd begun this conversation. "You said it depends on what we hope to gain from our efforts. What if we hoped to gain our independence?"

"As I said before, I don't think they'll permit that. As dearly as it costs them to have standing regiments in North America, it would cost them more if their American colonies broke away. They are, after all, the most powerful empire in the world. Imagine what their other colonies in other parts of the world might do if the Americans rebelled successfully. King George could not afford to grant independence to the American colonies."

"After the conflicts in Lexington and Concord," said Derby, "that might be where this is heading."

"I understand that," said Lee soberly. "Let us all hope that it doesn't come to that.

♦ ♦ ♦

We arrived in Salem on July 19 and learned that Ethan Allan, Benedict Arnold and a small force of Green Mountain Boys had seized Fort Ticonderoga in northern New York. The word was that Arnold and about 80 men overtook a small British garrison at the Fort that overlooked the southern tip of Lake Champlain and was close to neighboring Lake George. It was a small victory in one sense, but was reinforced by another quick victory at nearby Fort Crown Point. This was followed up by still another victory at Fort Saint-Jean in southern Quebec. In each win Allan and his men came away with a number of cannon which were transported over rugged mountain terrain to Boston where they were used by the newly formed Continental army in its Siege of Boston. The siege against British forces had begun almost immediately following the fighting at Lexington and Concord.

In quick succession, while John Derby and I were in England, a number of events took place, rapidly putting the American colonies on a war-time footing with their own mother country.

On May 10, 1775, the Second Continental Congress met in Philadelphia. The issues they confronted were dire. The delegates agreed that the only way to confront the threat of a militant British presence was to form a continental army. On June 15th, George Washington of Virginia was chosen to be the supreme commander of that army. Washington agreed to serve without compensation.

The next thing the congress did was appoint a standing committee to meet with foreign governments, as it was believed that eventually they would be needing outside help if they were going to confront the British Empire.

Then on June 17 the British drove the Americans from Breed's Hill in what was for some strange reason called the Battle of Bunker Hill. While the British were in fact victorious, the Americans took heart from this battle because the only reason they lost was that they ran out of ammunition. Up to that point they had been winning.

Two weeks later, on July 3rd, Washington came to Cambridge, Massachusetts, and took command of the Continental Army.

When we got back to Salem, Tom and I remained involved in our local militia, working at the *Gazette* when we could, but on call when needed by the militia. We considered volunteering for Washington's army, but deferred making a decision. By belonging to the local militia we felt we were doing our part, but we also thought that when we weren't fighting we could help to make sure that accounts of the war were accurate in the local press. If Washington wanted our militia to join his army we'd go.

One night as Tom and I were relaxing in a local Salem tavern with two room-temperature pints, I felt like reflecting on our time in the eighteenth century.

"Do you realize that we've only been here in Salem for about nine months?"

"Feels like half a lifetime."

"If you consider what we've been a part of, it's more than ten lifetimes for most people. We've actually lived what we used to read about."

Tom grinned. "If I'd had the maturity to realize that history is just a way of looking at life through a long-distance lens, I might have gotten more out of it in school."

"Agreed. In all fairness, though, the lens of a history book is pretty foggy. It doesn't allow you to see the human side of things. The way history is presented in most history texts makes it impossible to care for the people they mention. They're just names. You don't get to know them, so you don't care about them. The fact that you're young only makes it harder to appreciate history."

"Amen to that. Say, how you doing on that trip log you've been so diligent about?"

"I think I'm about ready to put a cover on it so that we can take it to the Social Library." Then I hesitated. This was the moment I'd dreaded because it almost certainly was going to be the first time on our trip back in time that we would strongly disagree.

Tom could see that something was bothering me. "What's the problem, bro?"

"Before I wrap this up I was thinking we might add an important message to the document. I was thinking that if we instructed the library to contact CAE before September 2015, that is before we even lifted off, we could include a request that Nevada not launch in the first place. You and I would not be trapped here in the eighteenth century. We could get back to the comfortable lives we'd known." As soon as these words left my mouth I saw his jaw drop. My worst fears were realized."

"Jesus, Gil, you're making an awfully big assumption. You're assuming we both want to go back."

"You don't? We never bargained for this. This is your chance to correct the biggest mistake you'll ever experience in your life."

"True, we didn't bargain for this. And granted, it's a lot harder living in this century than our own. But just because it wasn't in the original plans doesn't mean it's bad. I happen to like it here. I've found Jennie, and I honestly believe I can become an eighteenth century man. Sure, we don't have a lot of advanced stuff, but neither does anyone else in this century. Here people know how to cope, and if nobody else has a cell phone or a laptop, you don't miss it. I'm not at all sure I want to go back."

Now I was pissed. Sure, I'd adjusted okay to colonial life, but presented with the chance to go back to the twenty-first century I wasn't at all sure I'd choose colonial life for the rest of my years. Colonial life was a helluva lot bigger adjustment than acclimating oneself to two years into the future—the adjustment we'd signed up for. I just stared at Tom now, knowing that what I said next was critical to both our lives. Finally I said, "You know what this means don't you?"

"Yeah, it means that one of us is going to resent the other one for the rest of our lives. The only way this can work out halfway decently is if we both agree on one choice or the other. Right now it looks like there's little chance of that."

"You're really serious about Jennie, aren't you?"

"Yes. I am."

"Have you thought about living like this for the rest of your life? Don't answer that. Of course you have."

Tom pursed his lips pensively. "You don't think you could be happy here? You seem pretty content now, or is that just a brave act?"

"I'm not sure I know the answer to that. When I think about it I suppose I was getting sort of used to this lifestyle. A lot of my early doubts have sort of faded away in the last couple of months."

"Until we started to consider the possibility of getting a message back to Nevada before the liftoff. Then the possibility of returning to the twenty-first century became very real."

I tossed this around in my head before saying, "Yeah, I think you're right. I'd adjusted to having no other option, but now that I realize we have one, I'm not sure I want to pass it up."

"If we go back, it means we both go back and it means there will be no evidence that time travel ever worked."

"We'll know it worked." As soon as I said this I realized how stupid it must have sounded. "No, we probably won't, will we?"

"Probably not. If we go back to before we got here, how could we have memory of being here if we never got here?" Tom shook his head as if to rid himself of bewilderment. "Okay, this is beginning to remind me of the logical contradictions I used to think about when I read time-travel books. My guess is we won't remember any of this. Okay, how's it going to be? Are we going or staying?"

I had never been so confused in my life. I didn't say anything for almost a minute. Finally I said, "Give me some time to work this out. Okay."

Chapter 47

It took me a week to make up my mind. I handed Tom the manuscript.

"I want you to read it and give me your input. When you're finished, I'll incorporate your suggestions and prepare the final document."

Tom smiled as if he'd been wondering whether I was going to let him read it. "Glad to, though it won't be easy making corrections. Not like working on a computer."

"True, but better to send them a slightly messy document that's accurate than a neat one we don't agree on."

I was about to change the subject when Tom held up his hand and said, "Whoa there. Whoa. You didn't tell me your decision. Are we going or staying?"

I smiled. "Oh, it's in there. This way I know you'll read it."

♦ ♦ ♦

I had decided that I wanted to remain in the eighteenth century. I came to this conclusion because I convinced myself that I had carved out a good life for myself. I won't deny that the scientist in my wanted to be part of proving that time travel does work. What we were doing was momentous. If we went back, it would all be wasted. No one would ever know that we'd been here. So my reasons were both selfish and altruistic. I suppose many important decisions and choices are a combination of these two factors.

A few weeks after Tom gave me his corrections and suggestions and I'd made the appropriate insertions, we were ready to approach the Social Library. The Social Library was founded in 1760 by 28 men who each contributed 165 guineas. One Jeremy Condy, a Boston clergyman, was hired to buy books in London. The library actually opened in a brick schoolhouse in May 1761 with 415 volumes.

The Social Library was only open a few hours each week. Apparently they couldn't afford to be open more. The librarian, Jeremiah Weeks, was a tall, willowy, shiny domed man with rimless spectacles. I estimated that he was probably in his early thirties. He greeted us warmly, as I suspected he didn't get many visitors and was eager to meet those few he did get.

After we introduced ourselves Weeks asked, "What can I do for you gentleman?"

I tried to give him my most genuine smile as I said, "I have a rather unusual request."

"Come in, come in. Here, please make yourselves seated and be comfortable. You have piqued my curiosity. Pray tell, what is this unusual request?"

Tom and I had worked out a plan that we thought plausible. We even thought we knew how our dialogue with the library folks might proceed. The following is how we had imagined it might go:

"Well, sir," I would say, "it's this. I had this idea a year or so ago. At first it was nothing more than an idea, but as time went on I decided to do something about it."

"Yes, yes. What was your idea?"

"My father passed away ten years ago. He was a remarkable man. Uneducated but very literate and well read. Over the years he wrote letters to me that each in its own way was brilliant in its insights and wisdom. Much of what he wrote reveals much about the time and place in which we all live. I have saved some of these letters and written my own recollections of my father and even of my experiences so far in my own life. Together they shed light on him, our family and his community."

"That's seems quite nice," Weeks would say politely. "But how does that relate to the Social Library?"

"Well, Mr. Weeks, I decided that I would take these writings and create a package of historical documents that would be of great interest to a future generation. Sort of a time package." I wanted to say time capsule, but I was pretty sure that term wasn't in use in the eighteenth century. "In other words, it would be a package that would be sealed with instructions that it be opened on a certain date in the future."

"Hmm," Weeks would seem truly intrigued now. "I take it you have a certain date in mind?"

"Yes. It would be 250 years from the date of my father's death. That would make it September, 25, 2017."

"Good Lord, so far in the future. Why do you wish it to be so far off? Wouldn't you prefer that it be opened when perhaps the grandchildren of your father could appreciate what's in this 'time package' as you put it?"

"My father was something of a futurist. He had these grand visions of what life in the twentieth or twenty-first century would be like. I think he would want it this way."

Weeks might put his index finger to his chin and frown—not so much from disapproval as from concentration. "Interesting. Now don't take this the wrong way, but why would you think that a reader in some distant time would find recollections of your father's life and your life interesting?"

"My father was active in the war against the French. He was old for a soldier, but he wanted to do his part for the British effort. More recently, I have been directly involved in the confrontations between British regulars and our own militiamen. This time I, as a family member, was fighting against the regulars. I think this change in attitudes in a colonial family will be quite interesting to future historians."

"You mean you were actually part of the fighting?"

"In Lexington and Concord, yes. Here in Salem back in February I didn't fight, but I was a direct observer when Leslie and his men had to retreat with their tails between their legs. Then in Lexington I fought side by side with other militiamen against the regulars."

Then Tom might add, "Gilbert actually accompanied John Derby on the *Quero* when he took the Provincial Congress's depositions and other information to London to present to the Prime Minister and the Privy Council."

Weeks would purse his lips and nod his head approvingly. Clearly he'd be impressed. "I see. I see. And you chose the Social Library. Why did you pick us?"

"We want a library that hopefully will still be in existence well into the future," I said.

"You know I can't guarantee that."

"Of course not," I would say, "but I know you were founded 15 years ago with about 400 books. I can see by glancing around that you have far more volumes now. Salem is a growing town so in all likelihood the demand for your services will grow along with it. Of course nothing is certain in this life, but I am willing to take the chance that the library will be around in two centuries, if you're willing to accommodate our request. Even if, for some reason, the library isn't still in existence 250 years from now, someone will take the collection and hopefully open the time package on the designated date."

"You seem to know a great deal about us. Far more than the average resident here in Salem."

Tom would then say, "It was important to us that we know as much about you as possible before we came to you with our request."

"You know, of course, that I will have to consult with the trustees before I can give you an answer."

"Of course," I say.

The more we hashed this scenario around, though, the more it bothered us. Since we'd been in the eighteenth century we'd had to tell some white lies, but this would amount to such an enormous and such an elaborate lie that we started to search for another way to convince the people at the Social Library.

It wasn't going to be easy. We had two choices as I saw it: One, we could tell the truth including how we got to Salem from the twenty-first century and so on. In one sense this would simplify things. We wouldn't have to make up an elaborate lie. The downside, of course, was that Weeks and his trustees would immediately think we were off-the-wall loonies and send us packing. The other choice was to go through the elaborate scenario above that we'd pretty well rejected.

I opened by saying, "What I'm going to tell you, you will find hard to believe. Thomas and I have come to Salem from the future. We have colleagues and friends in the twenty-first century who are waiting expectantly for some word from us that we have actually successfully arrived here in Salem in the eighteenth century. The package actually contains an accounting of our trip and our lives once we arrived here in this century. That is why we must select a specific date. It is a date on which our colleagues will come to the library and hope to find our document." As I said this I paid close attention to how Weeks was reacting. It was a sight to behold. His facial expressions ran the gamut from amused to startled to disbelief. Frankly, I think what I'd said was so off the wall that he wasn't sure how to react. I had more to say, but I paused to see what he had on his mind so far.

Weeks rolled his eyes. "You will forgive me, gentlemen, if I tell you that I don't believe you. I won't deny that you've livened my day, but I think you must realize that this has gone too far. I know it doesn't look like I'm busy, but I do have things to do here. Now if you have something serious to request I'll listen. Otherwise, you should probably be on your way."

This was a critical moment so I had to chose my words carefully. "I understand how this must sound. Believe me, if someone had approached us back where we came from and said they were from a different century, we would have reacted exactly as you have. I know that what I've said sounds outrageous. Before we came to you we considered what we could say to you or what we could do that would convince you that we are telling you the truth. We decided that if we could predict certain events in the near future you would be persuaded that the only way we could know about such events would be because they had happened in our past.

"For instance, if I were to tell you that in November of this year the Continental Congress in Philadelphia will establish an American navy, would you believe us?"

"I would have to wait until after November to see if what you have said actually comes to pass. And if it does I might think you both witches. That, I believe, would be more likely than your coming to us from the future."

"But I thought people stopped believing in witches after the witch trials?" I didn't really think this at all, but I wanted to get Weeks's reaction.

"Where did you hear that? Just because the trials came to an end doesn't mean that witches no longer exist. I have my doubts, but many people believe there are covens in every community."

"In other words," I said, "you believe in witches yourself. Else why would you conclude that we were witches?"

"I said I have my doubts, but if your prediction comes to pass, I suppose I no longer would have those doubts."

"In other words it would be easier for you to believe in witches than fellow humans from the future?" I knew, as I said this, that I sounded argumentative, and that was the last thing I wanted right now. We needed Weeks on our side, not as an opponent.

"Yes, I suppose that is exactly what I mean. If you're going to convince me that you came to Salem from the future, you'll have to find some other way than by making predictions like some evil necromancer."

This wasn't going well, and we had about run out of ideas, when Tom whispered in my ear, "What if we took him to the spot off Great Misery Island where our ship went down. If the water is calm enough, he could look down and see for himself a space vehicle unlike any ship in the eighteenth century." I liked the idea. Our handlers in Nevada had advised against revealing the the ship. I'd never agreed with them, and now was as good a time as any to put such a revelation to the test. Sure, it would change us in the eyes of those who know us. We'd be celebrities, or possibly even freaks, but at least we wouldn't be condemned as witches. I whispered back to Tom, "Good idea. Let's run with it."

I turned back to Weeks and made him a proposition: "We understand what you're saying. We have a suggestion that we think will clarify things and maybe even make you famous." As I said this, I wasn't sure that fame was something that librarian Weeks was seeking. We all have preconceived ideas about people, and my idea of a librarian was that they were quiet, meek, timid. Fame and celebrity were the last things they'd want. But that view was my own hangup. Of course, if I was right, then tempting Weeks with fame was one of the dumbest things I'd ever done. Nevertheless, the cat was out of the bag so I continued with our proposal. "Last fall, Thomas and I arrived here in a ship that traveled through space. It's not like the ships that travel on the sea. Rather it travels at great speed through space. We use the term spaceship. The spaceship arrived near Great Misery Island, just a few yards from the shoreline. It is now at the bottom of the sea. If you could see with your own eyes this spaceship, would you then believe what we've told you?"

The librarian's eyes lit up as if his imagination had already taken control of his actions. "Yes, I suppose I would. But it won't be easy proving what you want to prove. If that spaceship as you call it is in deep water, then it will be nearly impossible to see it from the surface of the ocean."

Okay, okay. He was into it now. He wouldn't be asking questions like this if he didn't think it was worth the effort. He wanted to be shown. He wanted to believe.

"As I recall," I said, the water is about 18 feet at that point. I think you could see the shape from the surface if it was a calm day. Still, if you want to see it more clearly, you could dive down eight or ten feet and see it better. Do you swim?"

"As a matter of fact, I'm a good swimmer. I'd be interested in diving down as far as I could go, but if it's what you say it is, I think I'd like to get someone who does salvage work try to bring it to the surface."

"It's quite heavy," said Tom. " Might be a difficult salvage job."

"There are people in Beverly and Salem who do that sort of work. I've seen them raise good- size boats."

"I imagine they charge a good-size fee, too," said Tom.

Weeks nodded soberly. "Yes, they don't do it out of the kindness of their hearts. Still, if I'm convinced there is something off of Great Misery Island, I think I could persuade some of our trustees to get behind this. Our trustees are men of substance. Most of them are open to new ideas or they wouldn't have put their money and reputations into this library. I think, gentlemen, if you wish the support of the Social Library, then our next step should be for me to get a good look at your spaceship. I think we should arrange for me to take a look while the water is still warm enough to swim in. You've roused my interest. Shall we get on with it?"

I looked at Tom and then said to Weeks, "Sounds like a good plan."

I conferred off to the side with Tom. Finally I turned to Weeks and said,

"I suppose you're right. At this point it might be better for you and some of the trustees to read it."

Weeks smiled a smile of satisfaction. "Good, good. However, I believe that they will still want to see what lies below the surface near Great Misery Island."

"If you think so, but all this will take some time."

"Certainly if it takes a month or six months it shouldn't matter to the folks in the twenty-first century." Weeks tried unsuccessfully to suppress a grin as he said this. "If the library is extant two centuries from now, the document will be there." He leaned back in his spindly wooden chair with his chin resting between thumb and forefinger. "If all this is true, then it will be well worth our time. Both ours and yours. If it is not true, though, I fear that your life in Salem will be hell."

Chapter 48

A little more than a month later we again met with Weeks. This time he was accompanied by eight library trustees. When Tom and I entered the building Weeks greeted us somewhat nervously. Clearly his reputation as the steward of the community's bibliographic treasures was on the line. He cared greatly about the impression we would make on the trustees. The trustees, after all, controlled the purse strings. Obviously some, if not all, of them had read my document which ran some 50,000 words by my estimation. It was handwritten because I was unable to set it in type. I would have had to ask Sam Hall for permission to set type in the *Gazette* offices during the evenings. He would have wanted to read the document, and if I'd agreed to that, it would have meant spending the better part of every night setting type, plus it would have revealed our secret. It just wasn't feasible. Bottom line is the trustees had to read a handwritten document, which was slower going than a document set in type. All of them couldn't have read it because it had to be passed around and, since there was only one copy, it's more than likely that it didn't get to all of them. Still, this was our first big test. How Tom and I conducted ourselves today was critical, but even more important was the impression my document had made in the minds of those who managed to read it.

Tom and I had discussed what we'd do if the trustees and Weeks concluded we were nut cases or witches. Either conclusion would make our lives in Salem and probably the entire Massachusetts Bay Colony a living nightmare. People would no longer take us seriously. They would shun us or laugh at us or condemn us. Certainly it would make it impossible for us to earn a living. We finally decided that if they didn't believe us, we'd have to eat crow and say that the document, which was as long as a small book, was a work of fiction. Obviously a fantasy—the sort of fantasy that *Robinson Crusoe* was. Declaring the document a work of fanciful fiction, would protect us from being declared nuts or witches, but it would open us up to being called charlatans or flim-flam artists for maintaining that we were from the future. It was the kind of practical joke that would almost certainly be frowned on by these men of substance in the community. They would not take kindly to being made fools of for taking us seriously. As we made our introductions, I began to get nervous. We probably should have called it fiction in the first place. Everything would have been simpler, and if the document made it to the twenty-first century, everything would have worked out fine.

Weeks asked us to sit behind a small table facing himself and the eight trustees. It felt like an interrogation. The eight gentlemen had smiled courteously when we exchanged greetings a few moments ago, but now they sat grim-faced waiting to form judgment. From the looks of them, I suspected that they'd already formed an opinion. Weeks rose and said,

"Mr. Lee, Mr. Howard, the trustees of the Social Library have invited you here today to discuss the rather unusual proposal you have made to the library. The trustees would like to ask you a few questions if you don't mind."

"Of course not," I said in my most obliging voice. "Please feel free to ask anything."

A man sitting next to Weeks cleared his throat, more to get our attention, I suspected, than because of any physical need. I remembered from our exchange of greetings that he was Thomas Pynchon, president of the board. He was also the tallest man in the room—probably a good six five. He commanded the room, and not just because of his stature, but because of the way he carried himself.

"Gentlemen, I must say you have come to our humble library with undoubtedly the most extraordinary proposal we have ever entertained or are likely to entertain in the future. Ah, the future. That is the essence of what you ask us to consider. You will, I hope, understand that your request is an extremely difficult one for us to take seriously?"

"I can see why from your perspective, sir, it would be difficult to accept that we are indeed from the future. As we told Mr. Weeks, there was a time when such a suggestion would have been hard for us to accept. All I can tell you is that in the twenty-first century science has progressed to a point where many things are possible that people in the eighteenth century would not believe possible. In the twenty-first century people fly from one city to another in craft called airplanes. People can talk with each other at great distances using what is called a telephone. People can send pictures through the air and see them on screens in their homes. I know such things are hard to believe, but one day they will come to pass. Thomas and I know because we have seen and used these things and much, much more."

Pynchon responded: "Four of us have read your accounting and find it fascinating. It tells of things we can only dream of. Nay, I doubt if many have ever dreamed of some of the things you allude to, they seem so far from our experience. I have read several novels that talk of things that one could only describe as fantasy, but none comes even close to the fantasy you describe in your document. If we on the board agree to your request, we open ourselves up to public humiliation. Do you understand that?"

"Of course we do. We know how hard it must be to believe what we say and what that document says. We told that to Mr. Weeks because he had the same concerns as you have. We made an offer to him, which I will repeat now. If we can tell you now of events to come in the next few months, and if those events come to pass exactly as we've described them, will you then believe us?"

Pynchon pursed his lips as if analyzing what I'd just said to be sure it wasn't some sort of trick question. "I suppose we'd have to believe you, but I'm not sure that such a performance would prove you were from the future. It might just prove that you were possessed of some form of wizardry."

This was becoming frustrating and more than a little annoying. "In other words, it would indicate that we were witches?"

I think he detected the irritation in my voice. "You are putting words in my mouth, sir. I'm simply saying that if you demonstrated soothsayer like powers, it would not be such a stretch of logic to conclude that you were soothsayers."

"The simple truth of the matter is just the opposite. We are historians who've had the opportunity to look back in history from our vantage point in the twenty-first century and see events which we can tell you about. If we tell you now, it will look like prophesy, but in fact it won't be that."

A short, heavyset man with full gray whiskers spoke up now. His voice was surprisingly high pitched for a man of such size. "Mr. Lee, Samuel Cabot. Your verbal precocity is impressive, sir, but you must understand that no amount of verbal agility or oratorical eloquence can convince us that you have come to Salem from the future. I'm afraid even the most accurate of predictions will not convince us. If you are to convince us, you must find another way, or concede defeat and leave us as unceremoniously as you have the good sense to do."

I turned to Tom and conferred quietly with my hand in front of my mouth. "Shall we go to plan B?" He nodded and said, "It's our best shot."

I turned back to Cabot.

"Mr. Cabot, do you suppose that you might be convinced if we could show you the spaceship that brought us here?"

Cabot looked to his colleagues before answering. Seeing a number of nods of affirmation, he then said, "I suppose that would be convincing. Mr. Weeks has told us that you claim this spacecraft, as you call it, lies at the bottom of the sea near Great Misery Island." Seeing no disagreement from us he continued. "We agree that the only way to settle this matter is to take a look at your spacecraft, so I suggested to my colleagues here that we all go out to the island and see for ourselves. As you may know I have at my disposal a number of boats." A look of self satisfaction transformed his pudgy face. I've offered the use of one of these boats. I will also volunteer my town coach and Mr. Eppes here," he pointed to a distinguished-looking older man seated a few chairs away, "has offered the use of his landau to take us to Beverly Harbor where the boat we shall use is docked. The other trustees and I believe that we should take this little investigative trip as expeditiously as possible. Do you gentlemen suppose that you could make yourselves available tomorrow?"

It would mean that we'd have to take a day off from work at the *Essex Gazette*. I figured if we agreed to work that night to compensate for not being there during the day, Sam would agree. Or he might ask that one of us work while the other took the day off.

I said, "If we can persuade Mr. Hall to give us the day off we'll do it. I'm almost certain that he'll agree to at least one of us not working, so I'll say yes, at least one of us will be available. Just say the time and place where we can meet you."

◆ ◆ ◆

I met the trustees and Weeks in front of the Social Library at nine a.m. the following day. Sam Hall said that the paper was fairly busy. He was sorry, but he couldn't spare two of us, so Tom volunteered to stay and work. He claimed I was the better spokesperson for our cause.

Samuel Cabot seemed to have taken charge of our journey. When we were all assembled he said to the group, "There's been a slight change in our plans. Mr. Pynchon suggested that our trip might be easier if we went by land up to Beverly Farms and then hired two jolly boats, since the island is closer to Beverly Farms than it is to Beverly or Salem. I know, it's actually owned by Salem, but it's much closer to Beverly Farms. So that is the plan. Now if everyone is ready, I suggest that we climb aboard our carriages and head north." As he finished, his eyes lit upon me and he said, "Ah, Mr. Lee. Did you come alone or shall we expect Mr. Howard momentarily?"

"He's needed at the *Gazette*, so he won't be coming. Believe me he wanted to come, but it wasn't possible."

"Well then, let us be off."

Mother Nature couldn't have been more cooperative. The sky was clear and the sun's rays were comfortably warm. As we rode through Salem eyes turned to our little two-coach procession. I suspected that people were wondering if they were witnessing something important. After we were ferried across the river into Beverly I became aware that I was being surreptitiously examined by my fellow passengers. I supposed it had been going on from the very moment we set out. I kept catching furtive glances as if I represented some sort of alien species. I suppose, from their perspective, that wasn't far from the truth.

Normally when riding with strangers you'd expect some occasional friendly exchanges, but on this trip the trustees and Weeks seemed reluctant to address me. They chatted among themselves, but avoided eye contact with me. On a couple of occasions I tried to start up a conversation, but the response invariably was curt, inviting no ongoing exchange.

I had no idea what a jolly boat was. When we arrived at the small Beverly Farms dock area Cabot caught the eye of a man on one of the docks and within moments returned pointing to two open boats that I would have called longboats. They looked as if each of them could seat six to eight people including seats for two oarsmen. I gathered that we'd have to share the rowing duties, since no one was provided by the man Cabot had spoken to. There were ten of us, five in a boat, which made the rowing fairly easy, though once we got out to sea the island that had looked so close seemed a good deal farther. I had volunteered to take one set oars on one boat and was joined by Nathaniel Eppes at the second set of oarlocks. I estimated that it was about three-quarters of a mile out to the island, so rowing a boat with four other people in it wasn't as easy as it sounded back on shore. Fortunately, the sea was fairly calm and we got to our destination in good time, though I definitely worked up a sweat in the process.

As we neared the island I directed our little flotilla to the spot where I remembered our spacecraft going down about a year ago. Dear God, I prayed, let it still be there. Inwardly I laughed a nervous laugh. Why the hell wouldn't it be there? Who would have brought it up? If someone had raised it, it would have been common knowledge by now. We'd have reported on it in the *Gazette*. I was fairly comfortable that the ship was still there, but a little corner of my brain feared the consequences if it were not there. The Social Library trustees, who just happened to be some of Salem's most prominent citizens, would be pissed. Our credibility would be in the toilet. One part of my brain wrestled with these thoughts, while another part managed to pay attention to the task at hand. As we neared the spot, I held up my right hand, signaling to everyone that we should stop rowing.

"This is the spot," I yelled. "Or very close. The surface of the water is fairly calm so we should be able to see the ship below us." No sooner had the words left my mouth than every set of eyes in the two boats peered over the gunwales downward toward the water.

Someone in the other jolly boat said, "I see something down there. Can't make out what it is, though."

"Yes, I see it, too," said Samuel Cabot. "I have something here that will give us a better view." He held up something that looked a bit like a telescope, though, unlike most telescopes, it had only one section. "It's a glass that let's you see things beneath the surface. I designed it myself. It's similar to a common spyglass, but lacks the ability to magnify. The glass at the end has no power of refraction. Here, I shall try it." He then plunged the end of the device into to water and peered into it. A small wave splashed against the device, and he pulled up, wiping water from his face, forcing a smile as he did so.

All eyes were on him, wondering what Cabot would say as he again plunged the special looking device into the water. After about a minute, he pulled the device up and said, "Yes, there is definitely something unfamiliar down there. It appears to be in the shape of a large tube. A very large tube. I'd guess the diameter of the thing to be somewhere around eight or nine feet. It's difficult to say its length from this angle, but it must be at least that long, too. Perhaps a bit more."

"What sort of material is it made from?" asked one of the trustees. "Can you tell by looking through your device, Samuel?"

"It's hard to say. Doesn't appear to be wood. Too shiny. Looks like some sort of metal, but, of course, from here one can't be sure. We'd need to bring it to the surface." Cabot sat back now and thought for a moment, before he turned to me and said, "Mr. Lee, from what I can see through my glass here, I'm forced to conclude that what you've told us may have merit."

At this I allowed a smile of satisfaction to escape and was about to say thank you, when the other men in the boat asked to look through the glass. After each man had peered down into the water and voiced their enthusiasm for what they'd seen, Cabot said, "I think it would be prudent of us to bring this object to the surface for a better look." He now faced the others and said, "There is a fellow in Beverly who does salvage work and could probably bring the thing to the surface and deposit it on the island for closer inspection. If you're all willing to share in the expense, which shouldn't be excessive, I will contact him and make the arrangements. The others, with the exception of Weeks, who I'm sure earned a modest stipend as librarian, nodded or mouthed brief words of agreement.

Then Cabot said, "I'm sure Mr. Lee and his friend Mr. Howard will understand when I ask them not to discuss this matter with anyone outside of those of us here today. Quite candidly—and I'm certain Mr. Lee understands—if this proves to be something other than what you, Mr. Lee, claim that it is, the rest of us here will be laughingstocks. Our hard-earned reputations will be tarnished irreparably. However, if what Mr. Lee and his friend have told us proves to be true, which I still have grave doubts about, then we all will be viewed far more favorably. Far more favorably. I think this is a risk we should be willing to take, if for no other reason than to set these questions to rest, one way or the other. Are we in agreement on this?"

I could see that Cabot's words had been unsettling to the others. These men, if not always loved, were respected, prominent figures in Salem and the region. They couldn't afford to sully their names by backing some hair-brained scheme concocted by two scam artists.

Thomas Pynchon spoke up. "Good caution, Samuel. Good caution. If Messieurs Lee and Howard have been playing us for fools, then they will pay a heavy price for their knavery. I have not detected this kind of depravity in them, though admittedly we do not know them well. I think we must let this matter follow its natural course. We are all curious and openminded. I recommend that we do as Samuel recommends and bring this object to the surface. At the very least, it appears to be unlike anything any of us has ever seen before. It will be worth it to get a closer look. Once Samuel has made arrangements with this fellow in Beverly I think we should all meet here to witness the object as it surfaces and to inspect it when it's on dry land."

Chapter 49

Four days after viewing the spacecraft in the water the same group of men reassembled off Great Misery Island to witness the raising of the mysterious object.

Once again, I was present while Tom remained at the *Gazette*. He didn't seem to mind not being involved in the business with the Social Library folks. Had you asked me a few months earlier if I thought he'd mind taking a back seat for something so important, I'd have said, *'Hell, yes, he would mind.'* But lately he'd gotten comfortable in the routine of everyday colonial life, and, of course, he was spending much of his off time with Jennie Inglesby. When we were training back in Nevada he'd been aggressive, ambitious and eager to be involved in anything that he could learn from. Whether it was the pace of the eighteenth century or simply Jennie, something had changed him. Whatever the reason, he didn't resent my going off on these investigative junkets with the library people. He wished me well with a wide smile on his face.

Bobbing in the water above the spot where our spacecraft went down was a barge that I would guess must have been 50 feet long with a beam of maybe 18 feet. At the stern of the barge was a crane with a large winch or reel. Thick hawser was wound around the winch. The hawser must have been close to two inches in diameter—probably the thickest rope I'd ever laid eyes on. I still wasn't sure it was strong enough to pull up our heavy space vehicle. Even if it was capable of such a feat I feared that the weight of the sunken craft might capsize the barge. There were four sturdy looking workmen manning the barge and crane. One of them who seemed to be in charge yelled to us to keep a fair distance while they worked.

After 45 minutes or so it seemed to us in our two jolly boats that the workers had accomplished very little. It was hard to judge time in the eighteenth century since watches were a rare commodity possessed by a very small percentage of the wealthy. I'd only seen two watches so far, and they were pocket watches; not wristwatches. From what people told me they were not very accurate. The two I'd seen had no minute hands so you had to sort of guess within a half hour or so what time it was. To their possessors, though, this was a huge improvement over using the sun as a way to estimate time.

"What seems to be the problem?" Samuel Cabot yelled in frustration to the crew leader.

"We can't find anything to attach our hook to. The object seems to be smooth on all surfaces."

It was vitally important for our credibility that they get that ship to the surface, so I spoke up.

"The rear end of the craft is pointed downward toward the ocean bottom," I yelled across the water to the barge. I remembered this from our last inspection and now realized that, even if they could see the ship clearly, they probably wouldn't know stem from stern on a spacecraft. "There are several sharp projections and pipes at the rear of the craft that your hook might latch onto."

"The crew boss nodded and said, "Mebbe that'll help. We'll see if we can catch onto something down there, though it won't be easy." No sooner had he said this than one of his workers spoke up. "I can dive down and guide the hook. Can't stay down that deep for long, but I'll give 'er a try."

I broke into a smile when he said this. I knew that there were people who could dive more than 18 or 20 feet without gear, but they were few and far between. I had no idea that there were any in the eighteenth century. Divers in the eighteenth century had no choice. There were no aqualungs or other gear to help you breath underwater. A diver could go as deep as his comfort level allowed. I knew my limit was about ten feet, and that was not because of running out of breath. It was because the pressure in my ears killed me. The ones who could dive deep had the ability to pop their ears in such a way as to ease the pressure. I could hold my breath long enough for the deeper depths, but my ears couldn't take it. Now, with this fellow volunteering, maybe we had a chance to bring the ship up. As I considered this I watched the worker strip down to just his pants. No way in this century would he take off more, even when his audience was just men. As he removed his second shoe, he climbed up to the gunwale and dived into the water. When he emerged, shaking water from his hair and face, he spoke to another worker and told him to lower the hook down to the bottom and allow a yard or two of slack. When the worker on the barge said that the hook had reached bottom, the man in the water pulled himself down the hawser hand over hand. We waited. He'd been down a couple of minutes and those of us in the boats were getting nervous.

Suddenly he broke through the surface, breathless, but smiling. "Keep the tension on 'er. She's attached. Leastways, I think she is. Pull 'er up slowly."

We all watched slowly as two men put the weight of their bodies into turning the crank. Slowly the hawser inched up, winding itself around the winch. It was hard going as the spacecraft was heavy, even with the support of the water. The weight of the spacecraft pulled the stern of the barge down so that the gunwale was dangerously close to the surface of the water. It was close, but it wasn't taking on any water. At least not yet. The crew leader allowed a slight smile to escape as he smelled success. I began to breath again. As the spaceship broke the surface I studied the faces of the trustees as they stood in awe at what they were seeing. They turned to each other with words of amazement and seeming bewilderment at the sight of something so unlike anything they'd ever seen in their lives.

Just as we all sensed that things were going well, the barge lurched sharply and the stern lifted up several feet. The three workers were sent flying. One worker fell overboard. Just as suddenly, the barge righted itself. The diver in the water swam to the fallen worker and helped him get back on board the barge. Then the diver went under and was gone for just a few seconds. When he emerged, he smiled and said, "She flip-flopped and now the bottom is on the top. The hook's holding. You can continue pulling 'er up." The diver climbed aboard, and, with the crew chief, carefully replaced the two men at the winch. It was backbreaking work and it was obviously impossible to keep at it for too long.

After at least another half hour had elapsed, a small portion of the spaceship broke the surface and a cheer went up from the workers and those of us watching from the jolly boats. The crew chief said, "Pull her up a bit more so we can get an idea what we're dealing with." The men put their backs into their task as the winch squeaked painfully. I was afraid that, if the men didn't quit from exhaustion, the crank on the winch would break. After a few more screeching turns, about a foot and a half of the rear of the spacecraft was visible. The crew chief said, "Never seen anything like it in me life. It's too big and too heavy to bring on board. We're gonna have to pull her to shore and then muscle her up on land as best we can. Won't be easy. Thing's a lot bigger'n I thought she was."

I had no idea how they were going to accomplish this, as the barge had no visible means of propulsion. Certainly no engine. It did have a mast with a sail, but there was no wind. I doubted that even with a good breeze it would be enough to drag the barge and our spacecraft in to Great Misery Island.

Then the crew chief said something that showed me once again that, while our ancestors may not have had high tech, they did have ingenuity.

"Listen, lads," he said, addressing his crew. "I need someone to tie a line to that other hawser lying on the deck and then swim in to the island with it. I need another of you to swim in with him. Once you get there, see if you can slowly pull us in. If you can't do it directly, we'll need to work out some sort of winch system to handle the job."

The process was painfully slow, but after another hour and a half they had the spacecraft in the shallow water of the island's shoreline. The crew tied up the barge and waded in to the island. The crew chief continued to be creative as he instructed his men to form a makeshift winch by going around three tree trunks in order to give them more leverage when they pulled on the hawser. Suffice it to say another hour later the spacecraft ended up lying on the beach.

During this entire process I had a lot of time to think. One of the things I reflected on was the implications of this public viewing of our spacecraft in the year 1775. The immediate benefit to Tom and myself was that it was almost certain that we would be taken seriously. They would believe something that until now would have been almost impossible for them to believe. Because of that our credibility would be enhanced, and we would be able to survive in our new environment.

However, beyond the immediate benefit of our maintaining our credibility, I found myself fearing the longterm impact of the public viewing of our spacecraft by people in the year 1775. So far, our existence in 1775, as far as I could tell, was unlikely to alter the course of history in any way. I suppose the cynical could say that that doesn't say much for what Tom and I were doing with our lives. Maybe, but I'd like to think that we'd been living decent meaningful lives, but probably not the kind of lives that would attract the attention of historians.

The discovery of a spacecraft, however, was a different thing entirely. It's not only possible, but distinctly probable that such a discovery would make it into the history books. It's just as probable that it would change the thinking of people over the 240 plus years between 1775 and the future from which we came. I wasn't at all comfortable with this thought.

Somewhere in the recesses of my memory I recalled something that one of our trainers mentioned just before we lifted off from the desert in Nevada. He'd said, "Just in case you don't land in water, you should know that much of the metal from which your ship has been made will rust at a much faster rate than most ferrous metals. What that means is that if people see your ship they won't be able to preserve it in a museum or anyplace else. Within two weeks it will rust so badly that it will begin to disintegrate and lose it's shape. In other words, the evidence will be gone."

He said the ship would resist rusting while we were en route to the future because it would only start to oxidize when in an environment which contained oxygen and some moisture. En route through space to the past we would be in an oxygen-free environment. Once we landed, however, rusting would begin immediately.

As we surrounded the beached spacecraft I divided my time between staring at the ship and observing the behavior of the men around me. Both the workers and the trustees stood for a few minutes in awe of what lay before them. This huge cylinder lay silently with the nose cone facing the water. The skin of the cylinder reflected the brilliant sunlight. Along one side of the cylinder was written in boldface eight-inch type the words **United States of America**. Below that in five-inch type: Anno Domini 2015.

Gradually the men started talking. At first it was just a few words of astonishment. Then they began to seriously discuss what lay before them. I heard several comments about the words United States of America. I tried to pick up as much as I could, but it was difficult with so many talking at once. Clearly, though, United States of America had them thinking. It was obvious that they realized that they were witnessing something remarkable—something of historical significance.

After maybe 15 minutes Thomas Pynchon stepped closer to the silent, but majestic, mysterious metal object and said in his stentorian voice, "Please give me your attention for a moment." When the conversational buzz quieted down, he continued. "I think we can all agree that we are witnessing something that no man has ever witnessed in the history of this planet." Nods of agreement from the others surrounding the ship. "In light of this remarkable situation I think it is imperative that those of us who are today fortunate enough to witness this should not discuss it with anyone else. That includes our wives, children, parents or anyone we know. I know that will be difficult. Here is my reason: We don't know what we are dealing with right now. Should word of this get out before some of us have had the opportunity to question Gilbert and his friend Thomas, who knows what the consequences could be. Think of the questions to which we still need answers. For example, are there more of these spacecraft? Are there more people from the future here in Salem?" I started to assure him that there were not, but he put his index finger over his mouth, saying we'd have an opportunity to clarify everything. Then he resumed speaking to the small crowd. "What was the intention of sending this craft here? Will more be coming? We need to know the answers to these and other questions before we speak freely to others in the community, lest there be panic in the streets." The men, workers and trustees alike, said 'aye' and nodded yes. We'll see, I thought. Somebody was bound to leak it. I just prayed that the rusting would begin soon.

Then Pynchon said, "I believe someone has cows on the island. It's only a matter of time before they discover this thing so I think it best if we find them and get their pledge of silence, too. Again, only until we know more than we know now."

I was impressed by Pynchon. He was not only the leader of the Social Library, but a real leader of men. We'd see if I was still impressed after he and his friends finished interrogating us.

Chapter 50

They didn't waste any time sitting us down for their questions. As we landed the two jolly boats back in Beverly Farms, Pynchon asked me if I'd mind meeting with the trustees at the library that night. He asked me to bring Tom, too.

We met at eight o'clock. I generally kept time by checking the hall clock in Mrs. Inglesby's rooming house. Amazingly everyone arrived more or less on time.

Pynchon began by thanking us for coming. He and the trustees were polite, but not overly friendly. I attributed this to a sense that they were more than a little uncomfortable in our presence. We were fascinating, but also quite strange from their perspective. I could understand that. We weren't frauds, but the fact that we really were from the future made it a lot more difficult for them to deal with us. It's as if they thought that we possessed some mystical powers that they should be concerned with.

Samuel Cabot began the questioning. "Mr. Lee, can you tell why you came to Salem in the year 1775?"

"Yes, sir, I can, though to be perfectly accurate we arrived here in 1774. Just about a year ago."

"Right, right. But to my point, why did you and Mr. Howard come here?"

"We came here because certain scientists in our century believed that time travel could actually happen. So far as they knew, it had never happened in the history of the world, but they believed that scientific knowledge had progressed to the point where it was possible. Our coming here was a grand experiment. That's why it's so important that we place our document with the Social Library. The document is a record of our trip traveling here on the spaceship and our life here over the past year."

Cabot pursed his lips and thought for a moment. Then he said, "I suppose I can see that, but why here? What makes you think that this library will even exist in the twenty-first century?"

"Quite frankly, sir, the people who sent us here thought they were sending us two years into the future. That is, they thought they were sending us from 2015 to 2017. Obviously things didn't go as they planned."

"Obviously," said Cabot with a smirk. "What went wrong?"

"The computer program had a glitch." As soon as I said this I realized Cabot would be totally confused.

"Computer? Glitch? I'm afraid Mr. Lee your language of the future needs translating."

"A computer is a kind of machine that controlled our space vehicle. A glitch is a malfunction of that machine. Essentially, what I meant to say is that there was an error in the calculations made by this machine —clearly a very big error."

"Clearly. All right then, back to my original question. What makes you think that this library will even exist in the twenty-first century?"

If I weren't so nervous, I would have enjoyed this. "Because, Mr. Cabot, Thomas and I know it will survive—not as the Social Library, though. Coming from the future we have the advantage of knowing your history. Briefly put, in a few short years another library called the Philosophical Library will be formed in Salem. Then, about 30 years later, in 1810, your library will merge with the Philosophical Library and form the Salem Athenæum. The Salem Athenæum will survive at least to the year 2015, so our hope was that our colleagues would be able to retrieve our accounting of our trip and know that they'd been successful. As much as a miracle it may seem to you in 1775 that we are from the future, it will be equally exciting for them to know that they have succeeded in sending us here."

"I take it you cannot return to the year 2015 and tell them yourselves?"

"That's correct, sir. Their technology hasn't progressed far enough to accomplish that." I didn't tell him that if we got our document to CAE before liftoff there was a good chance we could go back. I didn't tell him this because I had decided, as had Tom, that I liked it in the eighteenth century despite its disadvantages.

"Technology. That is another unfamiliar word, sir."

"It means the practical application of scientific knowledge."

"Hmm," interrupted Nathaniel Eppes from his seat. "I would think that, if their technology as you put it could send you here, it could also take you back?"

Tom stood up. "Perhaps I should explain." I was glad to see him get involved and get me off the hot seat. He proceeded confidently. Tom had a better knowledge of astrophysics than I did anyway. "The spacecraft that brought us here is the thing you brought up from the bottom of Salem Sound near Great Misery Island...."

"Yes, yes, we know that," said Cabot impatiently.

"I know you do, sir. What I'm trying to say is that that object is only part of the spacecraft we started out with back in the twenty-first century. The larger part of the craft was called the thruster, and that part was dropped off once we left the Earth's gravitational pull. That was accomplished soon after we left orbit around the Earth. We needed the thruster initially to overcome the force of gravity and to break away from orbit, but once we were free of the gravitational pull, the ship you pulled from the water had it's own power source for the remainder of the trip. The point of all this then is that we no longer have a thruster, so we cannot lift off Earth for a trip back to our century. We cannot make a round trip."

"We are learning a great many new terms tonight," sighed Thomas Pynchon with a warm smile. "Thruster, round trip, technology. I suppose, with time, we'll come to have a better understanding of such terms, but one thing I would like explained now is how you can fly into the sky and somehow find yourself in a different century. I can't conceive of men flying at all. However, if that were possible and apparently it is, why would flying in the sky bring you to a different point in time? Why wouldn't it simply take you from one place on Earth to another?"

I said, "Your question is an excellent one, Mr. Pynchon, but it would take a long time to explain it. I assume you have other questions tonight, so if I might make a suggestion, perhaps we could set aside another evening for a discussion of the science behind time travel. Thomas and I could prepare a chart to help us make things more clear. In the meantime, I assume you'll be going back to the island to inspect the ship more carefully. Thomas and I can begin our explanations there by pointing to certain parts of the ship. Then, if you'd like, we can explain the entire process in another session. That is, of course, if you would like us to do that."

As I said this I hoped that the ship had already started rusting. The sooner it rusted away, the sooner the evidence would be gone. Our colleagues at CAE felt that it would not be good if we landed in a part of the world where the ship and its technology could fall into the wrong hands. That wasn't the danger in the eighteenth century. No, the danger now was that public awareness of the ship could alter the course of history. Tom and I couldn't control the thinking and the memories of the trustees and Librarian Weeks, but once the evidence was gone it would be their word against that of everyone else. If the ship rusted rapidly enough to disintegrate, it would be a win-win situation. The trustees would have seen it to certify its existence and verify our credibility, but no lasting evidence of our arrival would be available to perpetuate the story of men from the future visiting Salem. Once the ship became a pile of oxidized dust, the trustees would hesitate to perpetuate the tale of the visiting men from the future.

Pynchon conferred with the other trustees and then said, "We agree with your suggestion Mr. Lee. We look forward to such an evening soon. In the meantime, I have another question for you."

"Fire away."

Pynchon furrowed his brow looking confused. As soon as the words left my mouth I realized what I'd done. "That's another expression we use in the twenty-first century. It means please feel free to ask." I grinned and added, "It does not mean take out your gun and shoot."

Pynchon and the others shook their head as if they were having trouble keeping up. They did not see the humor in this. I could understand their confusion. Finally, the room quieted down and Pynchon smiled tolerantly.

"I think it will take some time getting used to you, Mr. Lee. I hope you understand." I smiled and nodded. He continued with his next question. "One of the other trustees has asked me to ask you this: We find it hard to understand that you and Mr. Howard were willing to leave your lives in the twenty-first century, knowing that life would, I presume, be more difficult here without your advanced scientific marvels. We also are simply in awe of your ability to leave the people you knew and in particular, the members of your own families. Would you be willing to speak to these points?"

"Yes, of course. I'll speak to the last point first. Neither Thomas nor I had any close living family members, so it wasn't much of a sacrifice to leave. Yes, we had friends, and it was not easy to leave them, but we were young and you might say somewhat impulsive when we agreed to take part in this experiment. Our travel here took twelve months, so we aged one year since we left our century. Actually, we aged more. I can explain that when we meet next. At that time we can explain, too, how you can travel only one year and go back in time more than 200 years. But back to your question: The original plan was for us to travel two years into the future. The intention was to travel from 2015 to 2017. Two years wasn't nearly as big a sacrifice as two centuries. As you can see, things didn't go exactly as planned. Instead of going forward in time, we went backward, and two centuries; not two years. It demonstrates how difficult time travel is. So the answer to your first question is this: No, we would not have been willing to go back in time 240 years. That wasn't what the people in charge of the project proposed to us. It's not what we expected. Two hundred and forty years would have seemed too much of a break with the life to which we were accustomed. Going two years into the future was exciting and challenging, but it would not have been a major change from the existence we had known.

"Being transported to the eighteenth century has been exciting, and we have gradually adjusted. We have made friends here and respect your culture. Gradually we find ourselves thinking as if we were born in this century. It amazes us how well humans can adapt."

"I suppose we can understand your thinking on this. So, Gilbert, what about the first point—leaving the marvels of the twenty-first century?"

"At times I do miss some of those things. I could take another whole evening telling you about some of those marvels. Since I've been here in Salem I've realized just how advanced they are. However, after being here a year, I also realize that most of them were not necessary to lead a good life; they only became necessary after we got used to them. I suppose we would miss them more, if everyone around us had them, and we didn't. Obviously, that is not the case in 1775. Yes, there are times that I miss them, but as I said, it's amazing how we humans can adapt to our surroundings. Thomas and I have reflected on this a great deal. Having lived with the technological conveniences of the twenty-first century and without them we can see that with those conveniences and marvels there is also a downside."

"Downside?" said Cabot with a mystified expression.

"It means liability, disadvantage."

"Sorry, but... "

"I understand. Anyway the downside or disadvantage of having certain scientific marvels at your disposal is that you become dependent on them and find yourself at a loss when they are not available." I could see nothing but blank stares from my audience as I said this. It dawned on me that, since they had no clue as to what I was talking about, they couldn't even imagine how they'd feel if these things were taken away. I needed somehow to give them an example they could visualize. "Imagine, if you will, if you no longer had the wheel available to you. Somehow the wheels on your carts and carriages disappeared. How would you cope? How would you carry goods to market? Fish from the docks to the markets? How would you move people great distances?" This was something that hit home. This was something they could understand. Still, they questioned my example.

"Yes, we would, I suppose, be crippled," said Jeremiah Weeks, "but that is almost impossible to believe. Even if one wheel broke, we would not lose the use of all wheels. We would replace the broken wheel."

"Excellent point," I said. "This makes *my* point. In the twenty-first century, they have means of conveyance that are faster and more powerful than a cart or a carriage, which makes those means of conveyance immensely valuable. Some of them are so powerful that they can carry hundreds of people at speeds of hundreds of miles an hour." I could see that this blew them away, so I continued with my argument. "However, as valuable and helpful as they are, when they fail to function the inconvenience is all the greater or in the case of a collision, all the more serious."

"Are these flying machines you're talking about?" asked one of the trustees.

"Yes, they're the machines we call airplanes." They gasped. It wasn't going to be easy for them to accept all that I was telling them. "It's also true of carriage-like vehicles that travel on the ground on wheels. They travel at speeds of 60, 70, 80 miles per hour. There are other carriages that are tied together and pulled along the surface in what we call trains. These trains are pulled on steel rails. Here's why when these marvelous inventions don't work for some reason they are missed all the more. The trains that travel within great cities are powered by electricity. If the electricity...."

"If I may interrupt again," said Pynchon, "I'm afraid your century is so far advanced from our century that we're going to need another explanation. The word electricity is not new to my vocabulary. I seem to recall that it has its origin in the Greek. And, I also recall that Dr. Franklin of Philadelphia discovered that lightning is a form of this electricity, but I don't see how lightning or any form of lightning could pull any form of conveyance. Certainly not this train thing you mentioned."

"Well, sir, as the years progressed after Dr. Franklin did his experiments, other scientists learned how to harness..." I noted puzzlement in my audience and quickly adjusted. "They learned how to put electricity to practical use. Electricity, in fact, became one of the major power sources for hundreds of scientific marvels in the twentieth and twenty-first centuries."

The evening went on like this for almost three hours. Finally, Pynchon ended it by noting the obvious: that we were all mentally exhausted: They, from trying to assimilate so much new and startling information, and we from trying to explain it in ways that they could understand. Since they still had a thousand questions, despite their exhaustion, we agreed to meet again the next night after we'd gone back to Great Misery Island to examine the spacecraft more carefully.

These were busy men; yet they were willing to set aside their normal obligations in order to learn as much about us and our story as they could. They were like kids in a candy store in that they were not inclined to be patient.

Chapter 51

Sam Hall, at the *Gazette*, was becoming impatient with Tom and me. Workers in the eighteenth century didn't get much time off. For that matter, things hadn't changed much over two centuries. In the twenty-first century American workers got far less time off than their European counterparts. Sam really couldn't afford to have us be off very much as he had a small staff, and we had become two of his most valuable employees. That's not vanity talking; it's a fact. Well, maybe a little vanity, too.

I mentioned this to Pynchon and he, being an acquaintance of Sam's, but more importantly, somewhat of a honcho in Salem, said he'd talk to our boss. They worked out an arrangement whereby Tom reported to work the next day, and I went to the island with the trustees. The rest of the agreement was that this would be the last time hopefully that I would take time off because of the needs of the Social Library. Somehow Pynchon, in pleading our case to Hall, described needing some special knowledge we'd acquired up in Halifax—knowledge that was helpful to the Social Library. Pynchon told me he apologized profusely without making my commitment to the trustees seem too mysterious. Sam agreed, no doubt because he's a nice guy and probably because he preferred to have a man like Pynchon owe him rather than resent him for not being cooperative.

As we neared the island I crossed my fingers. I wasn't disappointed, either. As soon as we laid eyes on the spacecraft it was obvious that it had started rusting. If I didn't know that it was supposed to rust that fast I would have been shocked. Even with my knowledge, I was amazed at the amount of oxidation that had taken place already.

Clearly the men around me were shocked. These were men of the world, every bit as smart as men I'd known in my own century. They exclaimed to each other how much rusting had occurred in the short time they'd been away from the ship.

I saw no reason to play dumb.

"Gentlemen, the rusting you see on this metal is intentional." At this, the furrowed brows and frowns told me that I'd better continue. "There's a reason for this, and as I explain it, I think you'll understand the wisdom behind that reason. Our colleagues, the twenty-first century scientists behind this adventure of ours, did not want our spaceship to fall into the wrong hands, meaning rival nations who might copy the technology and then build their own ship capable of traveling through time. Of course, as you well know, we didn't travel to the future. We found ourselves in the past. I still believe it's good that the spacecraft will rust away to the point where it is unrecognizable because if it remains intact it can be documented. If it can be documented, it could alter the course of history. I don't know how it would change history, but I believe it would. I think we can all imagine possible ways that could happen—"

"Yes, of course, said Samuel Cabot. "If a record of this event was made by us, it would in ways unpredictable, change history. That has never been done before and who knows what havoc it might wreak."

"Yes, exactly. Now those of you here will know what happened. Some of you may even tell others what you have seen, but this ship will not be recognizable for very many more days. At some point it will be little more than a pile of dust."

One of the other trustees then said, "So it would behoove us not to make too much of this because soon there will be little evidence to support our claims. Is that what you're saying, Mr. Lee?"

"Yes, I'm afraid it is."

"How Machiavellian," he said bitterly.

"I know it may seem that way, but if you think about it, it might be better than altering history by letting the ship survive."

The man continued. "It's your history, sir, not ours. Because you wish to protect *your* history you're saying that if we tell our wives or our most trusted friends about what we've seen and about what you've told us, we might become laughingstocks."

"I suppose that's possible. Or they may just think that you were mistaken."

"Or that we were duped by two charlatans."

I pursed my lips and nodded my acknowledgement. "Or that. Look, I'm not saying this is a wonderful situation. I'm simply saying that it's probably for the best, though, to be honest, only time will tell. I suppose the best thing I can say about this is that all of us here share a fascinating secret. Because of that shared secret I suppose we will always be bonded together."

Thomas Pynchon forced a wry grin. "You've thrown another word at us, Gilbert. I suppose I can divine its meaning. Our joint bonding gives us much to think about. Ah, well, it appears that we'll all have a long time to grope with those reflections. I for one confess that I honestly don't know if I will take anyone else into my confidence about all this."

"I assume," I said hopefully, "that the board will agree to accept our document with the provision that it will only be opened by one of the people we name on a date in 2015 that we designate?"

"I see no reason why we should not accept it."

"Then we would like that date to be October 25, 2015." This would be one month after liftoff and would mean that we would never be able to return to our century.

Chapter 52

On our way to work next day Tom and I debated the wisdom of telling Sam Hall about how we got to Salem. We knew we shouldn't, and for the same reasons we'd given to the trustees and Jeremiah Weeks. Merely telling him didn't prove that we came here from the twenty-first century, and because of that we risked being thought kooks or charlatans. Neither designation would enhance our standing with Sam Hall. Quite frankly, it was a lousy dilemma. If we told Sam and he believed us, it would help him understand some of what he now viewed as our quirks. More importantly, he was a terrific employer, a brilliant journalist and a first-rate conversationalist. Tom and I would be able to look forward to years of great heart-to-heart chats.

"But if he didn't believe us things would be worse," I pointed out. "He'd almost certainly want some solid evidence. I suppose we could always take him out to Great Misery Island while the ship was still recognizable as a spacecraft."

"We could, but what would be gained by that? He'd still be frustrated because he wouldn't be able to use it in the paper."

"Sam gave us a chance when we knew virtually nobody except Henry Woodbury. He's been real helpful, too. A good boss. I just think we owe it to him, even if he can't use what we tell him."

"Can't argue with that. But haven't we sort of pledged to keep this a secret between us and the Social Library people?"

"Not exactly," I said. "We've made it clear that if they tell others, it's at their own risk. Risking their credibility, that is. The only way we can avoid losing our credibility with Sam is to show him the ship while it still looks like a ship."

"Think we should tell Pynchon and the others that we're doing this?"

"No, because then they'd want to haul a helluva lot of people out to the island in the next few days, and the secret would be a lot harder to contain. The ship will be dust at some point, but if a couple hundred people see it, some reference will remain a couple hundred years from now. No, if we show Sam, we have to keep that as our secret."

"Of course he could then tell Pynchon and the others that he knew."

"Not if we pledge him to keep quiet."

"Maybe."

"Then there's Jennie," I pointed out. "You've already told her. Does she believe you, or would you want her to see the ship now?"

"Jesus, Gil, I can't take this. It's getting so damned complicated."

"Yeah, it has. It gets worse. Since Henry Woodbury and Jeremiah spend time on the island, they've probably already seen the ship. Do we owe it to them to explain things?"

"I'm afraid we're losing control of this." I considered what we'd been talking about for a minute; then said, "I think we should tell Sam at the very least. Take him to the island soon so he'll know we're not nut cases."

"Agreed," said Tom who then changed the subject abruptly. "I just thought of something. Remember what the guys said to us just before liftoff?"

"You mean 'You guys are out of your mind, but we sort of envy you'?"

Tom forced a smile. "Yeah. Do you realize what we've done? We've created a potential firestorm here in the eighteenth century when they're already in the middle of their own firestorm?

"You mean the Revolution?"

"Yes, something that's going to dominate these colonies for the next eight years."

"And it's just beginning. Well it's a damn good thing the geniuses back in Nevada designed the ship to rust itself into oblivion. Even though a few people know the truth, it gives us a fighting chance to keep this under fairly tight control."

"Maybe. I think too many already know about it."

Prologue Conclusion:
Retrieving the Package

Salem, Massachusetts, October 25, 2015

As I entered the Salem Athenæum, the young woman behind the desk was busy entering something on a laptop. She looked up as I approached the desk.

"May I help you?" she said with a warm smile, a smile that came naturally. I was immediately attracted to her.

I looked around the stately room and saw that the place was not busy. It appeared that I was the only visitor in the place—at least the only one in that elegant main room.

"I'm Chris Carver. From the Center for Advanced Exploration in Nevada. You, or someone here, contacted us a few weeks ago about a time capsule or something that you have here at the Athenæum. Apparently it's addressed to me and two other colleagues of mine."

Her smile broadened. "Oh my gosh. Yes of course. I was wondering who would show up. We're all agog about the package. All very mysterious."

"You mean what's in the package?"

"Well yes. When you see it you'll see that it's quite old; yet it says on the wrapping that it should be given to the Center for Advanced Exploration in Nevada on October 25, 2017. I have no idea what the Center for Advanced Exploration is, but I'm fairly certain that Nevada didn't exist when this package was wrapped. It looks so old. How old is it?"

I was hoping I could just take the package, thank her and leave without getting into the provenance of the time capsule. I was even prepared to donate a decent sum of money to the library for watching over the package. What I didn't understand, though, was that the package looked old. I couldn't wait to see for myself. How could it look old, if it was sent this year? I looked up and saw that the librarian was expecting an answer.

"I honestly don't know. Shouldn't be very old at all."

"You don't know? Yet it's addressed to you and your colleagues, and as I recall, it gives the names of two men who sent it to you. What's really mysterious is how something this old could be sent to someone as young as you. From the looks of the package, I would guess that you weren't even born when this was left with the Athenæum."

"That is mysterious," I said. "When the Athenæum called the CAE a few weeks ago they said that they had a an old package in their archives that said it was to be opened on October 25, 2015 by ONE OF THE FOLLOWING PEOPLE: Christopher Carver, Matthew Haywood, Hilton Siegel. Whoever it was who notified us—"

"It was me," she said. "Trish O'Connell. I spoke with your director and I told him that the out side of the package said PLEASE OPEN ON OCTOBER 1, 2015. We've been aware of the package for some time now and all of us, the board and myself, couldn't wait until the first. All of the board members were present when we opened it. Then came a new surprise. Inside the outer wrapping it said the package should be opened on October 25, 2015 by one of the three men I just mentioned. I suppose the two layers of wrapping were to give us time to notify you people so you could be here by October 25th. Now this mysterious package is even more mysterious because you seem puzzled yourself. I was sure you or one of the other two would know what this package was all about."

"I think I do, but I'm not sure. The fact that you say it looks old has me puzzled. Can I take a look at it? Can I take it with me?" I held my breath as her brain processed my request.

"I can show it to you, but I can't let you take it right now. First of all, it also says that whoever picks it up will pay the Athenæum the equivalent of one hundred times what was paid to the library when the document was left off, or something like that. You said you had an idea what the package was all about?"

"If I'm right, it's a long weird story. Tell you about it sometime soon over a drink." I gave her my most charming smile.

"I might even accept. I have to hear *that* story. Come on over to this table. You can examine the package there. The board of trustees would like to meet with you before we let you actually take it from the building. They're willing to meet as early as this evening if you are. Once you've satisfied them I'll need you to fill out this form." I looked at the sheet she held out and saw that it simply asked for my name, address, phone number and email. I quickly filled that out. She then asked to see some ID to verify what I'd given her. She was no longer smiling. She looked a bit sheepish as she said, "We can't let part of the collection go without good reason. I'm sure you understand."

I did understand, and I didn't like it. This complicated matters by a factor of ten. The CAE didn't want anyone to know about our project yet; not until they could announce it themselves in order to justify continuing the project. Continuing the project meant sending another vehicle farther into the future, hopefully one that had the capability of making a return trip back to the present. How we at the lab handled this, though, was tricky, because the next phase would cost far more billions than the first phase. If word got out from the Athenæum or from anyone other than our lab back in Nevada, we'd have to defend ourselves against charges that we were involved in this secret cover-up program. It *was* secret, but that was only to protect the program until we could announce success. After all, if we failed and it got out, the project would come to a crashing stop. Now some may think it should have been open to scrutiny from the get-go, but that's not for me to decide. Right now I had to make a decision—and quickly. What was I going to say to the board? Right now I had to answer Trish.

"Yes, of course. Tonight will be fine. The sooner the better." As I said that the fog of my confusion suddenly lifted, and I knew what I had to do. "I'd like to open it now, though, if you don't mind."

She hesitated for a minute before answering. "I suppose that would be okay. After all, it's yours, right?"

"Yes it is, even though your board seems to need to be reassured of that fact."

"You have to understand that if this is some valuable, historic document, they can't just let it go without at least knowing what it is."

"And if they're not convinced it belongs to me, they won't want to lose it. Right?"

She grinned. "Right." Then she said, " Give me a minute to got get the package.

Why would I agree to let her see what was in the package? Why would I agree to let the trustees see the contents? After all, if I wanted to play hard ball, I could get the lab's lawyers to force them to give up the contents without viewing it. Of course, the Athenæum could demand some kind of payment for safeguarding the document for whatever time it had been here. Hopefully that would be taken care of by the promise Gil Lee and Tom Howard had apparently made about paying the Athenæum the equivalent of one hundred times what Gil and Tom had paid the library. That seemed reasonable, but in the end we would probably win our right to take the contents of the package. The problem would be that it might become a legal battle that could stretch out for weeks or even months. The folks at the library would probably go ahead and look at the contents anyway, but being a positive thinker I figured that an old prestigious institution like the Athenæum would prefer not to have that kind of litigation or even the threat of that kind of litigation. Almost certainly they wouldn't want to pay lawyers to fight our lawyers, who, because they worked for the government, had virtually infinite resources. Besides, I was counting on their patriotism.

Aside from my concerns over gaining access to the package was my curiosity as to why the package even existed. And why it apparently looked so old. If our guys had landed successfully two years into the future, why couldn't they have contacted the CAE more directly? Why couldn't they have telephoned? Or more to the point, why couldn't they have simply appeared at the door of the CAE?

I'd done all this calculating in a matter of minutes. I was about to begin unwrapping the package, when I remembered something vital to the future of the program: Opening the package with just one witness could hurt the program more than help it. If a few reliable witnesses were present when I opened the document they would see what it was and later on, when we at the lab needed proof that it wasn't a huge scam, their testimony would give the project the credibility it would desperately need to go ahead. I'd have to pledge the trustees and Trish to silence until the lab released everything to the press, but it was a risk worth taking if it would guarantee the credibility of the program.

"Okay," I said. "Let's leave the package as it is until tonight. We can open it then so that you and the board can see what's inside."

"So I guess I won't be getting that drink."

"Why not?"

"All the mystery will be revealed tonight."

"Probably not everything. I'm staying in town tonight so let's still meet."

She seemed pleased with that as she handed me the package containing the document. "You can at least look at the outside of the package now," she said. "You must be curious." The package was about nine by twelve and maybe two inches thick. It was wrapped in some kind of heavy tan stock, cracking from age along the edges. It was sealed with two off-white ribbons that were tied with square knots. It looked to me as if it had never been opened. Then she showed me the outer wrapping that had been removed on the first of the month.

The first thing that came to mind as I inspected the package was how old it did look. The stock was faded and cracked as if it were centuries old. If this was a written record by my friends and colleagues Gil Lee and Tom Howard, it could only have been written and packaged within the last year or so. Such a package would never appear as old and worn as this one did. As I stood there staring at the package a million things ran through my mind. Why did it look so old? Why had Gil and Tom sent us a package if they could have contacted us more directly by phone or even in person? The most logical answer to that was almost too unbelievable to accept. Was it possible that they had somehow gone back in time instead of forward?

◆ ◆ ◆

I left the library for a quick bite before the meeting. While I was out I made a call back to my boss in Nevada to tell him the news. There was a long pause after I told him what I suspected had happened to Gil and Tom. I heard him tell someone about it, and then I heard an explosion of voices in the background. This should have been a big day for the lab, and in a way it was, but no one was going to celebrate. At least not for awhile. If we were right, going back in time presented as many problems as it did reasons for celebration.

All the trustees arrived early for the meeting. They must have been as eager as I was to discuss what was happening. At first there'd been doubters among the trustees, but Trish assured them that I hadn't pulled a fast one—that this wasn't some kind of scam. She told them that the package had been virtually hidden from view in the stacks in the library's basement under a layer of dust that looked as if it hadn't been disturbed in decades. Most, if not all, of them sensed that they were about to witness an historic event of major proportions.

I struggled with one of the ancient ribbons. I wanted to untie the knot rather than cut the ribbon. The less damage to the package and its contents the better. Seeing I wasn't getting anywhere Trish grabbed the package and said, "Here, let me do it." Within a minute she'd worked both knots free and returned the package to me.

"I know you want to open it."

I carefully pulled the decaying paper away from the document it had been protecting for God knew how many years. The document appeared to be a couple hundred loose pages of manuscript. Upon closer inspection I noted that there were two entirely different kinds of paper. The first third or so of the stack looked like paper I used in my home printer back in Nevada. The remainder of the stack was uneven in texture and slightly rough along the edges. Clearly it was handmade. I guessed that Gil and Tom had used modern stock while writing in the spacecraft and used the handmade stock when living in whatever time period they ended up in.

The top sheet was the title page and said, **An Accounting of our Trip Through Time, by Gilbert Lee and Thomas Howard, Salem, Massachusetts, 1775.**

I gasped and nearly fell over when I read this. It had to be some kind of joke. As soon as that thought crossed my mind, I knew it wasn't it. There was something about the paper and even the ink on the paper that seemed all too authentic. I noted that it was handwritten. This would make the manuscript harder to read and my first inclination was: *Why by hand?* Then I figured that to set it in type they would have had to use someone else's facilities, which would have meant that that someone else would have known what Gil and Tom were saying in the document, ergo the cursive. Fortunately the writing was fairly clear.

I looked up for a moment at Trish and the others, who just stood there stunned. I expected a question or a comment, but everyone seemed paralyzed by what they were looking at.

I understood what they were going through. It was a tough one to swallow.

"Well," I said.

"Is this what I think it is?" asked Trish.

"What do you think it is?"

"First of all the package has your name on it. It has two other names, too, but you're the only one claiming it. The names don't look like they were written recently, either. What this looks like is that someone from the past is somehow communicating with you. What I don't get is how they would even know you exist."

I smiled sheepishly. I couldn't help it. I'm professional enough to have recovered from my initial shock. This was sort of fun, in a harmless way.

"That's because those two guys are friends of mine. We've played hoops together." I flashed another of my award-winning smiles.

She rolled her eyes. The board members at the table had doubtful looks on their faces. They weren't sure what was going on here. "All right, all right," said Trish. "I know you're having fun, but I think you had better tell us what's going on here."

Time to get serious. "I will tell you, but I need everyone's promise that you will tell no one else about this. At least not until you read or hear about it in the news. Do I have your promise?" I made eye contact with each board member at the table.

A smallish, dignified looking man spoke now. He'd been introduced to me as Marc Cunningham, president of the board of trustees. "We're not going to be saying anything outside of this room. At least not until we know better what's going on here. So what *is* going on Mr. Carver?"

"First of all, I work for the federal government. I work with scientists in a top secret lab out in Nevada called the CAE. The Center for Advanced Exploration. I assume at least some of you know that because that's the place Ms. O'Connell called a few weeks ago."

"If it's top secret, why are you telling us?"

"After I've finished explaining, you'll understand why it's important that all of you know. What we're doing is top secret now, but at some point fairly soon, we'll need to make it public, and what I'm showing you today will make it easier for the public to digest what I'm going to tell you."

Oh, by the way, I didn't make the decision to show the Athenæum people the package contents all on my own. Before I left Nevada the project director and I discussed the very real possibility that I might be in a situation where I'd have to reveal what we were doing. He'd finally decided the more he thought about it that it would be beneficial to the program if we had some reliable witnesses that would be willing to come forth when asked, but would not blab before that. He'd conferred with a couple of his key people and they'd agreed. So here I was about to let that cat out.

I read the first two pages aloud. When I put the two sheets down, I noted that everyone was staring at me, stunned. They were shaking their heads slowly back and forth. I could tell that the reading had taken their breath away, as it had mine. Finally, Cunningham said, "This is real, isn't it?"

I was numb. I nodded ever so slightly. "It is. I've been involved in this project from the start, and I'm still not sure I believe it. It's the result of a project in a government lab out in Nevada that was designed to send two people forward in time. We chose 2017 as the destination year because it was close enough to when Gil and Tom began their trip to make their adjustment to a new time period fairly easy. The changes would be minimal, and they'd only be away from the people they knew and cared about for a couple of years. It was a sacrifice, but not that big a one to deter them."

They began to catch the fever. At that point I told them what had gone wrong with the mission. In a very real way, the mission was still successful. It was the first time anyone had ever gone back in time. Still, I was less excited than I would have been if things had gone as planned. When it became clear that they were convinced the document was legit and I had a legitimate right to it, I said, "good, I assume I can plan on taking the manuscript with me."

"As you can see, it looks very much like my friends ended up in the past, and not the recent past, either. It looks very much like they're back in the Revolutionary period."

A gray-haired woman of about 50 said, "Which means they won't ever come back to this century. Or do you have a way of bringing them back?"

"We don't. As hard as it was to send them to a different period in time, it would be much, much harder to bring them back. Dear God, what have we done?

After some animated discussion they said that they'd like Trish to make a copy of the entire document for their archives so they'd still have a vestige of the real thing. They further asked that when the lab unveiled its project to the world that they would give mention to the Athenæum. I said yes to both requests. I also reminded them that we owed them a payment.

Happily the meeting went very well. I had tried to put a positive spin on the mission despite my sadness at knowing I would never see my friends Gil and Tom again.

♦ ♦ ♦

We had that drink, and a couple more, too. Trish was without a doubt the most outstanding librarian I'd ever known. Truth is, she was the only librarian I'd ever had much conversation with other than to ask for a book.

As God is my witness, when the clock hit midnight I said I'd better go. I had an early flight the next day, and I had to be sharp for when I arrived at the Nevada lab. This was too important to screw up. No pun intended. This was a huge victory for the lab. You could say it was a enormous botch up, but you couldn't overlook the significance of the fact that the CAE had done something no one had ever done. This was more than just a victory for the lab, more even than a huge feather in the cap of the United States. This was something the whole world would go crazy about. There haven't been many times when I would have let my professional instincts override my hormonal instincts, but this time I did.

On the plane back to Nevada I speculated on would happen next. Almost certainly the lab would be able to get the money for a follow-up project. Everyone would want a project that sent a ship capable of a round trip to the past and back. From everything I'd heard from the guys in Nevada, that was not very likely. Even if they could send such a vehicle back to 1775, who would prepare it for the return trip. It's not like a car or small boat or small plane where one or two people can drive out to a destination and back. A space vehicle capable of a return flight would have to be huge and it would have to contain the fuel needed for the return trip. It would have to be aimed properly and ignited with the proper apparatus. In short, you'd need a sizable ground crew and sizable superstructure just to get the thing launched. We could do it in Nevada, but I didn't see how it could be done anywhere in 1775.

Unless—! Unless the guys in Nevada were even smarter than I thought they were. Even if they were, how soon could they have such a vehicle ready? The ideal situation would be to have it ready within five to ten years so Gil and Tom would have the opportunity to return if they wanted to.

Why wouldn't they?

The End

A special thank you for editorial input and advice from Jeanne Scott, Kimberly Scott and David Brody.

Richard Scott is a retired editor, writer, and publisher, having been president and publisher of the David McKay Company and president and publisher of Fodor's Travel Publications. He's also been managing editor of American Bookseller and Bookselling this Week. In the 70s Mr. Scott was co-host with Isaac Asimov, Brendan Gill and Nat Hentoff of a nationally syndicated talk show called In Conversation. He lives with his wife Jeanne in Salem, Massachusetts.

Made in the USA
Middletown, DE
29 June 2020